THE ROYAL WULFF MURDERS

THE
ROYAL WULFF
MURDERS

KEITH McCAFFERTY

VIKING

VIKING
Published by the Penguin Group
Penguin Group (USA) Inc., 375 Hudson Street, New York, New York 10014, U.S.A. • Penguin Group (Canada), 90 Eglinton Avenue East, Suite 700, Toronto, Ontario, Canada M4P 2Y3 (a division of Pearson Penguin Canada Inc.) • Penguin Books Ltd, 80 Strand, London WC2R 0RL, England • Penguin Ireland, 25 St. Stephen's Green, Dublin 2, Ireland (a division of Penguin Books Ltd) • Penguin Books Australia Ltd, 250 Camberwell Road, Camberwell, • Victoria 3124, Australia (a division of Pearson Australia Group Pty Ltd) • Penguin Books India Pvt Ltd, 11 Community Centre, Panchsheel Park, New Delhi – 110 017, India • Penguin Group (NZ), 67 Apollo Drive, Rosedale, Auckland 0632, New Zealand (a division of Pearson New Zealand Ltd) • Penguin Books (South Africa) (Pty) Ltd, 24 Sturdee Avenue, Rosebank, Johannesburg 2196, South Africa

Penguin Books Ltd, Registered Offices: 80 Strand, London WC2R 0RL, England

First published in 2012 by Viking Penguin, a member of Penguin Group (USA) Inc.

10 9 8 7 6 5 4 3 2 1

Grateful acknowledgment is made for permission to reprint an excerpt from "Falling in Love Again," music by Frederick Hollander, words by Reg Connelly. Copyright © 1930 Frederick Hollander Music. Copyright renewed. All rights administered by Chrysalis Music. All rights reserved. Reprinted by permission of Hal Leonard Corporation.

Publisher's Note
This is a work of fiction. Names, characters, places, and incidents either are the product of the author's imagination or are used fictitiously, and any resemblance to actual persons, living or dead, business establishments, events, or locales is entirely coincidental.

LIBRARY OF CONGRESS CATALOGING IN PUBLICATION DATA

McCafferty, Keith.
  The Royal Wulff murders / Keith McCafferty.
      p.   cm.
  ISBN 978-0-670-02326-4
  1. Fly-fishing—Fiction. 2. Murder—Investigation—Fiction. 3. Madison River Valley (Wyo. and Mont.)—Fiction. I. Title.
  PS3613.C334R68 2012
  813'.6—dc23   2011036189

Printed in the United States of America
Designed by Carla Bolte

ALWAYS LEARNING   PEARSON

For the most important people in my life—
my wife, Gail; my son, Tom; my daughter, Jessie.

And for my mother, Beverly.

It has always been my private conviction that any man who pits his intelligence against a fish and loses has it coming.

—John Steinbeck, *America and Americans*

ACKNOWLEDGMENTS

Every writer faces a day when he has to stuff his manuscript into a box and work up the nerve to hand it to someone. And then hope that he or she tells him honestly that no, he would not have been better off starting campfires with the paper. For me, the person I trusted with the box was Dominick Abel, my literary agent. It was Dominick who coached me through the drafts that helped form my story into this book. And it is thanks to Dominick that you hold it in your hands,

I also owe a big debt of gratitude to Kathryn Court, president and publisher of Penguin Books, who believed in my work, and her more than able assistant, Tara Singh, who put up with my endless tinkering of the final draft.

I carried around the kernel of an idea for *The Royal Wulff Murders* for a couple of years before sharing it with Elliott Anderson over a beer at BO's Fish Wagon in Key West. Elliott didn't live to see the published work. But his encouragement, in that great gravel voice of his, is not forgotten.

The early chapters of this book were coaxed into life in a converted garage office heated by a woodstove. It's a great place to write—old fishing lures hanging from the latticework, apple tree blossoming outside the window, Pearl, the Wonder Cat, curled on my desk, eyeing the finches on the feeder. But when Pearl died, the office became too lonely to bury myself in seven days a week, and the next winter too long, so I completed some of the later parts of the book among good company in warm cafés. I want to thank Jen Vero at Sola Café for having the best laugh in Bozeman, and Jess Wilkerson, Pam Butterworth, and Tiffany Lach for making me feel welcome and special. I owe big thanks to Bruce Muller at the Home Page Café, who'd rather be back in his native Zimbabwe than running a café (any man who has hunted down a man-eating lion tends to feel cooped up indoors), and his wife, Frankee, Montana's only certified tea master, who makes the best pot of Darjeeling outside Darjeeling. At the Home Page, strangers became acquaintances, acquaintances friends. They created an atmosphere of fellowship I have come to treasure, and include Pard Cummings, Ginny Arnold, Jen Waters, Lawrence Stuemke, Whitney McDowell, John Glover, Chuck Stafford, Arnie Duncan, John Neustadt, and Alex Komsthoeft. Steve Pieczenik deserves special mention for his irascible good nature, his encouragement, and his professional advice. It was also here that I met with one of the founders of the Whirling Disease Foundation, Dave Kumlien, who was kind enough to answer my questions and bring me up to date on the problems of invasive species that threaten our trout rivers. Any errors of fact in the book are entirely my own.

I'd also like to thank Bill Morris, Steve Dunn, Keith Shein, and Bob and Duncan Bullock, best friends who kept prodding me to finish the damn novel. And my high school teacher Mary Coleman, who so many years ago was the first to assure me that I had the ability to write.

As always, the deepest thanks are reserved for my family. My wife, Gail Schontzler, my best and most honest critic, not only helped make the book better, but her love and support made the endeavor possible in the first place. My son, Thomas McCafferty, was the person I trusted with the initial draft, and he made many valuable suggestions. My daughter, Jessie Rose McCafferty, often sat across from me, writing her own novel at stream-of-consciousness pace while I laboriously plodded to get in my 800 words. She would give me a look as if to say "Get on with it," and I'd have to put the sentence I was writing in my head onto the screen where it belonged. I'd also like to thank my brother, Kevin McCafferty, who forces a fly rod into my hands now and then and whisks me to a river to renew my spirits.

My father, Keith McCafferty, once said he'd do anything for me on the condition that I escape the polluted steel-mill towns and impoverished Appalachian hollows of my boyhood, where the sun was always obscured by haze and fish turned belly-up in creeks that ran red with mine tailings. He instilled in me the love of nature and trout streams. My mother, Beverly McCafferty, gave me the love of books and made sure I became the first person in the family to graduate from college. Without their guidance, I would be working in a steel mill or digging coal, if I was lucky, or otherwise buried in those great mountain folds that have been so abused by the profiteers, and where so many dreams have perished.

AUTHOR'S NOTE

As I write this note, I am sitting in the old Explorer alongside a riffle of the Madison River where I imagine Sean Stranahan fishes in the last chapter of *The Royal Wulff Murders*. I use the word "imagine" because the Madison Valley on the page is not exactly the Madison Valley of Montana. It has been altered to suit the story, although the character of the river and its fishing are accurately represented. Similarly, the characters in the book, while fictional, are cut from the collective cloth of my neighbors. Montanans are a self-reliant people who by and large have resisted cultural homogenization and who speak their minds colorfully, often with absolute strangers.

One thing that I have not fictionalized is the danger that invasive species pose to thousands of trout streams throughout the West. The plot of this story is not only plausible, it has precedent. Several years ago a private hatchery operator pleaded guilty in federal court to deliberately planting trout infected with whirling disease into waters in New Mexico, Utah, and Colorado.

I do not flatter myself to think that I speak for all trout fishermen, but one thing we can agree on is that our fisheries are under attack on fronts ranging from agricultural dewatering and mining sludge to New Zealand mud snails and headwater logging. It's not the angler who kills a trout for dinner who is the problem; it is the angler who sits idly by while others pillage the resource with impunity. Al

McClane, the late fishing editor of *Field & Stream*, wrote, "A mountain is a fact—a trout is a moment of beauty known only to men who seek them." If we do not bestir ourselves by joining organizations such as Trout Unlimited and Montana River Action, our trout will disappear, moment by beautiful moment.

THE ROYAL WULFF MURDERS

Prologue

The fishing guide known as Rainbow Sam found the body. Or rather, it was the client casting from the bow of Sam's drift boat, working a fly called a Girdle Bug in front of a logjam that parted the current of the Madison River. When the float indicator pulled under the surface, Sam winced, figuring a snag. The client, whose largest trout to date had been the size of a breakfast sausage, reared back as if to stick a tarpon.

The body submerged under the driftwood shook free of its tether, bobbed to the surface, and floated facedown, the hook buried in the crotch of the waders.

The client's reel screamed. The bloated corpse took line, steadily, implacably, in the manner of a large carp. Leaning hard on the oars, Sam closed the gap between his boat and the body. Calmly, in a voice that had coaxed a thousand neophyte anglers, he instructed his client to drop the long-handled net over the dead man's head. The catch so enmeshed, he angled his ClackaCraft downstream at the pace of the current, fanning the oars gently toward a bay at the bank.

"We got him!" The client beamed.

Sam thought, "Holy shit." But he made a mental note to convert all his monofilament leader material to Orvis Super Strong in the future, just the same. The eight pound tippet had held like a stout steel cable.

"I'll tell you what, Buddy," Sam muttered as he stepped out of the drift boat and gingerly lifted the meshes of the net over a hank of flowing hair. "You may not be God's gift to trout fishin', but you just got yourself a whopper of a story."

Sam worked the hook from the waders, then rolled the body faceup. For the next few moments neither man spoke. The client, his florid face suddenly ashen, leaned over the gunwale and threw up, starting with the tin of kippered herring he'd had for a snack after Sam's bankside lunch. He was a big eater and it took a half-dozen heaves to get it all up.

Rainbow Sam just stared. It wasn't only the ruptured left eye socket, from which a splinter of stick protruded like a skeletal finger, that riveted his attention. It was the lower lip, grotesquely swollen and purple as a plum. He bent down for a closer look. In the center of the lip was a trout fly. It was a Royal Wulff, a hair wing dry fly pattern about the size of an evening moth. Tied on a size 12 hook, Sam decided. The barb was buried in the flesh; from the hook's down-turned eye dangled a strand of monofilament leader material.

"Ah, shit," Sam said, having recovered from the shock of the mutilation. "I think I know this kid. Goddammit anyhow."

For the angler was a very young man, little more than a teenager, Sam thought. He had floated past where the kid was wade fishing only a few weeks before, on a stretch of river not far upstream. He remembered the occasion because the fisherman wasn't cut from the same khaki-and-GORE-TEX cloth that stamped most Madison River pilgrims. Sam disapproved of anglers who dressed like pages out of catalogues. They projected a *GQ* quality that might serve one in good social stead at an upscale fishing lodge, while emphasizing particulars to which trout paid no attention.

By contrast, this man's waders were stained and patched and he fished without a vest, let alone one sporting the obligatory ten pockets. "How are you doing, Mr. Sam?" the young man had called out that morning as Sam glided by. And Sam, momentarily taken aback before realizing that the angler had read his name from the logo stenciled on the bow, had tipped his cap in reply. It was a grace note in the day, considering that wade fishermen and boat anglers competed for the same water. Tensions could become strained on a popular river like the Madison.

"Now why the fuck did this have to happen to a nice kid like that?" the fishing guide muttered to himself.

He waded ashore, sucking the back of a tooth.

"Stay here," he said. "I'm going to call the sheriff. Don't touch anything while I'm gone." Sam's client, having clambered out of the boat, was sunk to his knees in the shallows, a string of drool hanging from his stubbled chin. A few feet away, a school of tiny fish flashed under the yellow wash of vomit. The man nodded dumbly.

Rainbow Sam climbed the steep riverbank. For just a second he took in his surroundings, the river reflecting lavender evening clouds and the deeper purples of the mountains, its current running between banks of wild roses. It was part of what attracted anglers from around the world to the Madison—the setting and the water quality, a champagne of intoxicating clarity that poured in one effervescent riffle from Quake Lake to the small fishing town of Ennis. And then, too, there were the trout, with their ruby stripes and polished flanks, as hard as metal and as perfect as God ever made.

Well, Sam thought, this poor bastard has caught his last one.

He noted the nearest residences: a log mansion sporting panoramic riverfront windows and, just upstream, a chinked-up homestead cabin with a rusted half-ton in the drive. He spat, automatically registering the twenty-first-century-Montana paradox: Big Sky native cheek by jowl with summer gentry—which house being the eyesore depending upon your point of view. Well, one ought to have a phone, anyway. He cinched the belt around his waders and began to walk.

CHAPTER ONE

Blue-Ribbon Watercolors
(and Private Investigations)

Sean Stranahan leaned back in the swivel chair in his studio, paint-stained Crocs up on his desk, a tumbler stenciled with the emblem of The Famous Grouse in his right hand. A half-finished trout fly, a caddis pupa imitation resembling a wingless moth, was gripped in the clamp of the tying vise in front of him. His eyes, fatigued from the close work of fly tying, drifted to the newspaper open on his desk, then to the fluttering leaves of the aspens outside the window. He took a sip of tap water from the tumbler. The afternoon was beginning to ebb and he'd have to make a decision soon if he was going to go fishing. A smile played across his lips. That is, he thought, if it was still safe to drive to the river. His eyes returned to the story in the paper.

"Body Found in Madison River," ran the headline. Rainbow Sam was quoted in paragraph four. He said he hadn't seen skin that white since swimming with the Polar Bear Club in Lake Superior. Initially, he had said since peeling the D cups off a biker chick at the Harley rally in Sturgis, but when the reporter reminded him that the *Bridger Mountain Star* was a family newspaper, Sam had come up with the tamer quote. Details were sketchy. The body of an early-twenties white male, clean shaven, shoulder-length blond hair, had been discovered half a mile below Lyons Bridge at 7 p.m. Wednesday by fishing guide Samuel Meslik. Cause of death unknown, pending autopsy. No mention of a trout fly, nor of a stick jammed into an eye socket.

Stranahan turned to the sports page and found the box scores of the Red Sox-Yankees doubleheader, which the teams had split. He had moved to Montana from a chapel town in Vermont near the Massachusetts border only three months earlier. He really didn't care about baseball, especially when the Sox were eight and a half games back at the All-Star break, but found himself reaching for that toehold on the past nearly every time he opened the newspaper. Beth loved the Sox. He pictured her sitting in the kitchen of their farmhouse, drinking coffee from her favorite eggshell mug, her reading glasses pulled down on her nose.

He folded the paper and laid it on a corner of the desk.

The phone rang. Welcoming the distraction, he picked it up. Maybe this was a print catalogue, calling to tell him that one of the watercolors he'd submitted had been chosen for a limited edition release.

"Stranahan."

"Why do you have to answer the phone like that?" It was his sister, who lived not far from Stranahan's old home in Vermont. "Why can't you use the Christian name Mom and Dad gave you?"

Stranahan sighed. "Contrary to popular opinion, I am a business-man. The way to deal with a publisher, not that I am overwhelmed with experience, is to answer tough, then soften up. It creates an illu-sion of intimacy."

"Tough?" she said. "You're not tough; you just look like you are. Oh, Sean, when something happens like it did to you, people start letting themselves go. Appearances count in this world. You're over thirty now. How are you going to pull yourself up if you're sleeping on a couch? If Beth knew what she'd done—"

Stranahan interrupted. "I don't want to talk about Beth. It's not her fault."

He glanced at his cluttered studio, watercolors hanging on the cracked plaster walls, fly-tying feathers decorating the floor—the place looked like the dirt ring in the aftermath of a cockfight. His eyes settled on a tea saucer he'd scattered with breadcrumbs beside a mouse hole in the baseboard.

"Are you still there?"

"Really, Karen, I'm fine." He tried to put a positive note in his voice. "The Trout Unlimited banquet's coming up. I have a painting in the auction. My work will get some exposure, and a couple more sales or a limited-edition contract and I can move into a proper place. All I really need to do is get back to work."

"What happened between you and Beth—it's not too late."

"Stop," Stranahan said, firmly but gently.

"But . . ."

"I'll call you soon. Say hi to Carl and the twins."

"I love you, too, Sean. Even if you didn't say it first."

"Ditto." That started the trill of laughter he'd intended and he replaced the receiver halfway through it and stared out the window of the studio.

In the three months since he'd said good-bye to New England, Stranahan had done a lot of staring: out the truck window; at the forested ridges that defined Bridger, the Montana town where he had settled—stopped might be a better word; into hazy middle distance; at the door of his office. He didn't know what he was looking for exactly, only that he thought he'd know it when he saw it. And talking with his sister reminded him that a good part of him was still mired in the East. He had wanted to ask Karen if she had seen Beth around town but had been afraid of the answer. Maybe she was with the lawyer who had handled the divorce, Ken Whatshisname. What a milquetoast name, Ken. The man even looked like a Ken doll, his blond hair holding the tooth tracks of his comb. Who put sticky stuff in their hair anymore? In Vermont?

Stranahan heard steps in the hall. His pulse quickened. The steps ceased in front of the door. He could imagine someone reading the etched letters on the frosted glass window—BLUE RIBBON WATER-COLORS. Underneath, in a discreet script that he devoutly hoped would be overlooked by all passersby, were the words "Private Investigations." If Beth ever saw that door, Stranahan thought, she'd laugh him out of the building. True, he'd worked as an investigator for his grandfather's law firm in Boston during college summers, but that had mostly been punching numbers on a phone. Later he'd done divorce cases, repossessions, assorted minor-league snooping for a couple of years in his late twenties, out of an office of his own, before devoting himself to painting full time. But when Stranahan applied for gallery space at the Bridger Mountain Cultural Center in the spring, the building manager had said that while he was *eminently* qualified—that was the word she used—the center already housed a number of painters and she liked her tenants to represent a variety of interesting occupations.

"Well," Stranahan had said, wracking his brain for résumé credits, because the cultural center was nonprofit and the rent was ridiculously cheap, "I'm a licensed private investigator in Massachusetts." He winced at his words, even though the lie was only one of tense.

The manager, an outdoorsy, gap-toothed blonde in her forties, had tapped the eraser of her pencil against her front teeth thoughtfully.

"That's an interesting combination," she'd said. "The way you look, that dark knight thing that makes a woman look at you twice. Um-hmm, you know what I mean"—she'd looked him up and down frankly—"I like that a lot. Just don't bring any guns in here."

Stranahan stared at the reverse lettering on the glass, trying to resolve the indistinct human shape in the hall. Whoever it was seemed to be dressed in patterned clothes, but the glass distorted shapes grotesquely. The person had been standing outside his door for half a minute. Making up his mind? Her mind? To knock and ask him what? For a painting? Or for the goods on a rotten husband? He was about to get out of the chair and save his visitor the agony of decision when the footsteps sounded again, fading down the corridor.

"There goes money," Stranahan said out loud. And under his breath, in spite of himself, "Or love." Talking to himself was a habit he had picked up since the divorce, when the moorings started to shake.

He glanced out the window at the declining day and came to a decision. Picking up a scratched pair of dollar-store reading glasses, he turned his attention to the half-completed fly in his vise. He added a few hackle fibers from a Hungarian partridge to simulate legs, then completed the size 14 pupa with a whip finish and painted a coating of clear nail polish to freeze the thread. He gave it a minute to dry before opening the jaws of the vise and sticking the fly into a patch of sheep's wool on his Red Sox cap. Then he picked up the fly-rod case hanging from its carry strap on an old-fashioned hat rack and went out the door, down two flights of steps, and into the angled sunshine of a July afternoon.

His '76 Land Cruiser, which, during the weeks of his cross-country journey, had served as his home—the studio, he reminded himself, was a step up in that regard—squatted heavy and boxlike under the spreading ash trees along South Gallatin Avenue. He rolled down the windows to let the breeze in and stuck the rod case in the back beside his easel and paints. He shut the liftgate and straightened up.

Turning, he caught sight of a woman walking up the street toward him. She had auburn hair and wore a sleeveless, flowered dress that clung to her body in the heat. The vitality of her stride was reminiscent of a teenage girl's, but she had seen more of life and he placed her as being roughly his age. She looked vaguely familiar. The woman gave him a passing smile and, stopping a few steps beyond, raised her right arm, cocked an imaginary pistol at her head—Stranahan saw a flash of gold ring—and dropped the hammer with her thumb.

She muttered, "Just like me. I'm always forgettin' somethin'," and started back toward him.

"At least you know which way to go to find it."

She paused, lifting her eyebrows in a question.

"Oh," Stranahan said, "I get in the truck, half the time I don't know which way to turn the wheel."

She chuckled. "Honey," she said, "men never know where they are going. You're just one who has guts enough to admit it."

She swung on by him. "You have a good day now," she said. She left a scent hanging in the air, like oranges.

CHAPTER TWO

A Stick in the River

The sheriff of Hyalite County, so-named for the opal ore that studded the volcanic peaks south of Bridger, placed her hands on her hips and said, "Hmpff."

"What we have here," Martha Ettinger said, looking from her deputy to the logjam in the river where Rainbow Sam's client had hooked the corpse, "is a case of simple drowning. Or not. Enlighten me, Walt. Humor me with some of that big-city cop perspective."

It was Thursday morning, the day after the body had been discovered. The previous evening there had been scant opportunity to search the area where the angler had received his prodigious strike. By the time Ettinger and Deputy Walter Hess had taken statements from Sam and his client—a banker from Atlanta named Horace Izard III—then waited for Doc Hanson to drive in from Bridger, pronounce the bloated, trout-belly-white body dead, and arrange for transportation to the county morgue, it was nearly dark. Ettinger had wanted to wade out to the logjam herself, but neither she nor Hess had packed waders with felt soles, which were necessary to keep one's footing on the treacherous boulders. Sam had offered his services and, when they were politely declined, his waders. Client Izard had seconded the offer, but as neither man had been able to hit a toilet bowl with any consistency in more than a decade, owing to an inaccuracy of aim by the appendages their bulging stomachs concealed from view, and as both wore a twelve shoe, their waders were comically large. It had been decided that Walt, who was only marginally taller than Martha at five-foot-ten, would venture out in Izard's waders, which looked more hygienic than Rainbow Sam's, despite traces of vomit.

The deputy hadn't taken a dozen steps before Sam had snorted, raised his eyes to Martha, and said, "Your deputy's goin' right in the drink."

Walt made it a little more than halfway to the logjam, shuffling carefully in the clown-foot wading boots, before slipping on a rock and taking a header. Rainbow Sam, who moved well for a big man, ambled casually downriver, waded out in his jeans, grabbed Hess by the collar, and, for the second time that day, dragged a waterlogged body to the bank.

Back on shore, Hess had thanked Sam sheepishly and grinned at Martha, who raised her eyes in exasperation.

"We'll come back tomorrow," she said.

Sam wondered if there would ever be a time when he didn't have to deal with morons in the water.

Put on the spot, Walt grimaced, spit a stream of tobacco juice from the corner of his mouth—he'd been a Chicago cop, taking a dip of snuff was a Western adaptation—and said, "I see it like this, Marth. Our John Doe here, he's out of state, reads *Fly Fisherman* and *Field & Stream* like they was Matthew, Mark, Luke, and John, buys hisself a fly rod . . ."

"Which we haven't found."

"Which we haven't found. Anyways, he has this rod but never learns how to cast. He's fishing, hooks hisself in the lip on his back cast, slaps his hand to his mouth, and falls into the river. He gets washed into a logjam and poked in the eye by a stick, starts swallerin' water, and next thing you know he's fishing that great trout stream in the sky."

"We don't know for sure yet he drowned," Martha pointed out.

"No, but them's the odds."

"Walt, did you, like, forsake the English language when you came out here, or were you always this much of a hick?"

"I fancy myself sort of the American Crocodile Dundee," Walt said, deadpan. He slapped the foot-long bowie knife strapped to his waist.

Martha blew out her breath.

"Yeah, you're probably right. That's the scenario I come up with, too. But I'll take exception with the nonresident assumption. He's casually dressed, his waders are patched up; it makes me think he could be local. Plus, the guide says he saw him here a few weeks ago, so if he was on vacation it was a long one."

"What bothers me," Walt said, "is how come no fishing license? No wallet, for that matter. No car. Leastwise, none nearby."

"And no rod and no fishing vest," Martha added. "Plus, the wader belt he's wearing is inflatable but he doesn't pull the cord to inflate it. If he falls in, you figure first thing he does is reach for the cord. It smells, doesn't it? Let's go have a look at that logjam. Maybe his wallet and his license washed out of his pockets and got caught in the jam."

"Not likely. If you remember, Sheriff, he was wearing one of those shirts with zipper pockets and they were zipped. I checked."

"Humor me, Walt. And do me a favor. This time, try not to fall in the river."

The logjam had formed itself into long commas of debris around an exposed boulder in the middle of the river. The body had become wedged underneath the mass of roots from a tree that had washed down during high water. Ettinger and Hess searched this area first.

It wasn't easy. The current swirled around the boulder, scouring out a pocket of deep water that pressed against the roots and threatened to upend the sheriff and her deputy with each mincing step they took. Bending down to look under the tangle, Hess took in a few cups of the Madison over his waders and whistled.

"Hooey, Marth, that's cold as my ex-wife's udders!"

Ettinger harrumphed. She had spotted something blue back under the root ball and was reaching as far back as she could, her arm immersed in the icy water and her wader top within an inch of the surface. The tips of her outstretched fingers grazed across what felt like fabric. She pinched her fingertips together, but the cloth pushed away.

She plunged her arm farther under, the water seeping into her waders. "Mother"—she felt her nipples stiffen and sucked in an involuntary breath as the water sloshed against her chest— "of"—she grabbed the cloth—"mercy!" she exclaimed, shuddering as icy water seeped underneath the wading belt and tingled against her belly.

"Aha!" She withdrew her arm triumphantly.

"Looks like Mr. John Doe lost his hat," Hess said. He waded over to examine the ball cap, which Ettinger pinched between her fingers.

"MOCCASIN HOLLOW SEMEN SALES. JULEP, MISSISSIPPI," Walt murmured. "Foreigner, just like I said." Above the brim was a stitched emblem of a Jersey bull, walking on his hind feet, approaching a cow who looked coyly over her shoulder at him. WE STAND BEHIND OUR PRODUCT, read the back.

"Amusing," Martha said. "Very amusing."

She turned the hat over. Inside the crown, a small square of sheep's wool, attached by two safety pins, held four trout flies.

Ettinger said, "You ever know a fisherman to wear one of these patches *inside* the hat? I thought the whole purpose was to dry the flies, so you pinned it to the outside."

"Don't reckon I do," Hess said.

Ettinger withdrew a submersible point-and-shoot from the breast pocket of her khaki shirt. She snapped a photo of Walt holding the hat and another of the logjam. Then she withdrew a ziplock from her wader pocket and sealed the hat inside it.

Hess shook his head. "This ain't no crime scene, Marth," he said.

She ignored the comment and stuffed the ziplock inside her wet shirt. "We'll have a closer look-see later."

For the next twenty minutes they searched the tangle of branches that formed the logjam, Hess on one side, Ettinger on the other. They found nothing else.

"What do you say we go back?" Hess said.

"Let's give it another few minutes."

"Marth," Hess said, "just what is it we're looking for? 'Sides the rod?"

"Think, Walt."

Walt went back to searching.

"I'm waiting," Ettinger said.

"I'm thinking," Hess said.

A minute later Hess straightened up. "Is this what we're looking for?"

Ettinger waded around the downstream side of the jam and bucked the current to come up alongside the deputy. A willow tree had been swept against the logjam, its branches partially submerged. Walt was pointing to the end of a half-inch-diameter branch that had broken off short near the trunk. The stub was splintered, and clinging to it was an inch-long thread of fleshy tissue, pale as a blanched earthworm.

"That looks like eye matter to me," Ettinger said. "But this is *downstream* from where what's-his-face, Izard the Third, hooked the body. If our theory about him drowning holds up, how could he poke his eye out with this branch and end up twenty feet upriver?"

"Maybe that Southern gentleman and the guide were wrong about the position of the body."

"What about the hat, then; why was it upstream?"

"It came off his head and he swept on past it and ended up here."

"That fishing guide was pretty positive about the body's location, Walt."

Hess rubbed his forehead with a sunburnt hand.

"Then how in God's name . . ." He stopped. "Aw, Marth, are you thinking what I think you're thinking?"

"Now *you're* thinking," Ettinger said. She took a snapshot of the tree limb, then fished around for another plastic bag in her wader pocket. Clasping the bag between her teeth, she opened the saw blade of her Swiss Army knife, grasped the stick a foot below the break, and started to make sawdust.

CHAPTER THREE

Back Casting

In Sean Stranahan's philosophy of life, any man who had a fly rod, a quarter tank of gas, and four decent tires was never too far from home. So while it may have been true that he wasn't sure which way to turn when he left the Bridger Mountain Cultural Center, the fact remained that no matter which point of the compass he headed for, he'd be home in time for an evening caddis hatch. Within thirty miles of Bridger ran four of the greatest rivers in trout fishing lexicon: the Yellowstone, the Gallatin, the Madison, and the Jefferson. He settled on the Madison's Bear Trap Canyon because he loved the barren hills and because the newspaper story on the man who had apparently drowned in the Madison's current—albeit a good sixty miles upstream—exerted a perverse magnetism.

At the river, clouds of caddis flies pulsed over the willows like dust swarming through shafts of sunlight in a musty room. Stranahan knotted the fly he had tied in his studio to the point of his leader. He worked the fly line out in tight loops, then dropped it gently to the surface. Immediately, the current swept it in a bow downstream. He flicked his wrist to roll a loop of line upstream, erasing the bow so that his line was straight and the fly, which imitated the immature stage of the insect, drifted naturally beneath the surface. Manipulating fly line was second nature to Sean, as was tightening it when the first fish took and then letting the trout run freely to jump once, twice, three times before it sulked in the current. Stranahan worked the trout in and cradled it underwater while removing the hook. The iridescent violet, ruby, and silver sheens trembled as the small rainbow trout twisted, catching angles of light. He released his hold and the trout arrowed away into the current.

He looked across the river. It always looked different after he had caught his first fish, more potent somehow. Although it had taken him time to adjust to the steeper gradients of Western rivers, Stranahan could now read the tapestry of currents as naturally as a field general interpreted military maps, and plan his campaign accordingly.

Fishing was something he was very good at and had been since he was a boy, armed with a pole and a bobber, dunking worms for bluegills in the pond at his grandparents' farm in western Massachusetts. Whenever the family arrived for a visit, Stranahan would immediately snatch his pole and a rusted gardening trowel from the trunk of the car, then jog straight to the pond to dig for bait. His mother would call to him to show a little more courtesy for his grandmother and grandfather, who would come out of the house waving, but his father always said, "Let him go, Marge; it means so much to him."

But if afternoons of dancing bobbers proved to be the most joyful and innocent of his childhood, the magic of fishing that transformed his life was experienced in darkness. After dinner, his grandpa and father would drink George Dickel and smoke pipes out on the porch. Sean would sit on the railing, listening to the crickets rubbing their legs, watching the weeping willow in the yard for the first lantern of light from the abdomen of a firefly. He would tap his foot impatiently on the peeled-paint floorboards, waiting for his father to tap out his pipe.

It had become a father-son ritual. His dad would take the pipe from his mouth, examine it—while Sean held his breath—and put it back between his teeth. The sigh escaping Sean's lungs, which would become an irritating habit that Beth commented upon more than once, was incubated on those interminable evenings. At last his father would knock the pipe on the porch rail, watch it with a critical eye until it lost some of its heat, and replace it in the pocket of his shirt. Then from his pants pocket he'd withdraw his car keys, which he'd casually toss over.

"How about getting the tackle box out of the trunk?" he'd say. "Unless you're too sleepy to fish. If you're too tired, Grandpa and I can go alone." His father and grandfather would exchange winks. "How 'bout it?"

Sean had never been too sleepy to sit in the bow of the old wooden rowboat moored at the dock. His father manned the oars, positioning the oldest and youngest generations of Stranahans to cast toward the indigo shoreline, where the cannibalistic bass—the big game of the pond—hunted frogs and bluegills as well as the young of their own kind. Sean's favorite plug was a Crazy Crawler, a treble-hooked contraption with hinged metal wings that opened and closed like a wounded bird as it was reeled across the surface. He would never forget the first time a bass inhaled the lure, shattering the moonstone surface of the pond. The jolt of the strike had taken Sean completely out of the current of ordinary life and into a dimension of sensation and urgency, where time was measured in heartbeats and minutes passed that could never be recaptured in the imagination—minutes that could be relived only if you were lucky enough to catch another.

"There you are," he said, speaking around the stem of his own meerschaum pipe. The trout walloped on the surface, heavy sounding, then swung in an arc far downstream. There was nothing showy about this one—it exhibited none of the frantic antics of the first fish. For perhaps five minutes the trout bulled stubbornly before surrendering ground, a few feet at a time, to the pressure of the graphite rod. It wavered, thick-shouldered, in the thin water near the bank. Sean reached down but the trout fought back into the current, exhausting the fathoms of its heart. When it swung back in, he reached under its belly and lifted.

It was a brown trout, heavily muscled, with a sprinkling of dime-sized blue and crimson circles on its sides. An old male, the fish had a jutting lower jaw and curved teeth that brought blood from Stranahan's fingers as he backed the hook out. When it was free, the brown settled to the bottom in a foot of water, its gills flaring as it regained strength. Watching it, Stranahan sat down on the bank. Twenty inches, he thought. Maybe better. Twilight was an amber smear on the horizon; the river glittered in the slanted light. In a few minutes the polish would fade from the surface, the current's mercurial song would slide into bass notes, and the wild night would claim it against further human intrusion.

He said, "You'd have liked this place, Pop."

CHAPTER FOUR

The Woman Who Sang Old Standards

The Cottonwood Inn, with its spacious dance hall, Polynesian-mahogany ceiling beams, and high-arched windows, had been, in its earliest incarnation, a terminus station on the southernmost spur of the Chicago, Milwaukee & St. Paul Railway. It was a place where women carrying parasols against the sun disembarked with their banker husbands for stagecoach rides that would take them one hundred miles up the Gallatin Canyon into recently designated Yellowstone National Park. Built at the edge of wilderness in the 1920s, the inn was a place where you could get a meal, a room, and a whore for a sawbuck.

When Sean Stranahan walked through its double patio doors on his way back from fishing, it was a place where ten dollars bought you a beer with a whiskey chaser. It also offered, Thursday through Saturday nights, a couple dozen songs from one of the artists who made the Northern Rockies circuit. As the inn stood opposite the cultural center, Stranahan had made it a habit to stop in most nights for a Moose Drool Ale. He was a little sheepish about liking the place. It was, after all, a yuppie enclave in cattle country, but one could reasonably argue that the cowboy bars fronting Main Street were no more authentic, not with ceiling-hung TVs tuned to ESPN and electronic poker machines drowning out the jukebox.

Besides, the Cottonwood Inn had Doris Sizemore, a broad, beaming ranch woman who had raised eight children with a string-bean husband who wore overalls every day she had known him before he

21

wasted away from lung cancer—this being Marlboro country literally. She took orders with a pencil stuck in abundantly curled hair, barked them back to the kitchen, and had a wink and smile for everyone. Regulars like Stranahan she made a point to sit down with once in a while. She was a good listener who made people open up by praising them to kingdom come and then talking a blue streak until they'd become as exasperated with her as they were with their own mothers. Doris was the only person west of the Charles River who knew about Stranahan's divorce, the deaths of his parents, even his sleeping quarters in 226A across the creek. She called him Stranny, which his mother had called him as a child to avoid confusion, because his father was also named Sean. He had hated the name, then came to like it once nobody called him that anymore.

"Who's singing?" Stranahan asked when Doris brought him the Missoula brew in a long-necked bottle.

"You haven't seen her?"

Stranahan gestured at the stage, where a microphone was cocked over a battered piano. "On break when I came in."

Doris clucked, giving him her mother hen look of disapproval.

"I wouldn't know her real name, but she calls herself—get ready for this—Miss Velvet Lafayette. She's a cupcake, though, if you like red lipstick and a long-legged woman. And she's a good singer. Suspiciously good, if you ask me."

She pinched her lips. "A God-fearing woman like myself has a nose for her kind. I could sum her up in one word." She waited a beat. "Trouble. T-R-O-U-B-L-E."

"I was just asking," Stranahan said.

She looked sideways at him. "A man is never just asking. Especially one lonely as you are, Stranny."

He rolled his eyes as Doris bustled away. It was just like her to make something of nothing . . . of a woman he had never even seen. Hell, walking in the door, he figured the talent would be a hippie with a six-string and a songbook of mountain treacle. But he kept his eyes on the stage as he took a pull from the bottle. Something nagged at his brain, an association he had tried to make earlier. But before he could resolve it there was a rustle of silk and a woman brushed his elbow as she walked to the stage, weaving with leonine grace between the tables. She trailed a scent like oranges.

"Thank you," the woman said to the scattered applause.

A wolf whistle pierced the room. Stranahan didn't have to turn around to identify the maker. It was Phil Halverson, an unshaven logger who had one of those pinched faces typically associated with cousin kissing and hog calling, and whose deep-set eyes were as black as a coon's under his grungy hat with a McCulloch Chain Saw logo. Everybody called him Punxsutawney Phil, after the famous ground-hog, because he began every conversation by telling you whether he'd seen his shadow that morning. If he had, then it was going to be a bad day. With the town of Bridger being on the east or sunny side of the Continental Divide, Phil had a lot of bad days.

"Ah, crawl back into your hole, Phil," Doris said in a booming voice, and there was another scattering of applause.

"And I thank you, too," Miss Lafayette said as she took her seat at the piano and spread her fingers against the keys, "even if some women don't hold that kind of Cro-Magnon appreciation in high esteem. Back in Mississippi—that's M-I-S-S-I-S-S-I-P-P-I, something every schoolchild knows how to spell by the time he's knee-high to a sunflower—romance isn't always 'May I have this dance, ma'am.' Sometimes it's a whistle from the kudzu. Sometimes it's just a look, you know, under a willow tree at a picnic on the bayou. And some-times, even if you don't want it to happen at all, it happens just the same; it happens just like this."

She dropped her head over the piano.

Falling in love again
Never wanted to
What am I to do?
Can't help it.

She had a husky contralto voice that painted each note with a smooth, sweeping brushstroke while letting the song stand by itself. Stranahan thought her a little theatrical in her gestures, but the voice was like her name, with none of the hysterical palpitations that pop diva vocalists used to turn singing into a gymnastic event bordering on orgasm.

Men cluster to me like moths around a flame
And if their wings burn, I know I'm not to blame
Falling in love again
Never wanted to
What am I to do?
Can't help it.

She wore a black sleeveless dress with a floral appliqué of hibiscus that clung like crimson fingers to her right hip and wrapped around the bodice to flower over her left breast. Her auburn locks draped in loose waves across her shoulders; between stanzas, while her fingers rippled over the piano keys in jazz counterpoint, she closed her eyes and tilted her chin so that her hair fell in a waterfall down her back.

And the songs were real songs: "Wayfaring Stranger," "But Not for Me," "The Nearness of You."

Stranahan sipped his beer and let her voice wash over him. He scarcely acknowledged Doris when she took the empty chair next to him as the set was coming to an end.

Velvet Lafayette bowed her head as the applause sounded. She waited until it had completely died before opening her eyes and smiling.

"That's very kind of you. I'll be playing here the next couple of nights, so make sure you tell your friends. Y'all have a good night, now." She stepped off the stage, bowed slightly to exchange some pleasantry with a young couple at a front table, and then walked directly toward Stranahan. She looked to pass him, then caught his eye. She said, "I certainly hope you figured out where it was you were going this afternoon. A man ought not get too lost, lest someday he can't find his way back."

"Thank you for your concern," Stranahan said gravely.

She flashed a smile and Stranahan followed her with his eyes as she climbed the coil of the stairway toward the guest rooms on the upper floor.

He turned to find Doris staring at him.

"Now Doris . . ." he began.

"I'm 'ought not' going to say a single word," Doris said.

CHAPTER FIVE

Awakening

Standing on the inn's veranda, Stranahan looked toward the peaks in the Gallatin range, midnight blue under a silver moon. He had noticed a flyer advertising Miss Velvet Lafayette, Queen of Hearts—A Riverboat Song Stylist and Jazz Pianist from the Mississippi Delta, taped to the door on his way out. The picture showed a younger version of the singer standing in front of the paddle wheel of a gambling boat, holding a playing card—the queen of hearts—over her breast. He must have seen the flyer earlier. Thay was why she had seemed familiar when he had passed her on the street.

He could not deny the attraction he felt toward her, even if he told himself he was just a sucker for a Southern accent. Or maybe Doris had it right. Certainly he had been lonely enough the past few weeks. But there was an undercurrent of tension that had passed between them, the spark that had been missing from his marriage almost from its beginning.

Sean took a drink from his bottle of beer and sat down on a wrought-iron bench. He wasn't thinking now of Velvet Lafayette, or of Beth, but of a woman he had met in Boston a year after he left his grandfather's law firm. The woman, Katherine O'Reilly, had hired him to find evidence of her husband's affair, which he had accomplished by the simple expedient of waiting outside the man's office building, identifying him by a photograph, and then following him to the Park Plaza Hotel near the Public Garden. He had watched the man punch the elevator button for the sixth floor, evidently having arranged a room earlier. Sean waited until he was out of sight and followed suit. Stepping out of the iron cage into the long hall, he hung around, looking purposefully at nothing, until a woman with sharp facial features and hair that matched the color of her camel hair coat stepped out of the elevator, knocked on the door of room 605, and was let in. He caught only a snatch of conversation, but the name "John" registered as the door shut. Stranahan caught the elevator down and phoned Mrs. O'Reilly from the lobby; she said she'd be there in fifteen minutes.

"I'm not going to cry," she said when she met him on the hotel steps, although her hands trembled as she rummaged distractedly through her purse. Katherine O'Reilly was a handsome brunette in her midforties whose hazel eyes were a little too bright, betraying the emotion that her voice tried to cover up. She asked Stranahan for something to write on. He produced an envelope. After some more rummaging, she took a magenta lipstick from her purse and scrawled two words: IT'S OVER, K.

"That isn't too dramatic, is it," she said to Stranahan, but it had not been a question, and she held up a hand when he attempted to follow her into the elevator. A few minutes later she was back down.

"I didn't make a scene. I stuck it in the door," she said. She looked directly at Stranahan. "The Copley Square is right around the corner. I'm going to get a drink at the bar. Are you coming?"

He went with her out into a light winter rain and, after the Scotch—drunk in dead silence—stood awkwardly beside her in the elevator of Boston's oldest hotel. She looked at him intently, as if scrutinizing his face for sincerity. In the room, she stopped his hand when he reached for the light switch.

"No lights." She kissed the rain off his face. And what started then as an act of retribution softened into a genuine regard and tenderness that seemed apart from the crisis that had led to the hotel and surprised them both.

"I want you to know," she told him sometime that night, "that this wasn't an eye for an eye. I'm not leaving him because he had an affair . . . again." She laughed sadly to herself. "Men are men. No, I'm leaving because there's nothing to say. We slide by each other like ghosts. Why is it we always fall in love with the wrong people? Answer me that."

When he began to murmur, she said, "No, don't answer." She placed two fingers over his lips. "Sshh. Just hold me awhile."

But he wasn't able to sleep. When the wash of dawn suffused the room, Sean eased open the drawer of the night table and removed a few sheets of hotel stationery, then took a soft lead pencil from his jacket pocket. Throwing a hotel bathrobe across his shoulders, he sat down in a chair facing the bed and sketched Katherine O'Reilly as she lay on her side with the sheet drawn across her waist. He found her face beautiful in repose, as relaxed as a child's face, the corners of her mouth twitching into smiles at some unknown dream.

She awakened before he finished, and, seeing him sitting there, she walked naked behind the chair and bent down so that her chin rested on his left shoulder and her hair cascaded over his chest. For several minutes she watched intently as he filled in shadows with deft strokes of the pencil. Then she softly kissed his neck and whispered, "What are you doing in this dreary town? You should be following your dreams, wherever they take you. Start your life over, like I am."

Enveloped by her scent, Stranahan closed his eyes and let out his breath. It was like breaching a dam, and for the first time in what seemed like forever, he found himself thinking out loud with a fellow human. In the afternoon, Stranahan drove her to the furnished barn he rented behind a two-century-old farmhouse in Milton. In the loft he opened the old steamer trunk where he kept his watercolors and let her praise flow over him like warm water. She refused to accept the sketch he had made of her, assuring him that age had drained her of narcissism, and besides, who could she ever show it to? No, you keep it, she said, it will remind you where you were and who you were with when you followed your heart.

Follow your dreams, follow your heart. Stranahan caught himself repeating the clichés, but coming from her, they didn't sound like clichés at all.

"Are you making fun of me, detective?" She tapped him lightly on the nose.

"Here," she said. "This is the one I want. That's you, isn't it?"

The painting was an earlier, Norman Rockwell–inspired effort, a sepia-toned watercolor of a boy in a rowboat, his small hands gripping the oars while his knees locked around a fishing rod trolling line into the water.

"I'll keep it where I can look at it, wherever I go," she said. "This way, I'll never have to say good-bye to you."

Stranahan cooked for her, and they slept that second night in the loft, buried in blankets with the window cracked and snow sifting on the sill. Forty-four hours after meeting her on the steps of the Park Plaza, Stranahan dropped her off in front of the architectural firm where she worked.

"I know you told me no tomorrows," he said before she opened the door, "but if I don't ask if I can see you again, then I'll spend the rest of my life wondering."

She looked at him tenderly, then lifted the corners of her mouth into a sad smile. "In a few days I'm heading to Canada, where my sister lives. I need to get away while I decide what to do. I want you to remember me like this, not as a fifty-year-old woman when you're still a young man." She kissed him briefly. Then she opened the door and he watched her walk out of his life.

He had heard from her only once, early the following spring. She had addressed a postcard to the farmhouse. The postmark was Halifax, Nova Scotia.

Dear Sean,

I am doing well, enjoying my sister and nieces. I take long walks on the beach every day. There are still times when my mind goes into dark places, and sometimes hours pass of which I am hardly aware. But it's a good start, and I feel as if I have made the right decision. I want you to know that you gave me back my *soul*. I wasn't sure that I had one left. Best of luck in your career now. Follow your heart.

Love, Katherine.

P.S. If your fingers aren't stained with paint when you read this, perhaps then it was simply a dream, although one I will always recall with the fondest thoughts.

Stranahan had set aside the letter and examined his hands. He smiled at the umber stains under the fingernails of his brush hand. He taped the letter to the back of the sketch he'd made in the hotel room and framed it in a simple walnut frame. Within three months of meeting Katherine O'Reilly, he had cleared his pending cases and sublet his office, moved to Vermont, and begun to paint full time. He had already had some success in Boston, but it seemed only appropriate that the first painting he sold at a local gallery was derived from the sketch. It was titled *Awakening*, done with broad brushstrokes in pastel flesh tones and dove grays, and fetched him the grand sum of $400. Its subject bore no resemblance to his eventual métier in landscape and angling watercolors, but it was a start, and had led to everything else, including, he thought ruefully, his marriage and divorce and the long drive to Montana.

Tonight, listening to the voice of a stranger, he felt a stirring of intimacy that scared him a little. It was easier to bask in the sad reflections of a lost love, to imagine even that there was still something to go home to after he and Beth had exhausted all the avenues of their escape from each other. But the words of Katherine O'Reilly haunted him, for, long before the end, most of the words were gone from his own marriage.

Stranahan picked up his beer bottle and carried it back to the bar. It was after one. The bartender was wiping the counter and the only patron left was the logger Phil Halverson.

He looked at Stranahan down his whiskey purpled nose. "That was a helluva woman, voice like a fuggin' angel. I don't see the shadder come morning, you just might find me on the second floor, ten toes up, and ten toes down. Yeah," he said, nodding to himself, "ten toes up, ten toes down! What do you think a that?"

"It's a starry night. I think you're going to see the shadow," Stranahan said.

The logger wiped a finger under the filthy brim of his cap as Stranahan left, then stuck it in his mouth. He chased the taste of salt sweat with another swig of beer.

"Helluva woman," he said to himself.

CHAPTER SIX

The Scream

Martha Ettinger groped for the phone.

"Ettinger."

"Sheriff, it's Doc Hanson. Sorry to call so early, but something's been nagging me about the autopsy."

"What is it, Bob? He drowned, right?" She glanced at the bed stand clock radio. Five a.m.

"Yeah, he drowned. But, well, there's a couple a things. . . . I could explain, but it'd be easier if you came down to the morgue."

"That where you are now?"

"Yeah, I woke up and got to thinking, so I came on down. He's on the table in front of me as we speak, the poor fella."

"Give me forty minutes. I gotta feed the horse and the chickens, or else I'll have to drive back out here later on."

"Take your time. He isn't going anywhere."

Martha hung up the phone and sat up in bed. Her cats, Elsa and Sheba, which slept intertwined at the foot of the bed, arched their backs, yawned, and walked up and began to rub their heads against Martha's shoulders.

"Yeah, yeah," she said. "Give me a minute."

She padded on bare feet to the bathroom and opened the hot water spigot in the shower. While she waited for the water to warm, she pulled her flannel nightgown over her head and looked critically at herself in the mirror. Thirty-seven years old, she thought, and wearing every day for the world to see. Martha Ettinger had a round face that was saved from ordinariness by blue eyes that seemed lit from within; when she smiled, which she didn't when looking in the mirror, her face took on a glow.

"She'll have boys flying to her like moths to a flame," her father had been fond of saying, and that had been the truth. Problem was, they were never the right boys. The boy who might have been right, who had grown up on the neighboring ranch, had been too shy to approach her once she reached puberty. It had always been the football players and the rodeo boys who came on to her. She had lost her virginity at sixteen to a calf roper who wore skintight Wranglers and a belt with a buckle the size of an elk's hoof. She could remember lying on her back on the rough straw of a horse trailer, the roper's quarter horse, Charlie, peering down at her from the stall divider while the roper pumped obliviously away. She remembered thinking, *He doesn't even know I'm here.*

Both her attempts at marriage had ended on the same note. When her second husband, Burt, a cattle auctioneer from Miles City, opened his mouth about ten times too often in the Mint Bar one night, she stood screaming while a ranch hand beat him senseless. Flinging herself onto the hand's back, she was cast aside as if she were a bag of feed. Later, pacing the lobby of the emergency room while her husband's jaw was wired shut, she found that she was furious at her own helplessness to do anything when the fight started. It wasn't concern for Burt, who was an asshole and deserved the beating—the marriage had been on its way to the Dumpster for several years—it was her own inadequacy to handle the curves life threw you. She'd been brought up in a tradition of self-reliance, but had the misfortune of being pretty and had allowed herself to be subjected to the wills of alpha males ever since high school, losing most of her self-esteem in the process. She didn't know exactly how, just yet, but that was going to change.

The day after she filed for divorce she put in an application for the police academy in Billings. She was accepted to fill a gender quota but rose through the ranks on her own merits, which included several marksmanship trophies and a brown belt in karate. Ten years after graduating from the academy, while she was serving as deputy sheriff of Hyalite County, she'd been invited to a dance held annually at the Cottonwood Inn during the August Sweet Pea Festival. By Montana standards it was a gala affair, where schoolmarms in sequined flapper gowns vied for space on the dance floor with cowboys wearing jeans, Stetsons, and tuxedo shirts. A fight broke out over a divorce that one man had assumed to be final and another had assured him wasn't, and the next thing Martha knew she was standing over a two-hundred-pound drunk with the heel of her shoe dug into his ear hole.

"Move one inch, dirtbag, and you'll be the first man in Hyalite County to be deceased via a woman's high-heel shoe," she had shouted at him. The night before, she'd been watching *Hill Street Blues* resurrected on a cable channel.

Martha was only vaguely aware of a growing circle of dancers, among whom stood several of the city fathers, including the mayor, Stan Vogel. What they saw was an attractive, slightly chunky brunette woman, sweating and braless under a V-neck silk gown, who was totally in control of the situation.

With no handcuffs handy, Martha marched the man outside and stuffed him into the passenger seat of her date's Jeep Wrangler. Followed outside by a small crowd, she declined invitations for help—"He's not going to give me any trouble, are you, mister"—and drove away.

"Just like Gary fucking Cooper in *High Noon*," one of the dancers wrote in a letter to the editor the following day. The newspaper quote, minus the F-word, struck a chord with the city. Cooper was a native Montanan who had actually gone to high school in Bridger back in the 1930s. Two and a half months later, Martha Ettinger won a three-way race for sheriff by fifteen points. But the dance at the Cottonwood Inn had been the last chance she'd had to wear the blue silk gown.

"How are the boys?" Doc Hanson said by way of a greeting. It came out all one word—"Howrtheboys?"

"Too good to be longing for their mother," Martha said. "Derek's up in Alaska; he has a summer job with the Forest Service cutting trail. David's with his father down in Arizona, hawking Navajo turquoise to tourists, cruising the roads at night, looking for rattlesnakes."

"You don't say? What's a high school kid doing looking for snakes, for chrissake?"

"That's a story for a day when we don't have to attend business," Martha said.

"All right, fair enough. Just help yourself to some donuts and coffee and slip into these after." He handed her a paper suit, mask, and latex surgical gloves.

She decided to skip the donuts. Martha wasn't squeamish: she saddled her horse every November, stuck her .30-06 in the scabbard, and shot her elk, dressed it, skinned it, hung it in the barn, and butchered it. But the autopsy suite at the morgue, with its cold floor, body fluid drain basins, and copper smell of blood quelled any appetite she might have brought to the double bay doors.

She walked over to where the body was lying on a stainless steel table. Even with the bloating she could see the fine musculature and good cheekbones. Just a couple of days ago, she thought, this had been an attractive young man. Who had dyed his hair, she noted. She tried to avoid looking at the torn eye socket that the stick had gouged.

"Like I told you yesterday, the ocular wound was postmortem," Hanson said. "No bleeding; he was already dead. It could have happened when he hit that log after drowning, but so close on the heels of his death you'd expect more lividity. Makes one think he could have been dead awhile before fetching up. The trout fly's another story. Swelling, bruising. Almost like he'd wrapped his hand around the leader and yanked on it."

"Or someone else did," Martha said.

"Or someone else did."

"You got me out of my feather bed to tell me what I already know, or is there something else? Any signs of struggle? I'm taking shit at the department for hushing the newspaper and making this out to be a suspicious death. If it wasn't for the stick being downstream from the body, this is an accidental drowning, cut-and-dried. As it stands, I'm looking like a woman who reads too many detective novels."

"I've been accused of being too thorough myself, Martha. But every once in a while it pays off."

He picked up a surgical tool that looked like a cocaine spoon, lifted the blackened lip, and inserted the spoon into the mouth of the corpse. He scraped deliberately along the inner lining of the esophagus— Ettinger turned her head away, suppressing a gag.

The county medical examiner carried the spoon to a steel counter on which stood an old-fashioned microscope with a squat, matte black body. Hanson deposited a peppercorn of debris onto a glass specimen slide, added a drop of staining solution, then compressed the sample with another slide. He inserted the sample under the microscope lens and made adjustments, talking with his eye glued to the eyepiece.

"My parents bought me this microscope when I was twelve. That was 1963. It was state-of-the-art then. I've probably spent more hours looking through this eyepiece than most people have looking at television."

"What's your point, Bob? Cut to the chase."

He ignored her.

"I was fascinated with nature—not just the marquee attractions, the bear and deer and so on, but the world at my feet. Spiders, snakes—that's why I asked why your son was interested in snakes, 'cause I was. Insects. Chlorophyll cells in leaves. Whatever I could squish between slides, I looked at with this microscope."

He glanced up from the lens. "I wanted to be a marine biologist. Naturally, I'd never seen an ocean in my life. But here was Lake Erie practically in the backyard—my dad worked for Dayton Tire—and when I graduated from high school I chose U of M, Michigan, 'cause they had a program in limnology. Dad was a Buckeye to his core; he's called me a traitor ever since.

"Anyway," he held up a hand when Martha started to interrupt, "I'm coming to a point here. Limnology is the study of freshwater systems, lakes instead of oceans. I was all set to go on to grad school, but then I had a temporary lapse of sanity. The Vietnam War was coming to a close, and as a child of the sixties I thought I could make more of a difference in the world if I concentrated on helping people instead of writing scholarly papers on the taxonomy of mayflies. I'd already taken all the premed courses and had the grades, so I applied to med school and this part of me"—he patted his chest—"has regretted it ever since."

Martha blew out a breath and waited.

"So my point is, you're in luck. There's not another ME in the state who would check out the flecks of debris in this fellow's throat as thoroughly as I did, or who, if he did, would know what he was looking at."

"Which is?"

"Why don't you tell me?"

Martha bent her head to the eyepiece. A mosaic of dots and green oblongs filled the lens.

"What do you see?"

"Pointillism," she said. "Seurat's *Sunday Afternoon on the Island of La Grande Jatte*."

"I'm impressed with your art history, but it's blue-green algae," the medical examiner said.

Martha waited for the explanation. But Doc Hanson, having contained his excitement for several hours, would not be rushed. A coroner didn't get many cases that carried the romance of murder in Hyalite County.

"Now I'm going to have you look at another slide," he said. "This is a water sample, taken from the lungs. Man was a nonsmoker, by the way." He turned the microscope to a higher power, readjusted the focus, and stepped aside.

"Christ," Ettinger said. "They look like the face in *The Scream*. Worse."

"Nasty devils, aren't they? The benign ones that look like haystacks are copepods. The ones with the wicked mouths are cladocerans. They're aquatic invertebrates, eaten by carnivorous insect larvae and baby fish."

"We drink these monsters?"

"We do if we drink lake water," Hanson said.

He held her eyes, waiting for the shoe to drop.

"But he was drowned in the river, Doc. Right?"

"Was he?"

CHAPTER SEVEN

The Color of Blood

Stranahan looked up from his easel. There was something about the cadence of the footsteps in the hall that pricked his brain.

The steps stopped in front of the door.

"Come in," he said, not waiting for a knock.

The shadow in the frosted glass seemed to freeze. It was the same person whose silhouette he had seen the day before, he was certain of it. He held a breath, waiting. Then the shadow vanished, and he could hear the footsteps receding.

He swirled the hairs of his brush in mandarin orange and dabbed distractedly at the canvas. In his painting, a fisherman contemplated twilight with a pull at his pipe, the river parting at his waders in ripples that caught the last blush from the horizon.

The tapping of hard soles on travertine floor tiles returned. This time there was no hesitation. The doorknob turned and he was looking into the face of Velvet Lafayette. Mustering his composure, Stranahan managed to turn his attention back to his painting for a second—an old habit to establish authority—then raised his eyes querulously. She was wearing jeans that accentuated the length of her legs and a stiffly ironed white shirt with a red ribbon under the collar. Her lips were an off-color red. Her hair gleamed. She shut the door behind her without taking her eyes from him and stood silently, assessing him from a distance of ten feet. The corners of the room grew very still.

"So it's you," she said at length. "I thought I recognized your voice."

"A man has to do something besides drive in circles and drink beer at the inn," he said.

"I didn't know that you were a private detective."

"I'm more of a painter these days."

"But you do, ah . . . detect?"

"That depends."

"Oh?"

"I was going to say it depends on what you want. I don't do divorce work. Or repossessions." Divorce and repossessions amounted to 90 percent of the inquiries his Boston office had received.

"It isn't anything like that."

"Then please, have a seat. Let me clean this brush and we'll listen to your problem and see if there's something I can do."

"You're a good artist," the woman said, letting her eyes travel around the room.

"Thank you, but most of what you see is commercial work. Unfortunately, I have to eat."

"No, you really are good, Mr. Stranahan. That's an Irish name, Stranahan." She experimented saying the word, drawing it out with softened vowels in a pronounced Gulf Coast accent. "Stran . . . a . . . han."

"Call me Sean."

"I'd prefer to keep this strictly professional, if you don't mind."

"Of course."

Stranahan dipped his brush in a Mason jar of water, wiped his hands on a handkerchief, and smiled encouragingly.

"Miss Lafayette, what can I do for you?"

She parted her lips to speak, then her expression changed and she seemed lost in some private reverie. She was silent for so long that Stranahan began to wonder if she had forgotten his presence. He caught himself looking at her mouth, trying to place the color on his palette.

Presently her lips moved, she exhaled audibly, and he snapped to attention.

"I'm a very private person, Mr. Stranahan. What I have to tell you I have kept inside for a long time. I have to be certain that anything I tell you will be held in the strictest confidence. Can I trust you?"

"As long as you're not confessing to a felony, or divulging details of a crime that is under investigation, then, certainly, I will keep your confidence."

"Thank you."

He waited.

"Why don't you start by telling me about yourself? Your name, for instance." He raised his eyebrows. "You must admit it's unusual."

"No. Yes, I mean, of course you're right. That's not my real name. I got that listening to a radio show in Biloxi. KDAD. Kay-Dad. They played blues, Bourbon Street jazz; I used to sing along. I was just starting to make a little money in a couple of the bars down in Natchez and a friend—no, not a friend, friendly would be more like it, some guy who was hitting on me. . . ."

She paused a moment.

"Anyway, he said he could get me a spot on one of the big Mississippi gambling boats, but that I'd need a name, you know, showy. Something that said 'grits, gravy, and glitter.' So one day I was listening to Kay-Dad and the deejay says you take the name of the street you grew up on and the name of the dog that chased the mailman down that street and you put them together, that'll be the name you use if you ever want to check into a motel for illicit purposes. E-li-cit purposes, that's just exactly what he said."

Stranahan nodded noncommittally.

"Well, I grew up on Lafayette Avenue. That's in Red Lick. But the dog that chased the mailman was a schnauzer whose name was Brutus, so of course that wouldn't do. But our Siamese cat was named Velvet and I liked the way it rolled off the tongue: Velvet Lafayette, yeah, I liked that." She made an amused sound in her throat, like a cat purring.

"And?"

"Well, I didn't use it for e-li-cit purposes, Mr. Stranahan, if that's what you're thinking."

Now it was his turn to smile.

"I was going to ask your real name."

She hesitated a second before answering.

"Vareda."

He waited, but she didn't volunteer her last name, and as she was just starting to open up, he decided not to press.

"What do your friends call you?"

"I don't know that I have any, really. That's a word people use lightly, but a real friend, no, it's been a while."

"What should I call you?"

"Miss Lafayette would be fine."

"You've never been married?"

"That's none of your business." Her tone was suddenly sharp.

Stranahan looked thoughtfully at her. He was unaccustomed to Southern women and wondered whether all of them could vacillate so easily between demeanors. One moment she was wide-eyed, running on nervously about this and that, then she was flirting with him, or playing with words to amuse herself, and the next her eyes flashed at him in anger, with the accent drained from her voice.

"Miss Lafayette," he said gently, "why don't you sit down and tell me what it is you want me to do?"

He watched her lips open. Blood, he thought. They are the color of blood. Not quite fresh.

"Fish."

"Fish? Fish as in fish, or as in 'to fish'?"

"I want you to fish."

Stranahan rocked back in his chair. He'd heard a few odd requests, but no one had ever asked him to go fishing.

"For trout, I assume," he said.

"Yes, with one of those fancy fly casting rods, like the ones in your pictures. Like the one I saw you carrying to your truck yesterday. There *was* a rod in that case, wasn't there?"

"Yes. . . ."

"Mr. Stranahan, if you can promise me that you are a good fisherman, I will pay you handsomely to fish for trout in the Madison River."

Stranahan watched her parted lips, watched the corners turn up triumphantly.

"Do you think you might be interested in doing some trout fishing for me, Mr. Stranahan?"

Blood, he thought, and not quite dried.

Her story, Stranahan thought, seemed plausible, if not believable. Vareda, aka Velvet Lafayette, had buried her father, Jackson, the summer before. Or at least a part of him. The rest she had in a coffee can on the passenger seat of her Honda Civic. Her father had died of a heart attack while fishing on the Madison River and Vareda had booked work in Montana to pay for gas to drive up, with the intention of scattering the last of his ashes over his favorite riffle on his favorite trout stream in the world. It was a request Jackson had made in casual conversation over the dinner table, but she had remembered. She wanted Stranahan to find that riffle.

And how do I do that, he had wanted to know.

"Old Papa left his mark on everything he touched in his ever-loving life," she said, in such a way that Stranahan intuited immediately that it could have included her. "When he went fishing, he cut a notch in the adipose fin. He said it didn't hurt a fish to cut it there."

Stranahan backed her up. What was a cotton farmer in Mississippi—

she had told him she grew up on a farm—doing fly fishing in the Madison River?

"It's a long story, Mr. Stranahan, and I really can't see how it matters."

Let me be the judge of that, he had told her.

"I'm not asking you to think," she'd said sharply. "I'm asking you to fish. If you don't want the job, I'll find someone else."

Stranahan had tried a different tack.

"What makes you think I would be able to catch the same fish, or know it if I did? Fins grow back. And even if I did catch some trout with clipped fins, they could have migrated from someplace else in the river." That wasn't quite true, but he wanted to see how much she'd thought this story through.

"He fished here in July, the third week. Today is July eighteenth. Trout return to the same parts of the river after spawning. A fisheries biologist told me most of them go right back to hiding behind the same rock. The very same rock, Mr. Stranahan." She gave him a "so there" look. Then she sighed and her face fell. She seemed on the verge of tears.

Stranahan reached across his desk—she had finally accepted the chair he'd offered—and took her hand. Instead of jerking it away as he half expected, she squeezed it with surprising strength. The gold ring he had noticed on her right hand the first time he saw her had a Celtic design. It bit into his skin. On the back of his hand he could feel the rough pads of her fingers, calloused from piano playing. Her red nails were chipped.

He said, "I want to help you, Miss Lafayette. But you have to understand, the odds. . . ." He shook his head. "Your father might have fished any number of places. He could have left trout with clipped fins from Quake Lake to Ennis, and that's just the upper Madison. If you could narrow it down, then maybe, but it would be an awful big maybe."

"I have something that might help." She took her hand from his and brought out a postcard from her purse. "Go ahead. Read it."

The card showed the rustic interior of the Grizzly Bar, the snarling head of a grizzly bear presiding from the wall. It was a fisherman's watering hole, located about a half mile above the West Fork bridge. Stranahan had sat at that bar only a week before, drinking Moose Drool and watching the Yankees and the Indians go into extra innings. He turned the card over. The printing was small, to cram in as many words as possible.

> My Dearest Daughter,
>
> I drove here all the way from Yellowstone, couldn't leave this country before fishing the Madison. They say the whirling disease has wiped out the rainbows, but I've been dreaming about this river and never would forgive myself if I hadn't made a few casts in its famous "blue ribbon" riffles. Imagine my surprise when the first rainbow leaped out of the water! I must have caught 20 of them, nice size all, and on dry flies to boot. Remember those Royal Wulffs I tied, the flies you said looked like hookers? They were the ticket. I notched all of them—V for Vareda. You know how I like to say hi to old friends if I ever catch them again. I better go. There's a fellow at the bar here who says I need another beer. Says he loves my accent. See you next week.
>
> Love, Your Old Papa.
>
> P.S. Sure beats catfishing!

The postmark was Bridger, Montana, July 20—the previous summer.

"He died the next day," Vareda said.

Stranahan handed the card back. He felt ashamed for jumping to conclusions, for thinking that her father possibly had molested her. For immediately conjuring a Southern stereotype.

"Do you think that narrows it down enough?"

"Well, it still leaves twenty or thirty miles of the upper river, assuming he did his fishing not too far from the bar. Part of that stretch, you know, from Lyons Bridge on down, you're allowed to fish it from a boat. One of the guides would have a lot better chance finding a marked fish than I would."

"I hired one last summer," she said, surprising him. "He wasn't much help."

"You came here last summer?"

She shook her head. "I got his name from a fishing store on the Internet. I called him. He seemed like a rude man. He said I was crazy, but told me he'd keep his eyes open. He wouldn't take any money."

"What happened?"

"I called him back at the end of the summer and he said he might be able to help me, or he might not. He wanted me to come up and talk to him about it in person. I knew exactly what he meant. The son of a bitch. I wouldn't trust anything he had to say."

The defiant look was back on her face.

"Well, the chances are your father was fishing above where the guides put in. Most wade fishermen stick to the top section, from Quake Lake to the West Fork."

"How far is that?"

"River miles? Nine, ten."

"You'd have a chance, then."

"I don't want to get your hopes up. Those were older fish your father caught. To be fourteen inches long last year—what I think he means by a good fish—they'd have to be four, five years old now. That's a long time for a trout to live. If he really did mark twenty—and all of us stretch the truth so it's probably more like a dozen—well, there's no telling how many are left. I'd feel guilty taking your money."

"The last time a man said that to me he wanted to be paid the old-fashioned way."

Stranahan looked directly at her.

"I'm sorry. I shouldn't have said that. I didn't mean . . . I mean, I've never doubted your . . . honor. I just . . . I'm alone now, you get to be around a certain kind of man. . . ." Her voice was barely a whisper.

She composed herself. "This is what I want to do," she said with her chin raised. "My father—each other—since Mamma died, we were all that we had. I make good money, Mr. Stranahan. I'll give you a thousand dollars. Fish until it runs out. At least then I'll have tried."

Stranahan could see there was no use arguing.

"When I heard you sing last night," he said, "you said you'd be here through tomorrow night. How will I get in touch?"

"I'll call you." She got a pen. "Do you have a home phone?"

He almost said, "Your hand is ten inches from it," but what would she think about hiring a detective who lived in his office and took sponge baths in the men's room? "Call here. I'm old school. I don't have a cell. They don't work in most of the state, anyway."

She wrote the number down in a small black notebook, then put it in her purse and drew out five one-hundred-dollar bills.

"I'll give you the rest tomorrow night after my show. That's when I get paid. You'll come?"

Stranahan nodded.

"I still think you'd be . . ." He saw the expression in her eyes and stopped. "I'll drive down this afternoon and camp on the river tonight. I'll be back for your second set tomorrow."

"Then I'll see you at the inn." She held out her hand, insulating herself once more with a professional veneer. Stranahan took it. She stood up. Suddenly she seemed uncertain. Her lips parted, then closed.

"Is there something else?"

"Yes. It's a small thing, really."

"A small thing," he repeated.

"There's someone else who might be fishing in the river. He's trying to find those trout, too, you see. And I thought, well, if you saw him there, you could tell him to call his sister."

Stranahan looked up at her. His mind sighed. So that was it. Admit it, he told himself, you're a sucker. A pretty woman walks through the door, asks you to do some fishing for her . . . He shook his head, smiling at his gullibility.

"I think you'd better sit back down, Miss Lafayette," he said, "and tell me what this is really about."

CHAPTER EIGHT

Stone by Stone

At 9 a.m. Saturday morning, Martha Ettinger stood on the Route 87 bridge watching a dozen fishermen salute the Madison River with graphite fly rods, out-of-staters almost to the man, wearing hats that advertised fishing lodges from Panama to the Kenai Peninsula. The only Montana plate on the sagebrush flat that served as a parking lot was attached with baling twine to the bumper of a battered Toyota Land Cruiser.

It was a long shot. The chance that one of these fishermen had witnessed a man—or a strong woman, for that matter—lugging a waterlogged body into the river ten miles downstream three days previously, if in fact the deceased *had* drowned in a pond or lake as the algae and microcreatures in his lungs suggested, well, it was about the same as her chance of being invited to another ball at the Cottonwood Inn. Nobody fishing this high would have seen the drowned man, that was certain, but it didn't mean one of these anglers hadn't fished the downriver stretch in question earlier in the week. After her meeting with Doc Hanson Friday morning, Martha had spent the rest of the day with Walt, covering the river from the place where the body had been found up to the Route 87 bridge. They had interviewed 136 fishermen, campers, and sightseers, only one of whom remembered seeing anything remarkable. A birdwatcher, looking to add the violet-green swallow to his life list, reported spotting a bear on the riverbank at twilight on Tuesday, a mile from the West Fork bridge. Martha had pricked up her ears; the time frame was right and the body had been discovered not far below the junction of the West Fork and the main stem of the Madison. The birdwatcher said it was so dark the bear wasn't much more than an articulated blob in his binoculars. Maybe, he admitted, it wasn't a bear. He had never seen a bear before. He was from Illinois.

She trod down the embankment at the bridge spur and crooked a finger at the first fisherman.

"Sir, I'm Sheriff Ettinger. I'd like to ask you a couple questions."

The young man made one more cast, reeled up, and waded ashore.

As she worked up the bank, a few anglers weren't so polite. They continued to fish during the interview and Martha let them, studying their body language for nervousness, looking for mistakes in timing that caused the loops of line to collapse. She also made a point to see what flies they were fishing.

It wasn't a bad way to spend a day. The river was azure blue, the corridor of the current enveloped by a cool, clean breeze. "Big Sky Country" was the state motto, and never truer than here, Martha thought, where you could see mountains sixty miles distant. To the north spread a vast amphitheater of light, where weather systems developed on the limestone escarpments of the Gravelly plateau, dropped curtains of gray rain, sent lightning shivers across the valley, dissipated, and then built again in purple thunderheads on the western front of the Madison Range, all while you watched in a T-shirt with the sun poaching the freckles on your forearms.

Martha sat down on a rock. She dipped her hat in the river and let the cold water dribble down her forehead. Five feet away, a garter snake swam through the rushes at the edge of the bank. It submerged, poking its head under stones to look for sculpins; then its head periscoped, the red-and-black forked tongue flicking, tasting the air. Martha gave it a wan smile. Going stone to stone—that was what she was doing, too. And with about as much luck. She had questioned seventeen fishermen in the first two miles, but there was no public access on this bank of the river. Anyone she found from here to the dam either lived in one of the streamside mansions on the south bank or had to have walked all the way up from the bridge. There wouldn't be many.

In fact, she found only one more angler, a man standing ankle-deep in the slot of whitewater where the river shot out of the earthen dam of Quake Lake. To her right, the mountainside was a concave scar of rubble deposited in the wake of the disastrous earthquake that had dammed the river completely in the summer of 1959. In the collapse of the mountainside, nineteen campers who were sleeping in their tents had been buried alive. The bodies remained under this debris, and to Martha it seemed their spirits still persisted in the mists that hung over the outlet.

The fisherman who had chosen this lonely spot was broad shouldered, fairly tall, and seemed completely at home in his body. As she watched, he waded from boulder to boulder with a light dancer's step, effortlessly navigating heavy current in which she'd be hesitant to stick a toe. He cast with none of the gymnastic waving of the inexperienced; he simply pointed his arm and the line followed. She watched his fly dancing along the seams of the current. When he turned to acknowledge her, a heavy bang of jet-black hair fell over his left eye. He scraped it back with his finger, gave her a crooked grin, and waded downstream toward her.

"Beautiful morning," he said, removing his sunglasses.

"What?" The roar of the river was so loud she couldn't hear him.

He stepped out onto the riverbank stones, his pant legs dripping water. He wore felt wading shoes but no waders. The stem of a pipe protruded from the pocket of a threadbare blue work shirt unbuttoned halfway down his chest.

"I said it's a beautiful morning."

Maybe he wasn't as young as she'd thought. Traces of silver framed his temples and, as he smiled, lines radiated from the corners of his eyes. Martha caught herself smiling back, conscious of the sweat stains under her arms.

"How's the fishing?"

"Great. Catching's a little slow." There was that smile again.

Martha checked the fly hooked to the stripping guide of his fly rod and looked up.

"My name's Martha Ettinger. I'm the sheriff of Hyalite County. Did you know that a man was found drowned in this river a few days ago?"

"I saw the paper," he said. "But I thought that was down around the West Fork."

"A little lower actually, below Lyons Bridge. But fishermen get around. We're trying to talk to as many as we can to see if anybody saw someone fall in or noticed anything out of the ordinary. Were you fishing this Tuesday?"

He scratched at a stubble of beard.

"I fished in the evening. But that was down below Ennis, in the Bear Trap Canyon."

"It was a long shot," Martha admitted.

The man nodded. "Well, that's what fishing is, too," he said. "Every cast's a long shot and then sooner or later a trout comes up and your fly disappears." He gave a short laugh. "Later, mostly."

Martha brought her notebook out of her shirt pocket, added his name—Sean Stranahan—and his phone number to her list of question marks, which so far consisted only of the man who had maybe seen the bear. She thanked him for his time.

"Good luck to you, Ma'am," he said.

Martha hadn't heard a man call her Ma'am in ten years.

"Good luck yourself," she said. She climbed up the high bank and started walking back down toward the dead-end private road where Walt had agreed to meet her. *Martha*, she said to herself, *you're a lonely heart. You feed chickens in the morning and at night you brush*

*your cats and go to bed alone. The only way you'll ever catch a man
as good looking as that one is to arrest him.*

It wasn't such a bad idea. Arrest him, she thought, then jump his
bones and pump the truth out of him. Ask him, for example, why,
out of all the fishermen she and Walt had talked to, he was the only
one with a Royal Wulff knotted to the end of his leader.

CHAPTER NINE

A Light in the Window

After the sheriff left, Stranahan clipped the Royal Wulff from his leader. With its snowy wing and red floss body, it looked about as conspicuous on the surface as a hummingbird in a teacup, and that's precisely why he'd tried it. Any trout that managed to survive in this torrent didn't ask questions; if a fly looked like food, it ate it. He'd given the Wulff fifteen minutes to prove that point. It hadn't.

He examined the flies in his box and selected a nymph pattern with a tungsten bead at the head. To the leader he added a blob of biodegradable orange indicator that would float on the surface as the fly ticked the gravel. This was about as far from fly fishing as a boy drowning a garden worm under a wine cork, he thought wryly. But it was just about as effective, too, and today he was fishing for his living, rather than the other way around.

Or was he? What was he really doing here? When Vareda Lafayette had reluctantly sat back down in his office yesterday afternoon, he had asked directly if her brother was missing. She had insisted he wasn't. Her brother, who would be a senior at Ole Miss this fall, had a summer job working in a fish hatchery near Great Falls on the Missouri River. The hatchery was two hundred miles north of Bridger, but he had agreed to help find the trout their father had fin-clipped on his days off. It was his second summer at the hatchery, and, having fished his way around the state, he knew the Madison River. But he didn't have a cell phone and she hadn't been able to reach him. She thought he might have driven down and could be on the Madison now—that was all. But he was a kid and she wanted to hire Stranahan because he was a professional.

"How do you know I'm a good fisherman?" he had asked her.

She'd asked at one of the fly fishing stores for a reference and his name came up, she'd told him.

That must have been the Kingfisher, Stranahan thought. He'd fished upriver from one of their guide boats while the guide was preparing a bankside lunch, and had caught one trout after another swinging a marabou streamer, much to the consternation of the guide's clients.

"And then," she was saying, "when I found your studio and saw that you were a private detective, that settled it for me."

Stranahan had let that pass and got down to business. What car did her brother drive? A small sedan, if it was the same car he drove back in Mississippi. Blue, or maybe dark green. It had an Ole Miss bumper sticker. What did her brother look like? Auburn hair, like hers. He'd told her he was growing a beard. What did she really want: for him to fish or just have a look around? Both, she insisted.

"Okay, then," he said.

She stood up.

"Aren't you forgetting something?"

She looked at him with a cool expression.

"Your brother. He has a name, I assume."

"Of course he has a name. He's Jeffrey Beaudreux." She spelled it for him. "Jeffrey Jeremiah. We call him Jerry. J.J., sometimes."

"Thank you. Is that also your name, Beaudreux?"

"It was. A long time ago. Now, is that all?"

Stranahan hesitated only a moment, dreading that he might be the bearer of bad news.

"Miss Lafayette, have you seen today's newspaper?" he asked. "Or yesterday's?"

Again, the level gaze.

"Because a body was found in the river the night before last. You say that your brother could be fishing on the Madison. I'm not implying a connection, but it would be derelict of me not to mention it to you."

"Yes, I heard," she said, biting off the words. "But that poor man wasn't my brother, if that's what you're asking. That man had blond hair. Long blond hair. And he didn't have a beard. The paper said so."

"I'm relieved to hear that," Stranahan said. But he was looking at her back and she let herself out without turning around.

Stranahan had played the conversation over in his mind when he had driven up the Madison Valley the afternoon before. A part of him had suspected all along that the story about the trout was bullshit, or at least was parenthetical to the real reason she'd knocked on his door. Dutifully looking for a car with Mississippi plates, he'd checked every river access from Valley Garden to the West Fork Campground, where he'd thrown up his tent to spend the night. This morning, he had worked from the West Fork to the Route 87 bridge, which crossed the Madison three miles below the Quake Lake outflow. He had hiked the bank all the way to the lake outlet before starting to fish, to fulfill the second part of his verbal contract with Velvet Lafayette, or Vareda Beaudreux, or whoever she was.

So far, he had failed miserably. He'd caught only two small trout before being interrupted by the sheriff, and another two, slightly better fish, in the next hour. Each he'd brought quickly to hand, examined its fins for scarring, and released. He'd seen nothing unusual and hadn't expected to. Before the onset of whirling disease, a parasitic infection that had decimated the population of rainbow trout fifteen years earlier, the upper Madison had been home to more than three thousand trout per mile. It still nourished a little more than half that number. The chances of catching fish that another angler had caught and marked a year previously seemed ridiculously remote.

Like any good artist, Stranahan was a sensualist. For two summers during his college years, he had worked as a driller's helper, taking core samples from sites where the Massachusetts Highways Department sought to build bridges. J.D. Harris, his boss, was a rough, exuberant man who had hands like hams from wielding drill casings all day long, but he could lay two fingers against a rotating drill rod and tell you exactly what the bit was coming up against two hundred feet down.

Something like this sense of touch Stranahan carried to the river. It was a subtle form of expertise that the writers of the fishing manuals overlooked. They reduced fly fishing to a nuts-and-bolts proposition, leading their readers to believe that the man who had the highest modulus graphite rod, the line with the slickest space-age finish, the invisible fluorocarbon tippet, and the perfectly tied fly would so overwhelm a trout with technological superiority that it would open its mouth in defeat. Stranahan knew that success rested upon touch more than it did on technology, and that technique took a backseat to concentration and desire. You fished a river by feel and your heart rode with the fly. The minute you let your mind wander, you were lost.

He fished methodically back toward the bridge, taking at least one trout from every third or fourth pocket where the river paused long enough to catch a breath. None had a V cut from its adipose fin. But as he squatted down to bring a fine rainbow of seventeen inches to hand, he saw a glint of light in the distance. He had waded out to a gravel bar and was facing the west bank. The light flashed and vanished. Then it flashed once more, seeming to originate from one of the cabins on the bank, although "cabin" was hardly an adequate word to describe the colossal log structure, with its wraparound deck sporting enough rough-hewn patio furniture to stock the lobby of the Old Faithful Inn.

No doubt some millionaire Californian owned the place. He would keep binoculars on the sill to track the flight of osprey or spot bighorn sheep on the opposite mountainside. The light was probably the reflection off the lens. Even if someone was watching him, and Stranahan had an uncomfortable feeling that someone was, there was no harm intended—just someone fishing vicariously through the successfully bent rod of a passing angler.

Stranahan released the trout, trying to shake off the thought that there might be more to Velvet Lafayette's story than she had told him. He headed downriver with a brusque step. If one needed an excuse, the next decent riffle was around the bend, anyway. He felt supersensitive to his surroundings, the melody of the current more insistent now that the shadows were lengthening. He rounded the bend and felt the constriction in his chest ease. Tan caddis flies swarmed from the willows as he pushed through branches toward the river. The mucky earth that sucked at his boots held a faint smell of mint. Stranahan stepped quietly into the water and began to cast.

CHAPTER TEN

A Scent in the Forest

The host of the Beaver Creek Campground, a gaunt giant with the pinched face and corrugated cheeks of a Depression-era farmer, opened the door of his trailer at Martha's knock and said no, there were no abandoned cars in the campground.

"Anyone who hasn't paid up?"

"Everybody's square, Sheriff," he said seriously. Hair the color of an orangutan's sprouted from the V-neck of his undershirt and he had a faint, hoarse voice, thrown like a ventriloquist's, so that it seemed to emanate from somewhere else. His eyes were rheumy, the pupils blurred. Martha found she had a hard time looking at him.

"I have half a lung," he said, as if sensing her thought. "That's what you get after thirty years in a West Virginia coal mine. Whisper's best I can do."

"I can hear you fine," Martha said.

Walt walked up from the Cherokee, where he'd been stretching his legs. "Maybe you have someone who's paid up but the campsite seems to be abandoned, never see anyone around? Car might have Mississippi plates." He was thinking of the hat Ettinger had found at the logjam. "Anytime in the past week or so."

"I'll look."

The man disappeared into the trailer and came back holding a clipboard. A Manx tabby cat darted out the door and underneath the trailer.

"That's Suzy," the man croaked, his lips barely moving. Martha had to resist the urge to look past him and search the cluttered interior of the trailer for the source of the voice.

"Nice cat," said Hess. He squatted down and clucked to the cat.

"Well," the man said, scratching a stubble of salt-and-pepper beard that seemed incongruous with the flame thatch that flourished on his chest. "D-24's been quiet. I take a drive around, once in the morning to catch the late arrivals, make honest men of them"—he rubbed his fingers together to indicate payment—"and again about eight in the p.m. Haven't seen anyone there now in, I don't know, five-six days."

"Is there a car?" Hess asked.

"Last I looked."

"You get worried when a camp seems to be abandoned?"

"Well . . ."

"Just a little?"

"Sure. I suppose."

Martha frowned at Hess.

"What's the name on the register?" she asked the host.

He looked down the list. "Bill Johnson. Dillon, Montana. No street address. Occupants, one. Filled out the register Tuesday night, paid up through the weekend. Subaru, Montana plates, Bridger prefix. Sound like your fella?"

"This Johnson, what's he look like?" Ettinger said.

The gaunt man shook his head.

"Came in after dark. I usually take a stroll around the loops about ten, you know; the doctor says it's good for my heart long as I don't push it. There was a fella setting up a tent. I got the double vision half the time so I seen two of him, but I wouldn't recognize him if he knocked on this door. I just collected the money in the envelope. He paid cash, I suppose that's unusual. One night, two nights, no. But six nights, nine bucks per, that's fifty-four dollars. And left me a tip at that. Three twenties." He raised a pair of eyebrows as thick as scrub brushes.

"You have the ticket?"

"I'd have to dig for it."

"We'll check out the campsite while you do."

"One thing I remember," he said, "he was dang sure comic; didn't seem to know what end of the tent was what."

Site D-24 was secluded in the pines on the lip of a high bank. A small girl, her ringlets of blond hair catching the last of the sunlight, was dancing on the picnic table. She jumped down at the Cherokee's approach and dashed along a faint path toward the only other campsite within view, where she disappeared behind the flap of a khaki tent trailer.

Martha and Walt clambered out and took in the camp. A Subaru sedan with a paint-peeled hood was parked in the gravel tongue; a small dome tent was staked down by the table where the girl had been dancing.

"Why don't you take a walk next door, Walt, see what that girl was doing here. And see if anyone's noticed anything or seen anyone while you're at it," Martha called after him.

"Okee-doke."

Martha stood with her hands on her hips, looking down a valley of lupine and Indian paintbrush toward Quake Lake, its shoreline in purple shadow. The bare bones of lodgepole pine trees stuck up like porcupine quills from the surface where the Madison had flooded after the earthquake.

She felt the fine hairs on her forearms erect with goose bumps.

"This place gives me the willies," she said under her breath.

She told herself to calm down. She had moments like this when she felt scared and inadequate, like she was still a child. She would become dissociated from her body, wonder who this woman was who wore the uniform and packed a pistol on her hip. From habit, she placed her left hand against the side of her neck and felt her pulse beat against her fingers. Strong and steady.

Refocusing, her eyes glanced from the tent to the picnic table, from the fire ring to the car. The car and the table were coated with a fine pollen. The girl's shoes had beaten a tattoo on the middle boards of the table. The fire ring contained a few chunks of charcoal; a depression in the middle of the ring showed where someone had doused the fire. Everything had a long disused look. She peered at the windshield of the car. On the dash was a green card that might be the stub of a camping permit, but the refraction of a light through the tinted glass made it impossible to read.

Walt's approach interrupted her appraisal.

"Nope," he said when Martha lifted an eyebrow. "Girl's mother says she's a, quote, 'Razzle Dazzle.' That's some sprite dancin' group and she just loves to shake her booty—that's the mom's word, not mine. Their picnic table's too cluttered, so she come over here. I asked her if she'd seen anyone here, says she hadn't and they been camped three days. The girl's name is Mary Beth. Her eyes got big as saucers when she saw my piece. Good thing I didn't draw the bowie." Walt patted his hip. "She didn't open her mouth the whole time I was there."

"Can't say I blame her."

Walt twitched his nose. "I think I smell somethin' in the trunk of the car," he said. "I think I smell enough to take a closer look."

"That the Chicago way, Walt?"

"Nope. That's just the way it is. You play by the book, nobody gets to eat beans in the Big House. Besides," he said, "didn't that camp host say he was worried?" Hess gave her a wink and a grin.

"You son of a gun," Martha said.

She walked over and pulled the zipper of the tent flap. Peering inside, she saw a rumpled sleeping bag. Piled beside it were the bare bones of a camping outfit—Coleman stove, cook box, cooler, a tipped-over lantern. Using the side of her thumb, she snapped open the latch of the cooler and peered inside. An open package of hot dogs, a mustard bottle, and an empty Pigs Ass Porter beer bottle floated in a pool of water. A couple of blue plastic ice bags, the ice melted, eddied around the edibles. She wrinkled up her nose.

She knelt inside and patted her hand over the nylon tent floor. "There's not enough level ground for a chipmunk to lie down on," she said.

Backing out of the tent, she crooked a finger at Walt, then pointed to the frame of the car.

"Okay, we'll do it your way. I think circumstances are suspicious enough. You think there might be a hide-a-key?"

Walt knelt down on the ground and grappled under the radiator. "Ah-ha."

He stood up beaming, pinching the edge of a magnetic box between his thumb and forefinger.

"Let's work this with kid gloves," Ettinger said. "I don't want that latent fella bellyaching about smeared prints. And don't walk around except on this patch of grass. Maybe we can coax that crime scene examiner, the Blackfeet Indian guy with the girl's name, Little Feather, something or other Feather"—she knew the man's name and puzzled at her reluctance to let on to Walt—"get him to come down from Browning. He might be able to find some footprints or tire tracks from another vehicle."

"Whatever you say, Marth."

Walt pulled latex surgical gloves over his hands. He turned the key in the lock and opened the passenger door. He withdrew the card from the dash.

"What's it say?"

Walt peered at it, holding it at arm's length. Ettinger impatiently plucked it from his fingers.

"Buy yourself some reading glasses, for heaven's sake."

She examined the card. "Bill Johnson," she said. "Same name as the register. Same dates." She walked around the back of the car and checked the number on the stub against the license plate. It was the same, also.

"Check the glove compartment for the registration."

Walt rummaged for a second.

"Anything?"

"Montana map, pack of No-Doz. No registration or insurance card. There's a rain jacket in the backseat, fly rod case"—he shook it—"feels empty. You want me to pop the trunk?"

Martha nodded thoughtfully. She bent over to peer inside the passenger door as Walt walked to the back of the car. Her mind was turning cylinders, trying to get some tumblers to fall.

She sniffed, then used the blade of her Swiss Army knife to crack open the ashtray.

"Doc said the victim wasn't a smoker. There's nothing in the ashtray, but I think somebody had a smoke. Put your nose in here, Walt."

Walt shook his head. "I can't smell anything, but that don't mean squat. I lived too long in the city to have much nose left."

Martha eased the door shut with a bump of her butt and smiled sourly as Walt poked the key into the trunk's lock. She noted bright scratches on the bumper where it looked like someone had taken a key or the back of a knife and scraped off a couple of stickers.

The hood yawned open with a pneumatic hiss. Spare tire, hydraulic jack not original to the car, tow rope, a coil of bright orange tube for sucking air from a full tire to inflate a flat. And a cardboard box of tools, well used.

"Handyman," Walt said. "This ain't the ride of no CEO."

Martha put her hand on the carpet flooring.

"Damp?"

"Damn gloves make it hard to tell." She rolled up a sleeve and pressed the underside of her wrist here and there. "Maybe against the side here. Yeah, I think so."

Martha shut the trunk, set her hands on her hips, and looked out across the water.

"Okay, I'm going to think out loud for a minute," she said. "We've got a campsite nobody's been seen in for five days, a car that's been stripped of ID, right down to scraping off the bumper stickers. We got a generic name on the camper registration and license plates that have a Bridger prefix, even though the registration card says the camper is from Dillon. So I'm thinking the plates could have been boosted and our guy got too cute. We'll call the numbers in, see about that. In the meantime, assuming this is the victim's car, and I think there's a strong possibility, the question is—how does it get here when he's twisting in the current twenty miles downriver?"

"That's easy, Marth," Walt said. "The guy who killed him drives it up here, sets up a camp under a name he picked out of a hat so no one will make a connection to our floater. While we waste time figurin' out what's what, he takes a powder."

Martha grunted. "Doc Hanson says he drowned in still water 'cause there's algae in his lungs. 'Cause there's wicked microscopic bugs. So we're looking at a river backwater or a lake. But instead of leaving the body where he kills him, our killer drags him out of the drink, stuffs the body into the trunk of the victim's car, drives it to the river. Hauls the body out to the logjam, grunts it upstream to the head of the jam—the stick in the eye tells us that much—all this effort to make the case for accidental drowning look convincing. Then what? He changes plates, scrapes off the bumper stickers, removes any ID from the vehicle, drives it back here, throws up the tent—the camping gear must have already been in the car—and walks away."

She reconsidered. "No, I'm wrong about the order. He drives here first to set up camp. Remember how the host said he saw him wrestling with the tent at ten o'clock? That's barely twilight this time of year, be too risky to dump a body in the river that early. Maybe he leaves the man where he was killed long enough to drive the car up here and set up camp. Then, after nightfall, he drives back to the scene, wraps up the body, and puts it in the trunk. He dumps the man in the drink, drives back up here again, and abandons the vehicle. Walks away."

Walt pressed his lips together.

"Walks away, Marth? This camp is nowhere and grizzly country to boot. What do you think about an accomplice? There could be a second car."

Martha nodded her head imperceptibly.

"Yeah, maybe." She paused. "I don't know, though. Most murder is personal. No, I think he's alone, he ditches the car, he walks away. He could be a local, has his own car parked a few miles away. Or maybe he's staying in another campground or at the cabins at Slide Inn or up by the Grizzly Bar. It's what, six-seven miles to Slide? Walkable."

"Somebody might have seen him if he walked the road."

"Late at night, there's not much traffic. He could duck away if he saw headlights coming."

Walt said, "Be worth putting out the word in the radio and the newspaper, see if anybody spotted a man on foot."

"We'll do that. But right now what we do is ribbon off this camp-site. Then I need you to put a plastic sheet on the driver's seat and drive the car back to Bridger. We'll need to run the VIN number."

Walt nodded. "Okay. But 'fore we go, all your supposin' is based on supposin' that the killer put the body in the trunk of this car, drove around with him awhile, then put him to sleep with the fishes. Switched license plates, for the love of Pete. That's a lot of exposure. What I'm saying is, well . . . two things. One, why bother movin' the body at all? Why not leave it to be discovered by the lake, or wherever it was he was drowned? 'Cause it would be found earlier? It was found the next day anyway. Two, why drive the car here? Why not just remove the ID, wipe your fingerprints, and leave it by the river? Doesn't add up."

Martha tapped her foot on the ground.

"Unless there was something about the place where he was drowned that could tie the two of them together. But you're right," she said. "We're missing something and I don't know what it is. Hmpff. Come on, let's go see that Lurch fellow who runs the camp. See if our visit jogged his memory."

She walked back to the car.

"You coming, Walt?"

"I'm comin'." Walt swallowed, his prominent Adam's apple bobbing up and down.

Without turning around, he said, "You feel it? You feel the difference in the air? Like a chill. Normal police work, it just makes you jaded. But killin' does something else. It gets in your bones. You're around death, it gets in your bones. You can't be a normal person anymore. You try to talk to a lady, carry on a conversation, there's this gulf. You're not living in her world. It's like an eternal twilight, like you're doomed to live in fog where it's cold all the time. A boogeyman's life. You can't wash it off. It's no way to be. I moved out here to get away from it."

Martha felt a muscle flutter above her collarbone. She felt it all right. For the second time in twenty minutes the hairs of her arms lifted against the sleeves of her shirt. She could smell it, smell it in the earth and the pines. Or maybe just knowing sharpened the senses. She looked away from the sepulchral lake and its ice-pick tree trunks and took a couple breaths.

"It's a bastard all right," she said.

CHAPTER ELEVEN

Rocky Mountain South

"I knew you couldn't stay away," Doris said. "Didn't even have time to change your clothes, just shucked your waders and had to see her, didn't you?"

"Our relationship is strictly professional."

"And what relationship might that be?" Doris cocked a hand on her hip.

"One of mutual admiration, I suppose." Stranahan took a swig of beer, holding the sweating bottle with two fingers on the neck. Except for a cupped handful of water from a seepage spring on the riverbank, it was the first drink he'd had since dawn, when he'd brewed cowboy coffee at his campfire on the West Fork.

"Crowd's bigger tonight," he offered.

"They're not coming for the listening. It's the watching. It's like she's left a scent trail around town and all the men have followed their noses. Tell me honestly, Stranny: What do men see in her? She's superficial. No, she's worse than that. She's artificial. Every word she says, it's like honey pouring out of the comb."

"It's Southern, Doris. It's her heritage."

"Bullshit."

Stranahan had to smile. "There's the fact that she's a babe," he said. "That might have something to do with it."

"I've got a niece who's pretty as she is. She's one of the dairy Size-mores, three sections up on the Musselshell River. Deeded land right up against the national forest. Let me set you up with her. You'd have your own trout stream."

"You sound like my mother before she passed."

"She really knows how to milk a cow, if you know what I mean." Doris suddenly blushed. "I didn't say that, did I?"

"Yes, you did."

"I bet your mother wouldn't have said that."

The lights went down in the ballroom.

"No. Shssh. We'll talk about it later. And, Doris?"

"Huh?"

"There aren't any trout in the Musselshell. It's catfish and suckers."

Doris deliberately screeched her chair getting up and walked back to the bar. "Phil," she said to the logger, "I hear one word tonight and I'll toss your skinny ass right into the crick."

"It's only three hundred. There was some misunderstandin' on my pay tonight."

"I could talk to Doris," Stranahan said, pocketing the wad of twenties she'd handed over.

Velvet Lafayette lit a cigarette and waved the smoke away with her hand—the offer, too. She was flushed from singing. A sheen of sweat clung to the smooth skin of her chest, above the scoop neckline of a peach dress.

"Doris is that old farm girl sits with you?" She added a syllable—"gu-url."

"She's not that old farm gu-url. She's my friend."

"I didn't mean it that way. I'm from a farm; it's a takes-one-to-know-one thing, that's all." She lifted the hair from the nape of her neck and flipped it over the back of the chair. "It's hot up there; never thought I'd be sweating in Montana. My mama wouldn't let me use that particular word. A girl perspired, farm labor sweated. Look, I'm short two hundred from what we agreed on. I can send it to you next week. I'll be playing near Butte . . . or maybe it's Billings. A name like a snake. Near one of those B towns. That's west of here, right?"

"One's west, the other's east."

She waved a hand at the smoke, at the absurdity of directions.

"Forget the money," Stranahan said. "You've hired yourself a fisher-man. It's not like it's real work. I take my paints to the river, anyway."

"The least I can do is buy you a drink."

Doris walked over, stared down at them.

"Two Wild Turkeys. Ice." Velvet glanced at Stranahan.

He nodded.

She took another pull at her cigarette and tamped it out in an ash-tray.

"That's my quota. One cigarette when I'm done singing. Three, four a week, tops. Do you smoke?"

"No. I mean yes."

"You either do or you don't."

"My dad gave me a pipe. I puff at it to keep the mosquitoes away when I'm fishing. I'm like Bill Clinton. I don't inhale."

"I do. That pretty much applies to everything in my life. They can put it on my tombstone—She inhaled."

"I felt like somebody was watching me today," Stranahan said.

"The sheriff. You told me."

"No, I think there was someone looking through binoculars from a cabin. More like a log mansion, really." He looked at her, saying nothing.

"Why would anyone do that?"

"I don't know." Stranahan held her eyes. "Do you?"

"What do you mean by that? No, of course not."

Doris brought the whiskeys, said they were on the house, wheeled on a heel, and left. Stranahan sipped the drink thoughtfully. Liars embellish their version of the truth. They look off to the left, he'd heard once, something about the lobes of the brain. Liars offer explanations. She hadn't and he believed her, but it wasn't the same as thinking that she had told him the whole story.

She reached across the table and took his hand, squeezing it hard under her thumb.

"All I'm asking you to do is help me bury my father," she whispered. She let go of his hand, picked up her drink, and swallowed the amber liquid. Stranahan could feel the burn as blood returned to his fingers. She tinkled the ice cubes in the glass and set it down. She stood up.

"I'm no longer at the inn. I'm up the street a ways now. Walk me home, Mr. Stranahan."

"If I walk you home," he said, "it isn't Mr. Stranahan. And are you Velvet, or is it Vareda?"

"Vareda. Walk me home . . . Sean."

They walked without looking at each other along the footbridge that spanned Bridger Creek, then up Gallatin Avenue past two-story Victorian houses with leaded windows paned with uneven glass that reflected prisms of lamplight. After a few blocks, Vareda turned up a stone walkway toward a house with a trellised second-story balcony. The house looked like it ought to be fronting a square in Savannah, Georgia. The walkway led to a secluded backyard and stopped at a white country cottage with a shake shingle roof and a porch with a swing.

She patted the seat of the swing for Stranahan to sit beside her. Above them, the arms of an elm tree cast shadows that flickered across her face as the swing swayed back and forth.

Her voice came from the shadow.

"This is a bed and breakfast. Called Aberdare, after the mountains in Kenya. It's owned by a Kikuyu couple. He looks like an ebony god and she's like his queen. They have guest rooms on the top floor and keep this cottage for honeymooners and, well, anyone who wants to pay. The whole house is filled with African art."

"It's beautiful."

"I know what you're thinking," she said. "You're wondering how I can afford to stay here when I can't pay you properly. But when there's a cancellation or a room open, they offer it to musicians playing at the inn. All I have to do is play piano for an hour before the dinner meal—it's bed and breakfast and dinner, too—and they let me stay free."

"Rocky Mountain South," Stranahan said.

"Not any South I ever knew."

"What South did you know, Vareda?"

"The one where nothing's the way it seems to be to others," she said without hesitation. "But I've talked more than I should have. It's your turn. You're from Vermont, you said."

"By way of Boston."

"What brought you out here?"

Stranahan was silent for a minute. It was a question he'd asked himself many times over the past three months.

"Don't laugh," he said, "but when my wife and I separated, when I was done packing up the truck, I drove to a crossroads at the edge of town and sat there for half an hour. I didn't know where to go. My sister would tell you it's because after Dad died I spent so much time taking care of the family that I lost track of who I was, and my wife would say there wasn't enough of me left to be there for her, but I don't know. I turned west, I think, because my father had talked about taking me on a trip to the trout streams out here. He liked this quote of Hemingway's, something about where a man feels most at home, except for where he was born, that's where he's supposed to go. My dad figured that was the Rockies for him, though he'd never actually been to the mountains. So in a way I came here to complete his dream. And to find out if it was mine. I'm still not sure."

Stranahan was aware of the warm pressure of her hand. He felt her fingers interlace with his.

"Dad was a mechanic," he went on. "Anywhere we drove, my mom would pray that we wouldn't pass a car broken down, because he'd stop to help and we'd be late to wherever. I don't know how many times I remember him pulling off the road saying, 'This'll only take a minute.' He'd be rolling up his sleeves and the other guy would look up from under the hood and my dad would say, 'What seems to be the problem?' Next thing you know he'd pop the trunk and climb into his overalls.

"Well, wouldn't you know, the car that killed him, he'd put an alternator in it the day before. The kid driving was fiddling with a tape deck, not paying attention. He jumped a curb and busted a fire hydrant. Dad turned around and started coming back to help. The kid panicked, water shooting everywhere, and jerked the car into reverse. . . ." Stranahan snapped his fingers.

"I was sixteen. We moved out of the city, up to Adams to live near my grandfather, who had a rental house we could use. My grandfather was a lawyer in Boston, partly retired to the country by then. He'd always wanted my father to follow him into law school and into the firm, but all my dad's talent was in his hands."

"So that's where the painting came from." Vareda lifted his hand and put his arm around her. She laid her head against his shoulder.

"No," Stranahan said, "the painting came from my mother. She was the artist in our family. Well, that's not entirely true. My dad was an artist in his way. He tied trout flies. He even built a machine for milling bamboo strips to make fly rods. I still have one, his signature on the flats ahead of the cork. The action's slow compared to graphite. But that's what I like about bamboo. You have to relax into the rhythm of the rod. It makes fishing less of a contest." He stopped. "I don't want to bore you."

"You're not boring me, but it is getting cold."

"Well, I ought to say good night then. Will I see you tomorrow before you leave?"

He started to stand, but she pulled him back.

"You're not going anywhere," she said.

She put both her hands behind his head and pulled him into a long, slow kiss, and he knew that the scent of oranges was from the rinse in her hair.

"Stay here," she whispered. "I won't be a minute."

When she returned, pulling the screen door of the cottage closed behind her, a man's shirt was loosely draped over her dress. She swiveled around on the swing until she was lying with her head resting on his lap.

"Keep me warm," she said, and placed his arm across her chest so that his hand cupped her left shoulder. She wriggled the side of her body against him. "That's better. Go on now. Talk to me."

"My mother had a box of oils," he said. "I used to go into the closet and open the tubes to smell the paints. Nothing like it . . . no wonder so many great artists died young. I still use lead white for oil painting because it's a warmer color than zinc, but . . ."

"Gittin' high in Mama's clothes closet," Vareda said, and chuckled. He could feel his arm rise and fall with the movement of her chest.

"Something like that," Stranahan said. "She'd stopped painting by the time I was born, but there were a couple of her oils on the wall: Indian ponies and a portrait of a girl wearing a red dress and a sad face sitting on the floor of a dark room. It's very good. But she was a mother, that's all she wanted to be, and anyway, she never picked it back up."

"What about you?"

"She bought me sketchbooks, starting when I was about three years old. I'd draw birds and animals, anything I could find around the pond or in the woods behind our house. It wasn't something I had to think about, just natural."

"The woods? I thought you grew up in Boston and didn't move to the country until later, after your dad died."

"It wasn't the city exactly, about ten miles south, a place called Milton. The Blue Hills were my backyard. The only time I actually lived in Boston was when I went to work for my grandfather's law firm summers after college. He had a retired Boston police sergeant to do his snooping. Percy McGill. Black Irish, like me. The greatest character I met in my life. I can remember the first time I saw him; he stuck out this big hairy hand and said, 'Sean, you don't want to do this. It's like drinking blood. You can't stop, you just keep going 'til somebody sticks a stake in your heart.' To make a long story short, I did stop. I went back to painting and moved to Vermont and got married to the sweetest girl in the world. Something happened, or didn't happen." He snapped his fingers again. "The spark died. Maybe it was never there."

"No children?"

"She couldn't have them. I told her it didn't matter, but it mattered. She never felt like she was whole. But there's more to it than that."

"There always is," Vareda said.

She smiled sadly, then he watched her smile lift, transforming her face.

"And now you're here."

"Now I'm here."

"What am I going to do with you?" She looked at him, playing a little, letting the words fall with a buttery drawl.

"What do you mean, what are you going to do with me?"

"Well," she said softly, "I could let you go. I suppose that would be the smart thing to do."

"Or I could go," Stranahan said. "Save you the trouble."

"Oh, I don't think so. No, we women have our ways. At least we do in Mississippi."

She lifted her face to be kissed, then, taking his hand, stood with him and moved to the door.

Stranahan was dreaming. He was dreaming that a cat was lying on his chest, its front paws curled under its chin, its small motor purring. Stranahan scratched its cheeks tentatively. If he moved the fur the wrong way, the cat would leave, and he wanted it to stay for the comfort and warmth it provided. Then the cat was gone and it was Beth, moving from his touch to her refuge on the far side of the bed.

He reached out in his sleep and his right hand brushed Vareda's hair. She was lying with her head against his shoulder and his left arm was numb. He ran his hand through her thick hair, stroking her scalp with his fingertips. When she stirred, he eased his dead arm from under her head. She murmured something and rolled over, pulling him against her so that they lay together like spoons.

"This isn't going to work," she whispered after a minute.

"What isn't going to work?"

"Anything. Everything." She breathed in deeply. "You. Me."

"You haven't seen me fish yet," Stranahan said.

She laughed softly and rolled over, bringing her lips to the hollow of his neck. He could feel the air cool his wet skin as her kisses traced down his throat and across his chest.

"My . . . fisher . . . man," she whispered.

CHAPTER TWELVE

A Can of Worms

When Stranahan awoke, she was gone. He had known she was gone, feeling the difference, that humidity change and palpable hollowness, for some minutes.

The note was pinned down by the hooves of a carved ironwood Cape buffalo standing on the table before the window. Lifting the buffalo was like lifting a brick of black gold. Stranahan held the note out until the narrow, backhand letters came into focus.

> Dear Sean,
> I am leaving while there is still time. For me, but for you, too. This way you will remember only the best parts of me. I leave you all that is my father. Please keep our secrets. I trust you. Be careful. Vareda.
> P.S. Don't try to find me. I know how to disappear, even from myself.

Stranahan glanced around the room. He was looking for the coffee can of her father's ashes. But the only traces she'd left were a long auburn hair on her pillow and the earthy smell of her skin. He wound the strand of hair into his shirt pocket. Before leaving he read the note again, noticing the left-handed script.

Be careful. His lips formed the words.

"Of what?" he said out loud.

Stranahan folded the note into his wallet and stepped outside the cottage. It was early, the grass wet with dew. A grackle with iridescent feathers cocked its head on the clipped lawn, then darted its beak down and tugged at a night crawler. The night crawler elongated and snapped free. The grackle bit it sharply and cocked its head once more while the worm writhed in knots on the grass.

"I believe that Americans say it is the early bird that gets the worm."

Stranahan looked up to see a tall black man in cutoff jeans and a faded denim shirt standing by the back door of the house. He was watering the hanging plants suspended from the roof of the wrap-around porch.

"None of the other guests are up, but if you would be so kind as to take breakfast with me, both Ullana and I would be delighted. I believe we have huevos rancheros." The man's voice was deep and resonant, with a reserved British accent that belied his casual dress.

Stranahan climbed the steps to the porch. He shook the man's outstretched hand. The ebony face split into a smile.

"Joseph Keino. I believe you are Sean?" Stranahan pulled his head back slightly. "I am not a soothsayer, Mr. Stranahan. Miss Lafayette told me you might be coming for breakfast."

"You saw her this morning?"

"I saw her leave, yes, from the window. Very early. She spoke to me yesterday at supper."

Stranahan followed Keino inside to a table facing a side window off the kitchen. He sat down, absorbing the news while trying not to betray his surprise. So she had known beforehand that he would be spending the night with her. He felt slightly let down and shook it off. Hadn't she said that women like her had their ways?

"Sean—may I call you Sean? This is my wife, Ullana."

"Don't get up," the woman said. She held a breakfast tray balanced on an upturned hand and with her other hand set plates on the table. She bent to pour coffee. The edge of her palm, where she held the handle of the coffee press, was the coral blush of the inside of a conch shell. She was the most beautiful woman Stranahan had ever seen.

Her mocha skin was perfectly smooth. Her wide-set brown eyes were illuminated by flecks of gold around the iris.

"Thank you," he said.

"It is my pleasure." She turned, smiling, her long black braid shifting in the hollow of her back, and disappeared into the kitchen.

Stranahan found he was very hungry.

"This is delicious," he said at length, and, thinking to make conversation, asked, "How did you come to America?"

They talked about Kenya, how Keino had come to the states as an agricultural student and was back and forth until the political climate in his home country made an educated democratic man persona non grata. But he seemed distant as he spoke, as if he was thinking of something else.

Finally he said, "Sean, while we have been sitting here I have been debating whether to tell you something that might be important. I've decided to because I very much like Miss Lafayette and she made it clear that you were a friend to be trusted. Yesterday, when she was helping us with the supper, I saw her looking out the window. She seemed highly nervous. I cannot say if she was frightened, but that is what I felt."

Keino rose. "Perhaps it's best if you see for yourself."

Stranahan followed him into the kitchen. Copper pots hung from an oval track over a tile island where Ullana was chopping peppers.

"You can see the cottage," Keino said, standing before a small window. "But not the front yard or the sidewalk. She was not looking at the street. I asked her if she was expecting anyone. She said no."

They walked back through the kitchen and sat down.

Stranahan said, "It couldn't have been me she was expecting."

Keino tapped the side of his nose. "Where I lived, you trust this more than these." His fingers separated to touch his eyes. "I sensed that whomever she expected, she did not want to see this person. Later she spoke of you and it was plain to see that you did not affect her that way. She has asked a favor from me. She said do not let you leave without giving you her package. I will get it."

He stood and walked into an adjoining room. When he came back, a chamois cloth shirt in a forest green was draped over his arm and he was carrying a package wrapped in brown paper. It was the shape of a coffee can. He set the shirt beside it. The shirt cuff was mono-grammed MJD in gold thread and Stranahan suspected it was the one she had been wearing the night before.

Keino held up a hand as Stranahan started to speak.

"You don't need to say anything. I am doing this for Miss Lafayette. As I said, I am quite fond of her. But please take the package. And the shirt. She said you were to wear it when you fished for her. You do not need to explain these mysteries to me."

Stranahan said, "You overestimate the extent of my knowledge."

"No, I understand perfectly," said Keino. "She *is* a beautiful woman. And you . . . and I"—he smiled—"are men.

"Now let me show you the house before the guests awake. You are an artist, Miss Lafayette tells me. I have a collection of artifacts I think you will find interesting."

CHAPTER THIRTEEN

First Water

Stranahan hung the shirt on the hat rack in his office. He sat down and stared at the paper package for a long minute. Then he opened his fly-tying kit, removed the scissors, snipped the paper around the coffee can, and lifted the plastic lid. He thought he was prepared, but the pea-sized gravel of bone gave the remains a gravitas that was unsettling. He could smell smoke and something darker. Tentatively, he stirred through the ashes with a pencil. It seemed to be what it was supposed to be, what a human being was reduced to in a two-thousand-degree oven. But heavier than you'd expect.

He closed his eyes, trying to resurrect bone chips into the father of the woman with the bloodred lips. He pictured a man casting in the Madison River. He could see the Royal Wulff dancing in the swirl behind an exposed boulder, the strike, diamonds of water shedding from the line, the gray head bowing and thick, farmer's fingers engulfing the tiny scissors of a Swiss Army knife. But why would anyone want to clip a trout's fin? When he'd pressed Vareda on the point, she had said you have to understand farmers. They brand cattle, notch pigs' ears—they leave their mark. Stranahan wasn't sure he bought it.

He replaced the lid, unlocked the lower right-hand drawer of his desk, and set the can inside, next to a stack of Beth's love letters he had taken with him from Vermont. It seemed like a betrayal and he promised himself he'd move the can somewhere else soon.

Stranahan glanced at his watch. Too late to drive to the Madison and be back before cocktail hour at the Trout Unlimited banquet. He wouldn't have minded missing it; yuppie fly fishermen bored him to tears. But there was the matter of money. He didn't see fishing for beautiful women as an industry with much growth potential. Being on hand for the auction would bring him into contact with potential clients.

He turned to the half-finished canvas that he'd been working on when Vareda first came through the door. He worked best when his paintings were envisioned as story scenes. He'd lost the thread of this one—just what in hell was the man doing there, with the rod tucked under his arm and his pipe in his teeth? In the painting it was twilight, the river glinting to pearlescence through shadows of forest. Feeling for a mood, he found himself reeling back through the years to a summer night on Vermont's Battenkill River. He was following the cherry glow of his father's cigarette as they waded downstream. The river rose around his thighs, swirling, murmuring to itself. The over-hanging limb of a weeping willow dipped rhythmically into and out of the current. A trout rose. Then his father was casting, the line whistling in the darkness. There was a sudden walloping explosion and his father's arm came up and he turned to hand over the rod— "Here, take it now, Stranny"—and then that thumping weight pulling him into the lost dimension, the river magic where time stops and the human soul pulses out through the fingertips to merge with the wild.

He picked up his brush and began to paint.

There are many ways of feeling alone. There is the squeezed-chest loneliness of walking down a dark alleyway, and there is the self-reliant isolation of fishing a midnight river in wilderness. There is that delicious hollow feeling of standing alone in a slumbering city, waiting for the light to change on the metropolitan avenue shining under the street lamps after the rain, secure in the knowledge that the woman whose bed you have left is dreaming about you and it is two against the world—a loneliness built for two. And then there is the devastation of being left by someone you love.

Stranahan had known all these forms of loneliness, including the unfocused drifting that had been his life since moving west. But upon entering the convention room of the Holiday Inn, he found that a cocktail reception in a room full of people you didn't know engendered a form of uncomfortable solitude he'd just as soon do without.

The Trout Unlimited banquet hosted an eclectic mix: men with what-the-hell beards scattered among trust-fund complexions, women sporting spaghetti-strap dresses and muscular calves, graying Montana natives standing straight as ramrods, wearing bolo ties.

Stranahan bought a watered-down bourbon and Coke and studied the competition on the wall and the long table where the art was displayed. His eyes were drawn to a night scene of the Gallatin River, a thoughtful, moody oil that had Lee Stroncek's signature. Next to it was a Francis Golden watercolor of a steelhead river winding between buff-colored bluffs. Here and there a trout leaped from a teak pedestal, trying to escape polished-wood water. Stranahan's contribution, *First Water*, hung at the far end of the wall. The river flowed under a ceiling of mist. A single ray of sunlight shone on a distant pine as a man pulled on waders by the side of a beat-up pickup truck, the steam rising from a thermos coffee cup set on the wheel well. The painting was a cliché, a necessary nod to the popular market, but it was also the autobiography of a thousand mornings in Stranahan's life.

He heard the voice first—gruff, full of gravel, amiable.

"What these pictures need are naked chicks in them, you know, wearin' hip boots and goose bumps."

Stranahan turned to see blue eyes twinkling over a smashed nose and a broad expanse of beard.

The man stuck out a meaty hand.

"Rainbow Sam."

He took the hand, escaping the grasp with tingling fingers.

"Sean Stranahan."

"What I'm sayin' is the sport oughta let its hair down. Fly fishermen have become insufferable, seven X this and *ephemerella* that. It's goddamned pansified Latin gibberish. For chrissake, a trout's a phallic symbol and let's not forget it."

He pointed at *First Water*.

"Paint in some red-tipped double-breasted mattress thresher pulling up high-heeled hip boots and buddy, I'm telling ya, you'd have every man in the room puttin' up his hand to bid."

Stranahan had to smile. He said, "I'll think about that next time I put a painting in this auction."

The man squinched up his face as if he'd received a blow. "Shit, I didn't mean nothin'. It's a goddamned good painting. You just have to excuse me. I'm always putting my foot in it; comes from never shutting up."

"No offense taken," Stranahan said. Seeing an opening to bridge the man's discomfort, he added, "You're Sam Meslik, aren't you? The guide? It was your client who found that body?"

Sam's eyes lit up. "Yeah, I caught some strange things before—bats, beavers, hooked a buffalo in the Park once on my back cast, had to break him off, a'course, woulda taken too long to land and I didn't have a tag for him."

Sam chuckled, his voice trailing away. Then he seemed to recall the question and said, "Yeah, that was my first homo sapiens, though. The only good cast my client made all day. Dumb shit couldn't catch a turd in a cesspool."

He lowered his voice conspiratorially, "You ask me, it weren't no ordinary drowning. It coulda been, but then it coulda been something else, is what I'm sayin'. I'm not supposed to tell anybody this," Sam said—though he had told anyone who would listen in the past five days, including three bartenders and the checkout girl at the County

Market—"but you find a man drowned with a size twelve Royal Wulff stuck in his lip, you ask yourself how it got there."

Sam jutted out his lower lip and with his forefinger hooked an imaginary fly through the center of it. Stranahan could see V notches in several places in his upper teeth.

"He hooked himself on his back cast?"

"Yeah, but the hook point was forward." Sam tugged at his lip, indicating the direction of the pull. "I s'pose he coulda caught it coming forward, you know, on his delivery," Sam said, "but usually you catch an ear or hook yourself in the back of your neck. Right in the center of the lip, and the lip all blowed up bloodshot—just seems unlikely to me."

"So you figure someone hooked him on purpose and the fly broke off?" Stranahan prompted.

"You said it, I didn't. But it makes a fella wonder, specially when you see a two X tippet hanging off the fly."

"Two X, that's awful heavy," Stranahan agreed. In fact, two X tested out around twelve pounds and was way too stout to use with any dry fly smaller than a sparrow.

Sam continued, "Now why would a guy use a tippet that's so thick he can hardly poke it through the eye of the hook? The fly isn't going to ride right and the fish will shy away from the tippet. The way I figure, either he doesn't know anything about fly fishing or he's fishing for some mighty dumb trout."

"Not many dumb trout in the Madison," Stranahan said.

"Don't I know it. And I know the man could fish some because I'd seen him." Sam briefly explained the circumstances under which he had recognized the young man. "So I been sniffin' around. I don't have much faith in that woman sheriff or the clown she has for a deputy."

Stranahan would have pursued the conversation, but the emcee of the evening was clearing his throat, calling for everyone to sit down to dinner. The burly guide drifted away to sit at a table with the clients he'd been fishing with that day. Stranahan found an empty chair at an adjoining table beside a middle-aged couple from Texas. The Texan was a Lone Star icon in bolo tie and Stetson who emphasized his opinions with a finger that jabbed toward Stranahan's chest, the woman a bleached blonde, wearing a snap-up Western shirt unsnapped to reveal freckled, very deeply suntanned cleavage. From her ears dangled glass pendant earrings enclosing miniature trout flies.

Stranahan made what conversation he could, but his mind was on the auction. He didn't permit himself expectations. Although the *Boston Globe* had heralded him as a "poor man's Ogden Pleissner," which the writer had intended as a compliment, he was unknown here, and in the art world reputation was much more important than quality of work. Stranahan's reputation, such as it was, had been made on his New England riverscapes, their distinctive characteristic a singular lack of fishermen. He thought it was enough to create the mood of angling; let the buyer paint himself into the picture where and how he wanted. His downfalls were the same as his strengths: refined taste, a rich yet somber palette, and a sense of restraint. But cliché was what sold. Collectors of angling art, like collectors of wildlife or Western art, harbored illusions of sophistication, but they wanted to see trout jumping and mountains reflected on water. Stranahan's concessions to commercialism—painting an angler into *First Water*, for example—usually didn't go far enough; that was one reason he was living in his studio.

Coming last on the auction block wouldn't help. There was money in Bridger, but it was young money, in impatient pockets, and buyers were likely to get in on the action early. As he'd predicted, the Stroncek oil and Golden's watercolor moved at good prices, $950 and $1,100 respectively. Most of the other paintings went for between $350 and $650, sculptures and carvings in the same range. Two young women paraded down the rows of tables, holding the pieces high overhead, like ring girls carrying placards between the rounds of a boxing match. They wore matching white blouses, trout-print bandannas knotted at their throats, and crimson lipstick.

Stranahan felt a tap on his back and turned to hear Sam whisper raspily, "What's Montana coming to, eh buddy?"

The auctioneer's voice cut short further comment. "And now we come to *First Water*, a truly gorgeous oil by Vermont artist Sean Stranahan. This is it, so let's dig deep for the good fight to protect our treasured trout streams. Do I have five hundred to start the bid?"

He didn't, settled for $300, and from there the bidding inched upward. Stranahan felt his chest expand and seemed to lift fractionally off his chair, floating in suspension as the auctioneer's disembodied voice receded into the background. It was ridiculous, he knew, but he was always like this at an auction, even though any money the painting garnered was donated to the cause.

His chest eased a bit as the bidding reached $500. At least now he wouldn't be disgraced. But the bidding plateaued at $550. "I got five and a half, five and a half going once, going twice . . . and I got a six hunnerd dollar bill. Thank you, sir. Do I have six and a half?"

Stranahan was too late to see Rainbow Sam lower his hand, but an exaggerated wink was enough to betray the bid. Stranahan's fondness for the gruff-looking bear grew by bounds.

The bidding was picked up at $625 by the same ruddy-faced man who had helped trade it up to $500. He took it for $800 a minute later as Stranahan felt his back muscles sink into the hardback chair. It was more than he had hoped for. True, he'd once sold a painting for five grand at a benefit to save the Androscoggin River in New Hampshire, but that was a cause célèbre for one of the east's most hallowed trout rivers and he'd had the benefit of name recognition. Plus, the Madison Avenue executives and Boston Brahmins who were spreading like a cancer across New England buying and restoring farmhouses needed something other than molting deer heads and leather-yoke mirrors to adorn their walls.

After the auction, Stranahan found the man who had bought *First Water* and introduced himself. Richard Summersby had an iron handshake and said he was from the Santa Ynez Valley in California, where he owned a vineyard. He said if Stranahan ever got down Santa Barbara way, he should stop in for some grape juice. He smiled at his little joke and winked at Stranahan, rich man to rich man. He said he and his wife had a "bungalow" on the Madison River where they fished during the summer. The house, Stranahan suspected, was what realtors called a "two-two-eighter": two people, occupied two weeks a year, eight thousand square feet. The kind of trophy palace where Stranahan's painting would be introduced to the khaki clientele that wildlife and angling artists crave, before sleeping unseen through the winter.

Excusing himself, he found Sam in line for the bar. "What's yours, buddy?" Sam said.

"I should be buying you the drink."

"Nah, I liked your painting; it was real, absence of booty and boobage notwithstanding. But it's dangerous to put up your hand in that crowd."

It was the most genuine compliment Stranahan had heard all night. He said, "Guess I'll have a whiskey to celebrate. Bourbon and whatever. I'll get the second round."

"Won't be anyone to drink it," Sam said. "I'm outta here. The featured speaker is a personal friend of mine, and a fuckin' PC bore. He's going to give a spiel on the curse of whirling disease, how it passes from fish to bird to river, how we all gotta wipe our boots and hose our boats down so we don't spread it around and lose the resource. Yada, yada, yada. I mean, it's true, whirling disease is still killing trout despite the naysayers putting their heads in the sand and saying the rivers are recovered. Anyone who fished the Madison in the old days can tell you it's still a big fuckin' problem. But the way he talks you'd think we were worshipping the goddamned trout, not yankin' and crankin' em.

He went on, "Hey, I gotta free day tomorrow. How about doing a little fishing with me at Henry's Lake? Now those are trout that are trout. I caught hybrids there that went ten pounds. Damsel nymphs on the menu this time of year. Do you have a float tube?"

Stranahan didn't.

"Then I'll bring my extra. Meet me at Josie's, six a.m. You know Josie's?"

He nodded.

Sam handed Stranahan his empty drink cup. "I'm going to see if I can't get one of them mattress threshers to let me rub her fur the wrong way." He glanced sidelong at one of the bandanna girls who had paraded the paintings and, winking, disappeared into the crowd.

CHAPTER FOURTEEN

Damsels in Distress?

Josie's was a Main Street café famous for its down-home breakfasts and an anatomically correct, full-size fiberglass replica of a palomino stallion. Mounted on an electronic pedestal that pirouetted above the door of the redbrick building, the horse was both a Bridger land-mark and an initiation rite for the Delta Sigma fraternity of the branch college. Each fall, students of the freshman pledge class stole into town in the night, hastily erected a ladder, and—keeping a sharp lookout for police—sent one person up the steps to paint the horse's pendant masculinity the university colors, blue and gold.

Stranahan was staring at the belly of the beast when a vintage Volkswagen Bug rattled to the curb. Rainbow Sam opened the pas-senger door and began to climb out, a three-step process for a man his size. He was dressed in the same clothes he'd worn to the banquet. His shirttails hung over his belt and his face looked baggy and hag-gard.

"Thanks, baby," he said.

Stranahan recognized the woman behind the steering wheel as one of the bandanna girls—minus, at this early hour, her trout-patterned kerchief.

"Thanks, Darcy," she corrected him.

"I know your name, baby," Sam said.

"I want to hear you say it," she said. "Come here," she said, reaching over and pinching his cheek. She pulled him back into the car.

"Thank you, Darcy McGill," Stranahan heard Sam say.

"McCall," she said sharply, then relented. "I guess that's close enough." She released her grip. "Poor baby," she said, accessing the damage she had done to his cheek, which had turned as red as a cherry. Leaning forward, she impulsively kissed it. Stranahan could see dark roots at the part in her blond hair.

"I'll see you," Sam said as he shut the door.

"Yes, you will."

"Women," Sam said to Stranahan, and clasped a hand on his shoulder.

Josie's Café was vintage Main Street Montana. Battered oak floor, upholstered art deco chairs, waitresses who'd heard every story since Genesis, the smells of grease and flapjacks, and, on the knotty pine walls, bucolic black-and-white landscape panels of grazing cattle. In back of the counter, elk heads flanked the scabby shoulder mount of a Shiras bull moose. There was a jackalope above an empty table against the wall. Stranahan and Sam sat down under the fork-horn rabbit, cobbled together from the head of a mounted jackrabbit and a pair of small deer antlers.

The waitress, a heavyset woman who had a silver streak in a head of coarse black hair and an echoing stripe through her left eyebrow, smiled at Sam as she pulled a pencil from behind her ear.

"Honey, you don't look so hot," she said.

"Pam, I had a bad dream last night," Sam said. "I dreamed you and me got hitched and I woke up all sweating and commenced to screaming."

She shook her head. "That's so lame I'm going to forgive you," she said. "So what'll it be?"

Sam ordered a Mexican omelet with a short stack on the side.

"Hard day's night, a man's gotta eat," he said.

Stranahan ordered the number one—two eggs scrambled, toast and jam.

They made fishing talk until the dishes came, Sean picking Sam's brain about whirling disease, about which he knew little more than that it had struck in the 1990s and wiped out 90 percent of the rainbow trout population in the upper Madison River. The night's keynote speaker had indeed been a bore, talking in scholar-speak about invasive species in general rather than the malady itself.

Sam shifted his bulk in his chair.

"Not my favorite breakfast topic," he said, "but it's your basic parasite/host thing. There's this spore—*Myxobolus cerebralis.* In part of the life cycle it's carried in a little worm about yea big"—he held his thumb and forefinger a half inch apart—"called a tubifex. The spore bores its way into the bones of baby trout and upsets the equilibrium. The trout swims like a cat chasing his tail, and I don't have to tell you that's like ringing a dinner bell to a bigger fish. Bottom line is that once the trout gets WD, he's a goner. If a fish doesn't get him, a kingfisher or an osprey will."

Stranahan interrupted, "So then, when the trout dies, it releases the parasite back into the water. That means if a bird poops in another river or a fisherman cleans his trout in a different river than he caught it in, it can release the spores and spread the disease."

"You got it. But it can also be transmitted by mud, 'cause that's where the worms live. A fisherman can be a carrier, or a boat. Fish one river, drive an hour, step into another wearing the same wading boots, instant infection."

"I thought the whole point of the parasite/host relationship was that the parasite doesn't kill its host."

Sam grunted. "In the natural order of things, it doesn't."

He explained that whirling disease was native to Germany, where the parasite infected the indigenous brown trout, which had developed a resistance to the disease. The Western rivers where whirling disease was a concern—and there were 150 in Montana alone—were primarily rainbow or cutthroat trout fisheries. The American species were much more vulnerable.

"So then, what's this I hear about recovery in the Madison River?"

"Mostly bullshit. The people who are saying this figure that because the rainbow population has rebounded to about 60 percent of what it was in the old days, the fish are developing a natural resistance to the disease. But the biologists I've talked to think that the rainbow trout stocked in Hebgen and Harrison reservoirs have worked their way into the river system, inflating the numbers of healthy fish. This strain of rainbow trout we're catching today is different than the one we were catching twenty years ago. They run smaller and they don't like to feed on the surface as much. The upside is that they seem to have a little more natural resistance to WD than the original strain. But I stress the word 'little.' If somebody ever develops a rainbow that shows resistance *and* feeds on the surface *and* grows long as your fucking arm, I'd pull my pants down for him along with most of the other fishermen I know."

Their breakfasts arrived and they ate in comfortable silence, sipping ranch coffee so weakly flavored that Stranahan wondered if the beans had percolated or simply been steamed in the vicinity of the pot. When the waitress walked over to offer a second cup, Sam nodded toward Stranahan.

"So, Pam," he said, "I caught my friend here gawkin' at the Rocky Mountain oysters hanging off your horse. Does he look *Brokeback Mountain* to you, I'm starting to wonder?"

Pam looked Stranahan up and down. "Nah, I'll give him the benefit of the doubt. Josie'd let me, I'd take a saber saw and make a eunuch of that critter. A woman goes to work at five in the morning, she shouldn't get flashed by a two-foot candy cane unless she wants to."

"I'm tellin' ya," Sam said, "after Darcy last night I'm scared to see what color mine is."

Pam frowned. "I thought I saw her Bug out front. You," she rapped Sam on the back of his head with her pencil, "you treat Darcy right; that girl's had a rough time of it. She needs a good turn after that

Dolan fella. I'll take it personal if she comes calling and you're the subject of our discussion."

"Who's Dolan?" Stranahan said when she had gone.

Sam shrugged his shoulders. "Asshole out of Roundup. Left her at the altar, Memorial Day last. Her whole family in the Disciples of Christ and everybody's looking at their watches. The father, old-time Swede rancher, finds Dolan at the Crystal Bar brooding over a beer. Gives him a chance to be a man. Dolan seems to be thinking it over when the old man says the hell, he's scum anyway, and beats the shit out of him. Pool-cued his ass."

"You like to live dangerously?"

"No, but my pecker doesn't know from that."

Sam noticed Stranahan glance at his watch.

"Don't worry, Bud," he said. "The damsels don't get going till ten most mornings. We'll be fishing in plenty of time."

Stranahan drove Sam to the south edge of town, where a wood-tie bridge crossed Bridger Creek. A dilapidated trailer sat on a cement block under a canopy of ancient cottonwoods. As the Land Cruiser pulled to a stop, an Airedale as big as a deer bounded over and put its paws up on Stranahan's shoulders, stretching to lick his face.

"Down, Killer," Sam barked. The monster obediently dropped to the ground.

Stranahan transferred his gear into the camper shell on the back of Sam's pickup, which sported a "Whoa Dude! There is a speed limit in Montana" bumper sticker, referring to the state's infamous "reasonable and prudent" speed law. He climbed into the cab.

"Now we're livin'," Sam said, and gunned the engine to life.

As they drove up the Madison Valley, Sam pointed out the logjam where his client had hooked the body. Barely visible from the road, it was a rare stretch of the river that was banked by conifers. Sam pulled over at a turnout and let the motor idle.

"Secluded," Stranahan offered.

"Convenient. That's the word that comes to my mind," Sam said.

"You really think somebody killed him?"

"Ah, I don't know. Coulda drowned. Coulda *been* drowned. But here's the peculiar thing. Guy's wearing an inflatable wader belt, the kind that you pull the cord and a CO_2 cartridge inflates it? You figure he's got a bug up his ass about drowning."

"So what's so unusual about that?"

"He didn't pull the cord," Sam said. "Makes a man think that maybe someone else pulled the waders on him after he was dead."

"Did you tell the sheriff this?"

"She'd have to've been blind not to see for herself."

They drove in silence until turning onto the 87 cutoff.

Sam grunted, "Poor bastard seemed like a good kid, too, the kind never says a bad word to his mother." He shook his head. "But hell with it. Let dead dogs lie. Let's catch some trout."

"Ten pounds, you say?" Stranahan said, shifting mental gears and remembering the size of the fish Sam had told him about in Henry's Lake. "I've never even seen a trout that big."

Sam shrugged his shoulders. "Good clean living, it can happen."

"What we're looking for," Sam explained after Stranahan had bought a one-day Idaho license at Staley Springs and they had pulled to the side of the road by a grove of aspens, "are lanes of open water through the weeds." He indicated a point of land that fingered into the gray lake. "There's a ten-foot hole shaped like a T off this shoreline. We're going to work our flies through lanes in the hole."

Stranahan began slipping fins over his wading shoes while Sam rummaged under the camper shell through his gear. "Here, I want you to take this rod. It's a six-weight."

He held up a hand as Stranahan began to protest that his four-weight was heavy enough. "Hey, I just might know more about this than you do, okay? You hook one of those cuttbows in the soup, you got to reef on him."

Stranahan accepted the rod without further protest. At a glance he knew it was made by Winston, a Cadillac among rod makers with a factory in Twin Bridges, Montana. The reel seat was hand-turned German nickel silver, the rod blank looked lit from within, finished in a glowing forest green. Just ahead of the sweat-darkened cork grip, a few wraps of black electrical tape obscured the rod blank, where the maker's name and model number would be painted in white ink. The reel held a smoke-tinged, intermediate density line that would sink slowly through the water column.

Stranahan said, "What's with the tape?"

"Just covering up a nick in the graphite," Sam replied. "Here," he said, "use one of these." He handed Stranahan a slim fly with monofilament stubs to resemble eyes and a sparse marabou tail. "You gotta shake your rod tip on the strip, that's the secret. No, let me." Sam took the fly from Stranahan's fingers. "You need to use a loop knot with this fly, it'll free up the action." He tied the damsel nymph to the tippet with flying fingers, then raised the fly to his lips and bit off the tippet end extending from the knot.

"So that's how you got the grooves in your teeth," Stranahan said.

"A few more years and I'll look like one of those natives that file them into fangs." Sam harrumphed, handed over the fly, and, walking backward, they both eased their donut-shaped tubes into the water.

It was like sliding back into the womb. Stranahan immediately felt a soothing peace envelope him. Lazily, he kicked with the flippers, keeping a parallel course to Sam's. Looking toward the bank he saw a flicker of color as a male bluebird disappeared into a birdhouse tacked to a fence post. How had he managed to fish all these years and never think of float-tubing before this?

His reverie was broken by the crack of a rifle. Another shot rang out, echoing through the canyons of the Gravelly Range to the north.

Stranahan paid it little attention. He been in the Rockies long enough to dismiss distant shots as part of the soundtrack.

He heard a rasping noise and turned his head. Sam was pulling line from his reel and lengthening his false casts.

"How deep do we fish?" Stranahan asked.

"Right off the bottom if you can find a lane through the weeds. My advice is to count down. Fish out a dozen casts at a five count, then try 'em with a ten count."

Stranahan's first casts were awkward. He had to learn to keep the back cast high to avoid slapping the water behind him. But soon he settled into a rhythm that matched Sam's. The chitchat petered out and they fished seriously, working out the hole and then moving down the shoreline to the east.

After an hour without a strike, Stranahan replaced the damsel nymph with a tan-and-black leech fly, made a cast, counted to five, and was into a fish. He felt a thrumming strength as the rod bent into the cork. It was as if he'd laid his fingers against the base of a power pole. Stranahan dropped the rod tip and watched the core of backing on the reel grow thinner and thinner. Three hundred feet out, the fish porpoised, its back rolling out of the water like an otter turning over. Then it dug deep. He had never hooked a trout with such implacable power and felt his hands trembling as the fish's runs shortened.

Sam had kicked over during the fight to encourage him.

"Easy now . . . these cuttbows always got enough gas left for one more run."

Stranahan saw the fish weakly break water. Taking advantage, he pulled it onto its side and it slid toward him until the butt of the leader was only a few inches outside the rod tip-top. Suddenly it dove underneath the tube, tangling the line around Stranahan's waders. He felt a sullen weight as the fish came to the end of its tether, the float tube turning under pressure from the fish; then suddenly the line was limp.

"Son of a bitch," he muttered.

He looked at Sam and shook the rod tip to indicate that the fish was gone.

"That trout would have gone eight pounds, my man," Sam shouted. He spread his hands apart to show the size, and, as his shoulders opened, his upper body jerked perceptibly backward. The float tube collapsed with a burst of air. A half second later Stranahan heard the crack of a rifle, then the shot echoing away. Sam was down, pinwheeling his right arm frantically to keep his head above water.

Stranahan began to kick toward the limp smear of blue where the bladder of the float tube eddied among the wavelets.

"Hang on, Sam, I'm coming," he shouted.

CHAPTER FIFTEEN

In Hot Soup

When Stranahan reached the shattered float tube, he could see that the bladder that formed the float tube's backrest was still intact, rocking on the surface like a blue bobber. Looking down, he saw Sam's hand where it grasped the submerged part of the tube. He grabbed the hand and pulled. Immediately, his own tube flipped over and he felt the explosion of the water around his head. He reached up to unclasp the buckle that attached the seat webbing to the front of the tube. The water was murky with suspended algae and he had to feel for the buckle. After a few moments of near panic, his fingers found the clasp and the buckle snapped open.

Instinctively, he dove for the bottom and kicked free of the tube. He came to the surface spluttering. He twisted around, trying to spot the air bladder of Sam's float tube over the standing waves in the lake. There it was! He began to sidestroke toward the blob of color, his legs heavy from water that had seeped past his wading belt. Finally he was able to reach out and crook his arm over the bladder of Sam's tube. He dug his fingers into the collapsed material and pulled, seeing Sam's fist rise toward him, like a hand reaching from a grave. It was tangled in the straps of the torn float tube. He let go of his grip on the material and stretched his arm down farther, gripped the tube, and hauled. Twice more he hauled, released, and shot his arm down. First the hand, then Sam's entire arm climbed above the gray curtain of the lake surface. Stranahan grabbed the big man under his right shoulder.

He lifted Sam's head out of the water. His face looked waxen and life-less.

Breathe, dammit, Stranahan said to himself.

He looked toward shore. The stand of aspens had to be a hundred yards distant. He thought back to the Red Cross course he had taken in CPR, but the rules were predicated upon the assumption that the victim was lying on hard ground.

Maybe if he could squeeze the water out of Sam's lungs, it would get his breathing reflex going. He reached down and across Sam's chest with his right arm and pulled, but it was hard to get leverage. The slight movement must have been enough, for there was a gagging sound as Sam vomited lake water. The big man's breath was coming in shuddering rasps. After a minute, his body began to relax and Stranahan was able to get behind him and work both his arms under Sam's armpits. Swimming backward, he began to pull Sam toward shore.

Minutes later—it seemed hours—Stranahan felt his flippers dig into the soft silt on the lake bottom. He'd made it. Turning onto his knees, he crawled out of the lake, dragging Sam until only the rear half of his body remained in the water and he no longer had to worry about him drowning.

Struggling to stand with a few gallons of water inside his waders, Stranahan felt a tugging at his right leg. He looked down. The tan-and-black leech fly that he had hooked the trout with was buried in his wader leg, the leader and the line stretching back into the lake. Stranahan registered the probability that the line was still hooked to the rod, which he'd dropped into the lake, though he couldn't remember when that had happened. He freed the hook, then stuck the fly into a piece of driftwood so it would not wash back into the lake. He could come back and retrieve the rod later. It hardly seemed important.

"I'm shot."

Christ! Stranahan had been so occupied trying to get Sam to shore that he had forgotten the rifle shot. Bending over Sam's heaving chest, he saw a ragged rent in the waders. The checked shirt above the wader top was soaked through with blood. He ripped his shirt off, then twisted the cloth to wring it out and clamped it over the wound.

Sam screamed, his head jerking up off the ground.

Stranahan glanced wildly around, his eyes falling on the two-lane blacktop that bordered the lake. The blacktop ended a hundred yards farther along to the west. Beyond the break, he saw a shimmer of dust lifting from the gravel and knew a car must be coming. It was like a heat mirage, wavering in the sunlight. Twin images merged and he was looking at a truck in the distance. He hiked Sam's waders up to keep his shirt in place over the wound and stumbled toward the road, waving his arms, but the truck veered onto a side track and disappeared. It was a two-mile hike to the fishing store where he'd bought his license. Sam could die of blood loss before he ever reached help.

The next half hour was the longest of Stranahan's life as his hand pressing the shirt became tired and finally numb. He talked to Sam constantly, but the big man just breathed, an occasional bubble of blood blowing between his lips on the rattling exhales.

Finally, Sean saw another wafer of dust lift to the west and he stumbled to the road to intercept the oncoming vehicle.

The truck stopped, motor idling.

"What's the problem?" The man behind the wheel smiled under a well-tended mustache.

"My friend's just been shot," Stranahan said, gesturing wildly toward the shoreline.

The man lifted his hand off the steering wheel and raised the palm to Stranahan.

"All right, settle down." He had a deep, reassuring voice. "I'm going to get my bag out of the camper and we're going to help him." He was already out the door and walking to the back of the truck. "I'm a vet. What I need you to do is take the cell phone. It's in a holster under the dash. Get it. Reception's spotty here, but if we get a bar you're going to make some calls while I attend to your friend. Can you do that?"

"Yes," Stranahan said. "Thank God, yes."

"Don't thank God just yet," the man said. "He's got some work for us to do first."

CHAPTER SIXTEEN

"We Meet Again"

Martha was on the line to Walt, who was checking a quarter mile of fence line that had been snipped with a wire cutter to aggravate a ranch owner who just happened to be a Hollywood action hero with a reputation as an asshole, when the desk officer interrupted to say there was a call waiting. The pine jockey cocked his hand like a pistol and mouthed the word "Bang."

She told Walt she'd get back to him, set one phone down, picked another up.

"This is Sheriff Ettinger."

"Sheriff, it's Doc Svenson."

"Yes, Jeff, what is it?" Svenson had helped deliver a breech foal at her place seven years ago, the mare she now rode to hunt elk.

"I was out visiting a colt on the Culpepper Ranch down by Henry's Lake and got flagged by some fella. His buddy'd been shot. Bullet broke a rib in the left chest quadrant. He was aspirating blood so I'm assuming the lung was creased, could collapse easy. Hyalite Rescue drove up ten minutes ago. They're leaving with him for Bridger Deaconess. I'm not so sure he's going to make it. Thought you'd want to talk with the man that flagged me down. He and his buddy were fishing in float tubes. Says he had one heck of a time getting him back to shore. . . . No, he didn't see the shooter."

Martha interrupted. "What are you calling me for? You're in Idaho, right? That's Centennial County jurisdiction."

"I know, and I got them on the horn first thing after making the nine-one-one. They're sending somebody, but thing is, the guy who's shot is Sam, um . . . hey, what's that guy's name? . . . Meslik. Sam Meslik. Isn't that the fishing guide who found that body in the Madison?"

"Put him on the phone. Put his friend on the phone right now."

"Hello."

"What's your name?"

"Sean Stranahan."

The name rang a bell, but she couldn't place it. "Mr. Stranahan, I want you to remain where you are . . . ah, where are you exactly?"

She listened a second. "Yeah, uh-huh. Well, here's what's going to happen. In a couple minutes a deputy from Idaho's going to arrive. If he wants you to go back with him to county, you go. But if he takes your statement at the scene, which I think he'll do, then stay put till I get there. Got that?"

"Yes, Ma'am," she heard him say, and knew then where she'd heard the name. He was the fisherman she'd met on the Madison at the outlet of Quake Lake. The good-looking bastard who had been fishing a Royal Wulff. She felt her face blush with heat. She'd thought about him just last night when Sheba, her old Siamese, had curled up against her back and she had felt the warmth through her flannel nightgown.

Ettinger cleared her head. She instructed Stranahan to put the vet back on the phone and told Jeff Svenson to stick around, too. As long as he was there, she didn't have to worry about anyone changing the scene. She told him as much and he understood he was to keep an eye on the witness. Then she called Walt back and told him to get his ass to the hospital pronto and wait for the arrival of Sam Meslik. Warned him that someone wearing an Idaho badge might also want to stick their nose in the door.

"Fuck 'em," Walt said. "They'll huff and puff but underneath they'll just want us to take it off their hands. You know Monroe, the sheriff?"

"I haven't had the pleasure," Martha said.

"He's a butt scratcher. Draw a circle around his feet, come back next week, and he's still standing there."

"I get the picture. But what if Meslik kicks?"

"He's a goner, makes Monroe's job easier. Mark my words, Idaho won't interfere."

"Listen, when Meslik comes around, don't let him say one word that you don't get on the record."

"You don't have to worry about me. I can coax a statement out of a corpse."

"Let's hope it doesn't come to that," Martha said.

Ettinger pushed ninety up the valley floor. She pulled off the road behind Sam's truck a little over an hour after leaving Bridger.

"That you, Jeff?" she called out toward the silhouettes of two men who were sitting on a log at the shoreline.

The man wearing a straw cowboy hat gave her a wave. The other, hatless, shirtless, rose to his feet as she approached. An inflated float tube ebbed against the shore.

"Sheriff," the bare-chested man said. There was no smile for her this day.

"Mr. Stranahan, right? What a coincidence." She looked appraisingly at him, let the moment stretch. He looked ashen, but not nervous.

She thought she'd let him stew a bit.

"Anybody with an Idaho badge show?" She directed her question to the veterinarian, learned that a deputy had taken a statement and said he'd be in touch.

She nodded. She looked soberly out to the lake a long moment, then at Stranahan.

"That your float tube?" She pointed up the lake a couple hundred feet.

"It flipped when I tried to rescue Sam. It washed up a while ago."

"Tell me what happened."

As he told the story, she never once let her gaze stray from his eyes, interrupting only to ask how long it had been between hearing the first two shots and the one that had struck Sam. He said an hour or so, it was hard to recall. Had the third shot sounded closer? Yes. How much closer? It was loud. Location? If you had to guess, where would you say the shooter was firing from?

Stranahan pointed northeast, toward the foot of the mountain slopes. Then he rolled his eyes up and blew out a heavy breath.

"I can't be sure. I'm sorry."

The wind had picked up, blowing the bang of black hair that dipped over his left eye. Martha felt herself being drawn toward his old-fashioned courtesy, the angle of his chin, his deep green eyes. She shook it off. He wasn't going to get to her today. First the Royal Wulff fly he'd been fishing. Now Meslik. She didn't believe in coincidence.

"You're an artist, you say?"

"I have a studio at the cultural center." He hesitated. "I ought to tell you I used to be a PI. In Massachusetts. It's etched on the door, but that's only because the director thought it would add some pizzazz to the building."

"Oh, really?" Martha said. "I don't suppose you could show me your license?"

"I'm not licensed in Montana. The sign on the door is for show. I'm just a painter these days."

Martha glanced at the veterinarian. "Jeff," she said, "I'd like a few words in private with Mr. Stranahan. You don't have to stick around—I'll be in touch, though, or Walt'll get back to you."

Svenson shook his head in affirmation, met Stranahan's eyes, and nodded. "Sheriff. Sean." He headed back to his truck, punching the keypad of his phone.

Martha pressed her lips into a thin smile, as if to say, It's just you and me now, and what a predicament we find ourselves in.

"You wouldn't be neglecting to tell me anything, would you, Mr. Stranahan? Because now would be the time. . . ." She let the words ride.

I should have known better, he thought. *I should have known that a woman doesn't pay you to go fishing, place your hand on her heart, and then disappear without there being some kind of catch that has nothing to do with hooking a fish.*

"Somebody came to the gallery a few days ago," he admitted. "I was asked to do something, but it's not detective work, exactly."

Martha looked sternly into his eyes, no longer noticing their color.

"Exactly what was it?" she said humorlessly.

CHAPTER SEVENTEEN

Killer

By the time Stranahan left the hospital, Sam's condition had been upgraded from critical to stable. The doctor he'd spoken with had brought his fingertips together as if in tentative prayer, awarded Stranahan his professional smile, spoken briefly, and left. Stranahan had followed suit. He had to attend to Killer and needed a drink, though not in that order.

At the inn, Doris brought Stranahan a Trout Slayer Ale. She took a chair, hooked a leg to pull another closer for a footrest, and shut her eyes tight.

"Long night?" Stranahan asked.

"They're all long."

"Want to hear a story?"

"Is the Mississippi nightingale in it?"

Stranahan pursed his lips. "That's the sixty-four-thousand-dollar question," he said.

As Stranahan drove Sam's rig along the gravel ruts that led to the trailer, he rolled down the window, listening for Killer's bark and not quite knowing how to handle the beast. But the trailer yard was eerily quiet. Stranahan switched off the ignition and doused the headlights. Five minutes later he was still listening to the ping of the engine as it cooled down. *Woos,* he said under his breath.

Bracing himself, he stepped out of the cab and walked to the door. He knocked lightly.

"Hey, Killer. Killer, it's just me." Nothing.

Stranahan turned the doorknob. The door yawned inward with a metallic grating. The pleasures of living in a tin can, he mused. Maybe his office wasn't as bad as he thought.

He called the dog's name again, then searched the inside walls for the light switch. Flipped it.

The place was trashed. The kitchen table was ripped from the post that bolted it to the floor. Chairs were overturned. A stack of fly rods leaning in a corner had been tipped; rod sections lay crisscrossed on the floor. Sam had set up a fly-tying desk in a walled-off alcove. Dozens of plastic compartments that held fly-tying materials were scattered on the floor. He picked a squirrel skin from the floor and put it to his nose. It was obvious roadkill, torn and smelly. Stranahan approved. He wasn't above bagging a little roadkill himself to tie flies with.

He walked toward the rear of the trailer. The bathroom door was ajar. He nudged it with his shoulder and saw the lid of the toilet lying on the floor. The last door must be Sam's bedroom, he thought. He hesitated. Except for opening the front door, Stranahan had been careful not to touch anything. He knew it was police business now. If he had harbored any doubt about the intention of the shot that had taken Sam down, it was gone.

He turned to find a phone and stopped. A sound? He put his ear closer to the bedroom door. There was an utterance, like a breath. The hair lifted on his forearms. If the person who ransacked the trailer was on the other side of the plank, he could die right here, and for what? Still, he didn't turn to leave.

Long ago Stranahan had learned that courage could be an unearned commodity, that often those who possessed it simply lacked the common sense to be afraid. Or else they didn't care, the way that some combat soldiers came to expect death and thus were immune to the fear of it. He knew that because at times he had suspected he was one of those people, and that had puzzled him. For someone young, he had seen a fair share of death—most important, the early passing of both parents. And had found he could cope while others, like his sister, could not. People had always leaned on him in times of trouble, and rather than draw him into the fold of humanity, it had isolated him and rewarded him a measure of courage that seemed unearned. Was it this feeling of being set apart that led to the demise of his marriage? If he could just follow the thread back far enough, perhaps he might discover why he felt as he did, and why he was instinctively drawn both to gregarious personalities like Sam as well as to those who suffered his own specific malady, such as Vareda Lafayette.

He let out a breath and turned the doorknob. The dog was lying beside the unmade bed, its pupils dilated dramatically. Muscles underneath the skin shivered. Stranahan felt the heart beating in the cavernous chest. He rolled the Airedale onto its back to look for signs of injury, but it was unmarked.

Kneeling, he got his arms underneath and lifted. God, Killer was heavy. The angular head lolled limply, the tongue extended. Stranahan backed out of the room and managed to kick open the unlatched door at the front of the trailer but fell heavily descending the steps, the dog on top of him. His head was swimming a little as he stood up and half dragged, half carried the Airedale to his Land Cruiser.

He gunned the motor and reached inside his wallet. The veterinarian had given him a business card. Ten minutes later, Stranahan was knocking on the door of a ramshackle log home with dark windows.

"I got a sick dog," he said without preamble when Jeff Svenson opened the door in a T-shirt and boxers. The vet was accustomed to middle-of-the-night emergencies and pushed past Stranahan to the truck without speaking. The two men carried the dog into the converted clinic at one end of the house as Stranahan jabbered away from the rush of adrenaline, recounting his visit to Sam's trailer. They hoisted Killer onto a stainless steel table.

"This dog's been sedated," Svenson said. "Either Benadryl or diazepam would be my guess, but I'm going to run a blood test because you want to know what he's got in his system."

He seemed to see Stranahan for the first time.

"Trouble seems to foller you around," he said seriously.

When Stranahan said nothing, he added, "You better get on the horn to the sheriff. She's gonna want to see that trailer." He pointed a finger at a phone sitting on a medicine cabinet and turned back to his patient.

CHAPTER EIGHTEEN

Hook, Line, and Sinker

Half dreaming at six the next morning, Stranahan could feel a gnawing at the back of his head. It felt as if something was eating through his skull. His eyes came open. Underneath the blinds, where the morning sunlight fell in slats across the oak floorboards, a mouse sat on its haunches. It was chewing industriously on a cracker that Stranahan had placed there a couple days before. Its whiskers quivered.

"About time," he said out loud as the mouse arrowed back into the hole near the corner.

Stranahan decided he would take the mouse's appearance as a sign of luck. He dialed the hospital and was put through to Sam's room. Darcy McCall picked up the phone, said Sam was sleeping, his condition unchanged. His next call was to Svenson. Killer was up, baying for his master, and had just breakfasted on two pounds of ground horsemeat. He had a short memory, Svenson said with a laugh. His stomach was what had got him into trouble. The Valium pills that had knocked him for a loop had been ground into raw hamburger. Sean asked if he wouldn't mind keeping the dog a few hours longer. Not a problem, no sir, was the veterinarian's reply.

Stranahan got dressed, gassed up his Land Cruiser, and pulled up to the coffee kiosk on the road to the Madison River. Called Lattes and Lookers, it was a bikini barista hut that had drawn letters of complaint in the *Star*'s op-ed page ever since it had opened a month previously. A doe-eyed barista with vaguely Asian features leaned provocatively out the window, wearing a teddy. Stranahan ordered a latte grande with a double shot, no whipped cream, and paid $3.25 for the coffee and the view. He was running on three hours' sleep after a wee-hour confrontation with the red-eyed Sheriff Ettinger, whose annoyance at his midnight shenanigans had left him unsettled.

Two hours after sunrise he pulled up to Henry's Lake. The fly line was right where he'd left it, tied to a log at the waterline. He pulled until it came taut. At the other end was the fly rod he'd dropped into the water. He'd have to use the float tube to retrieve it.

He pulled his waders on, taking more time than necessary. "Just what is it you're afraid of?" he said out loud. He buckled the flippers and backed into the lake, his heart hammering.

Half expecting the dread of yesterday's tragedy to come flooding back, Stranahan was surprised to find that the water calmed him. The same male bluebird flitted low above the cattails before disappearing into the house on the fence post. The rifle shots that triggered yesterday's chaos seemed as distant as the Centennial Mountains that stood impassively behind the southern rim of the lake.

Passing the fly line hand over hand, Stranahan turned his attention to the north. The perspective was quite different than it was from the shoreline, where the sheriff had him try to reconstruct the shooting. The hills where he thought the shot came from looked to be a mile away. If it had been a stray bullet from some gopher hunter . . . maybe. But anyone intent on doing harm would have to have climbed quite high to sight over the shoreline trees. The range was just too far. No, the sniper must have been closer, perhaps in the field behind the bluebird house. The county road was only three hundred yards distant. Just this side stood an abandoned homestead cabin, its back as swayed as a broke-down horse. Someone could have rested a scoped rifle across one of the empty windows. . . .

Stranahan felt the line stop. He peered down through the soupy water where the line angled toward the bottom. He pulled it hand over hand until the rod came up, strewn with coontail fronds. The tape that Sam had wrapped on the base of the blank had loosened with the overnight soaking. Stranahan unwrapped it and read, or attempted to read, the two-line inscription in Winston's signature longhand scrawl. The top line was faint but legible: *THE WINSTON ROD CO. TWIN BRIDGES, MONTANA.*

The second line consisted of an interrupted scrawl: a capital *"M,"* a space, then an *"f,"* another, longer space, followed by three more irregularly spaced letters, an *"e," an "r"* and another *"e."*

Stranahan knew that the line inscribed the name of the person who had ordered the rod. He'd seen a few Winstons and guessed that the *M* and the *or* would be part of "Made for." The last letters formed the name of the owner. The three that were legible meant nothing to him, but of those he could make out, only *the "e's"* corresponded to letters in Samuel Meslik's name. The "r" certainly didn't. Stranahan guessed it was no accident that the rod blank looked to have been sanded, and that the sanding had erased more of the letters in the owner's name than in other words. The electrical tape had disguised an obvious attempt to erase the owner's name. But to keep the identity from whom?

"From me, among others," Stranahan said out loud. It suddenly occurred to him that he might be holding the rod of a dead man.

Sam, he thought, *you got some explaining to do.*

Back on shore, Stranahan unlocked the tailgate of the Land Cruiser and shrugged into his fly vest. He'd driven all this way. Why not? Fishing would give him time to mull over the increasingly coincidental events of the past couple of days, plus there was nothing like jumping back into the water where the shark bit you to stimulate the cerebral synapses. His hands trembled as he stripped line from the Winston and knotted on a fly that was a variation on a Henry's Lake standard—a Halloween leech pattern with a woven orange-and-black wool body. It didn't look like anything in nature—ample proof, if proof was necessary, that a trout could be just as gullible as a man.

Or was it the other way around?

It was a cool morning. Stranahan pulled on the chamois cloth shirt Vareda had left for him, finding that it was a little long in the sleeves. He looked at the embroidered monogram. MJB. Had it belonged to an old boyfriend? An ex-husband? He realized he didn't even know if she'd ever been married. Perhaps MJB was her father. He recalled what she'd said about him: "Papa left his mark on everything he touched in his ever-loving life." A man who even marked the fins of the fish he caught. A monogrammed shirt would be right in character.

Stranahan thought back. Velvet Lafayette/Vareda Beaudreux had walked into his life cocking an imaginary pistol at her head and telling a story about burying her father that he had initially bought—he smiled at the thought—hook, line, and sinker. Three days later she'd disappeared, leaving thin red lines across his chest from her fingernails, a Maxwell House coffee can, and many unanswered questions.

Was it only coincidence that the water she wanted him to fish had been leaching nutrients from the body of an angler who may have been given a shove into the Hereafter? Who had possibly been fishing with the rod he now held in his hand? Admit it, he told himself: On the morning Sam was shot he was still trying to recapture the sensation of her touch. He was closing his eyes to bring back the lingering scent of oranges.

Uh-huh, Sheriff Ettinger had said last night as he recounted a story that, under her persistent questioning, began to sound ridiculous even to him.

And you believed her when she said she had driven all the way from Mississippi to scatter her father's ashes in the Madison River? And why were you chosen to perform this noble deed? What I want to know is how this woman comes to be knocking on your door? You say she heard your name at a fishing store, but I'm having trouble making that connection. Maybe you could help me out. And while you're at it, tell me why you wagged your tail so quickly when she asked you?

"She paid me," Stranahan had said, a response that had made the sheriff narrow her eyes.

"Sure she did," she had said.

Stranahan lifted his rod tip and had a trout. He played it distractedly—it wasn't very big—and reached over the side of his tube to release it. The body of the woolly bugger made a neon smear against its jaw, as if the mandible were torn and bloodied. Stranahan flashed to the image of a Royal Wulff dry fly imbedded in a bloated human lip. A mystery within a mystery, and outside the mystery, hovering like a wraith, an enigmatic woman who couldn't seem to settle on a name.

He slipped the blood-orange woolly bugger from the trout's lip. As if miraculously healed, the fish slipped back to the smoky depths of Henry's Lake. If only life could be so simple for him, Stranahan thought.

CHAPTER NINETEEN

Dead Man Talking

The pine snags jutting from Quake Lake cast shadows that lanced across the surface. Martha Ettinger followed Harold Little Feather's eyes as he gazed at this reflective pool, oblivious to her presence. The Blackfeet tracker stood with his hands folded across his belly, his black braid falling down the back of his khaki shirt. He hadn't said one word since they had turned into the campground, and Martha thought better than to interrupt him. She had once seen Harold Little Feather turn his heel on a crime scene because the investigating officer wouldn't shut up.

"How can I hear the dead man talking when you're blabbering at the mouth," he'd said, and had kicked the mud from his cowboy boots against the step-up of his truck and gunned it for Browning. The department had disciplined him, Martha recalled, but his punishment hadn't been as severe as the officer's; he'd been saddled with the moniker "Dead Man Talking" ever since.

Little Feather squatted down. He plucked a stem of grass and stuck it between his teeth. He motioned Ettinger down beside him.

"Beautiful, isn't it?" he said. "See how the valley runs down to the lakeshore? Monkey flowers, alpine phlox, purple lupine, paintbrush that cutthroat orange. You get a different view down here. Wildflower colors bleed together. A lower line of sight. Like hunting elk. You bend closer to the ground, you can see under the tree limbs, spot that big bull before he spots you. You hunt, Martha?"

"Uh-huh," Martha muttered.

"What's your rifle?"

"Ought-six, pre-sixty-four Model seventy Featherweight."

"Good gun." Little Feather squinted against the sun. "You a tracker?"

"I can track an elk in snow."

"Then you know how a bull minds his head. Walks around where the trail goes between tree trunks so his rack doesn't catch."

She wanted to say *What are you getting at, Harold,* but held her tongue. After all, he'd driven all the way from the reservation as a favor to her, slept in his jeans on her couch, and helped feed the animals before making the trip to Quake in the Cherokee. A freelancer now and horse trainer on the side, he wasn't even officially on the department's payroll.

Martha raised her eyes. A Steller's jay, iridescent purple-blue with a midnight head, flicked overhead and perched on a lodgepole snag at the edge of the campsite.

"You're getting restless," Little Feather said. "You're thinking, He's an Indian, he's on Indian time, so I'll just shrug my shoulders. But let me ask you something: When you're tracking an elk, what's the most important skill?"

"Patience," Martha said. Her voice betrayed her own impatience.

"Same with the human animal," Little Feather said. "When do you need the most patience tracking an elk? Powder snow or hardpack."

"Powder."

"Why?"

"'Cause the prints aren't clear, it's hard to figure out which way the elk's going. Usually, you can tell because he drags his feet as he's stepping out of the track, but in powder it's a tough call."

Little Feather nodded his head and Martha felt herself flush with pride, then silently chastised herself for seeking a man's approval. After all the years . . . she closed her eyes and slowly shook her head.

Little Feather went on as if he hadn't noticed.

"So how do you tell?"

"I follow the tracks either way until they go underneath a tree, where the snow is thin. Then I can see the hoofprints. Or sometimes, if you whisk away the loose snow on top with your glove, you'll see where the track cuts into packed snow underneath."

"You sure you don't have any Blackfeet blood, Martha?" Little Feather smiled.

Martha felt herself swell again.

"Now here's the question I've been getting to. Where do you find the best track, the track that's so clear-cut you can spot imperfections in the hooves, where you can ID the elk's fingerprint so if you find his trail again someday, you know him by his name? Take your time, imagine you're up in the doghair. There's a foot of snow. You're following the trail. . . ." He fell silent.

Martha felt again the cold-blued steel of the Winchester's floor plate through her fingerless gloves. She shut her eyes, following a gypsy meander of elk tracks in the forest gloaming. Where did the tracks really pop out at you? She thought back to her last elk, a rag-horn bull that had bedded twice on the north slope of Mizpah Creek after she picked up the track.

"In its bed," she said suddenly, startling herself. "Where it has lain down to rest."

"Bingo," Little Feather said. "The elk's body compresses the snow, its heat melts it a little, then when it stands up, its hooves cut down. Elk leaves the bed, snow freezes back up like cement, tracks are sharp as a knife. Now, with all the foot traffic around this campsite, where do you think we might find a clear track of the fellow that drove the Subaru?"

"Under the tent," Martha said.

"What do you say we have a look? You say it rained last week; if the ground was softened, then there might be an impression."

They had carefully emptied the contents of the tent earlier; now

Little Feather and Martha each took a corner and folded the blue nylon up and over. The earth underneath was damp from condensation. Tufts of grass had yellowed. Millipedes were rolled into tight balls. Little Feather squatted with his back to the sun, reached for the belt knife in the sheath on his hip, held it gleaming, and traced the outline of a bootprint with a steel tip.

"Big fella," Martha said. She felt the skin pucker as the fine down of her forearm hair lifted in the breeze.

Sitting in the passenger seat on the drive back—Harold had asked for the wheel because he said driving helped him think—Martha sought to make conversation. But Little Feather cut his replies short and she backed off. She liked Harold but felt the gap in culture each time they met on the job. He'd saved her butt way back when, though . . . how long had it been, eight years? She'd been up against it with the sheriff—she'd made deputy only a few weeks before—when she went over his head and pressed the DA to indict a realtor who'd been accused of sexual assault. The alleged victim, a woman of less than sterling character who led with her 36 Ds, said the man had tried to rape her in an apartment he was showing. It was a his-word/her-word deal, but Martha believed the woman, and Harold had made her case by matching a footprint on the woman's blouse with the accused's Florsheim shoe.

Ettinger felt the car slowing, heard the click-click of the turn signal.

"Harold?"

"You have time," Little Feather said. "I'd like to take a look where that fishing guide was shot on Henry's Lake. Any chance it's related to the body found in the river?"

"I'm beginning to wonder," Martha mused. "You shed some light on that one, I'd appreciate it. But it's in Idaho; there's a jurisdiction question."

"Look at this wide open country. I won't tell if you won't."

Fifteen minutes later Martha was standing on the shoreline where she had interviewed Sean Stranahan the day before.

"Someone's been out in a float tube this morning," Harold said. "See here, the print of the fins, where he backed into the lake. And over there, that's where he came out."

"What's that have to do with Sam Meslik's shooting?"

The tracker shook his head.

"I'm just making an observation. Like someone in the checkout line at the market reads the *Enquirer.* Because it's there, you know."

"You ever hear of Sherlock Holmes, Harold? You're starting to remind me of him."

"Who's he?"

"British detective, back in the nineteenth century."

"Was he good?"

"He was a fictional character."

"Oh." Harold's voice was uninterested.

Martha felt like a fool. She made her tone businesslike.

"Give me your reading of the shooting here. I told you what this Sean Stranahan said. You think it was intentional? Or just some gopher slayer with bad aim."

"He hit what he pointed his rifle at." Little Feather's voice was definite.

"How can you be sure?"

"Lay of the land." He swept his hand at the field where an abandoned homestead cabin baked in hard sunlight. "If he shot and missed a gopher with his rifle pointed in this direction, the bullet would hit the ground, not the lake."

"Maybe it ricocheted."

"No chance. A bullet has to be moving at a low velocity to ricochet. Gopher hunters shoot .222s, 220 Swifts. Bullets leaving the muzzle at 3,500 feet per second plus. They disintegrate on impact. Gopher, he's a red mist with a tail."

"So, he shot from where? The cabin?"

"Could have. It's two-fifty to two-seventy-five yards. You got a good scope, that's reasonable range."

"What about the first shots? Stranahan said they happened an hour before the one that got Meslik."

"Can't say. Maybe a different guy? Maybe he *was* a gopher hunter."

Martha set her arms akimbo. She drew a line in the sand with the point of her boot.

"You going to scratch your name, or are we going to go look at that cabin?" Little Feather said.

"**S**omebody's been here last couple of days." Little Feather had stopped thirty feet from the cabin.

Martha wiped the sweat from her brow.

"Shadow in the grass. See it?" He pointed by lifting his chin.

"No."

"Grass is bent; you'd notice in low light. The angle of the sun emphasizes the shadow."

They approached the sagging structure.

"We're not going to find a print if he was just using it for cover," Little Feather said. "Have to hope he went inside."

Martha waited impatiently at the open doorway.

"You need a flashlight? I've got one."

"Nope." Harold ducked past her into the gloom.

Martha looked south to the Centennial Mountains, the isolated range of Big Bad Wolf teeth that formed the Continental Divide. She hated standing with her hands in her pockets.

She heard a murmur from the cabin.

"Harold?"

"Come in, stay along the left wall."

She moved up beside him, the warped boards creaking underfoot. The walls were covered with newspapers, peeling and yellowed. Curious, she stepped past a rusted box spring and sought out the date at the top of one of the few paper sheets that was intact. *November 26, 1920.*

"They used them for insulation," Little Feather said.

Martha didn't respond but turned her attention to the empty window facing the lake. A mist of windblown pollen had settled on the floorboards in the shape of a tapered rectangle. Shoe prints were isolated on the dust as clearly cut as ballroom steps painted on a dance floor. Martha reached for the point and shoot in her pocket.

"Looks like someone walked to the window and looked out, then backed away," Harold said. "Didn't shoot from here; there'd be superimposed tracks if he spent any time and the dust on the sill would be disturbed. The shot that hit that fishing guide was taken outside, prone position, a solid rest over his hat or maybe his boot—that's what I'd do. We'll look for a spent shell, something dropped out of a pocket, but if he's even half smart we won't find anything."

He noticed Ettinger looking down at the tracks.

"To answer your question before you ask, this is about a size nine, narrow width. Old cowboy boot, heels worn down from a pronated stance. Is it the same guy who left the track under the tent? That one was a boot, chain-link design like you find on a Bean hunting boot or a rubber-bottomed wader. Point is," he went on, "you buy waders or hip boots, the sole is oversize. That's a twelve track under the tent, but the same man could wear a ten street shoe, or a nine."

"You're making things difficult for me," Martha said.

"Your people have been making things difficult for my people since Meriwether Lewis shot that Blackfeet boy on the Marias River. What's that been, two hundred years?"

Martha felt her face redden.

"Hey, I'm joking," Little Feather said. "About that lunch you promised me? I hear the Continental Divide in Ennis makes a shrimp etouffee brings tears to your eyes."

Martha felt giddy as a girl when the big tracker pulled out the chair for her by an outside table. True, it was early afternoon and both were dressed in work clothes, but this was as close to a date as she'd had in several years. She hadn't meant it to be. She'd asked Harold to lunch as thanks for taking the time to help her at the campground. But subconsciously, she knew, it was not that innocent.

They talked over the day. Agreed that neither held any stock in coincidence, that there had to be a thread that linked the three points of the triangle formed by the river, the campground at Quake Lake, and Henry's Lake. Martha noticed that Harold leaned closer than he needed to to talk to her and she caught herself adjusting her posture, dropping her eyes, pulling back an errant strand of hair that had fallen across her face. *Fluttering like a damned fool girl,* she thought.

The conversation drifted to hunting, the different places they had been.

Harold was saying, "My brother Howard and I have a lodge up for a couple weeks in elk season, up in that Badger–Two Medicine country. Sacred hunting grounds. We pack in with horses November second."

"Lodge. A teepee, you mean?" Martha said.

"Eighteen footer, fifteen-pole Sioux design. Comfortable. You want to join us, let me know. Howard's wife rides in, too. We cook beaver, lamb stew make your mouth water, elk liver someone gets lucky. Bring your bedroll and your Winchester. You can ride my old paint, Chester. It'd be my pleasure to show you that good country."

Martha felt sweat beading at her temples, saw snow swirling on wintry escarpments, steam blowing from a horse's nostrils. She knew her foot was only a shoelace span from touching his under the table. His hands folded, inches away from hers. Darker. Walnut, like the tabletop.

"I'd love to," she said.

CHAPTER TWENTY

Fishing for a Commission

"Yeah, yeah, so fucking what?"

Rainbow Sam, propped in the hospital bed, his left arm suspended from a ceiling contraption to keep the pressure off his broken rib, scratched at his bandaged side. He grimaced.

"So I found the dead guy's rod. Man's bloated up like a fish. He's got no use for it. Why give it to the sheriff? You know how much it costs to buy a Winston new. Six bills, my man. Six big ones."

Stranahan just looked at him.

Sam exhaled. "Yeah, okay, I made a mistake. Fishing guide, trying to put food on the table, keep his dog in Kibble . . ." His voice trailed away.

"I feel for you, man," said Stranahan.

"Don't make me laugh, you bastard. It hurts my side."

Sam coughed. He groaned.

"You think you could sneak me a smoke? I'm going batshit in here."

Stranahan ignored him.

"What was the name on the rod? The name you sanded off?"

"I don't recall."

"Bullshit."

"No, man. It's the truth. I've got short-term memory loss from the shot. Retro-something amnesia. Shit, I didn't know Darcy when she walked into this room."

Stranahan waited.

"Fuck you," Sam said. "Do what you want with the bloody rod, I don't care."

"Bloody?"

"I have a client, limey from South Africa. What can I say? I'm an impressionable man." He managed a weak smile.

Sam reached to the bedside table and passed Stranahan a plastic bag holding a blob of shredded metal.

"That's what they took out of me, Kimosabe."

"The bullet?"

"Nah, the deputy took the bullet. This is what the bullet hit. It's a spoon, man, a fucking spinning lure I found on the bank last week. I hung it on my vest, you know how you just do things for no fucking reason."

"So, you're telling me you were saved by a spinning lure?" Stranahan examined the blob of metal.

"It deflected the path of the bullet." Sam shook his head. "It's an omen, man. The big fella's trying to tell me to give up fly fishing."

"Maybe he's just telling you not to take another man's rod."

Sam didn't respond.

"While we're back on the subject, where exactly did you find it, the Winston?"

"In the drink. Thirty, forty yards upstream from the logjam."

"How did you find it?"

"Shit man, what's it matter? I just saw it when I hiked up to the cabin to call the sheriff. The tip was sticking up. You see it, it calls to you. Glowing that Winston green, like the felt on the poker table in the back room of the Crystal Bar. So I waded out and got it, stuck it in the boat."

"How did you explain the rod to your client?"

"Izard the Third? He'd been ralphing up his noodles. I don't think it registered."

"If you hadn't scratched off the name, there's a good chance it would identify the man who drowned, you know that. It's evidence. I'll have to turn it over to the sheriff."

"Do what you got to," Sam said.

He shook his head and heaved a sigh. "I fucked myself in the ass big time, didn't I?" He reached his good arm across his body and pointed toward the bed stand. "Look in my wallet. It's on the back of my card, behind the license. I wrote the fucker's name down."

Stranahan found the card with Sam's name inscribed inside the outline of a leaping trout and turned it over. His skin pebbled for a second, and he felt a wrinkling of the muscles in his chest wall. But he wasn't as surprised as he could have been.

J.J. Beaudreux.

Jeffrey Jeremiah Beaudreux. Vareda's brother.

The button was flashing on the answering machine when Stranahan entered his office. He glanced at his watch. Half past four. After speaking with Deputy Walter Hess on the hospital room phone, he had driven to Sam's trailer and fed Killer, then let him outside to do his business. They were buddies now, but Stranahan felt relieved that Sam would be released after the doctor made his rounds in the evening, ending his sitter duties. He reluctantly punched the message button, dreading a callback from Sheriff Ettinger after her deputy told her the news about the rod. Now that she had the probable name of the victim, she'd want to pump Stranahan for anything else he might know, and he'd have to give up Vareda before he had a chance to speak with her. But the voice was a man's—authoritative, brusque.

"Mr. Stranahan, this is Richard Summersby. I bought your painting at the TU banquet. I have a job for you if you want it. I'm on the river." He gave a number. "I'm looking forward to doing business with you, Mr. Stranahan."

Stranahan hit Stop on the message machine and punched the numbers into his phone. The static, twice-removed pickup of a roaming cell echoed back to him.

"... ello."

"Mr. Summersby?"

A second lag. "That you, Stranahan?" The cell was going in and out.

Stranahan affirmed that it was, noting how quickly the Mister had been dropped.

"Are you a good fisherman?"

Stranahan could hear a muffled roaring in the background. The river? "I can catch a fish, yes." *What the hell?*

"The reason I'm asking is that I can't. I've been through about six fly changes and all I'm catching is God's green grass on the back cast. Do you have any suggestions?"

Is this what he was calling me about? Stranahan thought of his checkbook balance. He sighed. He'd play along with about anything.

"Where are you?"

"Down the hill from the bungalow. It's above Raynolds Pass."

"Have you tried a caddis?"

"An elk hair, a Goddard's, some foam bit of nothing I bought at Bud Lilly's Trout Shop. Nada, nada, nada."

"How much water have you covered?"

"I don't know. I started in, ah ... not a lot. I'm a deliberate fisherman."

"Here's what you do. Put on a size fourteen elk hair with a greased sparkle pupa on the dropper. Pick all the pockets, keep wading upstream. Never make the same cast twice. The trick with dry caddis is covering lots of river. Later, when you start to see trout stick their noses out of the water, clip off the elk hair and tie on a soft hackle, leave the pupa on the dropper and work back downstream, swinging the flies in the current seams, the slower parts of the riffles."

"Is that going to work?"

"It works for me, sir."

"You know, I'm going to try what you said. I called because I had some work for you. I haven't made up my mind how much I'll offer. The next hour will tell. Stay by your telephone, Stranahan. Good-bye."

Stranahan set down the receiver. He looked at his walls, at the combinations of colors that carried him back and forward in time. How much was his life's work worth compared to a rich man's like Summersby? When he was younger, he would have felt superior to any businessman. But that was before he took up a line of work that depended on their whimsy.

"Yes, sir," Stranahan said out loud. "Yes, sir, I will tie your fly on your leader. Where would you like me to make that cast? Behind that rock, sir? I'll put more of the ochre in that piece if you want me to, sir. No, sir, I didn't mean to make the trout look small. I know it was a big one, sir."

Stranahan mock saluted the telephone, noticed the answering machine was flashing for a second message and hit the button.

"Why did you have to make it so hard for me?"

The voice was a whisper. Then there was the undertone of the tape and a click as the message ended.

Stranahan felt his chest expand and fall. He had the feeling you get in deep wading, the pressure building, rising water everywhere. Once already he'd had to break the news to Vareda that the body found in the Madison River might be her brother's. He'd been relieved to learn that the description didn't match. But descriptions could be deceiving, and finding her brother's rod only thirty yards from the body cemented the connection. From the quiet desperation in her voice on the phone message, Stranahan wondered if she already knew.

The phone rang. He gripped the receiver.

"Mr. Stranahan?"

It was Summersby.

"I just caught a sixteen-inch rainbow trout. I'll make you that offer right now. I have twelve rooms in my place here and what I'd like you to do is paint a picture for each, plus a second one for the living room. That's thirteen, minus the painting I already have. So an even dozen. How's two thousand dollars each sound? I like to keep the math simple."

Stranahan collected himself. "It sounds like a deal to me," he said. He had been prepared to swallow his pride and take a far lesser amount. "What is it you had in mind?"

"You don't sound like you're overcome with jubilation," Summersby noted.

"I'm sorry. There may have been a tragedy in a friend's life. I just got the news."

"I'm very sorry to hear that. Why don't you come down here for supper tonight? Thrash out the details in person."

"I think I'll be out of town."

"Tomorrow then. Drive down in the afternoon and we can get a couple hours on the river before cocktails. Ann and I are having the neighbors for dinner."

"I'll do my best to be there."

"Good. Now, that soft hackle you mentioned. Let me open my fly box and tell you what I have. . . ."

Stranahan talked fishing for a minute and hung up the phone.

He walked down the stairs into the slant of afternoon light and found the Montana map above the visor of the Land Cruiser. He spread it over the hood, the metal hot to the touch. She'd said the town had a snake's name. Near Butte or Billings. He ran his finger west. Whitehall . . . Butte . . . Deer Lodge. Drew his finger south. Phillipsburg . . . Anaconda . . . Wise River. Anaconda. That had to be it.

There was no lake by the town, though. The closest body of water was fifteen miles away, on the Anaconda-Pintler Scenic Byway. Georgetown Lake. Maybe there was a lodge there, someplace she could sing.

The Winston fly rod was in the Toyota. The deputy had told Stranahan to bring it to the Law and Justice Center, but that could wait
until his return. Knowing Vareda's reticent nature, he thought seeing
it could elicit information that she might otherwise withhold. If not,
there was still Georgetown Lake. Stranahan felt like a cretin for even
considering it, but he'd been a trout fisherman so long that the
thought was automatic.

For lake fishing, a six-weight was a good all-around rod.

CHAPTER TWENTY-ONE

The Red Canoe

U.S. 90 arrowed west into the sun. Stranahan saw shocks of wheat shot through with gold, the rivers at Three Forks glinting under their bridges. On a bluff where the Madison, Gallatin, and Jefferson rivers joined currents to form the Missouri River, Lewis and Clark had camped for several nights, debating a course in their quest to find a water passage to the Pacific.

Stranahan continued on, crossing the Continental Divide at Home-stake Pass, then downshifting through the Batholith rock spires known as The Dragonback. Butte sprawled below him, a brick town dwarfed by the caldera that until the 1960s had been the world's largest open-pit copper mine. He remembered that Dashiell Hammett, the noir detective writer, had called Butte "Poisonville" in his classic novel *Red Harvest*. It had been a city of toxic waste and payrolled politicians. Today, denied its copper teat, Butte still clung to life with the stubborn blood of its Irish immigrants.

Half an hour later, Stranahan stopped at a gas station on the outskirts of Anaconda, where the skyline was dominated by a dormant copper-smelting chimney. He fed coins into a newspaper bin and slid out the *Montana Standard*. The lead story was about a brothel museum commemorating the working women who had serviced miners and frustrated husbands in Butte until the early 1970s. He leafed through the pages, looking in vain for a section on the local nightlife. He went back into the convenience store and asked the pimply attendant if he knew any clubs or bars that had live music.

"There's the Bean and Cup, that's a coffee house; the Stockman has cowboy bands. You have to go to Butte for funk."

"How about Georgetown Lake?"

"There's the Georgetown Inn. They have music."

Twenty minutes saw Stranahan to the lake. The water shivered under a light breeze, wavelets blinking copper in the evening slant of light. A hundred yards into the lake, float tube fishermen were rafted up like ducks. Farther out, a red canoe trailed a reflection under the peaks of the Pintler Range.

He turned into the asphalt drive of the Georgetown Inn, a rambling, two-story building with a fading coat of yellow paint and a broad, roofed-over porch. He climbed the steps. Beside the door was a placard denoting the inn's inclusion in the historic register.

"An American aristocrat sliding gracefully into decay. The hotel, I mean." Stranahan turned toward the voice. A man was sitting in an Adirondack chair under the porch overhang, a paper cup in front of him set on a varnished spool table. He motioned to Stranahan with his left hand.

"Have a seat."

"Actually," Stranahan said, "it's sort of important that I find a friend of mine who may be staying here."

"A him or a her?" The man's long legs, crossed at the ankles, stretched out in languor. He had a narrow face, hollowed cheekbones, silver hair parted in the middle. In elegant decay himself, thought Stranahan.

"A her. I'll ask inside."

"They'll just send you back out. I own the inn. Not supposed to give out names of our guests, though. We've had some well-known people here who insist on their privacy. Hemingway stayed, 1939 I believe. With Martha Gellhorn. They were living in sin at the time.

We have a photograph of him in our bar, drinking gimlets. One after another. Gary Cooper was a guest, he was the one who recommended it to Hemingway. Eric Clapton made a visit last summer. He's a trout fisherman. I kept hoping he would uncase his guitar some evening, but he turned in early so he could be on the water by dawn. Perfect gentleman."

Stranahan took the offered chair.

"You're English," he said.

"Am I? I thought it didn't show. Would you like a drink?"

Stranahan was suddenly very tired. He'd been up since six, had almost no sleep in three days.

"Is an Irish coffee out of the question?"

The man pressed a button on the wall. He spoke briefly into an intercom.

"It will be right out. I'm Jack Osgood, by the by."

"Sean Stranahan."

They shook hands, Osgood lifting almost imperceptibly from his seat.

"Don't mind me," he said. "I strike up conversations, it's what men of my station do. Dying art, don't you think? Some of my cousins would argue that Americans never did learn how to converse, but that's simply untrue. Perhaps you don't speak English, but you communicate in your pidgin idiom and I've had some wonderful conversations with your countrymen on verandas just like this one. Porches, you call them, but I prefer the Hindu derivation. Be that as it may . . ."

His fingers fluttered briefly.

"Now then, Sean, may I call you Sean? Who did you come here to see? I was teasing before. Let me help if I can."

"Her name is Velvet Lafayette. I thought she might be singing here."

"Is she beautiful?"

"I think she is."

"So do I."

A young woman with a pixie face opened the door, balancing two drinks on a tray. She set the Irish coffee in front of Stranahan, a tumbler of amber liquid for his host.

"It's Glenfarclas, Mr. Osgood. We're out of the Lagavulin."

"A pity," he said.

When she had left, he took a sip of the whiskey and said, "The woman singing here goes by a different name. Vareda Beaudreux." He arched his eyebrows.

"That's her real name," Stranahan said, covering his surprise. "Velvet is her stage name."

"I should be honored, then, that she has trusted us with her given name. The woman arrived this morning. I put her in the end cabin. Back in the aspens. She seems a private person. She's booked two nights and sings here tomorrow. She sent a demo CD. If she's as brilliant in person, I won't have made a mistake."

"You won't be disappointed."

Stranahan stood up to excuse himself.

"No need to hurry. She isn't there," Osgood said. "She asked about renting a canoe. I told her anytime, no charge. They're chained to the dock across the street. Here, I'll get you a key and you can paddle out to meet her. She'll be in a red sixteen-footer. Your transportation's on me."

"You're a generous man, Mr. Osgood."

"I'm trying to make up for a lifetime of sin. If it's in my power to advance the cause of romance, well . . . don't believe in it myself, of course. It would ruin my reputation as a cynic."

He turned to press the buzzer again. "I'll get you that key."

The red canoe wasn't in sight from the shore. Stranahan dug with his paddle, pushing past the float tubers. A motorboat idled by, a filament of spinning line trailing from a rod fixed to the stern.

There she was. Far out toward the eastern shore of the lake. He J-hooked the paddle to keep the canoe in line, noticing, as the gap closed, that the red canoe seemed to glide effortlessly as it angled toward him.

She was wearing khaki shorts and an oversize flannel shirt in a red-and-black check. A black ball cap labeled JOHNSON SEAFOOD FARMS under an embossed crawfish was drawn over her hair, her ponytail escaping through the hole above the adjustable band.

Stranahan set down his paddle. She pulled alongside, bow to bow, small waves lapping the Kevlar hulls of the canoes.

Separated by a paddle's length of pearlescent water, she looked imploringly at him from under the bill of her cap. Her eyes looked swollen and her cheeks were flushed. Her shoulders abruptly collapsed.

"How did you find me?"

"I used to be a detective, remember? It's starting to come back."

Her voice was a husky whisper. "If you're a detective, you know what I want to hear."

Stranahan regarded her solemnly.

"I know what you don't want to hear, and I'm very sorry to be the one who tells you." Much better to get it over with. "A fly rod was found near the body of the man who drowned in the Madison River. It was inscribed by the maker to your brother."

She looked down at her hands.

"You know your way around a canoe paddle," he said at length.

He watched her chest heave without sound.

"We had a pirogue," she said without lifting her head.

Stranahan set his lips in a grim smile.

"Now it's me who doesn't know what to do with you."

"Oh, just throw me in the lake." She wiped a tear from her cheek and made a murmuring chuckle in her throat. "Save yourself a whole lot of trouble. Come on. Let's go in. It's going to rain."

"The coffee can Mr. Keino gave to you. Those are my father's ashes; I didn't lie to you about that. Or about the trout my father marked. That's something you ought to know." They were sitting on the porch, a spool table between them.

"Vareda, it hardly seems—"

"Let me finish. I've known that my brother could be dead ever since I first read about that"—she hesitated—"body. I was hoping that you would find him alive. I thought that the hair, you know, being the wrong color . . ." She stopped to compose herself. "I'm ashamed to say that I didn't have the courage to drive down there myself to look for him."

"Why didn't you call the sheriff?"

"Don't you know me? That's something I just couldn't do."

No, Stranahan thought. I don't know you at all.

"But you do know me," she said, as if reading his mind was such an easy thing. "You know *me*. The things you don't know don't really matter."

A silence fell between them. A grid of electric wires enclosing a lightbulb suspended from the porch buzzed intermittently to incinerate moths.

"Vareda, I'm here to listen," he said in an understanding voice. "Just talk to me. Tell me so I know what's going on. I'm involved. A friend of mine was shot yesterday morning, in a lake not far from the place your brother drowned. I was there when it happened. Maybe there's a connection, maybe there isn't, but I'm going to find out."

"Shot? You mean he's dead and it . . . it's to do with my brother?" Her voice faltered.

"No, my friend's going to be okay." He didn't want to get side-tracked talking about Sam. "Tell me about your brother. Why was he in Montana? Did you follow him here? What was he involved in? The sheriff hasn't come right out and told me, but I know she thinks it was a murder."

"Murder?" She leaned forward, her eyes startled open. "Murder." Dropping her voice to echo the word, making it a statement.

"As in someone helped him to drown. Vareda, maybe together we can make some sense of this. I'm on your side here."

"No." She shook her head. Then abruptly looked away at the slate expanse of the lake. The wind had picked up. Waves were lapping the dock. There was the fresh smell of the rain coming, then the first drops on the roof.

Finally she faced him with a look of resignation. "I have to tell you. There's no one else I can talk to."

"You've got my attention," he said.

"Is that all I have?" Her voice held an undertone of sadness. Then, "Where was I?" she said absently. "I don't know where I was."

"You were going to tell me about your brother."

"But you're here now." She reached across the table and took his hand, held it to her cheek. "It's late and . . . somebody shot, I mean, it could have been you. It's all been a shock. I can't think about it anymore tonight. I'll tell you, I promise. But right now what I want, what I absolutely need, is for you to walk back to the cabin with me. I can't face being alone tonight."

"You won't run off again?"

"Oh no. You can't get rid of me, now."

When they stood, she laid her head on his shoulder, then lifted it for a moment to turn her cap sideways so that the bill would shield the side of her face from the rain.

"There," she said, nestling into him. "We fit."

Stranahan smelled the faint scent of oranges, mixed with pine oil and wet aspen bark and the petal odor of the rain. He knew that there was something off about her, something inscrutable behind the gears that shifted her moods; he was no fool to think that he was immune to her manipulations. But as they stepped into the rain, the questions that brought them together receded into the darkness.

Later, touching two fingers to his lips in the dark, "There now. Don't say a word. Just hold me."

CHAPTER TWENTY-TWO

Salt and Pepper

Jack Osgood twirled the porcupine quill between his fingers. Stranahan had extracted it from the bloodied carcass of a porcupine that he and Vareda had found near the step of her cabin shortly after dawn. Beside the carcass was a canoe paddle, the handle sweat-stained and gnawed to a nub.

"They come for the salt," Osgood said, taking a chair in the breakfast nook of the inn. "It's their Achilles, the salt. A porcupine is safer in a tree. He can climb a limb where the fisher—that is the rarest member of the weasel family, if you didn't know—has to attack from behind and can't get past the armor of his quills. But when the porcupine comes down to eat the canoe paddle, the fisher attacks his head.

"The relationship is cyclical. The porcupine population goes up, fishers produce more fishers. The more fishers there are, the fewer the porcupines. Fewer the porcupines become, fewer fishers to the litter. Fewer fishers, more porcupines." Osgood drew circles in the air with his coffee cup. "And round and round. The patterns of God, as intricate as the designs on the wings of butterflies. A man learns so many useless things. . . ."

He placed the quill on the table. "I'll leave the two of you to your breakfast."

Stranahan saw mirth dancing in Vareda's eyes. The weight of her brother's probable death seemed to have lifted with the morning light.

Even last night, when their resolve to only hold each other had evaporated, it had been a strained love, marked by melancholy and distance.

She whispered, "He looks like Peter O'Toole."

"Gone to seed and then some," Stranahan agreed.

"I know what," she said suddenly. "Let's get the canoe and go fishing."

"There are things we have to talk about, Vareda."

"On the lake. I promise. Come on, Mr. Fisherman." She shrugged into her flannel shirt, grabbed a handful of salt and pepper packets from a dish, and put them in the breast pocket.

"For the trout I'm going to catch," she said.

Sitting backward on the bow seat, Vareda trolled with the rod tip down as Stranahan had instructed, right forefinger trapping the line against the cork grip. The rain clouds of the evening before had torn apart and were disappearing beyond the mountain horizon. From the stern of the canoe, Stranahan watched rays of sunlight flirt with her hair.

She said, "I'll bet I've caught more kinds of fish than you," and rattled off a dozen, ending with long-nosed gar, which she said she'd caught in the pirogue with Jerry. "I thought it was an alligator. Those teeth. The long nose. Oh, I had an imagination as a child." Her dusky voice played with the words, extending them.

"Jerry," Stranahan prompted, digging with his paddle.

"Don't." Suddenly glaring at him.

The rod tip bent sharply. A trout jumped clear of the surface, a shard like silver metal, glinting. Vareda let the trout run, pumped the rod when it stopped, reeling up only when she dropped the tip.

Stranahan cautioned, "Easy around the boat now."

A moment later he lifted the net, the trout shaping the meshes into a bow.

"How beautiful he is," Vareda said.

She motioned him to hand over the net, held the fish steady through the netting, and banged its head hard on the canoe gunwale. The trout stiffened, then relaxed.

"You're just full of surprises," Stranahan said.

He opened his pocketknife and dressed the fish with swift strokes, spilling the vermilion insides overboard and running his thumb under the backbone to clear the clotted blood. He laid it in the shade under the canoe seat.

"Daddy smelled like earth," she began. "When I was little, I'd see him coming across the fields and run to jump up on him. That smell, there's nothing like a field of plowed bottomland to take me away. Yeah." Cocking her head to remember, talking to herself, the story coming out.

She said that after her mother's death, from ovarian cancer, her father just faded away. Each day he was thinner, his daily walks became longer, each night was darker than the last. Finally, he couldn't stand it anymore and drove off one morning before dawn. Vareda was living at home then, working at the catfish ponds that were part of the farming operation, when Old McGruder, the foreman, handed her a letter with his eyes averted. Her father had written all the heart-wrenching words he couldn't summon the voice to tell her, said he had to get away, and Vareda had spent a week in terror, afraid he was going to hurt himself. Then a postcard arrived of the Old Faithful geyser in Yellowstone National Park. Her father wrote that he had bought a fly rod and caught his first trout in the Firehole River. He had always been an old-fashioned man's man, liked hunting and fishing, had read about the trout fishing in the Rocky Mountains and wanted to try it. And that's how he began to recover, and when he returned home a month later he was a semblance of the man that Vareda remembered.

She looked at Sean.

"He said once, I'll never forget, 'The thing about fishing is that it gives a man hope. Each cast builds a little hope and if he can lose himself to that hope, then the worries and the heartache fade into the background. The wind inside him dies down for a while.' Papa said it was like the river was the window he had to climb through to reclaim a lost part of himself. Isn't that beautiful? I think so. It's what brought him back to me. Maybe that's why I have a thing for fishermen; I'm always grateful." She allowed the corners of her lips to lift in a brief smile.

"There are some people, they're born with the sunlight inside them. I wish you could have met him. Daddy would have liked you."

The canoe tapped bottom. Gravel grated under the hull.

"Do you mind stopping?" Stranahan said. "I have to answer the call, as they say."

"I love to pee in the woods," Vareda said. "Especially if there's a breeze, umm."

She helped drag the bow of the canoe onto the shore.

"Oh, you shock so easily," she said, and shivered deliciously, pulling her shirt snug around her like a jacket.

When he came back from his walk, she was gone. Off to catch the breeze, he guessed. He thought of the trout on the canoe bottom and started to gather sticks on the shoreline, building them into a teepee below the high-water mark. He added lint from his pockets and held a match underneath. He blew gently until the flames grew tall.

Vareda came back and rinsed her hands and her face in the shallows.

"Thanks for . . . out there," she said, sitting on the sand beside him. "I'm not trying to hide anything about Jerry, it's just that if I talk about him, it's like admitting he's really gone. It's hard to start."

"Tell you what, while you think about how to get started, I'm going to cook that fish you caught," he said.

"Oh, you're mad at me. Don't be." Stranahan felt the press of her lips against his ear.

"I'm just thinking," Stranahan said, getting up. In fact, he was thinking about Sheriff Ettinger. He'd told her about Velvet Lafayette. He hadn't told her about Vareda Beaudreux. She was going to want more than a few words with Vareda Beaudreux.

Stranahan found a flat piece of driftwood and set it beside the fire. He split the trout lengthwise along the backbone. Pressing the skin sides to the plank, he fixed the two halves in place with fishing flies, the hooks bent through the skin to attach it to the punky wood. He propped the wood at an angle next to the fire.

"This is called planking," he said, scraping coals against the wood. "Do it right and the fish cooks before the wood catches fire."

The orange trout flesh began to sizzle. Stranahan banked the coals, kept rearranging them until he judged the trout done.

"Do you still have that salt and pepper?" He teased the backbone and ribs from the halves of fish and dropped them into the fire.

Vareda sprinkled the smoking flesh. She examined the trout flies that pinned the fish to the plank. The hair had burnt away. She flicked a few curled strands of scorched feathers with a fingernail.

"This reminds me," she said, "I have a couple boxes of Daddy's fishing flies. I have his net and his rod, too. I brought them up here thinking I might use them to find the fish he marked. But there's too much to learn to do it myself. The first time I tried to cast I hooked my earring on the watch-a-callit—the back cast."

Stranahan thought about the fly in Jerry Beaudreux's lip. It was something Vareda didn't know about.

"I want you to have them," she was saying. "You can use Daddy's rod and maybe one of his flies will be on your line when you catch his fish. I have other things to remember him by."

Stranahan stood up and without a word walked to the canoe. He came back with the case he'd carried the Winston fly rod in, the one Sam had found near the body.

"This is the fly rod I told you about last night. Look at the inscription. Someone tried to scratch it off, but it was definitely your brother's name."

"It was a high school graduation present," she said in a flat tone. "Daddy had two of them made, the one I have has his name on it. They're the same. I remember now, Jerry saying afterward he figured Dad probably hoped he'd fish with it in a storm and electrocute himself. He was at that rebellious age—but don't get the wrong idea, he loved Daddy as much as I did."

"Vareda, we need to talk about him."

"My brother reminds me of you," she said. "He has to find answers to questions. I'm afraid that's why he's . . . missing."

Her kid brother, it turned out. Jerry had been born when Vareda was twelve, and from the start had preferred the back door to the front, eighty-foot loblolly pines to a two-lane town. When Vareda's father had taken up fly fishing the year his wife died, so had Jerry, who by then was a teenager. Father and son had made annual fishing trips to the Rockies in the three succeeding years, leading up to the heart attack that had taken the elder Beaudreux's life the summer before. That had been Jerry's first summer working at the hatchery up by Great Falls, and it had been their father's plan to fish his way north to visit him, but he had died on the bank of the Madison only days before they were scheduled to rendezvous.

Stranahan asked Vareda if she had ever accompanied them on their fishing trips. No, she'd been too busy divorcing her husband. "Marry young, marry dumb—it's the oldest Southern story there is," she said, and Stranahan did not press her to elaborate.

"Have you ever heard of whirling disease?" Vareda asked. She hugged her knees to her chest, then glanced up. She said, "Look, an eagle."

Stranahan turned to see the bird soaring against a ridge of pine, its head and tail falling like snowflakes as the eagle abruptly dived to the lake and emerged, flapping heavily, with a fish clasped in its talons.

Stranahan pointed to the bird. "I know enough about whirling disease to know that's one way it can be transmitted." He explained that the parasitic cyst responsible for decimating the Madison River's rainbow trout population was ingested by fish-eating birds, which could infect other rivers in turn by defecating into the water. The hardy cyst would survive the digestion process, then, once deposited, could begin the cycle of infecting infant trout. . . . He was just regurgitating what he'd learned from Sam.

Vareda frowned. "All I know is it's bad," she said. "Jerry told me the hatchery had a grant to study the disease, but there was something about the operation that bothered him."

Stranahan interrupted. "When was this?"

"Just a couple of weeks ago. I was still in Mississippi. He called me. I didn't understand much of what he was saying, just that he was real excited. That was Jerry—he had enthusiasm, but no common sense. I kept saying 'be careful' but it was cops and robbers to him—he's so naive, I'm afraid he did something terribly foolish."

"Back up a second. You lost me. What bothered him at the hatchery?"

"He saw something he says he shouldn't have, that he wasn't meant to. He thought it might have something to with the whirling disease. There was this truck."

"A truck?"

"Yes. He said there was this truck that was collecting some fish, and I think he said it wasn't supposed to be there or maybe he just hadn't seen it before."

The truck, Vareda told him, had arrived at the hatchery before dark but after Jerry had left work for the day. Jerry had been fishing—he was living in a tent in a campground on the Missouri River only a couple of miles away—and was driving past and noticed the truck and became curious, because a couple of men looked to be loading fish into a live well in the truck bed. The next morning he'd asked the hatchery manager, who dismissed it as a supply truck bringing chemicals to clean the runways. The manager had volunteered nothing about loading fish into the truck, and later Jerry had overheard whirling disease mentioned when the manager was talking to another employee who was around only occasionally. That confirmed Jerry's suspicion and he had started spying on the place after hours. When he spotted the truck a second time, he decided he would follow and see where it went. But when it turned south onto the highway, he chickened out. The first time he saw the truck was Tuesday, then on Thursday. He didn't see the truck over the weekend but decided if it came again on Tuesday, he'd be ready and follow it.

"I think when he talked to me," Vareda said with a sigh, "it was a way of working up his nerve."

Stranahan thought about Vareda's comment about cops and robbers and had an inspiration.

"Vareda," he said, "you never actually saw your brother after he came up here for the summer, did you?"

"No. I haven't seen him since Easter."

"The reason I asked—do you think Jerry would have shaved his beard and dyed his hair to disguise himself? To reduce the chance that the truck driver might recognize him? That would explain why the description in the newspaper wasn't a match."

"No. Yes. I mean, that makes sense. Jerry would do something like that, like it was part of a game." Her voice broke and a tear slid down her cheek.

"I'm sorry to press you on this, Vareda. But I think we have to accept the probability that he did come to harm and focus on finding who's responsible."

She wiped a tear away and looked far off for a second.

"Okay," she said. "I'm okay. You're right. Ask me what you want."

"Try to remember. What did Jerry say specifically, about the disease?"

"He just mentioned the name and then sort of skipped to the next thing about the truck. That's the way he is. He starts to get a thought out and then by the time he ends the sentence he's talking about something else."

"You said he called a couple of weeks ago. When exactly?"

"He called on the twelfth of July. I remember because I'd marked the dates for my trip on the calendar."

"Was that the last time you talked?"

"No. He called at the inn last Tuesday. I'd just gotten to Montana."

Stranahan registered the date as the day before Sam found the body.

Jerry had told her that he'd followed the truck to Ennis. It had stopped at a bar and he was waiting for the man to come back out. He called from a pay phone and told her he'd call again when he found out where it was going.

"He never did." Her voice caught.

"One man?"

"I think so."

"Height? Hair? Build?"

She shook her head.

"Did he say what kind of truck?"

"No."

"Nothing else?"

"No. Oh, wait now, he mentioned a dog. He said there was a dog riding shotgun. But we only talked a minute. It wasn't, like, a conversation."

"So let me get this straight. After he told you he was investigating, you got worried and came up here. Then, before you had a chance to see him, he called to say he was following a truck from the hatchery."

Vareda nodded. She was signing the register at the Cottonwood

Inn when Jerry called. She had called ahead and booked a couple places to play that she'd already sent CDs to. She just bumped up the dates. The original plan had been to meet Jerry in August. They were going to scatter their father's ashes together before caravanning back south.

"We were going to meet after I played the Bridger dates. I was going to drive up to Cascade where he worked."

"Is there anything else that could help? Something I haven't asked you about?"

"I . . . I drove up there last Saturday, after I met you. I thought if you didn't find him on the Madison there was a chance he had gone back to his campground. But I didn't find him there, so I asked at the hatchery. It was sort of on a back road and hard to find, but I found it."

"Who did you talk to at the hatchery?"

"Some man, I don't know who he was. He said Jerry had told them he was taking a couple of days off, going to go on a fishing trip. But he didn't say it right away like that. He had to think about it. I could tell he was lying."

"What was the man's name?"

"I didn't ask."

"Describe him to me."

"Uh, he had short hair. Cowboy boots. Sort of a rancher type. But not a presentable person at all, if you ask me. When I asked him who Jerry's friends were, someone I might contact, he got sarcastic, said how the hell should he know. He damned near shut the door in my face. I got paranoid. I thought maybe he was following me. I just had this feeling when I got back to Bridger."

Stranahan thought back to Joseph Keino at the Aberdare Bed and Breakfast. He'd said Vareda kept looking out the window.

"And you've told this to no one?"

"Just you." Her cheeks were wet with tears. "After I left that message for you, right after, I was sort of crazy. If you hadn't come last night, I don't know what I would have done."

Stranahan got to his feet and kicked sand over the dying coals.

"Come on," he said. "We're going to drive back to Bridger and you're going to tell the sheriff what you told me. And you're going to have to go to the morgue to identify the body." He held up a hand when she began to object. "I'm just doing what you wanted me to do in the first place. You got me involved in this, now you're going to have to trust me."

She toed the sand.

"One more thing," he said, after they had pushed off in the canoe. "Whoever killed your brother, if it's the guy who took a potshot at my friend, then what he is looking for, or whatever he's trying to cover up, he's getting desperate. He's going to sever any threads that can tie him to Jerry. You, me too for that matter, could be at the ends of two pretty short ones. When things are taken care of in Bridger, maybe it would be best if you disappeared for a while. Do you have a third name you could use?"

She had to smile. "Look at me," she said. "Promise me you won't do anything stupid."

Stranahan dug his paddle, feeling the resistance of the water.

Underneath, trout prowled.

Stranahan dug deeper.

He thought of the water down there, a worm twisting on a hook.

CHAPTER TWENTY-THREE

Muddy Water

"**G**et me a couple rocks, will ya, Walt?"

Martha Ettinger spread an aerial photomap across the hood of the Cherokee.

"Like these?" He held up a couple of river stones.

"Two more, Walt. There're four corners to a map. Use your brain."

"Aren't we Miss Testy this evening?" he said, bending down.

"Sorry. It's this"—she grabbed her hair with both hands and then shook it loose with a violent shudder—"sit-u-a-tion. I got everybody thinking I'm a half clip short. A man's got water in his lungs, he's found in the river, that's where he drowned. Only microscopic bugs say he didn't. If it wasn't for Doc's goddamned microscope I'd be having a better hair day than I'm having."

"Yeah, Marth, you got that Bride of Frankenstein thing going up top, I must say." Walt approached with the rocks.

"Gimme," Martha said. She pinned down the map.

"Any bodies of water we haven't hit? We been at this ten hours."

Martha pointed. "Here, here . . . here. Three to go—this pond's just a little way down from Quake Lake, where I met the fishing detective who saved Meslik's waterlogged butt. Hmm?" She flicked her lower lip, exhaling a sound like bubbles rising to the surface. "You know what I like about this? I like knocking on doors in an election year and asking voters if they've drowned anyone recently."

"Shit, Marth, none of these sunbirds vote. Come Labor Day, they've all flown back to LaLaLand."

The Lazy S was a typical ranchette rip-off: the property shaped like a stick of chalk with three hundred feet of riverfront, a stagnant-looking pond, and ten worthless acres of sagebrush running back into the foothills. A young antelope buck cocked a baleful eye at the Cherokee as it turned under the yoke-style gate, then dashed off at sixty per.

The chinked log home sported a green metal roof with swallow nests plastered under the eaves, a wraparound porch, peaked windows overlooking the Madison churn. The houses on the neighboring parcels were a comfortable football field apart. One small dwelling upriver, built from dark logs and set back into a grove of mature aspens, had obviously been there longer than the development. The others were of a generic mold, similar to the Lazy S but with different colored roofs. The contractors had dismissed the setback clause with Libertarian aplomb—this was Montana after all—and built them illegally within the floodplain. Another act of God like the earthquake of '59, Martha thought, and there'd be a few million dollars' worth of logs floating to Three Forks.

"Yes?"

The man who introduced himself as Lionel Sinclair—"Call me Tony," he insisted—had an open, handsome face and brown eyes that housed a welcoming light, dimmed only slightly by the straw Stetson that rode his forehead. The corners of his mouth twitched in bemusement as Martha trotted out the spiel she and Walt had fine-tuned through the course of the day. They would ask to see the pond, say it was part of an ongoing investigation without offering specifics, offer their apology for the inconvenience. At the pond, they would take a water sample to filter for the algae and aquatic invertebrates found in the victim's esophagus, although the university limnologist had assured them the species were common to many still waters in the county. What they were really looking for was a bootprint match, a link between a specific pond and the campsite where Little Feather had found the print under the tent.

Sinclair listened patiently, leaning cowboy-style with his right arm braced against the door frame. He had Walt by six inches, four if you subtracted the heels of his ostrich-skin boots.

"You understand, Mr. Sinclair, we're just trying to eliminate right now," Martha concluded.

"Be my guest," he said. "I got the Department of Resources permits for the pond. Only things I have to hide are a couple spots up the river where there's brown trout long as your arm."

"Feel free to keep them under your hat," Martha assured him, and turned with Walt toward the pond. Halfway across the sagebrush flat, Walt glanced back to see Sinclair still standing in the doorway, giving them a laconic gaze.

"Cocksure bastard," Walt muttered.

The pond, perhaps an acre in extent, was clouded with pinpoint algae and had no more than a few inches of visibility.

"Pea soup," Walt said with a note of disgust.

Martha was already striding off. "You go one way, I'll go the other."

"Won't have to," Walt said, pointing at a line of boot tracks in the mud. The tracks ended where a distinct drag mark connected the shoreline with the bank. Martha felt a flush of excitement. The impression was finely ribbed, like corduroy. There were no human tracks in the drag mark, or to either side of it.

"Might use that Indian tracker 'bout now," Walt said.

Martha grunted. Little Feather had told her he'd be at his sister's house in Pony, working horses. It was too late in the day to call him.

"I don't get it," she said. "If this is a mark where someone dragged a body out of the pond, then you'd expect to find two sets of tracks, one going down, one coming up."

"Maybe not, Marth. Say the killer is the guy who made the tracks going down to the water. Victim's in the drink. He pulls him up the bank, the body covers up the tracks he's making backing up, probably those of the victim, too. Wouldn't be any sign of either, you see what I'm saying?"

Ettinger grunted. She unfolded a tracing of the print found under the tent and placed it on the dried mud next to the tracks.

"'Bout the right size," Walt offered. Ettinger withdrew a photo of the track taken under the tent from her breast pocket. Walt nodded. "Tread's a match. I'd say we got us a crime scene."

"Maybe not. These prints are smeared in the muck. Makes them look bigger."

"Anybody tell you you're a pessimist?"

"I've been through two husbands. It comes with the territory."

"I hear you on that. Still . . . we might have something here."

"Let's see what kind of boots Mr. Sinclair pulls over his dogs."

"I'm beginning to feel a bit guilty," the tall man said when he saw the expression on Martha Ettinger's face.

When she said she'd like to ask him a few questions, he nodded and held the door open. He hung his hat on the antler tine of a mule deer mount that acted as a hat rack and led the way into a spacious living room done in a tasteful desert motif; Navajo rugs were scattered, a bison robe was draped over a sofa patterned with eagles. A slim woman sat at one end, facing the windows that overlooked the river. A heavy pair of binoculars rested on the sill. She was reading a book and didn't turn around.

"You have a nice place here," Walt said.

"Thank you."

Sinclair was bald with a rim of brown hair pulled into a ponytail; a white line of demarcation marked where the hat had rested.

"I keep waiting for that Propecia to kick in," he said. "Till then, I have to be careful of the sun." He chuckled, then crossed the living room and placed a hand on the woman's shoulder. When she looked up, he made a few fluid movements with his hands. The woman stood and turned to Martha and Walt. Walt instinctively straightened.

"My wife, Eva," Sinclair said from behind her.

The woman touched her ear and lips, shook her head side to side, then took Martha's and Walt's hands and pressed them warmly. She was dressed in creased jeans and a cream linen shirt with pearl snaps. Shearling-lined slippers cradled slim brown feet. Lustrous black hair was pulled back in a sterling clip. She wore a silver bracelet and turquoise rings on two fingers of her left hand.

The woman held out her right hand in the shape that indicated a glass.

Martha shook her head, then mouthed the words "No thanks," and could have shot herself for being an idiot.

"Ah, we could sit at the table," Sinclair offered.

"Actually, we'd like to see your mudroom, where you keep your boots."

He hesitated.

"If it's all right with you." Martha scrutinized his face, which showed confusion, then, with a brief nod of his head, dawning comprehension.

"This is about the antelope, isn't it? We reported it to Fish, Wildlife, and Parks; that's what we were supposed to do, I thought."

Martha tried not to betray her surprise. What antelope?

While they'd been talking, Sinclair had led them across the living room toward a side door. Walt glanced back to see the woman bring the binoculars to her eyes and look out the window. He felt a sharp tug on his sleeve and turned to see an expression on Martha's face that said, clear as spoken words, *Get back on the job.*

The mudroom was roughly finished but fastidiously organized. Waders hung upside down to air-dry on pegs. Boots were paired against one wall. A stack of fly rods stood at attention in a rack, a lineup of slim graphite quills. Martha peered at the flies hooked onto the keeper rings above the corks. She noticed that one was a Royal Wulff.

"If you're interested in the antelope, I honestly don't know much more than I told the warden."

"Why don't you explain to the two of us?" Martha said.

"I heard the shot. Woke me up. Just getting light so I looked out the window—our bedroom's upper level—couldn't see anything. Only when I went outside later that morning I noticed the doe. She was by the pond."

"Any idea who might be responsible?"

Sinclair hesitated. "I have my suspicion, but that's all it is."

"This is just between us," Martha said.

Sinclair told them that the new neighbor two houses downriver, Gus Gentry, had built a bench rest in his yard and started blasting at gophers with a scoped rifle. When Sinclair had approached him about it last Sunday—after all, he had twin nephews who spent the better part of their summer vacation on the river and liked to roam the property—Gentry had reminded him that there were no covenants prohibiting shooting on his own land. The man was an ex-Marine, a noted big-game hunter from El Paso, Texas, who owned a chain of high-end taxidermy businesses that specialized in mounting African trophies. Sinclair had told him he would bring up the matter with the homeowners' association and Gentry said, "You do that." The next day, Sinclair had awoken to the shot and found the antelope, a bullet hole in the center of her chest.

"This happened Monday morning, then?" Martha prompted.

"Yes. I registered my complaint right after. The warden said some-one would investigate, but no one has. My wife didn't enjoy looking at it, so this afternoon I hauled her out of the mud myself, drove up the Sheep Creek Road, and dumped the carcass in a coulee. I don't suppose I can count on you to do anything about this?" The accusa-tion was buffered by a smile that Martha imagined had helped make him what he was, in whatever business he was in.

"We'll have a word with your neighbor," she said distractedly. She was thinking of the drag mark at the pond. The corrugated pattern in the mud must have been made by the antelope's hair. She felt a letdown of expectation. So much for the idea that Sinclair had moved a human body.

"I could take you there, up where I dumped her."

"That probably won't be necessary. Mr. Sinclair. . . ."

"Tony," he corrected.

"Tony, your complaint, though I assure you we take it seriously, isn't what brought us here. I'd like to ask you about a set of footprints we found at your pond. Are they yours? Maybe where you dragged out that antelope?"

He nodded. "Hasn't been anyone else there to my knowledge."

"Mind showing me the boots you were wearing?"

"Sure."

He pointed to a pair of boots in the lineup. Martha couldn't help noticing that his finger was dead steady.

She picked up the right boot and registered the mud smeared at the edges of the sole. It was an L.L. Bean Maine hunting shoe, size eleven.

"Would you object to me taking these boots back to Bridger? Just for a day or two?"

Sinclair's eyes never changed, but he straightened a little.

He said, "Is this really necessary? I mean, I have nothing to hide, but it would ease my mind if I knew what it was you were looking for."

"And I told you it's confidential business at this point. We're just trying to eliminate, not to accuse. We'll get the boots back to you."

"That isn't my concern."

"Then let us take them."

"All right, take them." He bit the words short.

"And this rod, can we borrow it, too?" It was Walt, holding the fly rod with the Royal Wulff knotted to the leader.

Sinclair threw his hands up.

"Take it. Whatever. Want my hat, too?"

"No," Martha said. "And we do thank you for your cooperation. I understand why you're upset. I'll probably come back tomorrow to have another look at your pond. Until then, can you keep people away from it?"

He nodded. "I'm sorry. Just wish you didn't have to be so damned mysterious. Makes me wonder what's really going on."

Martha let him wonder. She thanked him again for his cooperation, then turned with Walt toward the side door.

"We'll let ourselves out here if you'd prefer," she said.

"That would be considerate of you. Now, if you don't mind, Sheriff, I'd like to explain to my wife." Sinclair smiled his smile. It looked almost genuine. "She's having a hard time understanding what this visit is about, as you can well imagine."

"As you can well imagine," Walt echoed as they left. "As you can well imagine. "Who talks like that?"

"People with an education, Walt," Martha said with an audible sigh. She knew that Sinclair would be a dead end. Taking his boots was just going through the motions, similar tread to tracks found at the campsite notwithstanding.

Walt said, "I'll bet there's a shitstorm of sign language going on in that living room. My, she was beautiful, though. Silent. Sorta like a panther the way she walked."

"I wonder," Martha said, "just how you say 'shitstorm' in sign language?"

Walt didn't take the bait.

"She looked a little Native American to me," Martha said. She was thinking of Little Feather and flushed.

"A man could cut his hands on those cheekbones," Walt said, nodding his head. "Yup," he said as Martha put the Cherokee in gear. "Per near cut your hand right off."

CHAPTER TWENTY-FOUR

Three Dollar Bridge

At a little past four, Stranahan swung the Land Cruiser into the dirt ruts that ran alongside the Madison River at Three Dollar Bridge. Usually there was a rusted tin box with a slot to put your money in, but this time the landowner had appointed an attendant, a wizened old stork in faded overalls whose tollbooth was a folding chair under a sun umbrella. Stranahan stuffed three ones into the coffee cup the man proffered, the two exchanged howdees, and that was the extent of the conversation.

Back at the truck, Stranahan pulled the Winston from its sock. Not the rod Sam had found in the river, but its twin, the one that had belonged to Vareda's father. She had pressed it on him, along with her father's two fly boxes and his net, in the parking lot at the Law and Justice Center in Bridger earlier that afternoon. A sheriff's deputy named Huntsinger had informed them that Martha Ettinger was out of town, but agreed to take a statement from Vareda concerning her brother's death and accompany her to the morgue to formally identify the body. Stranahan had volunteered to cancel his appointment with Summersby—they were to meet at his "bungalow" on the Madison at 7 p.m. to discuss his paintings—but Vareda insisted there was no need for him to hold her hand. She'd arranged for a room at the Cottonwood Inn and needed some time to herself. He could call her there in the morning. Was that all right? The tone of her voice was matter of fact—she had been reserved from the moment they climbed into their cars and caravanned back from Georgetown Lake. For Stranahan, the distance between them came as something of a relief. In a legal sense he was off the hook the moment the door to the sheriff's office shut behind her, and as he headed down the bank to try his luck with the Winston, his step was lighter than it had been for some time.

A few hundred yards below the bridge, the Madison necked down, then foamed and eddied in a pinball course among the boulders. Stranahan caught a couple Montana bonefish, as locals called the ubiquitous whitefish, then sat down on a rock and idly fished through his vest pockets for the fly boxes Vareda had given him. Opening another man's fly boxes was like leafing through a stranger's bookshelves, looking for clues to character. If a fisherman's flies lined up like obedient soldiers, chances were he had a mannered disposition. If they stuck up askew, hurriedly replaced as the angler sought and discarded the weapons in his arsenal, then he might be charitably called a spontaneous person, creative, given to inspiration—to put it succinctly, a mess. Stranahan tried to keep some order in his own boxes, but by the end of a fishing trip the streamer flies that imitated small baitfish would be fornicating with the smaller nymphs, curls of leader would be protruding from the lips of the dries, marabous would be kinked and matted. He opened the larger of the two boxes and was heartened to see that Vareda's father was a brother in arms. The fly box held a chaotic mix of streamers and nymphs, many of the bead-head variety, and was studded with weighted stone fly patterns that would drop to the streambed like anvils. Stranahan avoided such heavy artillery when possible, but it was a workingman's fly box that pretty much covered the bases.

The second box, a vintage Wheatley crafted in England, held terrestrials on one side, with the hooks held in clips. On the other side, peeking at him from under clear plastic compartment lids, were the delicate dry flies—Trudes, Adams, Wulffs, PMDs, mayfly cripples, and a smattering of less identifiable patterns. Stranahan glanced over them once, then looked more closely. On each dry fly, buried among the hackle fibers, was the odd strand or two of golden pheasant tippet. Pheasant tippet adds a barring effect that can simulate the mottled appearance of many insects. But on dry flies, which trout see as fractured shadows against the glare of the sun, the addition of a few fibers of tippet was superfluous. It was a signature of the tier rather than a nod to the quarry. Well, he thought, it matched the personality of the man. Vareda's father liked to leave his mark, whether it was on the trout he caught or the flies that hooked them.

Stranahan felt a faint tremor in the earth behind him. A Black Angus steer dance-stepped a few yards away, its eyes weeping a viscous fluid that had attracted a swarm of gnats. The steer was so close Stranahan could feel the heat radiating from its barrel body. How long had it been there? He snapped the Wheatley shut and splashed water on his face. It was time to drive upriver and pay Summersby a visit.

The sun was into its decline by the time Stranahan turned off 87 onto the gravel track that accessed the summer homes on the river. A quarter mile in he pulled into the sagebrush to let a white Cherokee pass, registered the county plates, and an instant later recognized the face behind the dusty windshield.

The Cherokee idled to a stop. The window powered down and Stranahan greeted Martha Ettinger's question-mark gaze with a sheepish smile.

"Evening, Sheriff."

"If it isn't Mr. Stranahan," she said. "I must be missing something, because for the life of me I don't know what you're doing here."

Stranahan told her about Summersby, Vareda Beaudreux, the fish hatchery, the words tumbling out in a rush. The deputy in the passenger seat listened with a toothpick bobbing between his teeth. Ettinger waited, her impassive face streaked with dried sweat.

"It just gets curiouser and curiouser," she said when he'd finished. "This sister happens to show up when her brother, if it *is* her brother, winds up dead. I think you could have told me earlier about that."

"I found out last night."

"So you say. Well," she pressed her lips together, "she's staying at the inn. Hmm. Why don't the two of you come to my office tomorrow morning, eight o'clock sharp. I'd like to see Miss Beaudreux in the flesh; she must be something to look at for a grown man to act such a fool."

"I'll do that." Stranahan swallowed. "Uh, Sheriff? Did the man Sam found have dyed blond hair?"

Ettinger looked at him. "I'm not even going to ask how you know that."

A few minutes later, Stranahan pulled up to a riverside mansion constructed with enough timber to put a herd of elk out of a home. Summersby stood outside the door, arms akimbo.

"Hey, what's this?" he said in a booming voice. "You're already wadered up. Have you been fishing without me?"

Stranahan pumped the offered hand and allowed that he had fished a few miles down the river earlier in the afternoon.

"Figured you'd get a head start, huh? Caddis flies should be coming off soon." With an "I'll just be a second," Summersby disappeared back into the house.

Stranahan shut up the Land Cruiser, twiddled his thumbs for ten minutes, and decided to be his own man. He walked past the house and down the bank. He started false casting before he got to the water, dropped a caddis imitation into a slick behind an exposed rock, and was releasing the trout that took the fly as Summersby walked heavily up behind him.

"As your host, I'm obliged to grant you the first fish," he said. "But not the second."

Stranahan smiled, then flicked his fly back out and caught another fish. A small brown that he skittered in and released to its mother, which he caught behind a lichen-patched rock on his third cast.

Summersby had yet to take his fly off the keeper ring on his rod.

"I see this is going to be an education," he said.

Summersby wasn't a bad fisherman. Stranahan coached him into one trout, but damn, the man made four false casts before he ever let his fly settle.

"I know, I'm slow," Summersby said, noting Stranahan's frustration. "But you get older, you don't see as well, even with glasses. I'm not as sure on my feet as you are. And hell, I catch a fish, I'm ready for a pipe." With that he drew a briar out of his jacket, loaded it, and struck a match. His eyes crinkled as he drew down the flame.

Stranahan had one of those moments when the veneer cracks and you suddenly see behind the bluster of personality. Summersby wasn't patronizing. His use of Stranahan's last name, his affected intimacy, it was done in the old-school manner of Catskill anglers circled before a hearth. Successful businessmen who were equally adept at chairing a board meeting, hailing a midtown cab, or casting a hexagonal sliver of bamboo. The kind of men who enjoyed a boasting rivalry and shared a tin cup of Kentucky's best afterward. Stranahan had under-estimated him. He'd been so intent on preserving pride in the face of money that it was he who had been guilty of patronizing Summersby.

"Let's go set our feet up on the porch rail," Summersby said. "Talk about the fine arts before the neighbors arrive. Hell, you scared every fish half to death with that magic wand of yours, anyway."

CHAPTER TWENTY-FIVE

The Proposition

"I suppose a man could get used to this. I mean, if he had to," Stranahan said. He leaned back in a willow-framed rocking chair and noted that indeed his boots were tipped on the porch rail. Below the deck, in the bright reflections of the backwaters, he could see a haze of evening caddis flies, the quick circles of trout.

The door of the back porch opened as a compact woman with loosely blown curls and a welcoming smile walked out. She was pushing a bar cart that clacked across the slatted floorboards.

"Hi, I'm Ann," she said.

"My superior half," nodded Summersby.

Stranahan took the woman's hand, said his name, and was drawn into a hug. She was so much shorter that her arms encircled his waist.

"Don't mind me," she said when she released him. "You just looked like you needed a hug." Impulsively, she hugged him a second time, adopting him into her family just like that. There was the faint scent of rose water. Stranahan saw her as a certain kind of churchwoman he had grown up around, supportive, never an unkind word. He noticed the way Summersby's eyes brightened and felt a flush of jealousy at the couple's happiness.

"You men have things to talk about, so I'm going to go back to the kitchen. I love your painting, Sean," she said.

"Thanks, that's nice to hear."

Stranahan heard Summersby's voice.

"Johnny Walker Black okay with you?"

Stranahan was still looking toward the door where Ann had gone back into the house. He said, "I sat in a hotel bar with a woman drinking Scotch on the rocks, a long time ago now, but it always brings it back." He was thinking of Katherine O'Reilly in Boston.

Summersby leaned an elbow on the rail. He tipped his drink.

"Well, here's to Scotch-drinking women," he said.

Stranahan turned to look at the river. He said, "She gave me a shove, made me quit my work in Boston and go back to painting. If it wasn't for her, who knows where I'd be?"

"See, that's the difference between an artist and a capitalist," Summersby said. "You taste your whiskey and conjure up beautiful women; I drink mine and"—he drank—"I see cylinders of peat and purple heather highlands."

Stranahan smiled.

"Which is a way of saying I've fished in some far-flung places," Summersby said. "Tierra del Fuego for sea trout, Atlantic salmon in Iceland, Scotland's River Dee, that's where Prince Charles fishes. Balmoral Castle is on the Dee. That river is as beautiful as the day it was made. They say every rock has its personal valet."

He went on: "The Kispiox for steelhead. In British Columbia. Where else? Christmas Island—bonefish. Key West—tarpon. When I was younger, I organized a trek up the Ganges to fish for mahseer. The monsoon came early, never caught a mahseer. But how many men can say they've fly-fished India?

"I'm telling you this because in my dotage I like to bring those places back to me, surround myself with them, as it were. All my life I've been mesmerized by water, that's something I'm sure you understand. Unlike you, I can't just shut my eyes and picture the river in my mind. I need visual stimulation. That's where you come in, or where I hope you will. You're more of a landscape artist than a fishing painter. Correct me if I'm wrong.

"See, I didn't think so. I don't want renditions of photographs. If I liked that kind of thing, I'd rather have the actual photographs. I don't want soft-focus sentimentality, either. On the phone I made you an offer, and that offer stands. Paintings of blue-ribbon trout streams, the Madison right off this porch, the Big Hole at Maiden Rock, West Fork of the Bitterroot, and so forth"—he waved a hand—"two thousand apiece. All expenses—gas, meals, motels, you keep track. And I want you to drive to BC and paint the Kispiox. My only stipulation is that you have the paintings ready before I come back next year. I realize June is a long time to wait for money, so I'll pay you for the first six now, front a couple grand for expenses. We'll settle up later. That sound okay?"

"Better than okay," Sean said.

"Then if I like what I see," he paused, "well . . . the world." He chuckled. "I've always wanted to say that." He flung his arms in an expansive gesture—"the world. But I'm serious. Same job description, higher pay, of course. You'll have to update your passport.

"Mind you," Summersby added, "I don't need to see sketches first, anything of that nature. I trust your judgment. Only thing I ask is that the paintings fit the wall space. I'll show you around and we can iron out the details—verticals, horizontals, medium, that kind of thing."

He stuck out his hand. "Deal?"

"Deal," Stranahan said.

Summersby poured another finger of whiskey and the two men clinked glasses.

CHAPTER TWENTY-SIX

Wild West

Slightly drunk on Scotch and the prospect of enough money to move out of his office and wash in a shower instead of the copper trickle from the cultural center's bathroom spigots, Stranahan greeted each dinner guest with a hearty jocularity that really wasn't his nature.

The Sinclairs were the first to arrive. Tony, the husband, had a firm handshake and an air of being the voice of better judgment in any room he entered. Stranahan liked the man despite misgivings—Sinclair lived in the house upriver where Sean had seen light shining from what he thought were binoculars on the day he met Sheriff Ettinger—and immediately fell into a conversation with Sinclair that started out about fishing, segued into Montana's environmental politics and the uproar over wolf reintroduction, then found its way back to higher ground as they debated fly patterns and presentations. He found his eyes darting past Sinclair's shoulder to his wife, Eva, whose sign language was answered in tentative hand movements from Summersby's wife. Summersby had mentioned that Ann was learning to sign. He'd said if there was a neighbor who spoke Pekingese, Ann would have booked a tutor. This far off the track a woman needed her friends.

Ann caught Stranahan's eye and winked conspiratorially. He winked back.

"... sheriff and ..."

Stranahan's ears pricked up. He hadn't been listening.

Sinclair went on: "Said they wanted to check the pond. My guess is it had something to do with that man who drowned downriver. Didn't give a damn about the antelope, though."

There was a rap at the porch door. Stranahan was nearest and opened it.

"Let me guess. You're that painter fella."

A darkly tanned man took Stranahan's outstretched hand. He seemed vaguely familiar.

"Lucas Ventura," the man said in a chesty voice. "Call me 'Lucky.'"

"Sean Stranahan. Did I see you at the TU banquet last Sunday?"

"Guilty," the man said.

Lucas Ventura was about Stranahan's height, thick through the shoulders, with black hair combed straight back to reveal a pronounced widow's peak. The V on his forehead was bracketed by heavy eyebrows; his manicured goatee arrowed down toward a swatch of chest hair that erupted from the collar of a lavender fishing shirt. FISH WORSHIP. IS IT WRONG? read the logo on the shirt. Stranahan thought Ventura looked like a jovial Satan. Forty or so.

"Tony," Ventura said, looking past Stranahan.

Sinclair said, "Where're the kids? We've missed them this summer."

"Ex-wife issues. Don't get married, that's my advice. Too late for you, Tony, but"—Ventura turned to Stranahan—"maybe hope for you. I used to say 'Keep your dick wet and your flies dry.' Now I'm regretting taking my advice."

"You look like you do a lot of it . . . fishing, that is," Stranahan said. The ovals of skin underneath Ventura's eyes were light where his sunglasses protected them.

"A dabbler in the art." Ventura made a dismissive wave with his hand.

"Don't believe him," said Sinclair. "Lucky was runner-up in the one-fly contest. Imagine how those guides in Jackson felt taking a backseat to a Hollywood movie producer."

Ventura's voice was self-deprecating. "Minor leaguer, retired."

Stranahan was impressed. Not by the man's film credits—he knew nothing of that business—but by the fishing. He frowned on competition in angling, but in the one-fly the angler had to fish a single pattern all day. The contest drew hotshot anglers to the Snake River from across the country. Winning didn't have much to do with luck.

"What fly?" he asked. He was genuinely interested.

"Small olive streamer fly I tied with Arctic fox fur. Most of the other fishermen were using Turk's Tarantulas, stones with—"

He cut himself off abruptly. "Now what the fuck is *he* doing here?"

And to Stranahan, "Pardon my French."

Stranahan followed Ventura's eyes, which had fixed on a man wearing a khaki safari jacket who stood half inside the front door chesting Summersby and then shoving brusquely past the host to jab a forefinger in the direction of Tony Sinclair.

"You. Outside." The man's belligerence was palpable.

"You've got to be kidding," Sinclair said.

"Do I sound like I'm kidding? I got a visit from the sheriff this evening. She asked if I shot an antelope on your property. Who do you think you are to accuse me without a shred of fucking evidence? I'll kick your ass."

Stranahan saw Sinclair take a step forward as the stranger's fist shot out, a sucker punch that caught Sinclair on the point of the shoulder. Sinclair recoiled, then charged forward. In a blur of grunting bodies the two men had careened through the doorway and were rolling on the porch. Stranahan threw himself onto the pile and grabbed Sinclair in a bear hug as Lucas Ventura locked onto the interloper.

Stranahan heard Summersby's voice. "This isn't the goddamned Wild West. I'm calling the authorities."

Ventura grunted between clenched teeth. "I've got a better idea, Richard. Let's toss Mr. Gentry here into Tony's pond. That ought to cool the bastard off."

Sinclair had calmed enough for Stranahan to release him and the three men half dragged, half carried the cursing party crasher the fifty-odd yards to the pond. Five minutes after Ventura said "one, two, three" and Gentry twisted out over the high bank of the pond to land with a silver splash, Stranahan had heard the whole story—the Texas taxidermist's obsession with firearms, the gopher shooting that had alarmed the neighbors, and the hole in the antelope's chest.

Stranahan tucked his shirt into his pants back on Summersby's porch, where the returning heroes were applauded by Summersby.

"By god, I've heard hundred-pound tarpon jump," Summersby said, "but I don't think I've ever heard so satisfying a splash as that one."

"You boys wash up now," Ann said from the doorway. "It's time for dinner."

It was a dinner without appetite, people talking a little too loudly and laughing a little too whole-heartedly with the ticking suspicion in the back of the mind that Gentry, who had been seen stumbling toward his house in the early twilight, might at any moment walk back rifle to shoulder and nothing but a glass pane between the dining room and a copper-jacketed bullet.

Ann and Eva Sinclair had been for pressing charges, but the men, standing on Western principles, prevailed and no phone call was made, nor unease betrayed.

Nonetheless, Stranahan noted that the table seemed to breathe a collective sigh of relief when Summersby tapped his dessert fork against a wineglass and proposed that the guests see Stranahan's painting, which had been hung on the landing of the hall stairway inside the house.

The work was fittingly praised and the night ended on the porch, on the side of the house opposite Gentry's property, women in conference to one side, the men sitting in slatted redwood rockers, sipping brandy from squat glasses that captured miniature trout flies in crystal. One neighbor had joined the party late. Apple McNair was a swarthy man, short but powerfully built with full beard and deep eye sockets. He drove in on a bicycle, accompanied by a heeler dog that had one blue eye and one brown one. It was McNair who owned the homestead cabin up the river past Sinclair's residence. Summersby, in an aside to Stranahan, remarked that he was surprised that McNair had responded to tonight's invitation, for the man was a bit of a recluse and gone as often as he was home. It wasn't clear how he had come by the money to own Madison riverfront. His only apparent income was from fixing up vintage bicycles and running a custom knife business out of a toolshed in his yard. The shed, the dilapidated cabin, and McNair's rundown Dodge Sierra Classic rusting amid bicycle parts had done nothing for real estate values, Summersby confided, but then with a shrug he added that his property wasn't bound by the covenants that restricted the newer developments. It was Montana. What could you do?

Stranahan felt uneasy with the rich-man-to-rich-man intonation and made a point of talking to the newcomer. It was a disjointed conversation, with the two men facing each other on the dark end of the porch. McNair seemed pleasant but was uncomfortable socially to the point of being practically mute. When Stranahan asked where he was from, the man had extinguished the cigarette he'd been smoking, flicked the stub, and uttered a single-word response—"North." He handed over a Damascus steel hunting knife from the sheath on his belt, evidently looking for comment. Stranahan tested the blade on his thumbnail and whistled appreciatively, then handed the knife back, holding the point and offering the sambar stag handle.

"You could skin a bear with that," said the man.

The conversation stalled and Stranahan found himself talking with Lucas Ventura about Lucky's Adirondack guide boat, which dated to the 1880s and was, he declared, the most elegant craft ever designed. He said they'd have to fish from it sometime—how about Saturday a week? He had to fly to L.A. for a few days. Stranahan said sure and they agreed to meet at the lower access road to Quake Lake, just above the dam. Stranahan figured it was the kind of invitation that wasn't recalled the next morning, let alone ten days down the pike, and excused himself to his host, saying he had an appointment in Bridger early in the morning.

"Nonsense," Summersby said. "You're not going any farther than that guest cabin." He pointed. "There's a new toothbrush in the medicine cabinet, Navajo blankets in the steamer trunk at the foot of the bed. You say you have to be back by eight. Hazelnut pancakes are at six a.m. sharp."

There was no point arguing. Summersby had been getting his way for more years than Sean had been alive.

As he walked to the cabin in a loose gait prompted by too much whiskey, Stranahan felt guilty about allowing himself to be wrapped in the soft arms of summer home society. He drifted into a fitful sleep, then awoke in the early morning and stepped out the door to relieve himself, passing a perfectly functional bathroom on the way. He stood looking at the heavens. All was dark in Sinclair's residence on the far side of the fence. Beyond Sinclair's slumped McNair's cabin and past it was the sprawling riverfront house belonging to Lucas Ventura. Two squares of amber light shone in Ventura's upstairs windows, a third from a sconce light on the porch below. A fellow insomniac, ventured Stranahan. He squinted, the lights bleeding together into a triangle, like candlelight flickering from a jack-o-lantern. His eyes returned to the surface of the pond, peppered at this lonely hour with the reflections of stars. He thought about the half gainer the taxidermist had taken and then he thought about a doe antelope with a small hole in her chest.

Stranahan was suddenly wide awake. He hurriedly dressed and threw his gear into the Land Cruiser. Lights out, he idled down the drive and pointed the nose of the old truck toward Bridger.

CHAPTER TWENTY-SEVEN

Antelope Dawn

Five-thirty a.m. The horizon dark, although the birds in the ash trees that lined South Gallatin Avenue said it would soon be otherwise. Stranahan listened to the haunting three-note whistle of a varied thrush as he walked the short block from his Land Cruiser to the cultural center. He noticed a midsize pickup parked outside the double front doors; the cab light was on, illuminating a figure in the driver's seat. The passenger door swung open.

"Mr. Stranahan, I'd like to have a word with you."

"Sheriff?"

"That's me."

"I thought you said eight." He bent to peer inside the pickup.

"I did. But then I thought maybe we should have a chat, just the two of us, before we roused your girlfriend from her beauty sleep. I heard through the grapevine that this is where you hang your hat."

Stranahan's voice betrayed his exhaustion. He was just too tired to be flustered.

"Let's go up to the studio."

"That won't be necessary. You can keep me company right here." She patted the bench seat of the cab.

He shrugged, got into the truck.

"Coffee?" She poured him a cup from a thermos without waiting for the reply. "Donuts in the bag." She gestured toward the dash.

"I was going to come down to your office this morning," he said. He brushed powdered sugar from the corners of his mouth.

"Good, huh? I like the old-fashioneds myself."

"I put something together this morning," Stranahan said carefully, "or might have. It's just speculation."

"Speculation?"

Stranahan nodded.

"Then speculate," she said. "I'm in the mood for a story." The police radio crackled. She dialed it down.

"First, I want to know if it was her brother, the man Sam found."

"She ID'd the body. Didn't betray an ounce of emotion, so Walt says."

"She wouldn't, not in front of a stranger."

"You must know her so well by now," Ettinger said.

Stranahan let it pass. He said, "I have a guess who shot Rainbow Sam." He waited, expecting . . . well, he didn't know what to expect. To be interrupted if nothing else.

"Go on."

"It could be the same man who shot the antelope at a pond belonging to Tony Sinclair. He lives up—"

Ettinger cut him off. "I know the name," she said. "I heard about the antelope. I talked to the guy Sinclair accused. There's bad blood between them, but he's got no evidence."

Stranahan told her about the fight on the porch. Ettinger made a clicking sound with her tongue to betray her exasperation at the antics of grown men.

"Here's the thing," Stranahan said. "I asked Sinclair when the antelope was shot and he said Monday morning, right at dawn. Sam was shot about an hour later, eight miles down the road."

"So?"

"So it seems like a coincidence. Plus, this Gentry's a real asshole."

"I can't arrest someone because he's an asshole."

Ettinger rested her chin in her hand and tapped her fingers against her cheek. Until now the conflicted feelings she'd had toward Stranahan hadn't included the thought that he might be on her side. There was no denying her initial attraction was stronger than she cared to admit, but with the shooting at the lake, not to mention the bizarre story he'd fed her about fishing for the woman, her regard for him was tempered by skepticism. Was it really possible he'd stepped in something and was just trying to help?

"Sheriff?"

"You got a number for Sam Meslik?" Ettinger said.

He told her he did.

"Call it."

"Now? I don't have a cell phone."

"Oh, for crissakes, get with the twenty-first century." She fished in her breast pocket. "Use mine. Put it on speaker."

"What do you want me to ask him?"

"Ask if he knows Gus Gentry. Do I have to tell you everything?"

Sam knew Gus Gentry all right. All the guides who fished the upper Madison knew the son of a bitch who'd posted his property and confronted any fisherman who tried to walk the bank, whether he'd violated the high-watermark rule or not. The two men had just about come to blows earlier in the summer when Sam was guiding an angler on a walk-in trip.

Stranahan brushed aside Sam's inquiry about the purpose of the call and was on the verge of hanging up when Sam said, "Aren't you going to ask me how I'm doing?"

"How are you doing?"

"Well, let's see. It's six in the morning two days after I took a bullet. Not so fucking good."

Stranahan laughed as he snapped the phone shut.

"You know, it's easy enough to test the theory," he said. "Just match a bullet from one of Gentry's rifles to the one taken out of Sam."

Ettinger scratched at a mosquito bite on her cheek.

"What do you think?" Stranahan asked.

"I think there's a problem you haven't thought about. It's called a search warrant. I can't see Crazy Conner—pardon me, Judge Conner—hearing what you just told me and then dipping his quill in the ink bottle."

"I thought of that," Stranahan said.

"And?"

Ettinger answered her own question. "The antelope."

"The antelope," Stranahan said.

"Maybe the bullet exited," Ettinger said. "Even if it didn't . . ." She frowned. "Coyotes? Eagles? There might not be anything left."

"Then again there might be," Stranahan said.

"Say there was and we found the bullet and that bullet matches the one we took from Meslik; there's still no proof it was Gentry killed the antelope."

"No, but your Crazy Conner, he might not laugh so hard if you had a bullet to match the one found in Sam's chest. He'd sign the warrant. Then you could get the gun and do a match. You could prove if it was Gentry's rifle."

Ettinger nodded. She turned the key and the engine came to life.

"Where are we going?" Stranahan said.

"We're going to Law and Justice, pick up the Meslik bullet from evidence. Then you and I are going to find that antelope. If I order the techs to drive eighty miles on a goose chase, I'll never live it down. All we have is proximity, a shot near the river, and another up the road at the lake. But if I come back with a matching slug . . ."

She noticed the expression on his face. "What? You have a better idea?"

"No. I'm just surprised. I've been thinking along the same lines you have, that Beaudreux's murder and Sam's shooting are connected. Gentry throws a wrench into that theory. I thought you'd be more dismissive."

"What else have we got?" Ettinger said.

She eased her foot off the clutch.

"Vareda?" Stranahan said.

"Don't worry. My deputy will drop by the inn and have a cup of coffee with her this morning. I can talk to her when we get back."

She pulled alongside Stranahan's Land Cruiser.

"Throw your fishing gear in the back," Martha said. "Waders, too."

"What for?"

"Humor me, Mr. Stranahan."

"**W**here's the Cherokee?" Stranahan said. They had crossed the bridge over the Madison outside Ennis, an hour passed in mostly silence as Stranahan leaned his head against the window and fitfully dozed.

"Cherokee?"

Martha was momentarily taken aback, her mind flashing to Harold Little Feather. Little Feather wasn't Cherokee. He was Blackfeet.

"You were driving a Cherokee at Ennis Lake."

"Oh. The Jeep? It's in the shop."

"How long have you lived here? Montana, I mean."

"Native born," Martha said. "But now that you're awake there's something I want to talk to you about that's more interesting than my upbringing."

She fished inside the breast pocket of her uniform and handed Stranahan a small plastic fly box. Two trout flies stood on their hackle tips in side-by-side compartments, the Royal Wulff taken from Beaudreux's lip and the one she had snipped from Sinclair's fly rod.

"Do you tie flies, Mr. Stranahan?"

"Since I was five."

"What's your opinion of these?"

"They're Royal Wulffs." Sam had told him about the Wulff in Beaudreux's lip with the heavy curl of leader attached. One of the Wulffs in the box had an inch of leader attached, too thick for the size of the fly.

"I know what they are. What I'm asking is were they tied by the same person?"

Stranahan reached behind the cab seat and fished for his vest. He unzipped a pocket and got out the magnifying glasses he used to tie on tiny flies.

"Can I take them out of the box?"

Ettinger grunted her assent.

Stranahan examined the flies. Both had bucktail tails with collars turned from medium ginger rooster neck hackle, better than decent quality. White calf tail wings, the one with the leader attached pinkish tinged. Stranahan knew what that was. The thin red bodies were bracketed by several turns of peacock herl. Standard black nylon thread for both, 6/o probably. Lacquered heads.

"Neither's tidy enough to be commercial," he said at length. "But for home ties, the proportions are similar and they use the same materials. Except for the bodies. The bright one's floss, the other is wool. Of course, the tier could have run out of red floss and substituted wool, or decided to experiment. Only other difference is the hackle is wound shiny side forward on this one, and this one it's shiny side to the back."

"Would a Wulff you tied look different?"

She said it in the flat tone he remembered when she'd interrogated him at the lake.

"Ah." He smiled. "That's why you asked me to bring my gear. And I thought we were going fishing."

She didn't return the smile.

"Okay." He opened one of his fly boxes and extracted a Wulff.

Ettinger pulled to the side of the road and took off her sunglasses.

"Pretty scraggly," she said.

"I prefer to call it personal flair."

"Good thing you have it," she said. "One of these flies was found in the lip of the poor sap your buddy fished out of the river. The pink stain on the wing is blood. But I bet you knew that. Your friend Meslik has a big mouth."

"You're looking down the wrong road," Stranahan said.

"Really? What road should I be looking down?"

"You should be asking me if the fly in Beaudreux's lip was from his own box. If he was hooked with his own fly. I can tell you with one hundred percent certainty that he was."

"How's that?"

Stranahan parted the hackle fibers on the blood-stained Wulff to reveal two strands of pheasant tippet, golden with barred tips. Then, ignoring the question in Ettinger's eyes, he rifled through the pockets of his vest for the Wheatley fly box Vareda had given to him, the one belonging to her father, and showed her an identical Wulff behind one of the little plastic lids.

"Those little strands of barred feather, that's the tier's signature," he explained.

"Whose? The dad or the son?"

"Vareda said they were her father's flies. He probably gave his son a box of them. Wasn't he wearing a vest when he drowned?"

The sheriff pressed her lips together.

"No, he wasn't. And he didn't have a fly box in a shirt pocket or wader pocket either. He had a couple flies stuck in a piece of sheepskin, that was it."

"That's odd," Stranahan said.

"Yes it is."

Under the best of circumstances, dead antelope stank. Rainbow Sam had gone into detail with Stranahan about the odor when they met at the banquet. You open up an elk, he'd said, it smells the way the Taj Mahal looks by moonlight. Antelope smelled like sagebrush dipped in cat guts. The best you could say about them was that they tasted so much better than they smelled. In fact, according to Sam, antelope that hadn't been run before they were shot, building up lactic acid in their muscles, were the best of all game—the meat fine-grained and tender, marrying perfectly with a mint jelly sauce or a creamy béarnaise.

But not even the most pungent of sauces could resurrect this one. Dead three days in July, the stomach had bloated to twice its normal size. Still, the body remained intact except for exposed tissue around the eyes, anus, and bullet hole, where magpies and jays had buried their beaks into what could only charitably be termed flesh. In fact, it was the flock of jays whirling above the kill that had led Ettinger and Stranahan to it in the first place. Ettinger took a camera from the glove compartment and snapped photos from various angles.

"Looks like you're in luck," Stranahan said. The bullet had entered the chest as the antelope stood head-on and had not exited.

"What do you mean 'me'?"

Ettinger handed Stranahan latex surgical gloves and snapped another pair onto her own hands. She drew the folding knife from her belt holster.

"Keep her spread-eagle."

Stranahan positioned himself.

"Brace yourself," she said, and inserted the point of the knife below the breastbone. A hiss of gas groaned from the body, ending in a drawn-out flatulence. Instantly the air was fetid with rancid body acids. The bullet, after wrecking the chest cavity, had worked back into the paunch, spilling green clumps of digested grass that smelled like silage.

"Don't you dare puke on my shoes," Ettinger said.

Ettinger cut around the diaphragm and half spilled, half dragged the ruptured spleen, liver, kidneys, and stomach onto the ground.

"Our bullet's somewhere in that mess," she said. She looked up, blood and offal from the elbows down.

"Look at me," she said seriously. "I mean it. Look at me."

"I'm looking." Both had become dead serious.

"Do you have anything to do with this? Anything that's happened these past few days, starting with your Southern belle?"

"All I did for her was some fishing."

"But what you've done isn't the same as what you know, is it, Sean? This isn't a game."

Stranahan held her eyes.

"I think you're doing your thinking from the waist down. You're over your head and maybe you don't know it."

"Is that all?" Stranahan said.

"That's all."

"Thanks for the advice."

"You're welcome."

"Let's find that bullet," Stranahan said.

A half hour later, Ettinger scraped the mangled remnants of a rifle bullet from the lining of the paunch. The front of the bullet had mushroomed to double diameter. Most of the exposed lead had fragmented, but the copper base was intact, the groove marks created by the rifling in the bore clearly visible.

"What caliber do you figure?"

".243 or .257," Ettinger said. "That reminds me. I got a call from a Centennial County deputy in Idaho yesterday. They found a kid who said he was shooting gophers near the shore of Henry's Lake the day you were there with Meslik. He was shooting a .222. Not the caliber of the bullet that hit Meslik. So that clears up the first two shots you heard."

"What was the bullet in Sam?"

"A .243." Ettinger unbuttoned her shirt pocket and drew out an evidence bag containing the bullet taken out of Sam. She touched the base of it to the base of the bullet from the antelope. "What do you think?"

Stranahan squinted. "The diameter's close."

"I agree. But even if it's the same caliber, it doesn't mean the bullet was fired from the same rifle. The .243 is a popular cartridge. But every rifle leaves marks on the bullet that distinguish it from bullets fired from another rifle, even if they are the same caliber."

Sean nodded. He understood that rifling marks were as individual as fingerprints.

"How long will it take ballistics to establish if these two bullets were shot from the same rifle?"

"State lab's in Missoula, four days if I red-flag it. But we have a technician in Bridger who can make a comparison that's 90 percent certain of standing up."

"So if it turns out the gun belongs to Gentry and he shot Sam because of some prior altercation about trespass . . ."

"Which doesn't seem sufficient motive to me," Ettinger interjected.

". . . how does that relate to the Beaudreux killing?"

"Damned if I know," Martha admitted.

CHAPTER TWENTY-EIGHT

Victoria's Secrets

On the drive back, Ettinger was silent until she pulled to the side of the road downstream from Lyons Bridge.

"Do you know where we are?" she said.

"Back to square one," Stranahan said. He knew damn well that she knew he knew. "That logjam is where Sam found the body. He showed it to me on the way to Henry's Lake the morning he was shot."

"Did you walk down to the river?"

"No. He just pointed."

She switched off the engine. "Pull on your waders."

It was a five-minute hike. They stepped over a fence and stood on the lip of the bank. Ettinger, arms akimbo, nodded to herself.

"What do you think? The location, I mean."

Stranahan looked back at the highway. Only a narrow slice of asphalt was visible. He could hear a car coming up the 287, a flash of red—it was gone. A driver who turned his head toward the river would have a few seconds at most to register a fisherman there, let alone see what he was doing.

"Just what I told Sam," he said. "Or maybe he told me. The word that comes to mind is 'secluded.'"

"What's that tell you?"

"You're testing me?"

"No, I'm asking your opinion to see if you come up with the answer I did."

"Well, it's a good place to dump a body . . . at night. This is a popular river. A guide boat comes down every fifteen minutes on a slow day. Damn risky in daylight. But just for argument's sake, why couldn't it be an accident? The guy falls in upriver and gets caught in the logjam?"

Ettinger hadn't told Stranahan about the broken stick found below the body that matched the stub in Beaudreux's eye. She said, "We have reason to think that didn't happen. No, I think the body was taken here after dark and dragged to the logjam." Without further ado she started wading toward midriver. Stranahan was surprised at how deftly Ettinger moved, for the current was strong and the footing suspect. The dark seam near the island was crotch-deep. Stranahan found himself beginning to float a bit; he crossed at an upstream angle and caught up with Ettinger in the eddy at the tail of the island.

"What do you want me to see?" he said, breathing audibly.

"I don't want you to *see* anything. There's nothing to see. The body was carried out to this island and wedged under the logjam at the top of it."

Stranahan sighed. "It's another test, right?"

"Oh, I thought it would be obvious to a bright fella like you."

"What's obvious to me is the guy had to be damned strong," Stranahan said, a note of resentment in his voice. "Some guys couldn't even wade out this far, let alone drag a body. Maybe your killer had help."

Ettinger was slow to respond. "That's such a good point that we're going to have to find out."

"You don't sound very happy about it."

"You'll learn why. Come on, let's go back to the shore."

"Now what?" Sean said when they were on the bank.

"Now you're not going to get the wrong idea," Ettinger said, and she began to unbutton her khaki shirt. In moments she was down to T-shirt, bra, and panties.

"Consider this a bikini under a T-shirt," she said.

She waded a few feet out, shook her head as if to clear it, then dropped backward into the river.

"Mother of mercy, that's cold. Come on, let's get it over with."

Stranahan didn't need her to spell it out. They were going to find out if he could drag her to the logjam. He grabbed her wrists. When he lifted she sputtered, her head going under. It was like wrestling a bear.

"Let's try another way."

He let Martha catch her breath, then tried wading out by holding onto her ankles. It was easier . . . a little.

"What happens if a drift boat comes past?" He grunted.

"I'll flash 'em my badge," Martha said. She gulped a mouthful that went down the wrong way and they stopped while her body was wracked with coughs.

"One more try," he said. "Turn around." He gripped her under her arms, wrapping her in a backward bear hug, one forearm smashing her breast. He repositioned his arms.

"Don't worry about it," she said.

Stranahan began to wade toward the logjam with his back brunting the flow, Ettinger's feet trailing in the current. With only the slot of deep current outside the comma of debris alongside the logjam to cross, he repositioned his grip—the muscles in his arms burning from the tension—jammed his boots crab fashion against the burgeoning current, and went under all at once, releasing his grip. He heard her curse as she went down with him.

Ten yards downriver they managed to stand and slogged back to shore. Martha disappeared behind a willow clump to wring out her underthings and change back into her shirt and pants.

"I think I could have made it if I'd had my adrenaline up," Stranahan said.

From behind the bush he heard her voice. "I weigh one-thirty-eight in my birthday suit. Think you could drag a hundred-and-sixty-pound man out there who was wearing waders? In the dark?"

"No," Stranahan admitted.

"Tell you the truth," Ettinger said, "up till today I thought the killer acted alone. Now I'm thinking two people, but I don't know. . . . I don't know what to think."

Stranahan was surprised at the loss of heart in her voice.

She stepped out from the bush, carrying her bra and panties in her hand. "What's the motive? What are we missing here, Stranahan?" She hitched up her belt.

"I told you what I think. I think you need to look at that fish hatchery outside Cascade. The last time anyone spoke to your victim, he was following a truck from the hatchery. He called his sister from a pay phone in Ennis and disappeared. A day later Sam finds him here."

"So she says."

"Why would she lie about it?" His voice was sharp. He was tired of playing her guessing games. "What does it matter what I think? One minute you all but accuse me of having a hand in this and the next you strip down to your Victoria's Secrets and have me drag you around the river. What are you really after, Sheriff?"

"I'm after the truth," Ettinger said. "And it's Maidenform. But what I really want is your help. . . . Yeah," she said, lowering her voice, "I'm asking for your help. Just between you and me, I'm alone on this one. My deputy's the guy you want for your back when you go down a foxhole. But upstairs?" She shook her head. "And the department's no help. It's an accidental drowning to everyone but me; why disturb the water, no pun intended."

"You didn't tell me what convinced you that it's murder. How can I help if you keep things back from me?"

"Oh hell, just give me a minute to get my waders on."

Wading to the logjam for the second time, Martha pointed out the branch that matched the stub in Beaudreux's eye, showed Sean where the body had been found twenty feet upriver. She told him about the microscopic lake creatures in the man's lungs.

"You see, this is no accident," she said, sitting down on one of the logs. "But our perp, he made mistakes. If you want someone to think a fisherman drowned here, then you park the fisherman's car nearby. Instead, he went to all the trouble to drive it twenty miles up the road to a campground and put on some plates that turn out to be stolen. It's like he's overthinking things or else he's not quite smart."

She stared into the distance.

"Where did Meslik tell you he found the rod, exactly?"

"He told me it was upstream from the logjam about thirty yards. He found it on the way back from calling you from one of those cabins. The one with the weathervane."

Stranahan pointed to a blond log home squatting on the west bank of the Madison, about three hundred yards up the river.

"I know the lord of the manor," Ettinger said. "Belongs to Terry Jarvis, a county commissioner. Did he say where in the river—near the bank, midstream?"

"He saw the tip sticking up and waded to get it, so I think it was out in the current."

"What's that mean—you think?"

"If it wasn't for the stick in the eye, I'd say he was dumped upriver and floated down into the logjam here."

"Only he wasn't. Here's the way I see it," she said. "Beaudreux was drowned somewhere else, a pond, a lake, somewhere he could suck the bugs into his lungs. Whoever it was killed him, he didn't want the body to be found there, maybe because it would tie the two of them together. So he puts the body into the trunk of the victim's own car—we're still waiting on forensics but I'm pretty sure—he drives it to the campground on Quake Lake, sets up the tent, and waits till it's dark.

We know this because the camp host saw somebody wrestling with a tent about ten o'clock. It was still light out then, and no, before you ask, he didn't get a look at him.

"Then after dark he drives here, parks upstream off the river road. He hauls the body into the river and holds on to him as he walks downstream. That way he doesn't have to fight the weight of the body. The current does the work. Now he can't approach the logjam head-on, because the current's fast and there's a deep hole at the top. So what he does, he walks the body alongside until he can easily get across to the lower end of the jam, then drags it back upriver through this slack water where we're sitting, and wedges it under the logs. The body snags on the branch en route—that would account for the stick in the eye. He knew the body would be found right away—your buddy found it the next afternoon—but he didn't care about that as long as it was in a place that didn't point the finger at him. If he got lucky, we'd think the drowning was accidental."

"What about the rod?" Stranahan asked.

"I think he meant to place it here at the logjam, maybe wrap some line around the victim's hand so we'd be sure to find the rod with him. If a fisherman drowns in a river as shallow as the Madison and you don't find a rod, it raises suspicion. So he needed Beaudreux to be found with his rod. My guess is that he accidentally dropped the rod and couldn't find it again. It was night, remember, and he was wading down the river hauling a dead body."

"What's wrong with just dropping it where Sam found it?"

"'Cause there are too many people like Sam who would steal the rod if it didn't come attached to a body. But either way, he's made a case for an accidental drowning. Have I connected the dots here? I'm asking you."

Stranahan nodded.

"As far as it goes. You've got a when and how; what you don't have is why or who. The fish hatchery is the only lead we have. Seems to me like that's the end you work from."

"Me, too. But there's a catch. Officially, this isn't a homicide investigation. The car in the campground, the hatchery, the stick in the eye, they add up to nothing. The fly in the lip, that was self-inflicted, just bad casting. Now the bugs in the lungs and the stolen plates, yeah, that raises an eyebrow. But it's not enough for a full-blown homicide investigation. There are no signs of struggle, no bodily injury. I could make a call to the hatchery, but I can't justify driving three hours out of my jurisdiction to question the owner about a missing employee. Now, if someone were to tip me off about a vehicle previously seen in connection with our victim—say, right here in Hyalite County—then we might have a thread I can follow."

Stranahan smiled. "You've been building up to this all morning, haven't you?"

"Me? I'm just flying by the seat of my pants."

"You want me to drive to Cascade and check out the hatchery."

"No, I didn't say that. Officially, I'm telling you not to stick your nose in this. I'm telling you, 'Don't talk to anybody. Don't do anything stupid.'"

"What if I followed that truck? According to Vareda, her brother said it had driven away from the hatchery on a Tuesday evening, then on a Thursday, also evening. He'd followed it the next Tuesday. Maybe that's the schedule—Tuesday and Thursday evenings. Today's . . . Thursday."

"Is it?" Ettinger said. "I've lost track."

CHAPTER TWENTY-NINE

A Montana Tail

At Three Forks, Montana, the Madison, Gallatin, and Jefferson rivers get a taste of each other's water, streaming together to form the Missouri River—fishermen call it the Mighty Mo.

Turning off I-15 at the Cascade exit, Stranahan fed his thirsty Land Cruiser fifteen gallons, crossed the bridge, and turned south onto Sheep Creek Road. He'd let his fingers do the walking at a pay phone and found the hatchery without trouble, though the old farmstead with its prefab outbuildings had no sign and no obvious evidence of its purpose. Stranahan drove past, stopped, and got out. He studied the clouds, holding his hands in the attitude of a man attending to nature's call. From this angle the hatchery raceways, filled with aerated water for trout rearing, were apparent, so he air-zipped up and motored down the road a couple of miles.

Stopping again, he traced his fingers along the spider cracks on the weathered dash of the Cruiser. If Vareda's brother had been killed because he'd followed a truck from the hatchery, then anyone involved had to be alerted, and Stranahan couldn't afford to be seen loitering. Parking and pulling down your zipper was innocent enough, but a man could feign peeing for only so long. He let out the clutch, turned around, and drove back up the road past the hatchery.

There was a turnout on the near side of the bridge he'd crossed out of Cascade and he swung over and geared up. One seldom caught fish at a town access, but he wasn't interested in trout; his eyes were on the bridge. Anyone driving from the hatchery would have to cross it before entering the on-ramp to the highway.

Stranahan had noted two vehicles parked at the hatchery when he'd passed by earlier: an older Subaru wagon and a three-quarter-ton pickup with dual rear tires; both were iconic ranch vehicles. That was of limited value—Vareda's brother had said the truck he followed was one he hadn't seen except on the Tuesday and Thursday evenings. The live well in the truck bed would be the giveaway, that and maybe a dog riding shotgun.

Lost in thought, he was unprepared for the strike. The trout walked on its tail a yard and crashed back to the surface, jumped a second time, and headed for the middle of the river. There it bore down and Stranahan, hearing a crunch of gravel, swiveled his head to see a truck cross the bridge. It was a flatbed pickup with two-by-four rails, one driver, but no dog and nothing in the bed but the obligatory waffle metal storage box. Stranahan turned his attention back to the trout, which gradually tired until it was finning near his boots. He held it alongside his rod so he could measure it later—the fish so big that his hands trembled—then he worked the hook from its jaw and released it. He decided to retire the lucky fly, a double-breasted streamer called a Madonna, and was placing it into a clip in his fly box when he first heard and then saw a second truck cross the bridge. This one was heading the other way, coming from Cascade. Another flatbed, also with slatted wood side rails but this one had a white metal drum in the bed. A rusty Ford half-ton in two-tone blue. It was just a glance. The truck went down the road, lifting a ribbon of dust that swallowed it from sight.

"Well now."

He snapped the fly box shut, then on second thought opened it and tied another fly on. If this was the truck, it would be a while before it loaded up at the hatchery and he needed to look like he was doing something purposeful when it returned.

An hour went by. Stranahan heard, then spotted a truck driving back. It was the half-ton, all right, going more slowly this time. Past nine o'clock, but there was plenty of light to see the white drum in the truck bed. The driver was a man, but without man's best friend for company. Still . . .

By the time Stranahan gunned the Land Cruiser to life, the truck had disappeared into the town. At the on-ramp, Stranahan turned south with only a moment's hesitation. North was nothing but rapeseed and canola fields stretching to the Alberta border, no major trout rivers. He pushed the Land Cruiser to seventy. Spotting the truck in five minutes, he lifted his foot off the accelerator and felt a flush of goose bumps lift the hairs on his forearms. Tired all day, he was suddenly wide awake. He might still be many miles from the answers he was seeking, but for the first time since the shot rang out over Henry's Lake, he felt like he was heading in the right direction.

At twilight, Stranahan closed to within fifty yards and held there, waiting for the driver to switch on his headlights. He'd no sooner thought it than the taillights popped on. The housing of the right rear taillight was cracked so that the light shone through in two colors— red over white. Following in the dark was going to be easier than he had thought.

"I got you," he said under the rumble of the old straight six. "You're in trouble, and you don't even know it."

The feeling of elation didn't last. Rather than continuing south toward Helena, the truck exited the interstate at Wolf Creek, then turned right onto Route 434, a winding two-lane heading west.

Stranahan switched the dome light on in the Land Cruiser and fumbled for his *Montana Atlas and Gazetteer.* He glanced at the grid map on the cover and leafed to page fifty-five. In twenty miles the 434 would T-up with the Montana 200. This was one of those lost parts of the state with so little traffic that drivers waved to each other for the company. He decided he couldn't stay a set distance back but would have to seesaw, fade out of the truck's rearview mirror now and then. It was going to be tricky.

He held back as the truck slowed at the intersection. It turned left. As the truck geared down to cross Rogers Pass, Stranahan decided to pass it. If the driver had noticed him turn off at Wolf Creek and questioned the coincidence, passing him would ease his mind. Besides, he wanted a peek at this man.

Stranahan closed on the truck halfway up the grade. Drawing parallel, he glanced sideways without turning his head and saw a shadow figure under a ball cap; then, as he passed and pulled back to the inside lane, he checked his rearview and caught the silhouette of a dog sitting upright in the truck's passenger seat. It must have been lying down when the truck had crossed the bridge back in Cascade.

Now there could be no doubt that this was the same truck Vareda's brother had followed. Stranahan accelerated up the hill and left the truck behind. He fingered a pen from the dash and jotted the license plate number on his map. Stranahan crested the divide, where dark forests closed in from either side. He pulled off onto the first two-track he came to, nosing the rig back into a stand of dwarf pines. He switched off the headlights.

Stranahan's fingers beat a tattoo on the steering wheel. Wherever the truck was headed, it wasn't the Madison River; it would have continued south on the highway if that was the target. So where? A river to the west? He reached over the truck bench for his fly vest and took out the LED headlight he used when night fishing. He shone it on the map. Route 200 continued on through Lincoln, which rang a distant bell. Oh, thought Stranahan, that's where Ted Kaczynski, the Unabomber, had lived. Recluse country. He followed the thread of road farther where it paralleled the Big Blackfoot River nearly all the way to Missoula.

Waiting for the truck to catch up, Stranahan thought again of the big trout he'd caught at the access in Cascade. A dollar bill was six inches long, give or take, and he placed it four times against the butt of his fly rod, turning it over and over, and still was an inch short of the imaginary mark he'd made when measuring the trout. A twenty-five inch brown. Except for the cuttbow he'd lost at Henry's Lake the day Sam was shot, it was the biggest trout he'd ever hooked.

A blush of light brought color to the pine needles screening him from the road. Then the headlights of the hatchery truck beamed up to the tree tops and glanced away as the truck passed, following the downhill grade toward Lincoln. Stranahan waited until it was out of sight before turning back onto the blacktop.

Forty minutes later, Stranahan turned into a campground along the Big Blackfoot River. He drove past a darkened trailer, then a family tent with a campfire out front, voices piercing the darkness. He idled along to an empty site and shut down the engine.

A quarter mile back up the river, the hatchery truck had turned off the road onto a steep grade that led to the riverbank. Stranahan had been too close behind to do anything but sail innocently past. He had found the campground by providence. He got his binoculars and started hiking upriver, easy going through a stand of stately Ponderosa pines, then not so easy where a fisherman's trail wound through a willow jungle. Feeling his way through the snarl, he found himself at a gravel bar where the river made a sharp bend. Just upstream he could make out the shape of the truck. He heard the yapping of the dog and a sharp reprimand from the truck driver, whom Stranahan could see as a shape moving in the bed of the pickup. Sean brought up his Zeiss Jena binoculars. The glasses had been commissioned by the East German army for picking out would-be émigrés attempting to climb the Berlin Wall. A gruesome relic of the Cold War, but the superb optics gathered light from the night sky.

The truck driver was using a hand net to scoop from the drum tank. After each scoop, he dumped the contents of the net into what looked like a five-gallon bucket. The man clambered down from the truck and, awkwardly holding the water-laden bucket, shambled to the river, where he dumped the bucket—a quick phosphorescent waterfall. The hat obscured any distinguishing facial characteristics the binoculars might have illuminated, but Stranahan had seen enough.

As he hurried back to the campground, he heard a sharp whistle—the driver calling to the dog—then the cough of the engine. He knew by the time he reached the Land Cruiser that the hatchery truck would already be on the road. Back toward Cascade, mission accomplished? Or farther on to the west and south? This could be just the first stop. Several of the state's better trout streams were only a few gallons of gas away, the nearest of them the Clark's Fork and its blue ribbon tributary, Rock Creek. Stranahan picked up his pace.

But as he reached the outskirts of the campground, he was startled to see headlights dipping off the road to search through the campground. The guttural vibrato of the motor told him it was the hatchery rig, and for a heart-pounding moment Stranahan thought the driver must have made the tail and was looking for him. But then the headlights arced away and the engine shut down. The truck had turned into an open site. Now the driver was getting out, stretching. A flashlight beam poked around. A whispery voice said, "This place looks all right, what do you say, boy?" He saw the darting of the dog at the man's feet. The truck driver was just looking to set up a camp.

Stranahan found himself at his rig, unsure of his next step. He could stay put—God knows some sleep would do him good—but then what? Follow when the man left? Come morning, the chances of him being spotted were much higher. Also, he was down to a quarter tank of gas. He checked the atlas again. The campground was thirty miles from Milltown, where state route 200 rejoined the highway outside Missoula. There would be a service station at the junction, and a phone booth. He could gas up. The sheriff had given him her cell number. He could put off a decision until he called her.

He turned the key to the Land Cruiser, snapped on the low beams, and motored slowly through the campground. Maybe he'd catch a better view of the truck driver. But the man was puttering with his back to the road, putting up a tent, the dog a few yards away, digging industriously at the base of a tree. Stranahan started by, then, without really thinking it through, stopped with the motor idling.

"You need a hand with that tent?" he called out.

The man straightened up, and Stranahan felt his face flush from the adrenaline rush.

"Thanks just the same," the man said. He bent back to his work.

Stranahan took his foot off the clutch. He drove out of the campground and made a left onto the blacktop. The truck driver had never turned, never offered anything but his back and his voice, which Stranahan hadn't recognized. But he wasn't thinking about the man. He was thinking about the dog that had stopped digging for just a moment, and lifted its head.

CHAPTER THIRTY

Blue Slipper, Moonlight River

"Hello."

"It's Sean Stranahan. I know it's late."

He gave her the short version.

"It's the same truck Beaudreux told his sister about?"

"The dog, the live well . . . hell yes."

"Let me get a pencil."

Silence on her end of the line. Stranahan looked around. He was standing in a phone booth with a hinged door around the side of a service station casino, semis snoring in the back lot. A trucker walked by, shirttails over his gut, fingernail flicking a cigarette. He stopped in a pool of neon light to fire up another.

"Okay, give me the plate number," Ettinger said. "Uh-huh, uh-huh. That's a Great Falls prefix."

Stranahan thought about telling her about the dog, but he could guess her reaction: "Everybody who's got ten acres owns a dog like that. You've got too much imagination, Sean." And she would be right.

He could hear Ettinger's sigh on the end of the line.

"So what's this fishy business all about?" she said at length.

"That's the question I'm asking myself. I have an idea, but I need to talk to someone who knows more than I do."

"I'm listening."

"Not you, someone who knows fish diseases. Look, you told me to follow this guy . . . no, you listen," he said. "In as many words you did tell me. So I just spent fifty bucks on gas I can't afford, and I'm two hundred miles from Bridger, and, dammit, I ought to be able to ask somebody a few questions. You owe me that much."

"Are you done?"

"No."

They talked another five minutes. Ettinger couldn't understand why the man would set up a tent, risk being seen the following morning. Maybe, Stranahan said, he was just going to rest a couple of hours, time it so he drove back to the hatchery before dawn, during the period of least traffic. Stranahan ran out of change. Ettinger called him back.

"Okay, you promise," she said. "You're not going to follow that truck any farther, right? You drive back here, ask your questions, then you come straight to me. Noon latest. Got that?"

"I got it."

Stranahan said good-bye and went to put down the receiver.

"Sean?"

"I'm still here."

"I spoke with Vareda Beaudreux when I got back this morning. We ran her through the system and she checks out—she's who she says she is, the drowned man's older sister, she doesn't have a record. I spoke with the coroner. Her father turned toes up on the Madison July twenty of last year. He was fishing, it was heart failure, no foul play suspected. But to tell you the truth I didn't get too far with that woman. Ask her to spell her name and she acts like you're digging for the secret of her soul. I'm sure it must add to her appeal, men like you who want too much mystery in their lives. Anyway, she said if I talked to you to tell you she was going to be singing in the Blue Slipper tonight."

"Where's the Blue Slipper?"

"It's in Missoula."

Stranahan let the silence string out. Missoula was five miles west on I-90.

"You weren't going to tell me?" he said.

"I just did."

"Thanks, Sheriff. Good-bye."

"You'll call tomorrow."

"Tomorrow."

Stranahan set the receiver down.

"Trouble with the law, huh?" The trucker, waiting to use the phone.

"Something like that," Stranahan said.

Parking on the grass lot by the Blue Slipper, a riverside honky-tonk in Missoula's old downtown, Stranahan walked past an old-fashioned carousel, the fiberglass horses asleep on their sticks, then pulled open the heavy door to the club. For just a moment he could hear the rippling of piano keys playing off the vast murmur of the river current and heaved a sigh—he'd been half holding his breath thinking that she wouldn't be there, half holding his breath thinking she would.

A kid wearing a Bob Marley T-shirt shook back a lion's mane of dreadlocks as he accepted Stranahan's $5 bill. Vareda was singing a Johnny Mandel standard, "Where Do You Start?"

He found a seat at a back table facing the elevated stage and ordered a draught beer. After a time he shut his eyes and let Vareda's voice wash over him. It was a largely college crowd and when the song ended, a lanky young man dropped to his knees in an attitude of supplication before being yanked back up by the girl beside him. Vareda didn't notice; her head was bowed and she seemed lost to the world. For his part, Stranahan enjoyed the anonymity, allowing himself to float above the scene before being brought back to earth as the waitress set the frosted mug on the table. As he raised it to his lips, Vareda lifted her eyes from the piano and looked at him. Then she turned away, saying, "I really need an accordion for this one," as the first chords of "Crescent City" dropped from her fingertips, her voice dipping into Creole French for the refrain, *Tout est en son temps—*

everything will happen in time. Stranahan listened to the lyric without illusion. He knew that what they had together ran deeper than simple infatuation, but he also knew it could never weather the petty griev-ances of a normal life. He could regard Vareda Beaudreux with a coldly measured eye if there was reason to, now or down the line. There was a measure of regret in his knowledge.

She walked over when the set ended. Without looking down she squeezed his hand in a stay-where-you-are gesture, then walked to the bar where she accepted an envelope from a ducktailed man who wore a disco shirt patterned with electric guitars.

"Follow me," she said. "It's about fifteen miles."

They walked to Vareda's car.

"This place is a bit of a dive, isn't it?" she said. "I thought the West would be, I don't know, windswept streets or something. Meadow-larks singing."

She still wasn't looking at him.

"You seem, I don't know . . . distant," Stranahan said as she fumbled for her car keys.

"It's just it takes me a while to come down after I play. And I didn't expect to see you tonight, so you don't seem quite real yet." She put the back of her hand against his cheek. Then she broke away and climbed into her car.

The taillights led Stranahan south through a seemingly endless strip of gas stations, big-box stores, and fast-food joints. Then the broad sparkle of the Bitterroot River was under the span of a bridge. Beyond the river was the countryside, the lights scattered and the ebony canines of the Bitterroot Mountains jutting from the valley floor.

The Civic's turn signal flashed. Stranahan followed the dipping taillights along the riverbank and then upstream toward a cluster of window lights. Ahead he could see two boxlike structures shaped vaguely like mobile homes.

Vareda turned off the dirt track well short of the lights and parked by the river. By the time Stranahan pulled alongside she was out of the car, fumbling with the long string of buttons that ran the length of her dress.

"Come on, Mr. Stranahan, get those clothes off."

"Here?"

She pulled the half-unbuttoned dress over her head and shook out her hair, her form pale in the moonlight but for the black strips of her underwear.

"Do I have to help you, sir?" she said, her voice falling into the now familiar mocking tone that always seemed to come at such unexpected moments. She ducked back inside the car, reaching over to swing open the passenger door.

"Leave your truck here. Hurry now." Then, in her Southern voice, "Oh my, I do have a handsome man."

When Stranahan was down to his shoes and shorts and was sitting beside her, she turned the key and pulled back onto the ruts.

"It wouldn't do any good to ask what we're doing?" he said.

"I thought you were a detective."

She said nothing else and a quarter mile up the road pulled the car around in back of the first of the trailer-shaped structures, which Stranahan could now see were railroad boxcars that had been converted into guest cottages. Mountain chic. *Where did she find these places?* Vareda was out the door and running down the bank, the shine of the water only a few yards away.

She waded out to her waist and dipped under, otterlike, to reemerge facing him. Water streamed off her hair and the swells of her body.

A few moments later Stranahan was beside her; the cool smoothness of her skin was in his arms as she locked her hands around his neck and just looked for the longest time into his eyes. Then abruptly she shuddered against him and kicked free, swimming into the deeper current of the pool.

"It was just so smoky in there tonight I had to get in the water. When I was a girl we swam every day in Bayou Pierre." Her voice floated out in front of him as the current took her downstream.

"Aren't there alligators in Mississippi?"

"Not in Bayou Pierre. We have moccasins and alligator gars, they're big. But the only thing I ever worried about was snapping turtles. I'd have dreams one had me by the toe and was pulling me under."

He started to say something, but she cut him off.

"Ssshh, now. Just float. Isn't it wonderful?"

It was like nothing he'd known, floating cool down the starlit river, the current softly bickering with itself, the mountains hung in the distance. Then the sound more insistent as the river took a bend in a rush, waves standing high to one another and Vareda's head bobbing, going under to surface and under again and Stranahan following, trying to keep his mouth shut against the rising turbulence. Stranahan kicked at an angle until he was out of the tongue of writhing water and then, verging on panic, craned his head around, his eyes straining into the darkness.

"I'm here," she said, her voice in back of him.

He swam to where she was kneeling in the shallows.

"I'm a little crazy," she said in a breathy whisper.

"I won't argue."

"I've always been a little crazy."

"Come on," he said, "we're almost to my truck. We can stay on the inside here, out of the current."

"Not yet. No, you come here to me. It's soft here. It'll be all right. See, I can lie down."

Stranahan bent to kiss her lips, tasting the river that swept by them. She fitted her body to him.

"Now I have you." The river rose and fell behind them. "It's just you and me now."

A coyote broke its voice in the distance. Quickly it was joined by another.

"They're crazy, too," she breathed in his ear.

Later, she spoke from the bed in the darkness of the boxcar.

"Why is it you can ask me about Jerry, dig into me like that sheriff did with her questions, but then I ask you what you were doing tonight and you tell me you can't say?"

"It's better you don't get involved. The farther you stay away from this, the better it will be."

"I just saw what used to be my brother. He was in a *drawer*. How could I not be involved?" She had turned away from him to stare out the window, a shoulder of mountain under a slice of moon.

"I'm asking you to trust me."

After a while, she said, "So what do I do? I have to go through Bridger again to pick up Jerry's ashes."

"I could do that for you. Do you want me to scatter them in the river, too, if I ever find those trout your father marked?"

"After what happened to him? God no. No, I'll take him back to Mississippi. When we were kids there was a willow tree that made shadow lines on the grass; he thought they made a map that would lead him back to our house. It was his favorite place. If that tree hasn't been swallowed up by the bayou, it's where he'd want to be."

"Do you want your dad's ashes back, too? Maybe they should be together."

"Oh, I don't know." Her voice was far away. "Everything's unreal now."

She was silent. He could hear her breathing. Then she reached for him through the darkness.

CHAPTER THIRTY-ONE

Fish Chasing Their Tails

Stranahan found Rainbow Sam attacking the chaos in his trailer. He was wearing boxers and a Moose Drool T-shirt stained under the arms. His left arm was still in the sling. Peeking above the bandages was a tattoo of a fly-fishing Mickey Mouse, a good one on the line. The big man's body odor was hard to ignore.

"How's the man?" Stranahan asked. He noticed Killer curled in a dog bed under the foldout table. "How's the man's best friend?"

"Good and not half bad," Sam said. "I got to wear this damned sling for a month, though, so I don't rip the stitches in my chest. Fuckin' inconvenient. Can't row my boat. I had to turn a booking over to Peachy Morris, who's good people, but I'm still gonna lose the client. Peachy couldn't catch koi in a Japanese garden."

He shrugged. "Sorry about the mess, but nothing you haven't seen, huh? What do you figure the bastard was after? Only things of value are my boat and my gear and he didn't take that. Scattered my sticks"— Sam pointed to the stack of fly rods in the corner by his fly-tying bench—"a fuckin' miracle none got broken. I got a mudroom where I hang coats and shit. He trashed that worse than anywhere else."

"You mind if I look at it?"

"I cleaned it some."

They went to the room—wool jackets sagging off wall pegs, stained parkas, a pair of camouflage duck-hunting waders. Hung from an elk's rack were hats you could wring enough grease from to fry fish.

Stranahan was suddenly woozy.

"Hey," Sam said. "You don't look so hot. You got to buck up, man, either that or take a nap."

"I know. It's a long drive from Missoula and I haven't slept in two days. Some coffee might help."

They returned to the main room, where Sam set a kettle on the burner. Stranahan sat at the table, disturbing Killer, who whimpered, arched his back, turned a circle, then lay back down with his head propped on Stranahan's shoes.

"So what's so important you drove all the way from the 'Root to see me?" Sam set the two cups on the table.

"I wanted to ask you more about whirling disease, how much you know."

Sam grimaced. "Too fucking much. I'm a consultant to the AAWD. That's the Anglers Against Whirling Disease. We were federally funded till the money dried up. There're still a few fisheries biologists involved, not much paid staff; some guides like myself volunteer. We're valuable 'cause we got our fingers in the water, so to speak. What's it to you?"

"I promised the sheriff I wouldn't talk about anything she's investigating," he said. He sipped at the coffee. "She's just covering bases. You understand that guy you found was Vareda Beaudreux's brother. He'd done hatchery work before, the word came up."

"No, how would I know that? It wasn't in the paper. Your squeeze, huh? I'm sorry to hear that."

He held up his big hands.

"Hey, I'm not asking for quid pro quo here. I'll tell you anything you want, bro. But I thought you had a pretty good grip on WD last time we talked."

"Go over it again. Figure I don't remember anything."

Sam scratched a finger under his cast and rearranged himself in his chair.

"It's caused by a parasitic spore, a tiny form of animal, really. Because it's an invasive species, the native trout, the rainbows and the cutts, don't have any natural resistance. Instead of acting as a host for the parasite and staying healthy, the way the system's supposed to work, the spores eat holes in the skeletons of the fish. Throws 'em off balance. The poor bastards chase their tails until something eats them, a bird, a bigger trout. It can be transferred by mud, 'cause that's where these little worms live that carry the spores in part of the life cycle. Or it can be transferred by a bird that's eaten an infected fish and drops a turd into another river."

"How come you only hear about it in Montana? Wouldn't it be in other rivers out west?"

"Don't think it isn't."

The difference, Sam explained, was that Montana was strict about its wild trout program. Other states could mask the problem by supplanting depleted fisheries with hatchery trout.

"Here's the kicker," he said. "The disease affects the fish when they are little, right? In the wild, they don't survive. But in a hatchery environment, you can baby them through the worst phase of the disease until they are big enough to fight it off on their own. Then you can go ahead and plant them into a river. Not in Montana, that would put you in the pen. But some states, if a river isn't certified as whirling disease free, then the state can buy infected fingerlings from a hatchery and dump the fuckers into it."

He thumped his fist on the table, causing Killer to jump.

"That's like saying you got six people HIV positive in Bridger, it's no longer an AIDS-free town, so shit, why bother testing blood bank donors before suckin' the juice out of their veins and pumping it into the public? I exaggerate."

Stranahan's hand shook on the coffee mug. His mind was racing, not just from caffeine.

"Why would a hatchery raise diseased trout?"

"One, it's a fucking pernicious disease. Once you got it in the system, whether it's a river or a hatchery, you can't get it out. You have to rotenone all the fish, bury them, sterilize the joint. In Colorado, there're sixteen hatcheries run by the Division of Wildlife, guys who are supposed to be on the ball. Eleven tested positive for whirling disease. It's a big-time problem.

"Two"—Sam held up two fat fingers—"you can't study a fish disease unless you got fish to study."

Sam said that the Anglers Against Whirling Disease worked with a number of hatcheries to learn about the infection process, how water temperatures affect it, how the disease affects different races in a species. Conceivably, a strain of trout could be developed that was resistant. Some already showed promise. Down the road, a depleted river might have a sustainable wild trout population again.

Sean was impressed by Sam's encyclopedic knowledge, but not surprised. Fly fishermen were a forward-thinking group. They tended to look deep beneath the surface of their sport and were well aware of environmental factors that affected it.

Sam went on. "Montana, though, we still got a hands-off policy. We can try to control environmental factors, but we're not going to experiment with planting hatchery fish, not yet anyway. That's a death sentence for any wild trout that remain. We're gonna keep that cat in the bag as long as possible. Take a wait-and-see attitude and give the native populations a chance to build up resistance."

Stranahan had one more question.

"Let's say you have a hatchery that's raising trout that carry whirling disease, either by accident or design. If those trout were dumped into rivers that aren't infected, what would happen?"

Sam sat back in his chair.

"That's not funny, bro! Tell me you're not saying somebody is dumping sick fish into our rivers."

"I'm just saying, 'What if?'"

Sam made a face. "It's strange you should mention this," he said, "'cause it's happened. Back in '08, a hatchery operation illegally released diseased fish in Arizona, figuring once the rivers lost their disease-free status, then it could legally profit by selling diseased fingerlings to the state to stock the same rivers. The owner was convicted but pled out and probably got nothing but a slap on his pecker.

"But to answer your question, it would depend on the river. You take Rock Creek; WD put a big hurt on the rainbows in the canyon stretch, but brown trout from downriver moved into the niche. Overall population stayed the same, but now you got browns where there used to be rainbows. Other rivers, though, the browns don't fill the niche, so the river ends up with empty rooms that weren't there before—that's what happened to the Madison. Same with the Gunnison in Colorado."

"Who would stand to benefit?" Stranahan asked.

"What? If whirling disease wiped out a river?"

Stranahan nodded.

"I don't know, but some sure would stand to lose. Fishing's a bigger business than most people think. Montana alone, we're talking five hundred million a season in license sales, outfitting industry, tourist dollars going into motels, fly shops, restaurants. They call this the Treasure State 'cause of copper and gold, but today the gears run on trout slime."

"Could a hatchery benefit from bad fishing?"

"Worst case scenario? Fish, Wildlife, and Parks could throw in the towel, start a stocking program. A hatchery could see some dough that way, especially if it had an inside track on supplying the state."

"Hmm."

"Hmm fucking what?" Sam said. "Don't give me all this 'What if' bullshit. Something's going on here. Something bad. Am I right?"

"I told you I can't talk about it," Stranahan said. He decided not to press any further. "Look, I got to go. I'm supposed to see the sheriff today."

"Yeah, okay, don't tell me. Fuck you."

"Fuck you."

Stranahan held his eyes a minute, then saw Sam's face crack. They both laughed.

"Hey," Sam said. "I have a sport booked for tomorrow. Half-day float. I haven't palmed him off yet. What do you say we take him down the river? You row, I guide. Split the take." He rubbed his fingers together.

Stranahan shook his head. He had forward momentum now and hated losing it.

"A couple hundred bucks buys a lot of paint brushes," Sam said.

Stranahan reconsidered. "I'd like to, but it depends what I find out from the sheriff. Can you wait till later this afternoon before giving your client to someone else?"

Sam nodded.

"Do you think we could float through the stretch where you found the body?"

Sam nodded again. "But I got to warn you, this time of year you have to get an early start. If my client's up for it, we'll be on the water by five-thirty."

Stranahan said thanks for the coffee and Sam saw him to his rig, Killer loping ahead of them.

"That shirt you're wearing belongs in a trash can," Stranahan said, gunning the engine to life.

Sam looked down. He shrugged. "I'm not a man to give up on a garment just 'cause it's got a little age," he said.

When Stranahan glanced into the rearview mirror, Sam was using his good arm to flip him the bird.

CHAPTER THIRTY-TWO

Dagger in a Dead Man's Heart

"Have a chair, Sean."

Martha Ettinger sat with her forearms on her desk, her hands folded, her khakis pressed, her badge polished.

"Thanks, Eric. You can go now."

The deputy who had escorted Stranahan through the Law and Justice Center shut the door.

Ettinger studied the man across from her, stretching the silence.

"Did you see Vareda Beaudreux?" she asked.

"I did."

"All petered out then, huh?"

Stranahan looked at her.

"That was a low blow. I'm sorry," she said. "I'm just mad at myself. I had no business involving you in this."

"I'm involved with or without you."

"So you are. Okay, you go first."

Stranahan gave her the short version of his conversation with Sam about whirling disease.

Ettinger frowned.

"It's interesting," she said at length.

"It's not just interesting. It's illegal. At least dumping the fish is."

"But it's not murder."

"But it's motive."

Ettinger sat back and clasped her hands behind her head.

"Convince me."

"Start with what we know," Sean said. "Our victim, Jerry Beaudreux, gets a summer job at a Montana hatchery. The work is basically janitorial; he cleans fish raceways, tanks, stuff like that. Dispenses pellet foods. Takes the truck into Great Falls to pick up supplies. He's a bright boy and a hard worker but he's young, and, according to his sister, he comes across as naive.

"Someone connected to the hatchery is trucking trout to the state's best trout streams. That's illegal whether they are diseased or not, by the way. Beaudreux becomes suspicious when he notices people loading fish into a truck after hours. When he asks his boss what's up, he's lied to. His imagination kicks in. He decides to play detective. The next week he follows the truck to Ennis, where the driver stops at a bar. He phones his sister to bring her up to date. That's the last anyone hears from him. A day later, Sam finds his body twisting in the Madison, forty miles upriver from Ennis."

Stranahan leaned forward and put his fists down on Ettinger's desk. "I think the tail was made. I think the truck driver confronted him, drowned him in that pond you've been looking for, and then, to deflect attention, dumped him into the river and parked Beaudreux's car at the campground at Quake Lake. Whatever this young man found out, it cost him his life."

"You have a suspect?"

Stranahan thought about the dog he'd seen on the Big Blackfoot River, the thin thread that tied it to a half-remembered name. He'd passed up one opportunity to tell her about it and again decided to keep the information to himself.

"No," he said at length. "And I'm not changing the subject, but did you ever get ballistics on the bullet that killed the antelope?"

"You can forget that angle. The tech says the bullet from the critter doesn't match the one taken out of Meslik. One's a Nosler Partition, the other's a Speer Spitzer."

Stranahan interrupted. "That doesn't mean they can't have been fired from the same rifle."

"You want to let me finish? The rifling marks on the bullets don't match. They're both .243 Winchester, but from different rifles. Gus Gentry may have had a beef with your buddy, but he didn't shoot him. At least he didn't with the rifle used on the antelope."

Ettinger continued. "But let's get back to your little adventure the other night. We ran the plate number you gave me. It's registered to the hatchery. Beaudreux allegedly told his sister it was a vehicle he'd never seen before, but there you are. I'm sure there could be an explanation—it was kept in a garage, parked in Great Falls, lent to someone. But we can't tie it to an individual."

"On the other hand it implicates the hatchery."

"That it does," Ettinger agreed. "But we're talking about a murder, Sean. As in somebody making somebody dead. And I'm supposed to believe this is over diseased fish? Could a hatchery make enough money on the deal to justify drowning a man?" It wasn't a question so much as thinking out loud. "Tell you what we'll do. I'll call in a favor and have someone make a discreet inquiry into that hatchery, see who runs it, who it contracts for, any connection it might have to whirling disease study. I don't want to raise an alarm and have them destroy evidence that could help us down the road."

"Thanks," Stranahan said.

"For what?"

"I don't know. Taking me seriously."

"Yes, well, your guess is almost as good as mine. What do you say we get a coffee and kick this around some more. I think better behind the wheel."

"You sure? You look like you need the caffeine."

Ettinger had pulled the Jeep up to the window of the coffee kiosk on the outskirts of town. She told the bikini barista she'd arrest her if she dropped her top another inch, ordered a grande half-caf latte with a double shot and a small regular coffee for Stranahan, over his objection. She took a sip and wiped her lip.

"I hate to say I'm addicted to these things," she said. She reached for the cell that was vibrating on her hip.

"Ettinger . . . uh-huh, slow down, Walt . . . you're calling from a pay phone you say. . . . What campground? . . . I'll be damned. . . . Give me the number. . . . Hell yes, secure it. I'm on my way. And Walt, stand by a minute, okay?"

She pulled ahead a few yards and asked Stranahan to hand her the notebook in the glove compartment.

She snapped it from his hand, flipped pages, and punched numbers. Waiting, she impatiently bobbed her head.

"Ms. Janice, this is Sheriff Ettinger. Your brother said he'd be at your place. . . . Great, could I speak with him? It's important. . . . Okay, I'll wait."

She drummed her fingers on the steering wheel.

"You really are bad luck, Sean. There's been a murder. It—"

"Harold? . . . Yeah, your lucky day. . . . Remember that fellow with the voice, the camp host over at Quake Lake? Well, he's on the floor of his trailer with a hole in his heart, body's in rigor . . . No, not a gunshot, a blade. . . . The knife's gone. . . . No, we don't know for sure it was a knife. Walt's holding down the fort until the ME gets there. You're up in Pony, I'm just outside Bridger. I could pick you up in Norris in twenty minutes. The School House Café, it's out of business . . . that's the one . . . um-hmm. . . . I'll have him sit in his truck so he doesn't muck up the tracks . . . whatever you say. Thanks, Harold."

She jammed her forefinger at the phone, started bobbing her head, and rolled her eyes when the connection went through. She spoke to Deputy Hess and then shifted her attention to Stranahan.

"You want to hitch a ride with the law, see how it's done on our side of the tracks?" she said with a mirthless smile.

"I don't know. Are you going to deputize me?"

"Like in a posse? Come on." She made a shooing gesture, flicking the backs of her hands at him. "Seriously," she said.

"If I'd known, I would have had you order me a twelve-ounce," Stranahan said. "Let's go."

Stranahan had not expected an Indian. Black hair in a braid, worn jeans, flannel shirt with the arms cut off. Tattooed elk tracks circled the upper biceps of his right arm; weasel tracks hunted around the left. Harold Little Feather had a knife on his belt, wore cowboy boots showing more mud than leather. He climbed into the Jeep smelling of horse flesh and sweat.

"No kit?" Martha said.

"It's a no-doubt murder; thought you'd book a crime scene investigator. Not much call for fingerprint dust breaking ponies."

"But you're still certified?"

"Yep."

"I got the kit," she said. "Closest CSI is Helena and he's got a tube up his pecker as we speak."

"What for?"

"Kidney stones."

"Better than a knife in the heart," Harold said.

Walter Hess had strung orange crime-scene tape tree trunk to tree trunk to cordon off the trailer. Down the camp loop road a young couple stood beside a girl straddling a bicycle; it was the little hoofer who'd been dancing on the picnic table in the abandoned site on Ettinger's first visit to the campground. The tyke was turning the bike in tight circles, her shoes scuffing the ground.

Walt lifted his chin toward the family.

"Daughter found the body. She knocked on the door wanting to play with the cat. No answer, peered through the window, saw feet poking out. Curious thing she was, she walked right in on him. Then ran around the loop screaming to high heaven. Campers were climbing trees. Figured she'd seen a grizzly bear; they had a sow with two cubs mosey through last week."

"When's Doc Hanson going to show?"

"Left town an hour ago."

Walt acknowledged the tracker. "I got the relay—the girl's pop used the pay phone over to Loop B—I was checking out that kitchen fire up at West Fork Cabins. I walked straight along the dirt lane yonder, staying on the grass so's not to disturb any tracks"—Walt pointed at the approach to the trailer—"opened the door with a handkerchief, two fingers to the carotid to make sure I was dealing with a body, neck in rigor, no other contact. Backed out, called in. Don't think anybody else been up here since the girl."

"You're not leaving me any excuses," Harold said.

"Seen too many crime scenes compromised in Chicago." He shook his head. "Those uniforms in the Third, they couldn't pour piss out of a boot if you wrote instructions on the sole."

"You did good, Walt," Ettinger said. "I could kiss you but I'm not going to."

Little Feather squatted down. To Walt: "Let me see the bottom of your boot . . . now the other. Make a clear track here where it's damp. You got a pronounced pronation on the right side, you know that? It's okay, I won't tell anybody. Which side of the drive did you go up?" Walt pointed. "Okay, best thing now, just stay right here."

He turned his back to them and walked off toward the dirt ruts that led to the trailer.

Ettinger turned to her deputy. "Go talk to the family. I'll stay here until Harold clears the path."

To Stranahan: "Keep everyone clear of the scene."

He nodded, but something had irritated his mind, something he'd heard or seen—what was it? A mosquito stung his neck and he slapped it away.

"Sean?"

"Sure, okay."

He watched Walt walk toward the family, the girl casting her eyes down as the badge advanced, kicking at the kickstand of her bike.

That was it.

"Sheriff?"

Ettinger didn't respond. She had the crime scene bag and was standing at the roadside, watching the Indian.

"Stay here," she said absently to Stranahan. She walked off toward Little Feather, who gestured her to stay on his side of the path.

A half hour later, the ME's station wagon pulled up alongside the county rigs. Doc Hanson climbed out, gave Stranahan a perfunctory nod, and walked to the trailer. Walt came by a minute later, tapped two fingers to his hat in acknowledgment, and also went to the trailer. He hooked the door open with a forefinger and entered. Stranahan could hear Martha Ettinger's voice inside.

"**S**heriff would like to see you." It was Walt, walking up the path. He jerked a hand toward the trailer.

The ME passed him on his way out. No nod this time.

The camp host's neck was outstretched like a baby bird's, his body contorted on the floor. A blood bubble blown out of his mouth had partly collapsed, so that it spread a red film over the side of his face. It was close inside the trailer and smelled like BO with a tang of cat urine.

Stranahan breathed through his mouth, his eyes roving. Ettinger told him, Don't be shy, have a good look.

He took a couple steps toward the body. The host's tabby cat, which had been watching the proceedings with wild eyes from the top of a microwave set on the kitchen counter, jumped down and crouched on top of the man's stomach. When Stranahan bent down, it retreated under the Formica table that stood on a removable pedestal so that the benches could expand into a bed. The cat opened its mouth from the darkened recess in a silent hiss. Bending over had been a mistake. Stranahan felt the bile rising in his gorge.

"You ever seen him before?" It was Ettinger, standing behind him inside the door.

Stranahan swallowed the acrid taste. "No."

"Then you can go back to the vehicle. Skeeter repellent's in the glove compartment. They're thick out there."

Two hours later, after the body had been stretchered out to the ME's Suburban, Stranahan, Ettinger, and Hess convened at the Jeep. Little Feather remained in the trailer, bagging fiber samples from the camp host's clothes closet and area rugs to compare against foreign threads that might show up on the body.

"Did you get anything back there?" Stranahan said in a low voice.

"Lots, sure, but I don't know if it counts for anything," Ettinger said.

"Tracks?"

Hess spoke up. "Harold plays it close to the chest. He'll tell us on Indian time."

Hess opened the door of his Cherokee and brought out a can of soda. He took a swig.

"It's warm, but it cuts the taste of that trailer. You want?"

Ettinger and Stranahan both took a swallow.

"You breathe in," the deputy was saying, "you swallow the bad air, it makes a gas in your stomach. You'll fart an hour later and smell it. You take a crap in the morning, déjà vu. That means same thing all over again."

Ettinger made a face.

"What? Am I wrong?"

"I won't dignify that with an answer," Ettinger said. "Let's focus here, go over what we have while we're waiting for Harold. Walt, you're the big city cop, you start."

The deputy looked down at the tips of his crocodile boots.

"Blood on my brand new Tony Lamas," he said. "If that leaves a stain, ever' time I pull them on I'll be revisiting that trailer. Have to throw 'em away. Time will tell."

"Walt!"

"Yeah, okay. First thing strikes me is no forced entry. The camp host either opened the door, or else left it unlocked." He took another swig of soda and spat on the ground. "Two, the blow with the knife takes him by surprise. No sign of struggle. One thrust below the sternum so's not to strike bone, the blade angled up into the heart; you figure its someone familiar with a blade, odds on a man."

"Or maybe any cook in a kitchen," Ettinger interjected.

"Three," Hess continued, "I'll go out on a limb and say it's related to the floater in the river. We're working on the assumption that the guy who drowned Beaudreux drove up here to set up the camp, leave the vic's car at the site, so's to throw us off his trail. Maybe he thought the host here spotted him when he was making the rounds, that he could make an ID. We know the poor bugger was half blind and only saw the figure of a man at the site, but the killer doesn't know that."

"Tying up loose ends." Ettinger caught her chin between her thumb and forefinger and massaged it thoughtfully.

"I've seen it before." Walt said. "It's like a delayed reaction. You kill someone, your mind starts playing tricks. You see witnesses where there aren't witnesses. You get paranoid. 'I can't take the chance he saw me,' you're thinking. Each day passes, you worry more. Finally you come back with a gun on your hip. Or a knife." He looked at Stranahan. "Once is happenstance. Twice is coincidence. Third time it's enemy action. Like Goldfinger said to James Bond."

"You're a film buff now, Walt?" Ettinger said. "I would have never thought."

She turned to Stranahan. "Well?"

Stranahan thought a moment, surprised she'd asked his opinion. "I was only inside a minute," he began, "so I'll have to take what Walt says on faith about the entry. The camp host had no reason to suspect anything, so the stabbing is the easy part. The tricky part would be getting here and then getting away without being seen. When did your ME think the man in there died? Last night?"

"The body temperature suggests last night, probably before midnight, any later and you'd think the table would have been made into a bed." Ettinger waved away a mosquito. "I think we're on the same page here. The killer knocks, enters, the vic has no idea what's coming and takes one in the ticker. Our man escapes into the night. So, unless it's someone actually camping here, how did he get here? He drives, he risks being associated with a vehicle. We can't rule the camper angle out, but"—she paused—"Sean, what was it you were going to say earlier? I was preoccupied."

"You'll laugh," Stranahan said.

"Do I look like I'm laughing?"

"What I was going to say is he could have ridden a bike."

"From where? This is nowhere."

"From that neighborhood on the Madison where I ran into you, where Summersby and Tony Sinclair live. Where Gentry, the taxidermist who whacked the antelope, lives."

"We ruled him out for the Meslik shooting. There's no reason to think he's mixed up with Beaudreux."

"I'm not talking about him. I'm talking about someone I met at Summersby's party, a guy who rides a bicycle. His name is Apple Mc-Something-or-other, I can't remember."

"What makes you say that?"

"A dog." Now it was out. "The guy who was driving the hatchery truck. I told you I didn't get a look at his face, but I did see his dog. It's a heeler. Apple . . . McNair, that's his name. Apple McNair. He brought a heeler to Summersby's party."

"So, it's 'The Case of the Dog in the Nighttime,' is it?" Ettinger said. "Why didn't you tell me about this?"

"Because I wasn't sure myself," Stranahan said. "I couldn't see the man, so all I had to make a connection was the dog. You know as well as I do that there are a lot of heelers in Montana riding shotgun in a lot of trucks. I knew it could be a coincidence, but when I saw the dog, McNair just popped into my head. The guy with his back to me, short and stocky. This McNair, same body type. I didn't recognize the voice, but then I only heard a few words and people use different voices to speak to their pets. Plus he rebuilds old bikes. I thought of that when I saw the little girl on her bicycle. McNair could have ridden up here, stashed his bike in the woods and done the last bit on foot. Bike's more inconspicuous than a car."

Walt spoke up. "That cuts both ways. If someone saw a bike, they'd likely remember it more than a vehicle."

Stranahan shook his head. "There isn't much traffic. He could spot headlights at a quarter mile, pull off to the side, and take cover till they passed."

Ettinger folded her arms across her chest.

"I know what you're thinking," Stranahan said. "I'm jumping at another thread. But your victim was stabbed. This guy McNair, he's a knife maker. He showed me one of his blades, said something like 'You could skin a bear with that.' Man has a one-off look. He gives you the heebie-jeebies."

"The heebie-jeebies? Come on," Ettinger said, but her face had turned thoughtful.

Stranahan continued, "He lives on the river. He's twenty miles from where Sam found Beaudreux, he's no more than eight to Henry's Lake where Sam was shot. Plus the neighbors say he's gone a lot. Fits in with being the delivery man for the hatchery."

Hess glanced past them.

"Here comes Harold," he said. "Now we can have a real powwow."

Stranahan caught Ettinger's scowl.

"Oh, for chrissakes, Marth. Lighten up. I got as much respect for the red man as you do."

"You're hopeless, you know that."

"I am what I am."

"Obviously."

Harold Little Feather passed them without a word. He set his gear and the evidence bags in the cargo space of the Cherokee.

He smiled. *What a day, huh?*

"Give me something," Ettinger said.

The tracker rolled his neck.

"Got to get the cricks out. Hands and knees all morning do that to a man."

He went on talking as he stretched. "I took a lot of samples, but routine, you know. Some fibers on the body. There's blood and fingerprints to sort out in the state lab, you know how long that takes. Some caked mud on the floor that's cracked off the instep of a left shoe, but no mud on the victim's shoes, or any shoes in the trailer. To me the mud smells like silt deposits you'd find in a river or a lake, but could have been tracked in from just about anywhere."

"Shoe size?" Ettinger said.

"Not enough to say. One thing, though, the mud under the instep tells me the shoe has a high arch. I'm guessing cowboy boot 'cause I found boot tracks outside." He led them around to the back of the trailer.

"As you can see," he said, sweeping his hand, "cheat grass, fescue, dandelion, hardpack earth. Maybe a Kalahari bushman could pick up a track here"—he shook his head—"nothing stood out to me. But the duff under the trees tells a story. See where the so-called backyard ends, woods all the way to the road, it's a natural line of approach if someone wanted to stay in cover. No need to go through the campground and take a chance of being seen. I got partials by those two lodgepoles"—he pointed—"the best impression is under this Doug fir."

"I can't make out anything," Ettinger said, peering under the low-hanging branch Little Feather held up.

Stranahan said, "Cowboy boot."

"'Bout a nine," Little Feather said.

Martha nodded. "I see it now. Mostly it just looks like a shadow. Good work, Harold. You say this is the same guy who left the mud inside the trailer? Couldn't just anyone be wandering back here?"

"The camp host, most likely, but he's an eleven. Wouldn't be any reason for one of the campers to be here. No, I figure this is the guy. It's fresh; see how the nap on the duff hasn't settled around the edge of the track. The grains of earth stand on end when they're disturbed, can take half a day for the nap to collapse. And I can't say for sure, but that bit of brown stain there on the pine needles, that could be blood he tracked over from the body. I waited to show you before I bagged it."

Ettinger nodded. "This is all you found?"

"All I found that matters. Think back, Martha. Nine cowboy boot ring a bell?"

Ettinger felt the hair on her forearms lift. The tracks in the abandoned homestead cabin above Henry's Lake were a nine cowboy boot.

"You're saying this is the same guy who shot at Sam Meslik on the lake?"

Harold's brow furrowed. "Somewhere between maybe and probably is what I'm saying. I'll have to check the print against the tracings and the pics we took at the cabin."

"Exactly what prints would those be? Exactly what cabin?" There was a cranky note in Hess's voice.

"Don't get your u-trou in a bunch, Walt. I didn't tell you 'cause no one in the department had an interest. Besides, Harold and I were snooping in Idaho, which I didn't want to explain. Now it comes together."

"My u-trou?"

"Underwear."

Walt glared a moment, then his eyes crinkled up. "That's a good one, Marth, I'll have to remember it."

Interviews bled away the afternoon. A few campers had seen the host drive around the loops the previous evening, checking registrations, which confirmed the ME's estimation of time of death as being later in the night, but that was where the observations ended. No one had seen a man riding a bicycle.

Harold was standing beside the Cherokee with the Manx tabby under his arm when Stranahan and Ettinger returned from their circuit. Hess pulled up in his county rig, said he was taking off for Bridger.

Little Feather and Stranahan climbed into the Cherokee with Ettinger. Harold stroked the cat's cheeks to calm him as they started back up the valley.

"Figure I'll leave him with my sister. He'd just starve on the rez."

"I assume Janice married a white man," Ettinger said. "What do you think about that, Harold?"

Stranahan, sitting in back, felt a tension in the Jeep. The question seemed out of place.

"Me, I'm for whatever gets you through the night. Greg's a good guy and my sister, she's always been a bit of an apple."

"Apple?"

"Red on the outside, white on the inside."

"You ever date white women?"

"You asking about my love life, Martha? I don't know what to say."

"Just makin' conversation."

An uneasy silence fell over the trio. Stranahan had the feeling that if he hadn't been there, the words would never have been spoken. In his experience, a third person often acted as a buffer to keep the tone of a conversation light, even if the words were not. But the silence continued as the Cherokee dropped from Quake Dam into the valley.

"Don't you think we ought to interview McNair?" Stranahan volunteered. They were passing the 87 turnoff to the riverfront community, where the old cabin slumped like a swayback nag in a herd of thoroughbreds.

Ettinger said carefully. "I'm not dismissing what you said. But if we knock on this guy's door asking to see a rifle, or a knife, or some size nine cowboy boots, and he has something to hide, then do you think he's going to produce them? Even if he was dumb enough to keep them in the first place? No, we'd drive away and any evidence he possessed would disappear long before I could get a warrant."

"But there's bound to be blood on the shoes, or maybe on the bike. The longer this goes on—"

She finished his sentence—"the more I wonder about your girlfriend."

They drove in a silence a few miles. Stranahan remembered that he'd promised to call Sam about fishing in the morning and asked to use Ettinger's cell phone.

"Reception will be touch and go," she said as she handed it to him.

"Kimosabe." Sam's voice crackled indistinctly. ". . . you on?"

Stranahan thought, why not? If nothing else, he'd be able to have a second look at the logjam where Sam had found the body. Vareda was in Missoula, two hundred miles away, and obviously the sheriff had no more use for him.

"Yeah," he said into the phone, "but I want to drive my own rig. I can spot your truck at the take-out. Can you hear me, Sam?"

"Ten-four, my man."

They agreed on a rendezvous and Stranahan handed the phone back to Ettinger.

"You come up the Madison tomorrow," she said. "I don't want you looking for anything bigger than a trout. We're clear on that, right?"

Before Stranahan could respond, the radio crackled. It was Walt, asking Ettinger to pick him up a grilled chicken cordon bleu sandwich at the Blue Moon Saloon on the way in. He'd already passed the joint, but didn't realize he was hungry till now.

"Must a been one of those subliminal message things," Walt said.

"Okay, sure."

"Fries and a Coke. In a bottle if they got it."

"Anything else, filet mignon, foie gras?"

"I don't eat Frog food."

The radio went quiet and they rode in silence for a few minutes.

Harold Little Feather spoke softly. "We passed the Blue Moon 'bout five miles back."

"Shit," Martha said. "I'm so screwed up I don't know where I am anymore. Walt's gonna have to settle for a slab of slow elk at the Ennis Café."

From the backseat, Stranahan could see the Indian shrug his shoulders.

"Man wants the Cordon Bleu," Little Feather said, "nothing else is going to do."

"Oh, fuck you, Harold," Ettinger said.

"You see, that's why I don't date white women. They make promises they never keep."

Stranahan could see the back of Ettinger's neck redden under the brim of her peaked sheriff's hat.

CHAPTER THIRTY-THREE

The Smoking Hat

Retracing the drive up the Madison Valley the following morning, Stranahan kept Sam's trailer rig in his headlights. To the west he could make out the Sphinx, a lion-headed peak with its subordinate sister, the Helmet, squatting in starlit shadow. Montana in its vicissitudes continued to amaze him. Yesterday afternoon had been eighty-five degrees, not a breath of wind to deter the mosquitoes. The temperature had dropped forty degrees overnight, blanketing the warmer river in a serpentine wafer of fog. When Sean took the oars of Sam's drift boat at blush dawn, it was cold enough that he chose his battered felt fedora over his billed fishing cap and pulled it down to the tops of his ears. Sam's client, a square-jawed ex-jock named Frankie DiBacco, who owned a tire dealership in Steubenville, Ohio, smiled under his watch cap, a drop of liquid teetering on the end of his nose.

"Let's try giving them a proper breakfast first," Sam said, handing DiBacco the streamer rod. "Cast to the bank, strip that double bunny in darting pulses."

The tire baron was a B-plus angler and Sam netted three browns for him before the sun set fire to Specimen Ridge in the Gravelly Range. The wind picked up, gusting down the coulees that cut through the escarpment. Stranahan felt cold air kissing his scalp.

"My hat!"

The angler, measuring the distance with false casts, dropped the fly and stripped, missing the half-sunk fedora by a yard. Sam reached across Stranahan, grabbed the six-weight from the client's fist, and shot a fore cast worthy of a permit tailing in the Marquesas. He snagged the fedora and pumped it in, the soaked felt putting a bow into the rod.

He snorted. "This hat fights better than any trout you've hooked, Frank. You're letting us down."

Stranahan wrung out the hat and stuffed it into his gear bag. Sam fished a hand up under the stern, found what he was rummaging for, and wedged a ball cap down on Stranahan's brow.

"That one won't blow off. Looks solid on you too, bro."

A half hour later, a bend in the river revealed the logjam where Sam had found the body.

The fishing guide checked his watch.

"PMDs ought to be starting up," he said, referring to the hatch of mayflies that bring trout to the surface on many fine July mornings in Montana. He directed Stranahan to pull over to the logjam and drop anchor.

"Frank, why don't you switch to that four-weight with the parachute dry there—yep, the one with the calf wing and purple body. Work into position at the tail of the slick. Bugs will start popping any minute now."

As the client waded away, Sam and Stranahan found a log at the side of the jam to sit on.

"I know you been here with the sheriff, so you know we hooked the body at the head of the jam. Don't really know what else to show you."

"Well, I don't know what I'm looking for," Stranahan said, taking off the hat Sam had lent him and scratching his scalp. He turned the hat in his hands, then stared incredulously. The front of the cap was embossed with a rainbow trout. Above the trout, letters in a stitched script spelled MISSOURI RIVER PISCES. It was the name of the hatchery where Beaudreux had worked.

"Sam"—Stranahan's voice was deliberately restrained—"where did you pick up this hat?"

Sam's look was evasive. "Client give it to me."

"Really? Who was the client?"

Sam muttered "fuck" and spat into the water.

"Okay, you got me, it wasn't a client. I found it on the dead man's stick."

Stranahan frowned.

"The fucking Winston." He shrugged. "You know, the rod I found in the riffle." He pointed upriver. "The strap had been cinched down ahead of the reel, you know, with the rod sticking out like a ponytail. When I picked up the rod, the hat come up with it. So what? The guy my client hooked didn't have a hat on. Figured it was his."

"Well, it isn't." Stranahan told him about the bull semen hat Sheriff Ettinger had found under the logjam. Ettinger had said they'd found strands of Beaudreux's hair clinging to the sweatband.

"So whose . . . ?"

Stranahan could see the light flick in Sam's eyes as his expression changed. The guide grimaced, showing the sharp V notches in his teeth.

"This is the hat the guy who killed him had on? Tell me I'm wrong, bro."

Looking upriver, Stranahan could picture a man—a short stocky man, in Stranahan's vision—walking the body down the riffle in the dark, clamping the rod under his arm because he intended to place it with the body. But why take off his own hat and cinch it around the cork? The breeze turning the aspen leaves inside-out gave him the answer. Hadn't his hat blown off only an hour ago? Certainly McNair—Stranahan had finally put a name to the killer—had understood that the hat could link the hatchery to the body if he lost it, so he had attached it to the rod, cinching the adjustable strap just ahead of the reel. No doubt he figured to remove it once he got to the logjam. Or maybe the hat the victim was wearing had washed off and floated away, to lodge under the logjam, and that had reminded McNair he'd better be careful of his own hat. But then he'd tripped up, entirely plausible given the conditions—slippery streambed, dead of night, trying to guide a water-soaked body down the river. He'd lost his grip on the rod, lost his hat attached to it in the process. In the dark, he'd been unable to find it.

Sam was saying something, but to Stranahan the words were white noise, like birdsong. His mind raced. All along he'd figured Sam's cabin was trashed because someone was looking for the rod. But McNair wouldn't care about the rod; the rod belonged to the victim—it wouldn't incriminate him. It was the hat. The hat implicated the hatchery. DNA testing, if there were hair follicles on the hat, could tie McNair personally to the victim. Perhaps, Stranahan thought, the man had returned to the river in the morning, risking the exposure because he wanted to find the hat. He could have arrived in time to see Sam, already there with the sheriff. . . .

Yes, that's the way it could have happened. It would explain why Sam's trailer had been ransacked, why his truck had been followed the morning they went fishing in Henry's Lake. It would explain the shot at the lake. It also would explain the imprint of a size nine cowboy boot inside the old homesteader's cabin near the lake. It fit together.

"You look like a man with a turd that's been prairie dogging and finally got it to drop."

"What?" Stranahan spun back to his surroundings.

"You know, prairie dogging, popping its head in and out."

"Popping its—Jesus. You're a sick man, Sam."

"So what gives?"

Stranahan looked back up the river.

"Sam," he said, "I have a serious question for you. What did you do with the hat after you found it?

"I put it on my head, man. . . . I dunno, I think I did. Yeah, I did. I'd left mine in the boat. Why?"

So, Stranahan thought, if someone had been watching, he'd seen Sam take the hat as well as the rod.

"Why didn't you give it to the sheriff?"

Sam shrugged.

He said, "With her deputy falling in the drink and my client going 'Europe' all over my boat, a regular fucking Ringling Brothers, I forgot, I guess. I didn't mean to, swear to God. I just stuffed it up under the stern and put my own hat back on. Forgot all about it till yours blew off this morning."

"Show me."

Sam showed him a recess under the aft decking.

"That's like a secret compartment," Stranahan said. He remembered seeing Sam's boat in his yard the morning they'd left to fish Henry's Lake—whoever had trashed the trailer had undoubtedly searched the boat, too. The compartment could explain why he hadn't been able to find the hat.

"It's just a recess where the flotation foam didn't get blowed in," Sam said. "So what?"

Stranahan tried to deflect the question with one of his own. "You ever hear of this Missouri River Pisces?"

"No bells," Sam said.

Suddenly there was a yelp from Sam's client, who had hooked a rainbow trout that made three jumps in succession, the first one higher than the client's head.

"You got yourself a Michael Jordan, Frank," Sam shouted, and after the fish was landed, photographed, and released, the question on Sam's lips was at least temporarily forgotten. Three trout later, when the PMD hatch was petering out, the anglers piled into the drift boat to continue downriver. Sam didn't mention the hat again until they reached the Palisades take-out.

"Don't suppose you could maybe keep this hat thing under your hat, so to speak?" he said. "Sheriff's already pissed that I didn't hand over the rod. This was an honest oversight, I swear to God."

"I can't do that, but she'll understand," Sean said.

"That's an outright lie, my man. But you do what you got to."

Stranahan shuttled Sam to the put-in at Lyons Bridge, where he picked up his trailer rig. As the dust it raised settled back to the ground, Stranahan faced another of those moments when he had reached a crossroads and didn't know which way to turn the wheel. To the west was Vareda, who had done a lot of talking with her eyes the night he had spent with her in the boxcar but had never once broached the subject of when they might meet again. She would have to return to Bridger for her brother's ashes before driving back to Mississippi, and she was still on a long tether with Martha Ettinger, but . . .

But nothing, Stranahan thought. Missoula was two hundred miles west. He turned his attention to the north and Bridger, four walls hung with unsold paintings, and a crumb dish in front of a mouse hole. That life seemed beside the point now. But to the south—to the south was the cabin belonging to a short, stocky man who had a heeler dog that had one blue eye and one brown eye. It was scarcely fifteen miles away.

CHAPTER THIRTY-FOUR

In the Crosshairs

By the time Stranahan neared the Grizzly Bar, the adrenaline flush was fading. Taking his foot off the accelerator, he let the Cruiser coast. There was a phone booth outside the bar where he could call Ettinger. Surely, the hat would be the last piece of evidence she'd need for a warrant. But then, looking at it from her point of view, he realized that without genetic confirmation, which would take days, and then only if there was evidence to test, the hat did not connect the body to McNair. It was Stranahan's recognition of the dog that turned the compass needle in the direction he was headed, and that—well, that and a buck ninety-five would buy you a shot of espresso without the steamed milk.

Stranahan put his foot on the pedal and continued south. At the gate across the road leading to the riverfront development, he faced a decision. He could pay a visit to Summersby, which would get him close to his quarry, but then what? He didn't intend to confront the man. That could lead to destruction of evidence, as Ettinger had pointed out. No, what he wanted to do was watch McNair's property from a vantage where he wouldn't be observed or have to explain himself, and, as his eyes lifted to the skirts of the mountains, it dawned on him how he might do that.

A mile past the gate to the river houses, Stranahan turned on to the Forest Service access road leading to the Sheep Creek trailhead. The road climbed through a sage plateau for a couple of miles before reaching the turnaround. Stranahan rummaged for his water bottle and binoculars; then, on second thought, grabbed his damp felt hat and an old UMass sweatshirt. Who knew how long this might take? Skirting the trail, he crossed an irrigation ditch that siphoned the water in Sheep Creek and started to climb the facing slope to the south. Stranahan remembered Summersby telling him that on crisp autumn evenings he could hear elk bugling from this slope. By the time Stranahan reached a saddle in the side ridge, he was lathered in sweat. Putting his back to a windfall and folding the sweatshirt under him, he gulped lungs full of thin air, waiting for his heart rate to go down.

He lifted the binoculars, centering the range-finding crosshairs on the chinked cottonwood logs of McNair's cabin. He could see the converted garage that served as McNair's knife shop, his rusted Sierra Classic in the yard. No sign of life, though.

Stranahan raised the glasses, bringing into view Sinclair's log mansion and, just beyond and downriver, the home of Richard Summersby. Ann, Summersby's wife, was sitting on the porch where Stranahan himself had sipped whiskey only a few nights ago—it seemed like a few years. She turned the page of a book and Stranahan lifted the glasses and looked farther downstream at the manse belonging to the taxidermist, Gentry. A rifle bench rest, constructed with weather-buckled plywood, glinted with pinpricks of light—empty brass shell casings reflecting in the sun, Stranahan surmised. Nothing stirred. He brought the glasses back to McNair's cabin, then looked at the house upriver from it. This was a log home built in similar architectural style as Sinclair's but with a blue roof rather than a green one. A gleaming Adirondack guide boat trailered behind a Ford Expedition told him the house belonged to Lucas Ventura, the movie producer and hotshot angler Stranahan had met at Summersby's party. Ventura had invited Stranahan to go fishing with him in the guide boat—when was that? Saturday coming up, a week away. Well, thought Stranahan, some other time, some other life. But he could understand Ventura's pride in the craft, with its arched spruce ribs, beautifully flared gunwales, and the tapering blades of the long oars that were strapped inside the hull.

In the sky, the sun moved with majestic lethargy toward Lobo Mesa in the west. A shadow darted up the mountain under the wings of a hawk. A mule deer doe and two fawns walked out of the draw below, contoured the hill, disappeared.

At 7 p.m. Tony Sinclair walked out the front door of his house. He pulled on waders hanging from a wall peg, circled an aerosol can of mosquito repellent around his head, and picked across the cobbles of a dry river channel toward the sapphire ribbon beyond, holding his fly rod backward so it wouldn't catch the brush. Stranahan pulled on his sweatshirt and stretched, his butt and legs aching from the surveillance. Just what in hell did he figure to accomplish up here, anyway?

Standing up brought into view the irrigation ditch he'd crossed earlier. It sucked two-thirds of the water from the creek; now Stranahan noticed that the other third formed a narrow stream that drained the escarpment all the way down to the river. The stream was obscured by a line of brush, but here and there pools gleamed like string lights, shards of brilliance in the otherwise dark monotony of the landscape. Below the last drop in elevation was a larger pool—a beaver pond? It was all but obscured by a stand of aspens and red willow. From the downstream edge of the pond, the creek flowed weakly across the sagebrush flat before emptying into the river through a ravine that separated McNair's cabin from Ventura's mansion.

A rim of algal scum bordered the pond. From the access drive to McNair's cabin, faint tire tracks led to a copse of trees below it. The color white caught Stranahan's eye. Through the lenses it looked like a bucket, turned upside down on the bank of the pond. A seat to take when you wanted to drown a worm and fish, but fish for what?

Stranahan felt his face flush, then a sensation like an ice cream freeze in his brain. The pond, the tire tracks, the bucket. McNair's cabin was only a few hundred yards away. If he owned a ten-acre plot like his neighbors did, then the property would include the pond. Sheriff Ettinger had mentioned checking bodies of water in the area, but this one would be invisible from the access road. A perfect place to do—to do what?

"Just maybe drown a man," he heard himself say.

A rolling shadow climbed the ridge Stranahan was sitting on. He shivered, as much from unease as from the chill. House lights flashed on in Summersby's place, then in Sinclair's and Gentry's. McNair's cabin remained swallowed in darkness. Stranahan started to switch-back down the ridge, thinking of his next move.

Back at the trailhead, he shrugged into his fishing vest. He grabbed his fly rod—it would provide an excuse should anyone inquire about his presence—and locked the Land Cruiser. A tide of anxiety rose inside him. For the first time since moving west, he regretted not carrying something to protect himself with.

Years before, when the investigative footwork he did for his grand-father's law firm danced into corners of Boston's Southie, before the yuppie restaurateurs turned grit into glitter, he'd asked Percy McGill if he should apply for a concealed weapons permit. McGill, the former police detective who headed investigations for the old man, was a hirsute Black Irishman who wore sport coats tailored to conceal the suede shoulder holster he wore over his cream linen shirts. In the office, the holster invariably hung from the hook of an old-fashioned hat rack under McGill's Panama fedora. He'd answered Stranahan's question by stepping to the hat rack and pulling his 9mm Beretta from the holster. Silently, he proffered the piece, holding it by the barrel.

Stranahan had felt the cool steel, the authoritative compact weight.

"Now aim it at my heart," McGill had said.

"But . . ."

"Full clip, nothing in the chamber. Aim the gun." McGill stood up, offering the broad expanse of his chest.

Again, Stranahan had hesitated.

"I could have shot you five times by now. Raise the damned gun."

Stranahan brought the Beretta to bear, holding it at arm's length with his left hand cupped under the grip. McGill gave him his dead look, his cop eyes. Stranahan felt his heart beating and smelled the sweat and cologne from McGill's body. The muzzle wavered.

McGill reached out and took the gun from Stranahan's hand.

"In real life," he said quietly, "pointing a gun at a human being is the most serious thing you can do. It has consequences. You're a good kid. You handle yourself okay. I've seen you stand up to people. I was surprised, frankly. But you don't have any police training and I think a couple years from now you'll be doing something else. You're too smart to run down boulevard scum all your life. But . . . "—he cocked his head slightly—"if you pack a gun, and you ever get in a situation where you have to pull it—that's a line you don't want to cross. You can go to court with a chance of doing time. It's legitimate self-defense, you'll still have to live with what you did. It will change you. It'll distance you from your wife, your kids, your good mother. Not to mention that old man who loves you like the son he lost." He pointed at the door to the next office.

McGill holstered the handgun. Then he reached out and clasped a hand across the back of Stranahan's neck.

"Come on, let's go down to Louie's and get a coupla meatball sand-wiches. Lunch's on me."

Stranahan had never thought about buying a handgun again.

Still, it would be good to have something. He unlocked the rig, found the canister of pepper spray he carried in grizzly country, and zipped it into a pocket of his fishing vest. Then he made a makeshift sheath for his pocketknife from a scrap of cardboard and duct-taped it firmly to his calf. He opened the blade, stuck it securely into the sheath and pulled his sock over it. He felt a bit foolish, and it was going to hurt like a son of a bitch pulling the tape off his calf.

He locked the rig and struck out along a game trail following the course of the creek, the circle of his penlight penetrating the tangled branches of the willows.

CHAPTER THIRTY-FIVE

Black Masks

The pond hid in leaf shadow, its surface still but for a riffle of pewter at the inlet.

Not sure what he was looking for besides footprints, Stranahan began to circle it, shading the penlight lens with his handkerchief to dampen its glow. The white object turned out to be a Styrofoam cooler. Stranahan lifted the lid. A half dozen empty Coors Light cans eddied in a few inches of melted ice. Stranahan dipped a finger into the water. Cold. Someone had been here earlier today.

Near the earthen dam that funneled the pond's outlet, a trail disappeared into a copse of aspen. Stranahan found a flattened bit of ground with tire tracks in hardened mud, commas of rut where a vehicle had turned around. Someone had parked here several times in recent weeks. Stranahan knew it would be easy enough to match the tread to a vehicle, although if it identified McNair's Sierra Classic, what would it mean? A man was entitled to visit his own property. But if it matched the hatchery truck?

Stranahan heard an owl hoot behind him. As he turned back toward the pond, he felt a presence. He became aware of a lifting sensation, as if the gravitational pull of the earth had been momentarily suspended. Instinctively, he backed into the trees. He was turning to leave when a shuffling noise caught his attention. There was a trilling purr as a raccoon, silver in the moonlight, emerged from the brush and lumbered down the bank. It was followed single file by three kits. The raccoons stepped into the shallows and hunted around, digging with their forefeet. When the larger raccoon flipped something onto the bank, the kits pointed their black masks at it, then dove in as one. In the ensuing tug-of-war, one kit emerged with the morsel and galloped up the bank, closely followed by the others. A crawdad, Stranahan figured. Now the mother raccoon had caught something else. This time Stranahan distinctly saw a torpedo shape glistening from the coon's teeth. A fish shape, about six inches long. The raccoon dropped it on the bank, where it was descended upon by the kits.

In the next twenty minutes, this scenario was repeated half a dozen times. Stranahan knew that raccoons were proficient anglers, but surely trout were more difficult to catch than this. He watched, baffled. Then, an explanation dawned and one more puzzle piece locked into place. He felt a flush of excitement.

The raccoons were leaving. Stranahan unhooked the woolly bugger from the cork grip of his fly rod, walked down to the bank and flicked the fly into the pond. He twitched it, felt a minute tug, then another. A shiver of wavelets popped up as the fish fought over the fly. Stranahan retrieved the woolly bugger. It was too big for the fish's mouths. He substituted a small wet fly, tying it on by feel because he didn't want to use the light more than necessary. Immediately he hooked up and skittered a small trout to his hand. He put the barrel of the flashlight in his mouth and twisted it on, but even without it he could tell that something was wrong with the fish. The head was lopsided, with a deep cavity under one eye. The rear third of the body was black. Stranahan had never seen a fish infected with whirling disease before, but it didn't take a book to confirm his suspicion. He whacked the fish on the back of its head with a stone.

Stranahan patted the pockets of his vest. Finding a ziplock bag that had once protected a disposable camera, more recently a bologna sandwich, he slipped the fish inside. It wanted for company only as long as it took to make another cast. A few minutes later there were five in the bag, all showing posterior discoloration, while one also had a misshapen mandible. One fingerling infected with whirling disease in the Madison drainage wasn't an anomaly, but a pond teaming with them? Now, Stranahan thought, the sheriff would have to act.

"Time to vamoose," he muttered aloud and, reeling in the line, heard the owl hoot a second time. He turned his head toward the sound. As he did, a blur shot toward him. He went down hard with the impact, his head smacking the water. He felt a viselike grip on his legs and struggled to turn his face up to breathe. For a moment he surfaced, sputtering, then felt his legs hoisted into the air and went under again.

He kicked frantically. His chest seemed ready to explode. An image of childhood flicked in his head, over and over, like a flashcard. He was running down a hill, his feet tripping forward so fast he was almost falling, tripping and falling toward a redbrick house, but the house was getting farther away, then farther. . . .

He swelled up out of the darkness, hearing a choking noise. He was on wet ground, his body convulsing. The pain was unlike anything he'd known, his chest breaking in half with each cough. He was swimming in and out in flashes; then a shot of light bounced off his head, and, mercifully, the noise of his body began to recede away.

When Stranahan came to, he was staring at a naked woman. She was a platinum blonde, without a pore or hair follicle on her body. The polished finger of a knife protruded from her navel. His eyes came into focus. He saw that the woman was a *Playboy* centerfold, tacked up on the wall of what looked like a workroom.

He lifted his head off his chest and spat, a thin stream of blood running down his chin onto his soaked fly-fishing vest. His lower lip burned like hell. Touching it with his tongue, he felt a lump. He tried to reach a hand to his face, but it wouldn't move. His hands were bound behind his back with something tight and sticky—duct tape? His feet also were bound and he was sitting on a chair, the chair backed up to a work table mounted with a heavy vise.

Hearing a keening whine behind him, he swiveled his head. The chair creaked under his weight. Apple McNair was hunched under a naked lightbulb that illuminated a grinding wheel, his face set in a tight-lipped grimace behind a shower of sparks.

"I see you've come around," he said, his eyes fixed to the wheel. "Twasn't sure you would."

McNair held a blade about six inches long up for critical inspection. He dipped the blade into a bucket of what looked like motor oil and wiped it with a rag.

He said, "D two seems to hold the heat longer than stainless. Why, I don't know."

He took the tip of the blade between his thumb and first two fingers and abruptly jerked his arm toward the wall behind Stranahan. There was no time to duck, just an instant shivering in the air. Stranahan turned to see the blade, trembling silver, neatly incising the airbrushed nipple of another centerfold, an amply endowed brunette playfully wielding a pitchfork in a hay barn.

"Oh, do me again." The obscenity of McNair's falsetto voice rang through the shed.

Stranahan felt the hairs lift at his temples.

"Look," he mumbled, the words stinging as he tried to speak around the swelling in his lip. "There's been an 'um mithunderstanding. I was coming back from fishing the river and I'd noticed the pond earlier. I was just going to ma—make a few casts." I'm sorry for trethpassing. I didn't know it was your land."

McNair snorted. "I seen your rig. Ask me, Sheep Crick trailhead's a strange place to park if you're fishing the Madison."

"Not if, if you want to fish the Quake outlet. It's longer to hike up from the bridge."

"You poking around the crick with a flashlight. I got eyes. I seen you from the house." His voice was flat. "You ain't here to fish no river."

McNair's head was cocked. His mouth sagged open, forming a black oval hole in the beard. There seemed to be a question in his eyes.

He doesn't know who I am, Stranahan thought suddenly. He never got close enough to look at me at Henry's Lake the morning he shot Sam, and he can't remember me from Summersby's party. He tried to recall the night. He'd introduced himself to McNair after nightfall, on the dark end of the porch. They had been two shadows talking. Stranahan had recognized the heeler dog only because it was sitting under the porch lamp.

As if the man could read his mind, McNair pushed up his safety goggles and looked hard at Stranahan. Below the simian shelf of his forehead, his right eye roamed.

"I seen you before," he said. "I know your voice."

There was a buzzing sound. McNair pulled a cell phone from his jeans pocket and turned his head.

Stranahan heard him say, "Yeah."

"Did you figure out who he is?"

The masculine voice at the other end of the line sounded metallic. The cell was on speaker phone.

"He just swum to. We getting round to it."

"Get around to it, then," the man said. "Find out why—" His voice abruptly stopped.

"Is this on speaker?"

Stranahan saw Apple McNair mouth the word "fuck."

"Shut your phone," the voice commanded. "Go into the house and wait for me to call you on the landline. This has got to be fixed, you understand me? We're going to fix this. Do it."

McNair snapped the phone shut. His grimy beard jutted at Stranahan. The voice dropped in register.

"Make yourself comfortable." He barked a guttural laugh, but his face had taken on a petulant, childlike look. He'd been chastised in Stranahan's presence and couldn't meet his eyes.

"It doesn't have to go this way," Stranahan said. He forced himself to speak through the pain and enunciate clearly.

The man acted as if he hadn't heard.

"Kidnapping's a serious crime. Cut this tape off and we'll call it even. Nobody has to get in this deep over a few fish, especially if it's your feet to the flames and someone else is calling the shots."

"Fish?" McNair's voice was quizzical.

"The trout in the pond. I caught a couple. It's doesn't have to be a big deal."

"The fish is the key that unlocks the land," McNair said cryptically. He nodded to himself. "Don't you know that?"

He walked past Stranahan, his face in profile, but his near eye, the roaming eye, rolling over to regard him from the corner of the socket. A frown tugged the man's brow into three deep folds as he shut the door behind him.

Stranahan's first thought was to scream. But the closest house, Sinclair's, was at least one hundred yards away. He had gone fishing and might still be out. His wife could be home, but Eva was deaf. Ventura, who owned the only other house within shouting distance, had told Stranahan that he'd be out of state, so probably only McNair would hear him. Then McNair would come back to silence him. Screaming would lose him what little time he had to gather his wits.

He glanced around, his eyes drawn to the knives driven into the pinups. The blade that had whizzed over Stranahan's head stuck out of the wall only a few feet away. Was there a chance?

Stranahan jerked up, almost losing his balance. A weight inside his head shifted, making him nauseous. He concentrated on breathing. The nausea passed.

You're going to get one chance, he told himself. *Don't fuck it up.* He hopped over to the pinup. McNair had not affixed a handle to the blade that pinned the brunette's breast to the wall. Bending down, he clamped his teeth around the steel tang. He pressed his head down. The point was driven into the unpainted fiberboard that was tacked over the old chinked logs. It didn't budge. He let go with his teeth and pressed the tang down with his chin. Then he nudged the tang upward with the top of his head. Up, down, sideways. The blade was getting loose. Again he took the tang in his teeth. He tugged. The blade came free so suddenly his teeth almost lost their grip.

Now what? He had the knife, but could he position it to cut the tape on his hands? He scanned McNair's work table, his eyes drawn to the bolted vise. If he could clamp the blade into the vise, then he could back up to it and slice through the tape that bound his hands.

He hopped to the table, trying to focus but unable to help thinking about the time ticking away. He knew he had at most a few minutes before the door swung open and McNair barked that guttural laugh. . . .

Stranahan studied the vise. The jaws were ajar a quarter inch or so, about the same width as the knife tang. A stroke of luck. He rotated the knife in his teeth until the blade edge faced up. Bending, he tried to nudge the tang into the jaws. The jaws were too tight. He pushed his chin against the steel rod that acted as the vise handle and inched it left. He knew if he opened the jaws too wide, it would be impossible to close them while holding the tang in position with his teeth. He tried to wedge the knife into the gap. Still too tight. He tried a third time. The tang inched partway down into the jaws and stopped. Stranahan gingerly released his grip with his teeth, praying the knife wouldn't fall out. Quickly, he bent to press the handle to the right with his chin, pressing as hard as he could to tighten the jaws of the vice.

"Now for the easy part," he muttered out loud, and winced. His teeth ached. Stranahan backed up to the table and tried to lift his bound hands high enough to reach the upturned blade. He couldn't quite reach it. He noted a sawed section of two-by-six on the floor. He swiveled his boots back and forth, toeing the board closer to the table. Then he turned and hopped up onto the board backward. It made him just tall enough. Lifting his wrists behind his back, he positioned them over the upturned blade by feel.

He sawed down with his wrists, not knowing if he was cutting tape or flesh. A searing pain like a paper cut made him wince. Fuck it, he thought, the worst that could happen was he'd slit his wrists and bleed to death. If he didn't get free, he was going to die anyway. He was sure of that much.

He sawed his wrists back and forth. With a jerk they broke apart. Swinging his arms out in front of him, he saw blood dripping from his wrists onto the floor. At least the wounds weren't spurting. Working with nearly numb hands, he got the knife out of the vise and cut the tape at his ankles. He lurched toward the door, his right hand tightly gripping the tang of the knife. He stopped to listen. Nothing. He pushed the door open and stepped outside. Stranahan's feet felt like wood blocks as he stumbled around the far corner of the workshop. He could see lights in Sinclair's house, beyond it more lights in Summersby's. The dull sheen of Sinclair's pond, where the antelope had been shot, was in a line with the two mansions, only a few hundred feet away. Now Stranahan could hear McNair's voice raised in the cabin. He patted the pocket of his vest. The fish were still there, but the pepper spray was gone. McNair must have found it.

Stay on the phone, he thought to himself. *Keep talking.*

Trying to pick up his pace, he caught one foot on the other and fell heavily. He pushed back up with his arms and shuffled forward. He could feel sharp pain as the circulation in his feet was restored.

Behind him, he heard a door open, then shut. McNair, coming from the cabin.

Stranahan panicked. Sinclair's house was still too far away.

"God-dammit." He heard the snarl of McNair's voice.

Only a few more steps to the pond. Stranahan stumbled down the bank, his shoes sticking in the muck, then waded into the water. He sank up to his neck. He could hear McNair banging about in the workshop, then the searching beam of a flashlight.

He tipped his head back until only his nose and mouth were above the surface. If McNair came his way, shone the light over the pond, he'd try to sink to the bottom. Then it would come down to how long he could stay down, as opposed to how long McNair searched.

But the flashlight beam was moving away, bobbing as McNair sprinted up the road. He thinks I've run back to the pond where he found me, Stranahan thought, where I caught the trout. But almost as soon as that occurred to him, the flashlight beam swung around. McNair was heading toward him again. Stranahan could hear the man cursing: "Fuck, fuck, fuck" as the beam shone around. He was maybe fifty yards away, then thirty . . . twenty.

The flashlight beam raced across the sage, flared on the far bank of the pond. Stranahan took a deep breath and ducked underwater. Reaching down, he felt into the mucky bottom for something to hold on to, to keep himself from floating to the surface. His left hand clasped around what felt like the branch of a log. He opened his eyes in the stew of algae and saw, diffused, the flashlight's beam on the water surface. His chest felt tight. He let out a few bubbles of breath, clamping down on the reflex to breathe. Deliberately, he started to count.

Forty-nine, fifty, fifty-one . . .

The light on the surface was gone, the water black. One hundred twenty-two, one hundred twenty. . . . Stranahan burst to the surface, gasping. Taking huge gulps of air, he craned his neck, looking for the light. There it was, by the door of McNair's cabin. The man was heading into the house. For what—to get a rifle? Stranahan waited a minute, pondering the odds of making it to Sinclair's house before being shot down. He thought he heard McNair's voice. Was he talking to himself, or on the phone again? Then he was coming out, his silhouette bulked by something he was carrying. It looked like a bag or suitcase, something blocky. But not, thank God, a rifle. Stranahan heard a clang as McNair pitched something into the bed of his pickup. Then he heard the engine turn over. The black beetle of the truck turned out the driveway, motoring with the lights out. Within a minute the sound faded.

Stranahan lunged out of the pond.

CHAPTER THIRTY-SIX

Lothar

"There he stood, bleeding all over my porch, a goddamned knife in his hand. I thought he—you're stepping in it, Sheriff."

She stepped to the side.

"Like I told you on the phone, muck up to his waist, he was shaking so bad he could hardly stay on his feet. A trout fly sticking in his lip. Lucky it didn't have a barb. I backed it out easy enough. Wrapped up his wrists, don't know how much blood he lost but it stopped with pressure. I said I'd drive him to the clinic in West Yellowstone but he's stubborn, just kept telling me to call you."

Tony Sinclair closed the door after Martha Ettinger.

Stranahan was sitting at the dining room table, his swathed wrists up on the distressed wood tabletop.

"Not going to drip blood on Mr. Sinclair's fine furniture, are we?" Ettinger said by way of greeting.

"No. Afraid I ruined one of his cowboy shirts, though." Stranahan's lip was twice normal size, his voice a mumble.

"Not going to die on me?"

He shook his head.

She took the chair opposite.

"Give me the ten-minute version first."

He dabbed his lip with a bag of ice cubes that Sinclair had given him.

"Humph," Ettinger said when he finished. "You're certain those trout you caught had whirling disease?"

"No, but they fit the description. They're still in a bag in the pocket of my vest."

"We'll have someone test them at the Bridger hatchery tomorrow."

"What about McNair?" Stranahan asked. "Did you get him?"

"We had deputies at Ennis and the 191 T-junction north of West soon as Mr. Sinclair called. I asked the Idaho sheriff to post someone at Last Chance with a vehicle description, but by the time I made the calls, response time after that"—she shrugged—"he could have slipped the net."

The kitchen phone rang.

Sinclair picked it up. "For you, Sheriff."

"Really? . . . Where?" She listened. "What, rolled over? . . . 'kay . . . I know where it is. . . . Yeah, the house is next door. I'll get what I can find. I'll meet you there in twenty."

She set the phone on the cradle.

"We got the truck," she said. "Guy camping up Beaver Creek saw it swerve in front of his car to turn up the forest road. It was out of control. Driver flipped him the finger and the camper called it in, bless his offended little heart. Walt says the truck rolled over five miles up the logging road heading for the Hilgard Peaks. He's up there with a couple SAR now."

"SAR?"

"Search and Rescue. Katie's on the way from West and she's got Lothar ready to go. You feel up to a manhunt, Stranahan?"

"I'm ready." On the tabletop was the bloodstained knife blade with which he'd cut his wrists free. He picked it up.

"Mr. Sinclair, I thank you for your help tonight. A deputy will be by to take your statement. Please give my apologies to your wife. You two must be getting tired of our intrigue."

"Not at all," the man said as Ettinger and Stranahan passed him. "Summers in Montana are more exciting than I thought they'd be." But he was talking to the door.

Outside, Stranahan saw the lights flashing from the county rig parked at McNair's cabin. Ettinger walked right by the Cherokee, striding toward the lights.

"I thought we were going to where the truck wrecked," Stranahan said.

"We are. We're just going to avail ourselves of some of Mr. McNair's unmentionables first."

"Lothar's a tracking dog?"

"Now you got the picture."

A deputy stood outside the door. He had McNair's heeler dog, was stroking its head.

"Heeler's are a one-man dog, but this one's dead calm," he observed. "Door was unlocked. He was sitting on the couch, come up to sniff my hand."

The place was a sty.

"Men live alone, they tend to become feral," Stranahan noted.

Ettinger grunted. From a pile of clothing on the couch she chose a wadded up T-shirt that wasn't too matted with dog hair and sealed it in a plastic bag. She paused at a gun cabinet with a glass front. There were indents in the rack for five guns but only four stood at attention. Stranahan examined the engraved numbers on the barrel of the lone scoped rifle in the rack to see if it was a .243, the caliber Sam had been shot with.

".257 Roberts," he said. "Maybe he took the .243 with him."

"Did you see him carry a rifle to his truck?"

"It was dark. He had something that looked bulky, but I don't think it was a rifle."

Ettinger dug her fingernails into her scalp. "You didn't happen to see if he had a gun rack in the cab?"

"No, I can't swear that I was ever even inside the truck, but I don't know how else he got me to his shop. But gun rack, no gun rack, doesn't mean much. McNair could just as easy keep the rifle on the back bench wrapped in a blanket."

The sheriff blew out a breath. "He's armed, you can count on it. We're wasting time. Let's get up there."

Twenty-five minutes later, the Cherokee's headlights lit up the road-block. There were three vehicles—Walt's county rig, a Chevy Diesel 4x4 with an ATV chained in the bed, and a white F-150 pickup.

"That's Casper. Katie's truck," Ettinger said.

As they got out of the Cherokee, Walt detached himself from the group of figures clustered around the hood of the big diesel and came up, his headlamp glancing up brilliantly into Stranahan's eyes.

"Turn that damned thing off," Ettinger said.

"McNair's truck's down yonder." Walt switched the light off and pointed down the hill toward the creek. "Looks like he came to the turn and slid over the edge. I was presupposing when I told you it turned over. Warren figures it just tipped on its side and stopped when it come up against the bank."

"Did you search the vehicle?"

"Only the outside. Didn't open the door. Didn't know if you'd be calling in Little Feather to do an evidence search and work the track."

"Harold went back to Browning," Ettinger said.

"Well, we don't need an Indian to foller this son of a bitch. We got the dog."

"Did you happen to see if there's a gun rack."

"Sure."

"And?"

"There's a two-gun rack in the cab. No weapons in evidence. I put the page out to the hasty team at SAR and they're geared up. But nobody's coming from the civilian side till you say the word."

"I can't say the word if we think he's armed, you know that."

"I do know that. That's why I called Katie instead of the other K nine. She's a park ranger so that makes her law enforcement."

"So there's just us five, then."

"Six, counting your buddy here. Who shouldn't be here, I might add."

"Mr. Stranahan's part of the investigation. I deputized him on the drive over."

Walt briefly raised his eyes to acknowledge Stranahan.

"Okay. Six then," he said.

Martha jangled the keys in her pants pocket, realized what she was doing indicated indecision, and stopped. Beside her, Stranahan let the news of his newly appointed position sink in.

"Let's look at the map," Ettinger said.

A twelve-volt lantern on the hood of the big Chevy illuminated the faces of the squad. Stranahan was introduced to the other deputies, who had gathered around a topo map spread on the hood. Jason Kent had sandy hair and was dressed in Carhartt overalls. A big man crowding fifty, he wore a weary face that reminded Stranahan of a farmer who'd seen too much weather. Sheriff's Sergeant Warren Jarrett stood ramrod straight and offered a hard hand. His black mustache was neatly trimmed and shopped around as his front teeth worked on a toothpick. He looked to have been born to wear the uniform. Katie Sparrow had a petite build and couldn't have been more than five feet tall.

"Pleased to meet-cha," she said briskly, glancing toward Stranahan before turning back to the map.

"What do we have here?" Ettinger cut to the chase.

"You mean besides rain coming on and the highest density of grizzly bears outside Yellowstone Park?" Sergeant Jarrett said without the trace of a smile.

Ettinger looked at Kent.

"You're incident commander, Jase. It's your show."

Kent rapped the knuckles of his big hand on the hood.

"Tonight's a nonstarter," he said. "If this was a lost hunter who wanted to be found, I'd say go. Do an attraction and containment with the Hasty Team, build a bonfire he could spot from a vantage, send an ATV up every trail. We'd round him up. But in the night, man who's probably armed, us shining flashlights, he'd more likely find us."

"I'm willing," Walt said.

"It isn't about willing," Kent said. His voice was matter-of-fact. "It's about assessing risk and not being reckless."

Ettinger set her right elbow on the hood and cupped her chin with her hand. She didn't say anything for a long minute.

Then: "Jase is right. I don't know if Walt has filled you in, but this guy's suspected of killing two people and may have put a bullet into a third, who was damned lucky to survive. And his intentions toward Mr. Stranahan tonight were less than honorable. If he feels threatened, he'll get one of us before we have a chance at him. Let's do this by the book. We'll have numbers up here tomorrow, we'll get an all-points out, we'll catch him in the net."

"We're here now."

It was Katie Sparrow, the K9 handler.

"We've got point-last-seen. Lothar can give us direction-headed. We'll work slow with no lights. We won't give him a target. But I don't think this guy will shoot unless we're pressing him."

"I don't, either," Walt said. "He's trying to get away. If we can follow him far enough to figure where he's headed, we'll have a better chance tomorrow than if we don't. I mean, he could pull a mountain man or head back down into the valley, be nice to know which."

"Can I say something?" Stranahan felt five sets of eyes turn toward him.

"What the hell happened to your lip?" Walt said.

Ettinger sketched out the details of the evening in three terse sentences. Walt whistled.

Stranahan said, "I saw McNair carry something from his house and throw it into the bed of his truck just before he took off. Like a suitcase, or maybe a backpack. Was anything like that in the truck?"

"Warren, you checked it out," Walt said.

Jarrett shook his head. "When the truck tipped over, a bicycle slid out of the bed. Other than that just a few rusty tools, vise grips, wirecutters, like that."

"Katie?" Ettinger nodded her chin toward the white pickup, where the shepherd sat bolt upright in the passenger seat, his ears in silhouette. "If it rains tonight, can your dog still work the trail tomorrow?"

"That depends how much it rains. But we got heavy air and damp undergrowth to hold the scent, conditions are prime right now. This guy's only got about a two-hour lead. Could I see what you brought?"

Ettinger motioned for Stranahan to retrieve the T-shirt from the Cherokee. Katie opened the ziplock. Walt dropped his head for a sniff.

"My Christ, Martha. That man's got odor like a yeller dog. Be 'bout as hard as follerin' a turd skidding down the icing on a wedding cake."

Katie zipped up the bag. Stranahan noticed the steel in her gaze as she looked at Ettinger. In profile, her cheeks and the corners of her eyes had a corrugated look. Sun and wind had made a map of her face.

"So whatcha' think?" she said.

Stranahan could see the sheriff's resolve waver.

"I think Katie makes a point," Ettinger said. "This is a chance we can't pass up. No lights. We'll only follow far enough to make an educated guess."

A short council of war later, Katie Sparrow leashed the shepherd, fed him the scent, and led him in a perimeter search of the truck. Lothar hit a low note and strained with his head down.

"He's got it," she said.

Stranahan watched the cluster of red and blue LCD bulbs from the dog handler's Carnivore Tracking Light cast rusty circles on the grass. It would make blood drops shine like diamonds in a coal mine. If McNair had injured himself he could be close by, which would place the team in danger much sooner than if he had disappeared into the timber on sound legs.

Sparrow held the dog at the forest edge as Stranahan and Ettinger, along with the two deputies—Warren Jarrett had a scoped rifle slung over his shoulder—came up to join her. Kent, as incident commander, would normally have remained with the rigs to relay radio messages, but as he and Jarrett had the most SAR experience, Walt had agreed to stay instead.

"Blood?" Ettinger asked.

Sparrow shook her head.

"Okay then, like we agreed on," Ettinger whispered. "Jase and Warren stay five paces in back of Katie, Sean and I bring up the rear. Everyone has the roadblock marked as a GPS waypoint, right?"

Jason Kent slowly shook his head. "I still don't like this," he said. "Katie, you're on point here. You're assuming the biggest risk. It's beyond call of duty."

"Let's just go," the handler said.

The team took up the track, the sheperd leading them west into the forest, then turning to climb until it reached a game track worn deep by the hooves of elk. The dog contoured, then left the track to climb straight uphill, the slope so steep that Stranahan found himself grasping onto lodgepole trunks to haul himself up.

"The son of a bitch has lungs," Martha whispered, her breathing heavy.

Clouds had slipped under the stars and Stranahan could no longer see the faces of the posse, only their profiles. There was a grumble overhead, a deep clearing of the throat that heralded the rain.

The dog hunted on through the first drops, then into a downpour so hard the rain bounced off his head. He stopped to shake.

"Well?" Ettinger said, water drops beading on the billed hood of her parka.

Sparrow shook her head. "The rain's going to wash the ground scent, especially in the open areas. Lothar will still be able to stay on him in the trees, catch scent that's trapped under the canopy, but it's going to be a slow go. If the wind picks up, we're FUBARed, pardon my French."

"Let's see where we are."

A copse of spruce trees just off the track offered marginal canopy cover. Warren Jarrett punched up the map page on his Garmin GPS, the contour lines highlighted on a green screen. He tapped the Out button to change the scale. The triangle icon showing their position appeared under a whorl of contours marking Wolverine Peak.

"We're about six hundred feet below the crest," Jarrett said. "He's climbed this high, I think we can assume he's going to top over into the Hilgard Basin. That's wilderness with a capital W."

"Then let's call it good," Ettinger said. "With the dog working this slow we're not going to catch up and I don't think we want to. I don't know about the rest of you, but I could use some sleep, even if it's in the Jeep. We need to save our strength for the big push tomorrow."

"Katie, you don't agree?" The handler was shaking her head.

"No. I'm just pissed off at God." She knelt down to let the shepherd nose at her face.

Kent spoke. "We go back down this trail now, someone could fall and break his leg. It'll be safer if we take cover until the storm blows over."

"Don't you ever get tired of being the voice of reason?" Ettinger said. Stranahan caught the exasperation in her tone.

"I'm just stating the obvious," Kent said.

So that was that. The group split up to shelter under the spruces.

Stranahan found one that offered enough dry space for both he and Ettinger to sit shoulder to shoulder with their backs to the trunk.

"Cozy, huh?"

"Don't get any ideas." Ettinger pressed up against his side.

"So I'm your deputy now, huh?"

"Deputy, slave, minion of my kingdom, take your pick."

"Are you authorized to do that?"

"I'm the sheriff. I can do anything I want."

Stranahan felt her take a deep breath, her side pressing into him, then she let it out in a long sigh.

"What did you expect, Martha—that we'd find McNair fast asleep under a tree like this one?"

"I'm just mad at myself for not seeing it before. If Walt and I had been more thorough, we would have found that pond. It didn't show on the map, but that's no excuse. And McNair. You were right about the guy and I wasn't."

"Don't be so hard on yourself."

"You think it's easy being a woman sheriff in this state? If I didn't expect a lot out of myself I'd never be wearing the badge."

They sat quietly for a while, listening to distant claps of thunder.

"So I know I already asked you," Ettinger said, "but you're absolutely sure those fish in the pond had whirling disease?"

"No, but the black tails, the misshapen heads, I'd be surprised if they didn't." Beside him, he sensed Martha shake her head.

"You don't seem convinced," he said.

"No, what I'm having a hard time wrapping my head around is why. Why is McNair, a guy who lives in a shack, driving a truck around the state dumping diseased fish into the rivers? And why put some into that particular pond? From what you said there must be hundreds in there. What's in it worth killing two people, not to mention the Meslik shooting? You take those kind of measures, the payoff has to be commensurate to the risk."

"Maybe there wasn't much risk. If it hadn't been for Vareda Beaudreux's brother driving by that evening, no one would have known the difference. I think this thing just got out of hand and snowballed."

"Even so, I'm still asking myself the same question—why? Is there a money angle we're missing? And who's this mysterious man he was talking to on the phone?"

"Have someone investigate the hatchery. That's my advice."

"Oh, I will."

"Do you smell smoke?" Stranahan said.

"No, do you?"

"For a second there." Stranahan tipped his head out from under the spruce. "No, it's probably just my imagination."

He wedged back against the trunk. He could feel Ettinger shiver against his shoulder.

"Here." Stranahan put his arm around her and pressed the side of her more firmly against him. "Don't worry. The minion of the kingdom won't get any ideas."

Stranahan could feel Ettinger's regular breathing and had nearly dozed off himself when he heard footfalls approaching. Warren Jarrett lifted the lowest spruce bough to peer at them.

"Rain's let up, Sheriff," he said.

Ettinger cleared her head.

"Thanks, Warren."

He backed away.

"Fuck," Ettinger said. Her body had become rigid against Stranahan's side. "He caught me sound asleep in the arms of a man. How's that look?"

"Is it really bad as that?"

"No, Warren's a boy scout. He won't tell anyone. But he'll look at me different. I'll seem weaker to him."

"Everyone here looks up to you. You're underestimating yourself."

"Yeah, right." There was a note of resignation in her voice. "Come on. Let's get back to the trucks."

CHAPTER THIRTY-SEVEN

The Playboy of King Salmon Drive

Lothar found McNair's campsite at midmorning. The fugitive had sat out the storm under a spruce tree about a quarter mile farther up the mountainside from the tree that Stranahan and Ettinger sheltered under. He'd torn the corner of a 7.5 minute series topographic quad to start a fire; they found a curled edge of the map in the ashes.

"Son of a bitch," Katie Sparrow said.

Ettinger bit down on her lower lip.

"Hey, Stranahan, get over here. Remember what you said? 'What did you expect to find, McNair asleep under a tree like this one?' Well, that's right where the bastard was, damned near close enough to hear us talk about him. To think we were that close"—she pinched her fingers together—"we could have ended it if the big man up there had just decided to cooperate."

"Maybe the big man did us a favor," Stranahan said. "If it hadn't rained, we would have got closer and he could have shot one of us."

They stood by the tree—Ettinger, Stranahan, Sparrow, Jarrett, and Harold Little Feather, who had driven through the night from Browning after receiving Ettinger's call from the satellite phone.

The shepherd cast in circles trying to pick up scent on the wet grass.

Stranahan shook his head. "I thought I smelled smoke. Remember me telling you that? It was this fire."

Ettinger compressed her lips.

"Fuck, fuck, fuck," she said. "We catch the bastard I'm going to kill him on general principles, guilty or not. You know what I mean?"

They were all tired as hell after a night in the pickups. Stranahan had actually slept under Jason Kent's diesel half-ton, in a sleeping bag the deputy kept in the cab.

Martha Ettinger scratched her head.

Katie Sparrow pulled a dog biscuit out of her pocket and took a bite, then put her lips around the mouthpiece on the water hose of her Camelback backpack.

"Ah," she said.

Ettinger looked at her with an expression she usually saved for Walt.

"I've been eating them for years," Sparrow said. "But only on the trail. You want?"

With the tip of his belt knife, Harold Little Feather pointed to a depression in the mud a hand span from the base of an alpine fir. The indentation was shaped like a narrow horseshoe.

"This is where he set the rifle butt when he was collecting wood for his fire. Tilted the barrel against the tree trunk. Recoil pad has a waffle pattern."

So he was armed. The news came as no surprise to Stranahan, but it cured some of the doubters on the hunt who couldn't understand why so many resources were being expended upon a person who had yet to be formally charged with a crime. Ettinger had held off processing the kidnapping charge with the DA until the department could do a proper investigation.

But there was no further progress. The rains came and went, Lothar shook his coat and worked into the wind, but couldn't pick up the scent. After three days, county funds began to dwindle. The manhunt, which had grown to include a chopper, ham radio operators, and a highbird radio repeater mounted on a single-engine

Cessna to relay messages among two dozen ground pounders, was scaled back once and then a second time.

On the fifth day after McNair disappeared, a team consisting of Stranahan, Walter Hess, and Martha Ettinger convened on the upper Madison River to conduct a second investigation of McNair's cabin, a CSI borrowed from Sweet Grass County having already been through it the morning after Stranahan was kidnapped. On that occasion, blood had been found on the instep of a size nine cowboy boot, which had been sent to the Missoula crime lab for a DNA match with a sample from the camp host who'd been stabbed at the Beaver Creek Campground.

"This place is a litter box," Ettinger said. "I can't believe how men live. All of you ought to be ashamed. Just look at this room. He's got a dumptruck's worth of shit in here.

"And the kitchen." She shook her head. At some time, the power had been shut off and the freezer had leaked a pool of blood onto the floor. It had gummed up and darkened, but still stank to high heaven.

"Maybe he got behind on his power bill," Walt said. "Then he made amends but never got around to cleaning the mess."

"Then it ought to be in the records. No man is an island, not one who owns land in Montana. There ought to be a paper trail—gas, phone, electric. Bank statements. Property taxes. Did somebody from county pick them up when they did the investigation?"

"I don't think so."

"We just conducted a detailed search here. You're telling me the man doesn't have records?"

"Maybe he keeps them in the knife shop," Stranahan said.

The knife shop was as he remembered. Stranahan took the team through what had happened that night.

"You're lucky to be alive, young man," Walt said.

Ettinger found the records under a display case of McNair's custom knives. They were neatly labeled in manila folders in a stack of Rubbermaid file boxes.

"Christ, he's even got collision insurance on that heap he wrecked up the creek," she said, sitting at McNair's workbench with the papers.

"Seems out of character, wouldn't you say so, Martha?"

"Yes, I would. Considering how he lives the rest of his life."

McNair had bimonthly pay stubs going back sixteen months from Missouri River Pisces, where he was listed as Staff, Temporary. He even had sales records for the knives, mostly sold at gun shows, from a client list that stretched several pages in a ring binder.

"He's making just enough to keep the grizzly bear from the door," Ettinger said at length. "But where did he get the money to buy this in the first place? Forget the cabin, the land's got to be worth what, a quarter million?"

"It might have been, it might not be now."

Ettinger looked at Stranahan.

"I thought riverfront was recession-proof."

"I wouldn't be so sure," Stranahan said. "I've been told that sales have slowed. Property values are climbing now that the fishing's coming back, but the market's still soft."

Ettinger raised her eyebrows.

"Sam Meslik," Stranahan said. "Guiding is a leisure dollar business. He's got his finger on the pulse of this valley."

"You don't say," Ettinger said, fingering the papers. "Look here," she said.

She spread out a few sheets of paper.

"Copy of the deed says he bought this place for . . . $137,000. Was that before or after values dropped?"

Stranahan looked at the date on the deed. McNair had only owned the place for two years. He said, "Whirling disease hit here in the mid-'90s. This is long after land values began to fall."

"Have prices gone up in the past couple years?"

"You could ask his neighbors. Sinclair and Summersby, they're board members of the homeowners' association. They'd know."

"I'd like to know how he paid for it," Ettinger said. "You look at these bank statements, he's got $600 and change in a checking account, no savings, nothing about IRAs or other assets."

She turned her attention to the papers while Walt and Stranahan methodically searched the shop.

"Two or three of these pinups are new. But most must be thirty years old," the deputy said, gazing at the glossy photos on the walls. "Yep. Back when women didn't barber their pubic hair. What do you think about that, Martha?"

Ettinger grunted. "Won't dignify," she said without lifting her eyes.

A minute passed. Ettinger pushed back in the chair and stared at the walls.

"You know you're right, Walt," she said in a thoughtful voice.

"What's that?"

"About the pinups."

"That's what I said."

"But what's it tell us?"

"The man likes a full bush?" Walt asked. "Can't say I blame him. I lean toward a natural look myself."

"No, Walt. That's not what I mean."

Stranahan spoke. "It means he brought these centerfolds with him when he moved into this place."

"Either that or found them at a garage sale or something," Ettinger said.

"No," Stranahan said. "He brought them. Here's a stack of *Playboy*s." He lifted the magazines out of a drab olive ammo box stacked against the wall and glanced at the spines. "They're all from the same year, 1979. Twelve issues, a complete set." He was rifling through the pages. "Some are missing centerfolds, maybe some of these tacked on the walls. Subscription address is a Jonathon L. McNair, 13 King Salmon Avenue, Kuskok Bay, Alaska."

"Let me see one."

Stranahan handed her a thumb-worn magazine with a crazed cover.

"Can you spot the bunny?" Walt said.

Ettinger ignored the question.

"I told you McNair was from Alaska, didn't I?" she said.

The two men looked at each other. Ettinger had been in the office during the last two days of the search. Stranahan hadn't talked to her since Tuesday.

"Well, sorry I didn't mention it earlier, but I just learned. Judy did a background check. McNair grew up in a place called Cordova, father was a commercial fisherman. Went down with his boat when the boy was ten years old. Mother took off—she was half Indian, an alcoholic. McNair and an older brother moved to Kuskok Bay to live with an aunt, the father's sister. The aunt was white, also an alcoholic. The brother attended Bristol Community College a couple years, that's right in town, then left for the lower forty-eight. McNair dropped out of school in the tenth grade. Stayed in Alaska for the next sixteen years, right till he came down here."

"What did he do for a living?" Walt said.

"Worked in canneries, did some commercial fishing, but there's no record of him running his own boat. Before he moved to Montana he was guiding for a couple lodges in Bristol Bay that cater to fly fishermen, taking anglers up and down the rivers in jet boats. Both outfits fired him. The people Judy called said some of the clients actually liked the man, or the idea of him, you know, Alaskan stoic of few words, most beginning with *f* and ending in *k*. But off the water he was too rough around the edges. He got in a fight with a camp cook and broke a steel fish cooler over the man's head. About killed him. Would have gone into the tank but the cook wouldn't press charges."

"So what brought him to Montana?" Stranahan asked.

"Judy didn't say. Consensus among the people she talked to was that he kept to himself. Basically hibernated all winter in a cabin, a real misfit or a typical Alaskan, take your pick. Just a fringe person, the kind in a small town you know mean trouble and never try to sit next to on a bar stool."

She pushed the magazine aside and wiped her hands on her pants.

"Ugh. I don't even want to think of the cooties on those pages."

"Why are you so interested in the magazines?" Walt sounded perplexed.

"Because it's odd behavior," she said. She pointed to an Alaska license plate nailed to the wall above the door. "That license plate's two years old, from the time he left Alaska. My guess is that McNair drove his truck down here on the Al-Can and brought his belongings with him—including these *Playboys*. Now why would a man of what, thirty-five, do that? And keep them all this time? Help me out here, boys."

"Don't look at me," Stranahan said.

Walt made a cross with his fingers, as if fending off a vampire.

Martha shook her head. "It makes me think that this guy dropped out of society in adolescence, that his thought process stopped moving forward before he came down here. These pinups are tokens of a time warp he lives in. And then there's the hostility, the way he's pierced them with knives. Maybe something happened back there to make him hostile to women, that turned him into a recluse."

She scratched her head. "Am I making too much of this? Walt, you took criminal psych classes at the academy."

The deputy shrugged. "Sounds reasonable, I suppose."

"Who do you figure"—Stranahan glanced at the address on the magazine cover—"Jonathon L. McNair is? The older brother?"

"That would be my guess," Ettinger said.

"What happened to him?" Stranahan said.

"Judy didn't follow up, she had her hands full as it was, but I think he's worth looking into."

She stood up. "Come on, let's get out of here. Walt, I'm putting you on hatchery detail. All we know is it's owned by an outfit in California. Dig deeper. I'll help Judy look into the family. Sean, you work the money angle. Talk to some real estate agents in the valley. Land sales are public record. You can use this." She took a card from her breast pocket and scribbled a note on the back. "Anyone has a question regarding your association with the department, tell him to call my cell."

"What is my association? I know I'm not legally a deputy."

"Helper-outer, how's that sound? I'll find a way to pay you for your time, if that's your concern."

"No, it's just that I might have to persuade someone I'm worth talking to. Helper-outer doesn't sound very . . . authoritative."

"Okay, consultant. Happy?"

"That has a better ring," Stranahan said.

At the Cherokee, Ettinger found a liter bottle of water and poured it over her hands.

She shook her head.

"Disgusting," she said. "Positively disgusting."

CHAPTER THIRTY-EIGHT

Tawdry Aubrey's Sons

Stranahan spent the following day on the phone, attempting to learn more about property values on the Madison. Sam was his first call, and subsequent inquiries with real estate agents confirmed what the fishing guide said. The disease had caused riverfront stagnation, with prime parcels simply not moving off the block for a dozen years, up until the past couple when anglers started catching more fish. During the same period, the asking price for similar properties on rivers that had escaped the depredations of whirling disease, the Big Hole for example, had more than doubled. This was interesting, but Stranahan still couldn't see how someone deliberately infecting a river to ruin its fishing could profit. Not unless the dynamic changed and property values, rather than holding, tanked in the wake of a disease outbreak. Then someone could buy up lots and, later, when the fishing came back, sell them for much more than his investment. Let the disease have its way and a lot that cost $150,000, say, might be bought for half that, then resold for anywhere from the original, predisease price to a quarter million or more when trout once again dimpled the river surface. Buy one large ranch to subdivide and a man could up his worth by millions.

He remembered something Apple McNair had said: *The trout is the key that unlocks the land.*

Well, thought Stranahan, this was one way that key could turn. But there was a snag. The investor had to know for a certainty that the river would rebound from the disease.

When his eyes began to water from staring at the computer screen in the cultural center's common room, he headed to the Bear Trap on the Madison, fly rod in hand. An hour and a couple of small brown trout later, he was hiking along the bank when the answer came to him. The quickest way for a river to recover from a depleted fishery was to plant fish back into it. And that, he thought, was where the hatchery came in. True, Montana had a wild trout program in place, meaning its rivers were sustained only by natural reproduction. No hatchery fish could be introduced. But state policy could change, especially if the disease affected the tourist industry. Sam had told him that fishing brought $500 million to the state each year, and already the fish and game department had come under pressure from angling groups to stock rivers decimated by whirling disease. The Madison's gradual recovery had stalled that movement, but if whirling disease became epidemic, those voices would become loud again, and they would be heard.

As he stepped into the next riffle and sent a soft hackle searching through the current seam, a biblical verse wormed into his head. "The Lord giveth," he said to himself, "and the Lord taketh away." Then as he cast a second time, he changed the words. "The hatchery taketh away, and the hatchery giveth back." An hour later he was in Bridger, repeating the phrase to Martha Ettinger over the phone.

"Let me get this straight," she said. "You're saying this hatchery is deliberately infecting rivers with diseased fish so that property values fall. Then, whoever is initiating the collapse is going to buy up river-front property, knowing that the fishing will rebound. And that the whole operation hinges on inside information, that whoever's behind this knows the state will renege on its wild trout program and stock the rivers with hatchery trout."

"That's what I'm saying," Stranahan said. He told her what McNair had said about the key unlocking the land. "Well, this is the key," he said. He thought a second, then added, "Maybe Missouri River Pisces is going to get a contract to help with the stocking. Then they'd be making money two ways."

"It sounds like a stretch," Ettinger said.

"It is. But it's how someone could make money with minimum risk. Thing is, there not only has to be prior knowledge that the trout fishing will come back, but also that the recovery will happen within a reasonable time frame. It can't take a decade or more like it did on the Madison. Then you'd just be paying property taxes and sitting on land you couldn't sell. You'd bleed to death."

There was silence on the line.

"You think this is another of my hunches, right? But remember—"

"No," Ettinger cut him off. "No, I'm thinking about something else I found out. I think you'd better meet me."

"I can be at your office first thing in the morning," Stranahan said.

"No, tonight. Drive out to my place. It's the old homestead up Hellroaring Creek with the weathervane on the gate. We can link into the Law and Justice computer system from here."

Stranahan ran his hand down the spine of Sheba, the longhair Siamese that had hopped onto the cherry table in Ettinger's kitchen. The cat rubbed its brittle whiskers on Stranahan's coffee cup.

"Was that your horse I saw driving in?"

"That's Petal. She's like a stone that changes color when you put it in water. She's white until it rains, then these big gray spots show up."

Stranahan had never seen Martha out of uniform and felt slightly awkward with her in the intimacy of the farmhouse. He sipped his coffee and looked past the kitchen into the living room, the chinked log walls nearly black.

"It was built in the 1880s by a Presbyterian minister," Ettinger said. "He was fleecing his flock, money from the men and the clothes off the women. When one of the husbands found out, he shot him."

"The Wild West," Stranahan said.

"Maybe then. Now it's just peaceful. It's only a few miles out of town, but I'm connected to the earth here. I can feel what it was like to live in a simpler time."

"I hear you," Stranahan said.

Ettinger smiled rather embarrassedly, as if to say, "This is who I really am."

Her voice didn't have the brusque tone he was used to. She was dressed in jeans and a blue-and-white striped shirt, like a French sailor's shirt. The color brought out the azure hue of her eyes. When Ettinger saw him looking at her, she dropped her eyes to the table, then tried to cover up her discomfort by reaching for the cat and putting it off the table.

"So," she said, the professionalism back in her voice. "The man on the phone."

"The man on the phone," Stranahan agreed.

"He's the one we're really after. McNair's only a pawn in this." She waited for Stranahan to nod. "Whether this is the kind of land grab you think it is or something else, two men dead, trout chasing their tails, this is the guy who works the strings."

Stranahan nodded again.

"So, I put Judy on the family. My instincts tell me that's where it starts. She got through to a corrections officer name of Yuto, up in Kuskok Bay. That's the town where the brothers moved after their mother left. Yuto's been around forever. He says that the aunt the boys went to live with wasn't much of a step up from the mother. Her name was Aubrey—Aubrey Anne Archer. The guys at the department called her Tawdry Aubrey. She bartended commercial fishermen places, guys who get drunk and fight because it's four men to a woman and they can't get laid. The aunt takes advantage of the equation in time-honored fashion. She hooks. Not formally, just by emptying the wallets of a string of boyfriends when they come ashore. According to Judy's source, each one of these guys really thinks he is her boyfriend, that he's helping her out, her suddenly having to support a couple of boys. Which is the point I'm coming to. Because she's working on her back in the evenings, the kids have to raise themselves. Apple being ten and Jonathon three years older, it's Jonathon who raises Apple. You see where I'm going with this?"

"Maybe," Stranahan said without conviction.

"You will. The boys, it turns out, are opposite sides of the coin. Jonathon becomes captain of the hockey team, senior class president, Captain von Trapp in the *Sound of Music*. Apple develops sort of a hero worship for him, but has none of the charisma and even then he's getting into fights, getting into trouble. By all accounts, Jonathon is protective of Apple and a good influence. A father figure to a boy who has no father, or mother for that matter. Understand, we're looking at this from twenty-plus years out. We could only locate a couple classmates who recall anything about Apple and they were dismissive; to them, he was just the short guy who trolled along in his big brother's shadow."

Ettinger cocked her head. "Listen," she said.

Through the screen door Stranahan heard it—"whoo . . . ooo . . . ooo . . . ooo." Then again.

"That's a great grey," Ettinger said. "I hear him about twice a week. A horned owl isn't as regular, it doesn't have that deep timbre in its voice."

"I wouldn't have taken you for a bird woman," Stranahan said.

"Oh, I'm lots of things."

She came back to the subject. "Anyway, jump forward a few years. Jonathon enrolls in community college. He's eighteen, can legally move out of the house. He moves into a place with two friends. Apple's still at home, a freshman in high school. We can date the *Playboy* subscription to this time, because the address on the magazine is where Jonathon was renting. Without the older son's presence,

Apple's grades drop, he gets in fights, truancy problems"—Ettinger shrugged—"he drops out of school in the tenth grade."

"Why did the older brother leave the house?"

"One of his old roommates says it was a girl. Jonathon had a girl-friend and he needed somewhere to be with her. Actually, he'd had a serious girl earlier who had drowned in a lake. The rebound girl, her name was Barbara Rouse."

"More the reason to harbor a resentment toward women," Strana-han said. "Apple is deserted by his mother, neglected by the aunt, then abandoned by the one person he looks up to. And a woman is to blame for that, too."

"It gets worse. According to the friend, it's the Rouse girl who lures Jonathon away to Washington. She has relatives in Olympia and encourages him to apply to Evergreen State. Jonathon gets accepted, he joins her in the lower forty-eight, and Apple levels off about a rung up the ladder from the bottom of society. He becomes the kind of person I make my living off of."

"Does he have a record?"

"Disorderly conduct. Disturbing the peace. Fighting. But under-stand, this is Alaska. You have to do something pretty bad to get into the system. If everyone who gave someone else a black eye was deported, there wouldn't be anyone left to catch king crab."

"Why didn't Apple follow his brother to Washington?"

"That's a good question. We have no record of Apple leaving Alaska until he came here. We also have no update on the brother. Evergreen State has him attending for the fall of 'eighty-seven, spring of 'eighty-eight. I had Judy people-search a few databanks. Nada."

"How about the girlfriend?"

"Barbara Rouse—R-O-U-S-E—graduated from Evergreen in 'ninety. Her parents live in Bellingham. Judy got a phone number and left a message."

Ettinger drummed the fingers of both hands on the edge of the table. She pushed back in her chair.

"So that's where we stand. I don't know how this ties in with your property theories."

"Neither do I," Stranahan said. "But when you were talking, it crossed my mind that the brother might have had something to do with McNair coming to Montana. Something got him out of Alaska and the brother was the most important person in his life. Did you think of that angle?"

"Sure. Also that the motive behind the move was to run away from something in Alaska. That might be more likely."

"How about the hatchery?"

"Walt made a couple calls, but something came up and he had to drive down the county. So that's on the back burner till tomorrow."

"What about McNair? Is anyone still looking for him?"

"Karl Radcliffe is going to take his Piper Cub up at dawn, see if he can spot smoke. But we pulled just about everyone else. We postered the trailheads to warn hikers there was a fugitive at large, but there're going to be people who ignore it, so spotting a campfire won't mean much. We've had people go to ground in the mountains before and what happens is they come out on their own. They get hungry. Even this time of year, unless you can catch trout in the cirque lakes, you're down to throwing rocks at squirrels and eating serviceberries. He could be anywhere now. Down in the valley, out of state, anywhere."

"So now what?"

"Punch the keys, make the phone calls. We'll know more tomorrow. But it isn't TV. Things take time. Even the bloodwork on the boot, which is flagged, is going to be another week."

"What do you want me to do?"

"You've done plenty already. Where's your Miss Beaudreux, by the way?"

"Halfway to Mississippi would be my guess. She came through Bridger to pick up her brother's ashes the day before yesterday, when I was out with Search and Rescue."

Ettinger shot him a quizzical look.

"I called the funeral director. That's how I know she picked up the urn."

"So you haven't heard from her?"

"Not since Missoula."

"And you really want to keep helping with this?"

"What do you think?"

"Then keep working the property angle. But take some time off to breathe a little."

"I am. Remember Ventura, that movie guy who's Tony Sinclair's neighbor? I'm going fishing tomorrow night with him, if he remembers. I'd forgotten about it till I saw the boat trailered in his drive the other day."

"We tried to talk to him," Ettinger said, "but he left for California before the shit came down. You see him, ask him about McNair, anything he knows beyond that he was persona non grata in the neighborhood."

Stranahan told her he would and a minute later got up to leave.

"Oh shit," Ettinger said. "I almost forgot. I asked you over here to look at a couple pictures," she said, leading him into the main room of the old cabin, where she had a computer set up on a butcher block made from the cross-section of a tree trunk.

"Doug fir," she said. "I got it at a farm auction. Said to be eight hundred years old, but I haven't gotten bored enough to count the rings. Here, this is what I wanted you to see. It's a page from the Kuskok Bay high school yearbook. Yuto got it from one of Jonathon's classmates and scanned a couple pages."

Stranahan bent to peer at the postage-stamp-sized headshots on the screen.

"It's from 'eighty-six, the year Apple was a freshman, before he dropped out."

She hit the plus sign to enlarge the section with Apple's photo. It showed a blank expression, dark eyes set in deep sockets, and a shock of unruly black hair. It was recognizable as McNair only if you knew that first.

"The dead look," Ettinger said.

"A mug shot," Stranahan agreed. "But that's just being a teenager."

Ettinger backed out of the page and clicked on another attachment to the e-mail.

"Jonathon, his senior year." Ettinger enlarged the photo to graininess.

The young man smiled knowingly at the camera. A bang of jet black hair combed to the side fell heavily over the left eye, which was noticeably puffed. It gave the face a lopsided look.

"Looks like he was in a hockey fight," Stranahan said.

"His expression says he won," Ettinger said. "Cocky bastard. Look how he lifts his eyebrow for the camera. Got that bemused look down. But I can see what the girls saw in him. You get the hair off his face, he's a good-looking boy."

"I can't see too much family resemblance besides hair color, can you? But it's a bad shot to make a comparison with."

"We'll have the book tomorrow. Yuto says there are several more photos of the older brother, team shots and so on, so we should have something clearer to work from."

She walked with Stranahan to the door.

"Thanks for coming over." She switched the porch light on for him.

Stranahan noticed the softness had come back into her voice. She looked tired in the light, and Stranahan instinctively reached out and took her left shoulder in his hand and gave it a squeeze. He felt the urge to lean in closer, but didn't. There was an awkward moment, then she bridged the space to kiss him lightly on the cheek.

"Thanks for standing beside me this past week," she said.

Stranahan idled down the drive with the windows open. When the great grey hooted, he stopped and shut the engine off. The voice echoed into silence, leaving the undertone of the current. The owl was the sonorous heartbeat of the night, the river song its breath, and these sounds resonated in Stranahan's chest long after he had retired to the futon in his studio, as the bass notes of nature do with those who sleep alone.

CHAPTER THIRTY-NINE

Ghost Village

At 8 p.m., the surface of Quake Lake shimmered with gold coins. The flat stone Stranahan skipped blinked away into the distance. He arched his back to get the kinks out after the drive up the Madison Valley.

It had not been a productive day. He'd spent the morning talking with real estate agents and coming up against a wall, learning nothing more than he already knew. In the afternoon he'd met with Sam, who had introduced him to an asthmatic rail of a man named Hoss Borger, a retired fisheries biologist who volunteered at the Anglers Against Whirling Disease Foundation. Borger sat down in Sam's kitchenette with his lips compressed as Stranahan talked about the possibility of someone transmitting whirling disease into Montana rivers.

The biologist hit his inhaler before he spoke.

"It shakes your faith in mankind," he said in a rasping voice.

Borger said more—about tubifex worms, sporoplasm infection, avenues of transmission—skimming a surface with which Stranahan was familiar. He did clarify a point. Stranahan had heard that the disease could be transmitted by anglers who dirtied their boots in an infected river, then released sediments when stepping into another. That had struck him as a flaw in his theory. If spreading disease was as simple as traipsing around with mud on your boots, why go to the trouble of transporting fish in an aerated tank. Why take the risk? Borger assured him that introducing diseased fish

279

into a river was by far the most certain conduit for infection. Then he passed the buck, offering the number of a biologist who specialized in disease control.

"I'm sorry," he said. "It's not that I don't take your concern seriously. But some days I tire easily."

After he left, Stranahan mentioned that Hoss was a big man's name. It seemed incongruous for someone so frail.

"You wouldn't have said that if you knew him before he got the big C," Sam said. "He says he'll drown himself before it goes much farther and I don't doubt it. He'll be sleeping with the trout before Labor Day." Sam jabbed a thick finger into Stranahan's chest. "So will you, Kimosabe, if you keep sticking your nose into other people's business."

On this unsettling note, Stranahan drove to Quake Lake to meet Lucas Ventura.

Maybe he wasn't coming. It had been ten days since Ventura had asked Stranahan to meet him at the boat put-in near the outlet. For all Stranahan knew, he was still in California.

But then he heard the rattle of a trailer and one glimpse of flaring gunwale told him his drive would prove worthwhile, after all. Ventura turned the Ford Expedition around and expertly backed the trailer hub-deep into the lake. He swung out of the cab wearing hip boots and grabbed Stranahan's hand in a hard, brief clasp.

"Glad you could make it, Sean," he said in his chesty voice. "Now if you could just release the lock on the winch, I'll pull the boat off."

Ventura handed Stranahan the bow line when the boat was floating free and parked the truck. He came down to the water with a gear bag in one hand and a fistful of fly rods in the other.

"Beauty, isn't she," he said. "Built in 1888 by a craftsman named Elbridge Ricketson. They have a museum for these boats at Blue Lake in the Adirondacks. A little tippy"—he tilted an outstretched hand back and forth—"but plenty stable to cast from. How about it? All set?"

"Let me just grab a rain jacket," Stranahan said, glancing at the sky. A bank of violet cumulus clouds were building to the west. Ventura seemed anxious to push off and was sitting on the rowing seat when Stranahan returned.

"Give her a shove."

Stranahan leaned against the folding back of the cane-weave stern seat while Ventura pulled the long oars in scissoring strokes.

"God," he said a second later. "It's a relief to be back in Montana."

"You were on business, I take it."

"Not really. I'm more or less retired, at least in a hands-on sense. But along the way I accumulated three wives who bore me five children. Most summers I get the kids up here en masse, but there has been some recalcitrance on the parts of wives one and two, a conspiracy if you ask me, and I had to see the lawyers about it. If it isn't one thing, it's another, right?"

"How are we going to fish?" Stranahan asked.

Ventura jutted his chin. "Last hour of light there's going to be a mayfly emergence about a mile uplake, Callibaetis duns sitting on the surface just pretty as sailboats. But I'm going to start you off with a pair of leech patterns under a strike indicator. Purists frown on that, but when that indicator goes down, baby, it goes *down*. I got a twenty-seven-inch brown on a seal bugger last October. Kype like a sockeye salmon."

Ventura kept up a steady stream of patter as he stroked the oars, and in what seemed like only a few minutes they had crossed the lake. Above them was scar tissue from the '59 earthquake, a giant scoop of rubble studded with dolomite boulders the size of houses. Ventura set the oars in their chocks. He lowered a mushroom anchor, taking care not to scrape the side of the craft.

Gesturing for Stranahan to hand him his rod, he deftly tied a dropper strand to the leader and rigged it with an olive-brown micro leech on the point and a purple one on the dropper.

"Cast crosswind. Mend to the right and let 'em drift. When the flies come under tension, inch them in with a hand twist retrieve. Mind what I said about breaking them off."

As Ventura instructed him, Stranahan noticed the concentration on the man's face, how the inverted Vs of his heavy eyebrows drew creases in his forehead. Stranahan remembered back to his first handshake with the man, thinking that he had looked like a jovial Satan.

"Does something about my face bother you?" Ventura asked in a serious voice. "You seem to be looking at me more than the lake."

"Nah," Stranahan said. "It's this whole place that bothers me—the water, the trees. Everything has a skeletal look. It gives you that little tick of dread."

Ventura's face relaxed. "It does that for me, too," he said. "Seven point five on the Richter scale, twenty-eight dead, nineteen still buried. See that post sticking up there? That's part of Ghost Village. The roof and some of the walls are gone, but underneath the waterline there's a cabin, one of eight that were swept away by the flooding and washed against this bank. Your flies, they're fishing in the living room. I've caught trout in just about all the submerged cabins. It's eerie. But then, I'd row this boat through the swamps of Hades if there were ten-pound browns cruising the surface."

Stranahan caught the first trout, a small rainbow. Ventura followed suit and then one-upped Stranahan with a decent fish of about two pounds. As he bent over the gunwale to release it, Stranahan noticed a vein in the man's neck twitching rhythmically. Ventura's face wavered in the surface reflection. Something about him gave Stranahan a vague feeling of discomfort. Instinctively, he looked up and down the lake.

As if sensing his mood, Ventura said, without looking over,

"Quake's always deserted this late in the evening. That's what I like about it."

For a time they fished in a silence that was uninterrupted by trout, and Stranahan found his uneasiness seeping away. His mind drifted back to the case. Twice, earlier in the day, he'd tried to call Martha Ettinger to see if she'd learned anything from Walt about the hatchery, or something more about McNair or his brother. When he got through, she'd been short with him.

No, she hadn't consulted with her deputy yet. In case Stranahan didn't know, she had a full jail and a county to run. She'd find time in the afternoon. If she didn't call back before he left, then good luck with the trout. End of conversation. She hadn't even asked where he'd be fishing.

Ventura's voice brought Stranahan back to the present. "Heard you had an exciting time when I was gone." He was appraising Stranahan's still-swollen lip.

"You could say that. How did you hear?" The paper had reported the manhunt, but Ventura had been out of state.

"Tony Sinclair called when I drove in from the airport. Told me you knocked on his door looking like a drowned muskrat. Said Apple McNair had kidnapped you. He wasn't too certain of the particulars."

Stranahan remembered what Ettinger had told him, that anything he could learn from Ventura about his neighbor might be helpful.

"The particulars are that the man is an asshole," Stranahan said. "I was fishing in the beaver pond on the Sheep Creek outlet stream and he jumped me, damned near drowned me, and then taped me up in his workshop. I managed to get away when he went into the house. Did Sinclair tell you there was a manhunt for him in the mountains?"

Ventura nodded. "But they didn't catch him, right?"

"Far as I know, he's still up there."

"Grizzly bear bait," Ventura said.

"That's what I'm hoping."

Ventura stripped his line in, snipped his leech fly off with his teeth, and bent to tie on another.

"A little odd to be going there at night, isn't it?" he mumbled, wetting the knot in his lips. "I shouldn't think there'd be a trout in that old beaver pond worth the effort. Besides," he continued, "it's private property. You know better than that."

"You're right. I shouldn't have. But I noticed it when I went out for a hike and thought I'd check it out. I figured I'd get there before last light but the walk took longer than I'd expected."

"So the man just overreacted to the situation?"

"You might say that," Stranahan said. "It was like setting off a Doberman. But I really don't know what he thought I was doing that got him so upset."

He saw his opening. "Look," he said. "You're his neighbor. What makes him tick?"

Ventura appeared to consider the question. "I think you're asking the wrong person," he said. "I doubt I've had three conversations with the man. He came over for my Fourth of July fireworks display last summer—I invite all the neighbors. But he didn't cause any trouble and it's not such a bad thing to have at least one person in the development who lives here year-round. For security reasons, that is."

"Seems like people were avoiding him at Summersby's party," Stranahan prompted.

Ventura grunted. "His place is an eyesore." He seemed on the verge of saying more, then bit it off.

Stranahan pressed. "You know where he's from, anything in his background might cause him to be so hostile?"

"What do you want to talk about him for?" Ventura said. "You can't let a guy like that fuck up your life."

Anger had crept into Ventura's voice. Stranahan could feel it as a heat. Again he noticed the vein in Ventura's neck. Suddenly he understood what had bothered him before. It wasn't pulsing with a normal heart rate, but throbbing.

Ventura gained control of his voice.

"I promised you some fishing," he said. "Up the lake there will be some better trout rising." As he reached behind to pull the anchor, Stranahan took advantage of the distraction to glance at his wrist. The second hand of his watch was coming up on the half-minute. He started to count the pulses in Ventura's neck. Two, three. . . . He counted to thirty-four as Ventura hauled on the anchor, then glanced back down as Ventura brought the anchor aboard. Sixteen seconds had passed. Thirty-four times four—one hundred thirty-six. It was twice a normal heart rate.

Ventura pulled on the oars, then dropped them and let the boat drift while he slapped at his forehead. He leaned down to reach into his gear bag.

"Damn bloodsuckers," he said. "You can always count on the mosquitoes when the wind dies down."

After spreading the DEET onto the back of his hand, Ventura tossed the tube to Stranahan. Stranahan found his hands were shaking and deliberately calmed himself to apply the repellant.

Ventura was digging his nails at the bite on his forehead. The movement made his slicked-back hair fall into its natural part to the side, and when he leaned forward to take the tube of repellent that Stranahan returned to him, a bang of hair fell across the left side of his temple. Stranahan felt a tingling on the skin of his forearms, then a rapid flush of blood up his neck. For a second, he couldn't breathe. Then the boat lurched forward as Ventura manned the oars.

Sitting back, Stranahan took a deep breath, squeezed his eyes shut, opened them, and . . . watched the face before him lose twenty years in the span of a second. The face he was looking at—aggressive, arrogant, a bang of hair over the left temple that half hid a purple eye—

was that of a teenage boy. It was the face that he had seen on Ettinger's computer screen, the face of Apple's older brother, Jonathon McNair.

Stranahan saw Ventura looking at him. He sought to cover the alarm in his expression. "God," he said, forcing a catch into his voice. "I had one of those moments when you can't breathe. Like bad heartburn."

"You all right?"

Stranahan burped, then inhaled audibly. He hoped he wasn't overdoing it.

"Yeah, I think so. It's gone now."

"That's good, Sean, because I wouldn't want you to miss out on the hatch. We'll be there in just a few minutes."

This is impossible, Stranahan thought. It's just because I was looking at the yearbook photograph and my mind's painting it on the first person who bears a resemblance. Ventura's a goddamn film producer, for chrissakes. He's got a different name, he's lived a different life.

Stranahan looked at Ventura for assurance, but the falling darkness was obscuring the contours of his face even as it dimmed the last glimmer from the lake surface.

"You'll need to extend your leader to five X and tie on a dry," Ventura said. "About a sixteen parachute Adams. I like a cripple pattern myself. Best to rig up now."

Stranahan tried to recall the voice on the telephone from McNair's knife shop. Could this be the same man? But that voice had been distorted by the speaker phone.

"See the dimples in the cove," Ventura said. "You're lucky, one of those trout will have your name on it."

Stranahan could see fish rising as he fussed with the leader. They were up into the most remote bends of the lake now, about a mile below the Beaver Creek Campground where the host had taken a blade in his heart. Ventura pulled on one oar to turn the boat into an alley of open water through the spires of the drowned pines. He let it glide nearly to the shoreline. The trees of the forest made a solid wall.

"Damned prostate," he said. "Keep her steady there while I hop out."

Stranahan put his hand against the barkless trunk of one of the snags poking out of the lake while Ventura stepped off the side of the boat in his hip boots. He waded up toward the bow, the water thigh deep, his back turned, one hand holding onto the gunwale. Seconds passed. Stranahan waited to hear the tinkling in the water. Dead silence. A trout swirled an oar's length away.

"I never asked where you were from?" Stranahan said. He tried to make the question sound innocent, but he could feel his heart beating in his chest.

"Someplace I hoped I'd never have to revisit, Sean, in any sense of the word." Ventura's voice was heavy, as if he had to forcefully inhale enough air to get the words out. "But it revisited me."

As he spoke the last words he shrugged his shoulders in a defeated gesture and turned, bringing a flat automatic to bear on Stranahan's chest.

CHAPTER FORTY

A Shot of Salt

Separated by the length of the boat, the men stared at each other through the gauze of twilight.

A sound came out of Stranahan's mouth, not his voice at all.

"You don't have to . . . this isn't something . . ."

"Please," Ventura said. "Just . . . please. Do you think I want to be here any more than you do? If I could make this go away with words, I would. You can't possibly know how much I wish that was true. But I can't." His hand shook on the pistol.

"Tell me," Stranahan said. He thought: *Get him talking.*

"I wouldn't know where to begin," Ventura said.

Stranahan noticed that he was holding an Adams dry fly. It seemed absurd. Mechanically, he completed tying it to the leader tippet.

Ventura's voice, coming out of near darkness, had a different tone. The authoritative, chesty resonance was back.

"Fishing's over, Sean. Place your rod on the bottom of the boat. Now put your hands on the gunwales, one on each side. That's right. If you move a hand for any reason, even if it's to itch your nose, I will shoot you. Do you understand? I'm just going to ask this once. What were you doing at that pond?"

Stranahan's mind raced. How much did Ventura actually know about him, other than that Richard Summersby had hired him to paint pictures and that he was the person McNair had attacked? Ventura couldn't know that Stranahan was onto the hatchery scheme or that he had guessed his tie to McNair. Still, he had to give him something.

"Your neighbor tried to kill my friend, Sam Meslik. He's the fishing guide who was shot on Henry's Lake. I thought McNair was gone and I was going to try to find a rifle at his house, so there would be evidence."

Ventura nodded his head thoughtfully at the part-truth, and for a moment Stranahan allowed himself the luxury of hope that this evening could still be put behind him.

Then Ventura shot him in the chest.

Stranahan felt a hot flash, a concentrated burning sensation like the blast of a blowtorch. Instinctively, he clamped both his hands over his ribcage. He could not draw breath. A scent, like phosphorous burning when a match is struck, invaded his nostrils. The burning in his chest drew to a point of pain and Stranahan felt his lungs expand, the point of pain draw sharper, then the gasping exhalation of his breath.

Ventura's voice rose from the blackness.

"Do I have your attention now?"

Stranahan was looking at his palms. Why wasn't there blood?

"You shot me," he said.

"Yes, but look at it this way. You're not dead. I pulled the bullet out of the cartridge case."

"Then . . ." Stranahan concentrated on his breathing.

"I shot you with ten grains of pistol powder behind a charge of sea salt. I thought there might be occasion to clear the bullshit out of the air."

"Salt?" Stranahan barely got the word out.

"From Brittany. It's expensive salt. The next cartridge is loaded with a Winchester SXT. Enough powder to blow it out your back."

He allowed himself a chuckle. "Must burn like hell, having your chest seasoned like that. Make you more tasty, huh?" Ventura waded up alongside the boat until he was standing by the stern. "Let me see your hands. Are you bleeding?"

"Maybe under my shirt."

"We can't have it on the boat, Sean. So take your hands—no, don't wipe them—put them back on the gunwales right where they were."

Stranahan did as he was told.

Ventura's voice was patient. "Now I'll ask you again—what were you doing at the pond? Tell me the truth and you get a story while we wait. I have a surprise for you. But lie to me . . ." Ventura let the words hang.

Stranahan felt the muscles in his chest shudder. Deliberately, he amplified the reaction, feigning convulsion. He had to buy time.

"Come come, Sean. Think about what I did for a living. I know theatrics. Answer me."

Stranahan knew that Ventura intended to kill him, truth told or not. His only chance was to convince Ventura that it was in his best interests to let him live.

"Diseased trout," he heard himself say. "McNair put trout in the pond that have whirling disease. He's planting them around the state. I was collecting evidence."

"That's ridiculous."

"No," Stranahan said. "It's the truth. He works for a hatchery, Missouri River Pisces. He planted fish in the Big Blackfoot River. I followed his truck."

"Why would he do that?"

"He's working for someone who's hoping property will go for a song if the trout disappear."

"Someone?"

"I don't know who."

"This scheme, how would that work?"

Stranahan explained that the state would stock fish if the disease became epidemic and ruined the fishing. It would kick-start property values. Someone who bought low could sell high.

"I don't think you know what you are talking about," Ventura said.

"Maybe I don't. But the sheriff knows what I know?"

"The sheriff?"

"Yes. Martha Ettinger."

"You're working with the sheriff's department?"

"She knows I went fishing with you tonight. She knows where we are. If I don't call her, she'll be at your house by midnight. She'll investigate you for my murder."

Ventura's laughter was a harsh bark. "I don't believe you."

"I can prove it," Stranahan said. "My wallet, it's in my vest. She gave me her card. Look at the back of it."

Stranahan heard a mechanical click. For an instant, he was blinded by a beam of light. Blinking his eyes, he saw Ventura, standing in thigh-deep water a few feet away, with a penlight between his front teeth. The light made a gargoyle mask of his face, accentuating the shadows. Ventura snapped the fingers of his left hand. He motioned with the pistol.

Stranahan fished the wallet out and deliberately tossed it high, hoping that Ventura would lunge. If he did, Stranahan would go for the gun. But the flashlight beam barely nodded as Ventura snapped it out of the air.

"Doesn't mean anything," he mumbled. The penlight bobbed as he spoke around the barrel. "It's just a telephone number."

"What it means is that anyone who calls that number, she'll tell them to cooperate with me."

"She doesn't know who I am. If she does, she has no reason to care."

The words were distorted, but Stranahan could feel a tension in them, a concentrated effort at delivery. He drew in a breath. *Here goes*, he thought. *Live or die.*

He said, "She knows you're Apple McNair's brother."

What effect the words had on Ventura, Stranahan couldn't say. The face looked grotesque behind the sunspot of the flashlight beam. He felt his stomach knot, drawing inward at the anticipation of being shot.

He went on quickly, "You can't talk your way out of your relationship with McNair, but you can distance yourself from him. I don't know anything that connects you to the people he's killed. Maybe you have something to do with the hatchery plot, I'm guessing you do, but that's a crime you can lawyer your way out of. But if I go missing, then you're a murderer."

The circle of light glanced off his face and Stranahan heard a click as Ventura snapped off the penlight. In the sudden blackness, he could feel his heart pounding.

"Let you go, just like that." The voice came out of the ink.

"Just let me step out of the boat. The shore's right here. I'll walk back."

"And tonight never happened?"

"I'll tell the sheriff that we went fishing, but you knew nothing about McNair." In the silence, Stranahan could feel the wavelets lapping the hull. He could try to roll the boat and dive under. Either that or go for Ventura. He'd been measuring the steps since the moment Ventura turned with the pistol. But slogging through the water, it would be slow. No, stay calm. Give Ventura time to think about his own best interests.

"You're a good liar, Sean," Ventura said at length. "For about a half a minute you had me convinced the sheriff was going to show up on a white horse. But I don't think she has any idea where you are, and I don't think she knows who I am, either. I said I'd tell you a story. That is, in return for the truth"—he hesitated—"but then, you learn to admire liars in my profession. It's what acting is, the so-called Method notwithstanding."

Stranahan took a chance. He pressed slightly on the gunwale under his right hand. Immediately, he felt the boat respond. It would roll if he pressed down hard enough.

Ventura spoke. "You are right, Sean. Apple is indeed my brother. He is a child, really, and I was father more than brother to him for a long time. The question is: Am I responsible for his actions? Am I my brother's keeper? It's true I own the land upon which he lives, so perhaps I am guilty of omission by not telling the neighbors. But that is not a crime. Apple is not my ward, and nothing he has done can be traced to me."

"What about the fish?" Stranahan said.

"Do you want to hear my story, or interrupt? Do you want to die without knowing why? I will get to the fish." Ventura hesitated. "Though in a sense that is where this begins."

In a reflective voice, he said, "He worships me, you know. There's no way around the fact that he is mentally ill, but some of the damage is understandable. Our father died when Apple was ten. We had a mother and an aunt who, together, added up to half a mother. One left to drink herself to death. The other was a whore by another name. What saved Apple were fish. We grew up on our father's boat, helping him commercial-fish sockeye and pink salmon. The silver salmon, when they turn into tidewater, have scales like Tiffany diamonds. Apple said once, I'll never forget, 'They're so shiny they make my eyes water.' Ask me why, I don't know, but as long as he fished he was happy. He didn't need anything else."

A shadow crossing the white pepper of the stars made Stranahan glance up. It was an owl, beating by on silent wings. Stranahan followed its flight, lifting his left hand where it grasped the gunwale and pressing with his right . . . and felt the boat tip. Then sway the other way. And thought about it—as good a way to die as another.

Ventura was talking to himself now, lost in his reverie.

"The change came when we moved to Kuskok Bay. Apple stealing wood, burning Mrs. Wilson's mail because she had looked at him a certain way. Petty crimes. Later, in high school, the"—he searched for a word—"deviations in his behavior became more pronounced. A woman in the Indian village woke up to find that a hank of her hair had been cut off. She told the newspaper she'd seen a devil with black eyes; she wasn't far from right. Another woman caught Apple sticking the hook of a trout fly into her pierced ear when she was in bed. Strange thing to do, climb through windows and touch people while they sleep. It's like counting coup."

Stranahan thought of the trout fly in Jerry Beaudreux's lip, felt the lump on his own lower lip with his tongue. He heard Ventura sigh.

"I could have turned him in," he said, "but I didn't want the trouble. By then I was left wing on the hockey team, the class president, got my hands on the perfect breasts of the prom queen. You would think Apple would be jealous, but he wasn't, not of me. He did get jealous of people close to me—girls, especially. And in oblique ways, he made sure I knew what he was doing. He'd leave muddy shoes in the hall, ones I hadn't seen before, so I would be the one who threw the evidence out. He'd take a locket of hair he'd cut off someone's sleeping head and tuck it into my shirt pocket. You understand what I'm saying, Sean?"

"I think so. He made you complicit. It gave him something on you that would make it harder to leave."

"That's it exactly," Ventura said. "Behind those black eyes there is calculation. There is resentment directed at happiness, at contentment, things he can't have. There is a violence of the heart.

"Do you know what the mistake of my life was? It was telling Apple I was running away with Valerie Morris after graduation. We were going to water-thumb our way to Washington, go to college—big plans for kids from nowhere."

Ventura fell quiet. Stranahan could feel a change in the night—the mosquito drone lower-pitched, the air turned damp warm. No stars now. He looked up and felt the first drops of rain.

"The sheriff told me that your girlfriend drowned."

Ventura didn't immediately answer. When he spoke, his voice had lost its reflective quality and sounded defeated.

"She was found in a lake where bush pilots tie up their float planes. It was on the eve of our graduation. Valerie worked there, hauling gear, fueling up the Beavers with additives—all the old De Havilland's ran on leaded fuel—odd jobs. Her body was trapped under a dock. There was a bruise on her forehead, so it was presumed that she had fallen when she stepped from the dock to the float of the plane tethered there, that she slipped on the float and hit her head on it. She drowned in three feet of water."

"You think Apple killed her, don't you?"

"I know he did . . . now. I wasn't sure at the time. The accident was plausible."

"The sheriff told me about a girlfriend you left Alaska with. Was that because you were afraid Apple might hurt her, too?"

"No. That was later. Apple had given up on me by then. I think killing Valerie was an act of desperation, and when it didn't work, when I left anyway, he dropped out of school. Dropped out of life, really. No, I left Alaska with Barbara looking forward, not backward. But how do you know this? I'm curious."

"The sheriff's department did a background check on Apple. People remember you."

"You still want me to believe you know the sheriff? Maybe you do at that. It doesn't matter now. What I was asking was how did you know I was Apple's brother?"

Stranahan had to think. He couldn't tell the truth, that it had been barely half an hour since he recognized him from the yearbook photo. Ventura would know then that the sheriff had no idea who he was. It would remove the only reason the man had for letting him live.

He said, "Your old girlfriend's parents."

"Barbara's?"

"They live in Bellingham. They knew you'd gone to California, knew who you'd become there. The sheriff called them." It wasn't true. As far as he knew, Ettinger hadn't spoken with Barbara Rouse or her parents.

Once again there was silence as Ventura let this sink in.

"I don't know," he said at length. "I changed my name. I changed my appearance. I did everything I could to put that life behind me."

"She knew," Stranahan said. "I think Apple must have known where to find you, too. Or did you contact him?"

"No, that is the last thing I would have done. But my second wife was an actress. B-minus, but even B-minus actresses are someone in Hollywood. Apple read about her in a magazine. It had a photo of the two of us, our place here. It named the valley. He knocked on my door two years ago August. He said someone had dredged up Valerie's name. Said he had seen them together down by the lake on the evening Valerie drowned. The man wanted money to erase his memory.

"I asked Apple point blank if he'd drowned her, something I had been afraid to do after she died. He said no, but admitted that Valerie had given him a ride home that day and maybe the man had seen them in her truck. Was I going to give him the money? The blackmailer, who was a drunk, only wanted $10,000.

"All this on my doorstep. Would I invite him into the house at least? Sean, he is my brother. I let him into the house. I tried to explain that the authorities would see through this drunk and dismiss his allegation as a belated attempt at extortion. Well, then, Apple told me, would I give him some sort of job so he could stay in Montana? I told him I didn't work in Montana, which was true, though I did have business interests in the state. He told me he'd driven down on the Al-Can and planned to fish some rivers. He said he'd check back with me in a couple weeks. I was not encouraging and hoped sincerely that he would give up trying to reestablish our relationship. When I shut the door, I hoped I had seen the last of him."

"What happened next?"

Ventura made a snorting sound. "Do you really think my talking will help you? Don't insult my intelligence."

He continued. "I'm telling you this because for years, understand, I've kept it inside. It creates a cancer, a gnawing in your gut that doesn't go away. But how do you tell someone that you ran away from your boyhood life because you suspected your brother had murdered your girl? And that you did nothing about it?"

"How can you be sure he killed her?"

"You notice that the mailboxes for our community are at the gate? After Apple left, what do you think I found there?"

"I don't know. A letter."

"Come on. You can do better."

Stranahan remembered what Ventura had said about his brother climbing through windows.

"Hair," he said.

Ventura grunted approval. "Now you're thinking, Sean. Yes, it was a lock of hair. Apple had torn open a bill in the mailbox and put it inside. Valerie was blond. The hair is blond. I know that you need follicles for DNA testing and the hair looks like it was cut. So maybe I can never be sure. But in my heart, I know it's her."

"Why don't you turn him in?"

"No, I have other plans for Apple now."

"So you know where he is."

"Oh, yes. And closer than you think. Sean, as soon as I saw Valerie's hair, I knew that this night was a possibility. I just didn't expect that you would be a part of it."

"What . . . ?"

"Just listen. You had questions about the fish. Missouri River Pisces is jointly held by two businesses in California. The business does not carry my name, but I do have the controlling interest. Why? The simple reason is that trout are my passion. You were correct in believing Apple was placing fish infected with whirling disease into Montana rivers. You also were correct to assume that someone who owned land along the rivers intended to profit when fisheries depleted by the disease were planted with hatchery-reared fish.

"What you failed to discover"—Stranahan heard a sloshing sound as Ventura, who had been standing only a few feet from the boat, waded toward the black outline of a log jutting from the shore—"what you failed to find out is that there was a second component to this operation."

Stranahan saw Ventura's shadow compress as he sat heavily on the log. He was making himself comfortable, had rested the hand that held the pistol against his right thigh.

"As a fisherman yourself," he went on, "you must know that a great deal of money has been spent to find a solution to whirling disease. Where those efforts have largely failed, I have succeeded. I will not bore you with too many details. What I will tell you is that a number of years ago, I made the acquaintance of a man who had studied whirling disease as a graduate student at the state university. This was before the malady manifested itself in the West and became front-page news. At the time I met the man, he was a geneticist that a film company had hired as an expert for a movie I had a piece of. We had fly fishing in common, that is how I came to know about his past. He understood that brown trout in Europe could withstand the ravages of whirling disease. His aim was to find a strain of trout native to our side of the pond that might do the same. Understand this was thirty years ago. He was just a student with no grant money. The customary avenues of obtaining trout for testing were closed to him. His professor told him, 'You're a fisherman, Marty'—the man's name was Martin Dollack—'go catch some fish, infect them with the spores, see what happens.'

"This he did. One of the populations he tested was from an alpine lake in the Mission Mountains. The rainbows had been aerially planted and were remarkable because they showed no effect of whirl-ing disease when exposed to the spores. But Marty's findings were based on an insignificant sample and his professor never submitted them for publication. He graduated, moved to California, and never thought about whirling disease again until about fifteen years ago, when it became news in the angling fraternity. Thinking his old research might be of value, he contacted the state fisheries. A biolo-gist asked him about the lake, but he couldn't remember the name and wasn't sure it had one—am I boring you, Sean? No? Anyway, the biologist thanked him, but said it wouldn't matter what lake it was, because it had probably been stocked many times since his graduate days—they bomb those alpine lakes with fingerlings on a five-year rotation—and the strain he tested would have died out or been diluted by crossbreeding. In those years, you see, the state stocked whatever hatchery rainbows were cheap and available, a cocktail of genetic strains. So the strain he had studied was not only untraceable but probably nonexistent. No one was interested in a thirty-year-old study that couldn't be genetically replicated.

"Except for me, that is. I was quite interested and had already invested in several hatcheries. They were vanity projects, I admit. I wanted to develop rainbow trout that were the biggest, the hardest fighting, the most likely to take a fly from the surface. So I questioned Mr. Dollack. I ordered maps and he was able to retrace his steps and pinpoint the lake. My next step was to look up the stocking data. What I discovered was that the alpine lakes in that area had been written off the program fifteen years before because they fell within readjusted borders of the Flathead Indian Reservation. I put in a call to the regional biologist and asked him, as an interested sportsman, mind you, if any of the lakes that were no longer stocked still sup-ported trout. He said that one could, if it was deep enough to avoid freezing out and had suitable spawning habitat in the inlet or outlet stream. Ah, I thought, so there was a window of light, just a chance that the original strain might have survived. I thanked him and thought to pursue this thread, but I was up to my neck in a cutthroat business and when the movie was wrapped the entire matter was put on hiatus."

Stranahan heard a metallic snap as a flame flared in the darkness. He caught the cherry glow of a cigarette.

"A pernicious habit, Sean. But I find it moderates the anxiety."

Ventura smoked in silence a few moments.

Stranahan thought of something Vareda had said—"They can put it on my tombstone: She inhaled." All that seemed so long ago, now.

"The geneticist passed away," Ventura said. "I heard about it after I moved up here. It reminded me of our discussions. By then, I had a controlling interest in Pisces and was in full pursuit of the perfect trout. I dug out my old maps and put on my hiking boots. The lake that my friend had fished turned out to be a beautiful tarn with a low-gradient inlet stream of small spawning gravel—I had my hopes up. And sure enough, I caught trout. Not big, but thick-shouldered. Broad stripes, rosy cheeks, just as nice a rainbow as a lab ever made."

Ventura sounded animated. He was completely absorbed by his story. Stranahan noted his own shallow breathing. He felt dreamy in a shifting-color way, as if slipping toward unconsciousness, and tried to snap out of his lethargy. He focused on the burn in his chest. He was gathering himself to tip the boat; better to go down swinging. He had a gut feeling there wasn't much time left.

"Absolutely of no use, understand," Ventura continued. "The fish were adults and the disease only affects the young. But the next time I came back I had a seine, I had a five-gallon tank with an aerator, I came off the mountain with my sample. I infected the fingerlings with parasites from other diseased trout and crossed my fingers. The fish manifested no signs of disease. I decided to take another trip. Sean, I studied those trout over the course of the next two years, crossbred them with other rainbow strains, subjected the smolts to conditions they might encounter in a riverine environment, all the while masking the experiments so that employees like the young Mr. Beaudreux wouldn't suspect. There was only one person at the hatchery I could trust, so most of the research I did on my own. I didn't want anyone spilling the beans prematurely. I could see the state preempting the study and taking the credit. You see, I'm a vain man. I like money, but I like recognition more. Anyone in my business who says otherwise is a liar.

"So I waited until I was sure of the product. And that product, Sean, was a rainbow trout that would thrive in Montana rivers regardless of whether those rivers harbored the spores of whirling disease. What's more, it was a trout with a fast growth rate to an acceptable adult size—two to four pounds—and we had grown some to eight pounds.

"It was time to act. Like other hatcheries, we accepted funding from the Anglers Against Whirling Disease Foundation and periodically reported our progress. I hinted we might have something promising, feeling out the response. I approached the state fisheries with the same careful steps. And I found out that"—Ventura paused for effect—"no one cared.

"Can you imagine that? I tell you, it was a slap in the face.

"And why? Why because their reasoning is entrenched in the conservative, because Montana has a wild trout program and the state's commitment was to improving the existing fishery, not finding a new trout to supplant it."

Ventura uttered a bitter laugh.

"They were devoting their efforts to working with irrigators to ensure tributary flows so that the baby fish could grow past the danger stage in water temperatures unfavorable to whirling disease; they were spending their money educating the public about transferring disease from river to river. It was a Band-Aid approach, not a cure. Basically, everyone was just hoping that the trout would develop genetic resistance. When the Madison River rebounded, the state took it as a victory, conveniently overlooking evidence suggesting that the river was naturally restocking itself with fish that migrated into it from the reservoirs. The Madison trout were not recovering on their own at all.

"So here I am"—Stranahan could hear the bitterness in Ventura's voice—"here I am with a Christmas gift wrapped in a blue bow that no one wants to open. What arrogance!"

"So you said, 'Fuck them,' " Stranahan prompted.

"I said fuck them. I said if they don't want to solve their problem, I'll solve it for them. I'll pollute their rivers with infected fish until there are no wild trout to catch. I'll wait until public outcry demands that the state institute a stocking program. And when that day comes, I'll be a hero, for I have the trout that will save Montana's rivers. It's called the Ventura strain. It has a ring, don't you think? The only thing that held me back was that I didn't want to dirty my hands. I couldn't see myself driving around in the dark with a load of rainbow-striped contraband, you might say. It would be unseemly."

Ventura paused.

"Then Apple knocked on your door," Stranahan said.

"Yes, Sean. Then Apple knocked on my door."

CHAPTER FORTY-ONE

A Shaft of Steel

"**A**pple was the last piece of the puzzle. When he came back from his fishing trip, I said I might have a job for him, after all. I didn't mention the lock of hair. Acted as if I hadn't seen it. I had the riverfront property next door with the homestead cabin. I had papers drawn up to put it in his name, though it is I who really own it. I also placed Apple on the hatchery payroll as a driver.

"And, well, I was on my way to realizing the dream. I already owned several properties on streams that had declined due to whirling disease or else had historically offered marginal fishing, like the Blackfoot, where mining had compromised the fishery. That land would appreciate, the only question was how much. I would buy more land as the disease spread and opportunity knocked. Little or no risk with Apple doing the lifting. Then, like a fool, the hatchery manager hires that Boy Scout Beaudreux. Apple was not supposed to kill the young man. He says it was an accident. I say maybe."

"He had a trout fly stuck in his lip," Stranahan said. "That part didn't make the papers."

"So probably not. It confirms my suspicions."

"Shooting Sam, stabbing the camp host, it didn't stop with Beaudreux."

"No, it didn't. What will happen tonight, it's something that should have happened a long time ago."

"What's that?" Stranahan had a dreadful feeling he already knew. He shifted his weight as far as he dared to the left-hand side of the boat, the side that faced the log where Ventura's black bulk was sitting.

"I'm going to write an end to a Shakespearean tragedy," Ventura said flatly. "If Apple was caught, he would open his mouth. You are the witness to his crime, the pressure to bear that would make him talk, and I would become a casualty of his sins. But I will wait to kill him until he is through with you. As far as your sheriff is concerned, you will have killed each other and I . . ."

Stranahan rocked hard to the right, tipping the boat. He felt the shock of the water before the sentence was finished. Surfacing, he pushed the stern of the boat away from him, hoping that Ventura would think he was dragging it as a shield. He lunged in the opposite direction.

Ducking under, he heard Ventura's garbled shouting. Then, a muffled explosion. A shot? Another voice rising against the first. Stranahan reached forward, pulled his arms against his sides, reached forward, pulled. He swam underwater until his outstretched hands scraped the trunk of a pine snag. He grabbed the trunk and slowly lifted his head. The shoreline was a thin band dented by the phosphorescence of the water. He craned his neck. There, farther up the bank. He could see the boat and beside it the figure of a man. Ventura must have righted the craft. The sleek silhouette began to glide toward him, a spot of light glinting in and out, then sweeping in his direction. The widening V of the beam tugged at his head.

"I got you sumbitch."

It wasn't Ventura's voice. Stranahan had a moment's panic as the guide boat closed the gap. Thirty yards. Twenty.

He ducked and swam underwater until his lungs were tight to explode. He surfaced, coughing. His chest felt wheezy. The beam of light was snapping around on the snags farther out. Stranahan swam toward shore, then crawled through the shallows on hands and knees to fall exhausted on the scum of detritus that rimmed the shore. As he tried to stand, a flash of light swept over him and for a second he saw his silhouette against the mud. *Goddammit.* He tried to run, but his left leg was shaking. He hopped on his right leg and fell hard. He must have hurt himself when he bailed out of the boat and hit the lake bottom. He lay flat a second, heart hammering. A cone of light swept over the shoreline to his left. Turning from it, he began to crawl toward the forest, dragging his cramped leg.

Finally he reached the trees. He grasped at the trunk of an aspen to pull himself upright. Then he heard a scuffing noise and abruptly he felt his body yanked backward. A tangy, organic odor filled his nostrils. He turned his head. The outline of a man, black against the stars. Ventura? No, not tall enough, and the smell was familiar: the animal stench of Apple McNair.

Stranahan grabbed at a clump of willow brush, felt his skin ripped off his palm by another terrific yank. The grunting turned to a rhythmic panting. He was being dragged up the shoreline facedown, steadily, without apparent effort.

He screamed. The panting intensified. He was being pulled faster.

He screamed again.

Faster.

Why wasn't he already dead? It occurred to him that Apple must be following Ventura's orders, that he was being dragged to the older brother farther up the shore. Ventura must have arranged for Apple to meet him here. Stranahan saw a last chance to plead for his life.

He craned his face to the side when McNair paused for a moment, his breath stentorian. The outline of the guide boat was by the shore, only yards away. A spot of brilliance shone through the shallows where a flashlight lay submerged. It illuminated a humped shape at the shoreline.

"Don't be a fool, Apple," Stranahan gasped. "Lucky's going to kill you. He's going to make it look like you killed me, then turned a gun on yourself. Like you're a crazy man."

McNair muttered something Stranahan couldn't understand.

Stranahan plunged ahead.

"Why do you think he came in the boat? So they'll find your footprints on the bank, not his. He wants you to kill me, then he's going to shoot you. He's leaving this place alone. I can help you. We can figure this thing out."

McNair's grunt was punctuated with a rattling cough. "Ha!"

"Think, man, think!"

But McNair was dragging him again. Then he gave a big yank and Stranahan's face smacked down against the shape that bulked against the shore. He breathed in and got a mouthful of mud. Then, abruptly, he felt Apple's grip release.

Stranahan rolled onto his side. He seemed to be wedged against a log. He tried to get up, pulling on the log. Stranahan heard a gurgling sound and felt the log give under his hand; his fingers groped along it, tangling in a wire of human hair. And something else, hot and wet where the log pressed against his leg.

Stranahan heard Apple's high-pitched giggling, discordant and broken, his lungs gulping breaths between the words.

"Lucky's . . . luck . . . run out." The last words tumbling from a heaving breath, followed by what sounded to Stranahan like laughing sobs.

McNair let out a primeval scream. He was crying, his body rocked in spasms of despair. And accompanying the sobs was something else. A beating rush from somewhere beyond, like the quick padding of an animal.

"He shot me. My brother . . . shot me."

McNair dropped to his knees and started to hack at the body of Lucas Ventura, the knife in his fist plunging up and down, his wailing not of this earth.

Stranahan got to his knees, tried to stand.

McNair was back on his feet, looming over him.

"Don't this beat all," he wailed. "Don't this . . . beat . . . all!"

And he threw himself at Stranahan, the blade in his hand slicing down as Stranahan rolled with the blow, hard as a fist on the muscle of his shoulder. He felt the hot spray of blood on his face. As the hand rose Stranahan grasped it, saw the blade poised over his chest, felt the downward bearing of pressure and his own strength ebbing. And then something black jerked through the front of Apple's ragged T-shirt. There was a gushing heat over Stranahan's throat and chest as McNair's body spasmed, the hand holding the knife bricking rigid and then abruptly going limp, the knife dropping away.

Above him, Apple began to reel, pulled backward as if grasped by a giant hand. For a moment he stood tall, the steel finger of a blade protruding from his chest, the tip gleaming dully. Then Apple McNair toppled forward on top of his brother.

Stranahan rolled up onto his knees to see a second figure, struggling to its feet a few yards away.

"Jesus H. Christ!" a voice roared. "That man flung me like a Lab throwin' water."

"What the hell, Walt, you stabbed the son of a bitch." It was a woman's voice.

"He had a knife. He got me with his knife," Stranahan gasped.

"Shit man, that wasn't a knife. That pipsqueak blade? Now this"—he saw the man bend over McNair's crumpled figure and a whooshing sound as the man yanked and held in his hand what looked like a short sword—"this here is a knife!"

Then the blackness around him began to whirl. The voices of the man and the woman were merging, growing indistinguishable—they floated above him like his mother's and father's voices when he was coming out of a deep sleep—"had to use the knife . . . no other choice . . . Crocodile Dundee, never hear the last of it . . . shit, if I shot I might have hit him . . . hurry up, dammit . . . he's bleeding bad . . . talk about a pickle. . . ."

Stranahan felt a pressure on his shoulder, swam into consciousness to see the woman's face inches away, felt her breath against his mouth, and passed out.

CHAPTER FORTY-TWO

Spirit of the Bear

He was in and out. Once, when he awoke and his eyes had adjusted to the darkness, he saw a figure in a chair beside the hospital bed, hazy but familiar. Then felt cool skin against his burning forehead, fingers stroking his hair. The face stayed in soft focus, haunting his memory. When he shut his eyes there was a scent of oranges.

He imagined people talking to him. From a distance he watched his own mouth open in reply but didn't hear any words. At times he surged toward a light, only to have it recede into distance. For hours he wandered a forest that led from darkness to darkness. At one point cascading colors shimmered behind the lids of his eyes, like Northern Lights. The shimmers grew more intense, became milky swirls against a silver of dawn. The room took on shapes and he was suddenly awake.

"Shitfire!" was the first word he heard. "The coma kid is up and kickin'."

"Sam," Stranahan whispered.

"Fuckin' A," Sam said, "We thought you was a goner."

Stranahan ran his tongue over his cracked lips. "Vareda, I . . . saw her."

"That woman's hardly left this chair. She was outside smoking a cigarette when I come in. She calls me 'Dayshift,' 'cause she's the nightshift, been sleepin' right here on the floor. I mean that's a woman, you're talking tits and wits my man. Give you a look that cut you right to the bone."

309

He winced. "Oh, shit, me and my mouth, I didn't mean nothin. . . ."

Stranahan lifted a feeble hand. He felt himself reeling backward and fought to clear his head.

"Could you get me some water?"

"Oh sure, I'll just get the nurse. She was—"

Stranahan cut him short. "No . . . nurse. I don't want anyone to know I'm . . . up. Just talk to me. How long . . . have I been here?"

Stranahan heard a tap turn in the bathroom. Sam returned carrying a plastic cup.

"This is, ah, Thursday. Two nights. Here. Just sip at it."

Stranahan swallowed, the water cold going down. He took a gulp.

"That's probably enough." Sam took the cup from him.

The big man shook his head. "That Apple feller got his shiv in the artery. You was spurtin' it out all the way back to town. The sheriff, she was pushing against it and when she got tired, the deputy applied pressure and they took turns drivin'. Fuckin' ambulance never showed. There's a stink about it in the paper. Anyway, I hate to say it, but fuckin' law enforcement saved your life. You were down to seven pints of blood."

Stranahan had a thought. "I'm B negative. That's rare. Lucky they had the blood."

"They didn't. Guess who's O negative." Sam turned a beefy finger at his chest. "Universal donor, my man. They had me in the hospital records."

Stranahan managed a thin smile. "So this means I'll get to be as full of bullshit as you are?"

"Be a better fuckin' fisherman, I know that." Sam reared back and laughed, then caught himself and put a finger to his lips. "That nurse has ears like a mule deer. Here, the Indian fella brought you beads. The nurse don't want them on you, but Vareda hung them on your neck the last couple nights. There's a bear claw—the Indian says it's supposed to infuse you with the courage of your spirit animal."

Sam rummaged in a small daypack wedged into the corner and brought out a necklace of rough wood beads with grouse feather dangles and a hooked bear claw, black with an amber tip. Stranahan clutched it to his chest.

"So what do you think is going to happen to the Blackfoot River and those other streams where McNair dumped the fish?"

Sam's massive shoulders gave a shudder. "Too many variables to call the shot. If the river doesn't have the right kind of tubifex worm, then the spores can't survive and it could be okay. Or it could be a fucking disaster. Depends on the river and how many diseased fish they polluted it with. Just got to cross our fingers. Might not know for months. Shit, it could take a couple years before an age class turns up missing."

Stranahan felt a flutter of panic.

"Sam, I have to talk to the sheriff. She doesn't know everything that's happened."

"Don't worry, man. You talked to her plenty."

"I did?"

"All the way back to town. They were tryin' to keep you conscious."

"How do you know?"

"When Vareda got back in town, Sheriff told her the story. She told me."

"I thought she'd gone back South."

"Only if you think Idaho Falls is the South. She had a gig there to make the gas money to drive the rest of the way to Mississippi. Said she had a premonition when she was on the road. But I don't think so. I think she heard about you before she ever got out of state. It was all over the radio. Anyway, she shows up here smellin' like a citrus grove, sees me, and lifts her nose like I'm a bowel movement the nurse forgot to flush. But the doc told her about the transfusion and she worked her away around to liking me all right. Now we're like this." He held two fingers together.

"Bring her here," Stranahan said. "Before anyone knows I'm up."

"Okeedoke, but she might have stepped out for a while. She don't get a real night's sleep on the floor."

Sam heaved his bulk out of the chair and left the room. Then the furniture started to whirl.

When Stranahan came to, a high-angle sun was shining through the slats of the window. A face swarmed in the periphery of his vision, finally settling into focus.

"Not the girl you were looking forward to seeing. What, you were expecting someone prettier? You hurt me, Sean." Sheriff Ettinger placed her hand over his forearm. It felt strong and cool.

"Sam told me what happened at the lake. Right now you're about the prettiest woman on the face of the earth. But I would like to see Vareda."

"We'll get to her," she said. "You feel like listening for a minute, maybe answering a few questions?"

"Right to the point, aren't you?"

"It's considered a failing in a woman, I know." Ettinger switched on a light at his bed stand.

"You truly are a beautiful woman," Stranahan said, and saw her face redden. He managed a weak smile. "The last thing I remember out by the lake was you giving me CPR. Your lips pressed against mine."

"You gagged up bile into my mouth," Ettinger said. "It wasn't a romantic occasion."

She assumed a brusque tone.

"Anyway, I'm afraid when you hear what happened, it's Walt who's going to be the pretty one. McNair was dragging you up the shore by the time we got there. Couldn't swear who was who until we were right on you. Too much chance of a bullet going through McNair and hitting you. That's when Walt pulled his pigsticker. The man saved your life; you can bet he'll let you know about it."

"I remember," he said.

"Yeah, but what you don't know is that the shot—you told me about it, remember?—well that was Ventura shooting McNair. Got him in the right chest quadrant. McNair responded by stabbing his brother, Doc found at least twenty wounds. Used him as a pincushion. Walt said he had Rasputin strength, even though the bullet wound would have been fatal. That was a dead man walking who dragged you up the shore."

Stranahan squeezed her forearm. "How did you know where to find me?"

"Remember the yearbook? We got it. It had better photos of Apple's brother. Walt said it looked like McNair's neighbor. He'd taken a statement from Ventura a couple years ago when a grizzly bear got into the man's garbage can. Walt doesn't have a full attic, but what's in there stays there. And I remembered you telling me you were going fishing with him. A lightbulb went off in my head."

"So that was it? Walt just knew?"

"No, he wasn't sure. But before we could run the name we got a call from the Rouse woman. Said she'd heard from her parents that we were trying to contact her. I asked her if there was any chance her Alaska beau had changed his name to Ventura. She confirmed immediately. Her old college roommate had seen his picture in a magazine and made the connection. She said it was sort of exciting to see who he'd become—What? Why are you smiling?"

"Oh, just that it's exactly what I told Ventura," Stranahan said. "I had to convince him you knew who he was. I thought he wouldn't take a chance of killing me if he thought you were on to him. I told him you knew right where to find us. But you didn't. So how did you . . . ?"

"Pedal to the metal."

Ettinger said she and Walt had hit every access up the Madison on the way to Ventura's house. When they got there the driveway was empty, so they'd started knocking on doors. Tony Sinclair said he'd seen Ventura's rig pull out trailering the boat.

"So now," Ettinger said, "we're figuring he's meeting you at a lake. We drove to Henry's first because that's where your buddy Meslik got shot. Quake was next on the list. We found the boat trailer but couldn't see the boat from the ramp, so we figured you'd gone east up the lake. We drove on up to the Beaver Creek access below the campground. Still no boat, so you had to be in-between somewhere. It must have taken an hour to hike through those goddamn woods. It's just one log fallen on top of another. We were about to give it up when we heard the shot. You know the rest."

"I get flashbacks about your deputy's knife," Stranahan said.

"You and me, both. I'll be doing paperwork on Walt's little stunt the rest of my year. Just don't gush over him too much. His head's about two sizes bigger than his hat and it's only been three days."

She thought of something. "You have some of Sam Meslik's blood in you. Did you know that?"

Stranahan nodded.

"Walt's got a bet with me, thinks you're going to turn into the Wolfman."

"What do you think?"

"I think a couple days in the sun and mothers will be locking their girl children behind closed doors."

"That good-lookin', eh? Did I tell you how pretty you are?"

Ettinger blushed.

"Here's what I don't understand," Stranahan said. "Why did McNair kill his brother? It was supposed to be the other way around."

"I don't think we'll ever know for sure. But Harold was able to follow McNair's tracks through the woods from the highway, right on down to the lake. What I think is that when McNair headed for the hills, Ventura had arranged a meeting point. A where and when. Maybe not at the lake that night. Maybe they'd already met and then set up the rendezvous at the lake, Ventura telling Apple that he could have his way with you. He could have dropped McNair off on the highway before he met you at the landing. One way or another, McNair was to join the two of you right where Ventura pulled the boat in. My guess is that McNair showed up before the appointed time. Harold found a bunch of tracks where he thinks McNair had waited in the trees. So he might have heard Ventura turning traitor on him. Or maybe he went in expecting as much. I think he was smarter than we gave him credit."

"If that's true, it makes Ventura sound like a fool."

"You said yourself that he was worked up. I doubt he was planning to talk so much. He just got going and couldn't stop. People who've kept secrets for years, they're desperate to get it off their chests. When he started telling you about his brother, it was like a dam bursting."

Stranahan bit on his lip, which was still swollen where McNair had stuck him with the fly.

"Do you think McNair drowned Beaudreux up at that pond where he got me? Think that's where the boy followed him after he called his sister in Ennis?"

Ettinger was nodding her head. "I was getting to that. We drained it to remove the trout and found one of those lanyard things fishermen wear instead of a vest. It had a plastic sleeve with Beaudreux's license in it. Probably came off his neck when Apple drowned him. And Doc confirmed that the pond contained the same species of invertebrate monsters that he scraped out of Beaudreux's throat. I think what happened was Beaudreux followed McNair from Ennis and investigated that pond the same way you did, with a fly rod in his hand."

"Dumb as me, huh?" Stranahan said.

Ettinger grunted.

"What about the camp host?"

"Probably the way we figured. McNair thought he'd been spotted and killed the old codger. Life's easy to put together in hindsight, huh?"

Stranahan thought a minute, the hum of the hospital punctuated by the bickering of house sparrows on a windowsill feeder.

"The day Sam was shot. I never could figure it out. How the hell did McNair know to find us at Henry's Lake?"

"The way Walt has it figured is that Ventura overheard Sam talking to you at the TU banquet. Apple had probably told him that he'd lost his hat in the river and that Meslik had found it. I'm guessing he trashed Sam's trailer after the two of you departed for the lake, and when he didn't come up with the hat, he drove to Henry's and shot Sam. If he couldn't get his hands on the incriminating evidence, then he figured to eliminate the man who could produce it. I doubt it was on Ventura's instruction. He was just a loose cannon."

A nurse entered the room carrying a tray of meds.

"I was just leaving," Ettinger told her.

"Aren't you forgetting something?" Stranahan held her eyes.

Ettinger sighed.

"Can you give us one more minute?" she said to the nurse.

They listened to the footsteps retreating down the hall.

"Your Mississippi nightingale is halfway to the land of cotton by now," Ettinger said. "When Sam told her you had come to, he said she got this frightened look on her face. He said he had to just about push her into the room to see you. But you were asleep. She told Sam she'd come back in an hour, but she never did."

"Oh," Stranahan said.

Ettinger smiled at him with an expression he took for compassion.

"Forget about her, Sean. Any woman who loses her father on the riverbank and her brother in the drink, it's a bad sign. Specially for someone who spends as much time around water as you do."

Stranahan looked away for a long moment.

"I was right about her, though," he said. "She wasn't guilty of anything."

"Sean, the only thing she was guilty of was stopping a few hearts."

Ettinger leaned forward to squeeze his hand, and Stranahan caught her eye appraising the necklace peeking from the folds of his hospital gown.

"Sam says Little Feather gave it to me when I was touch and go. Supposed to infuse me with the spirit of the bear."

"Harold," Ettinger said, in a tone that Stranahan had never heard before, and left the room.

CHAPTER FORTY-THREE

The Lady of the Lake

When Stranahan heard footsteps in the hall, he lifted the brush from his palette. His heart began to race.

Nearly three months had passed since Vareda Beaudreux had tapped at his door, shut it behind her, and stood there in her white shirt with the red ribbon and her lips the color of blood. The badger-hair tips of his brush now reflected this hue the best he could match it, and the nearly finished painting awaited the final application. It was, he thought, one of his best pieces. During the last several days, as his moods shifted and the shapes that swam behind his eyes flowed through his right hand, he'd had second thoughts about sending it to Mississippi.

It was the letter that inspired his effort. When he was released from the hospital, he had tried to call Vareda at the number Martha Ettinger provided. But he'd been unable to get past the farm manager, McGruder, who had rebuffed him in a kindly low-country drawl, saying that Vareda was going through a period of adjustment and thought it best to keep to herself for the time being.

When a month passed and he still hadn't heard from her, he wrote a businesslike letter, revealing the details of the events that had come to light after McNair's death. He intended to end the letter by vowing that he'd keep fishing for the trout her father had marked, then had ruined his carefully guarded prose with a postscript that used the L word twice. He'd looked at what he had written, debating how much of himself he was willing to reveal, and sent it anyway.

If he had learned anything that summer, it was that risk mattered in a life stagnated by indecision. Risk had almost killed him, but it had brought him into the moment, and the colors were so much brighter that he had no intention of retreating into the hesitancy of his past. *What the hell*—that was the new philosophy he'd confessed to Sam after an autumn day's streamer fishing on the Yellowstone, where he had caught a six-pound brown with a hooked jaw and pectorals dusted gold. "Fuckin' A," Sam had said, nodding his head sagely.

The letter sent in reply to Stranahan's missive had a Biloxi postmark. It lay folded and many times read in the third drawer of his desk. He had tucked it underneath the coffee can of ashes, which he still dutifully carried down to the Land Cruiser on days when he went fishing up the Madison Valley.

"My dearest Sean," Vareda had written, "Last night I dreamed you were here. It was cold like Montana must be in the winter. When I opened the door, the snow came in with you and I shivered. I kissed your cheek. It was rough and cold, but your lips were as warm as honey toast. If you had been lying beside me when I woke up, you would have been devoured.

"I know it must be confusing, trying to reconcile the feelings you know I have for you with the distance I've placed between us. It is not my intention to be mysterious. But I am encompassed—isn't that a fine word, encompass?—by forces that isolate me and which I fear I have once again succumbed to. A time will come when I can see you again. Until then, know that I am yours, as much of me as you can hold in your thoughts. I love you with a passion I have never known for another man. You are my love. *Vareda.*"

In Stranahan's painting, droplets of water fell from the canoe paddle. The bow angled obliquely into the foreground, the water underneath was dimpled with reflections. The mood was somber, the expression on the woman's face hard to place. Apprehensive, hopeful, or infinitely sad? Perhaps all of those.

Stranahan heard the tapping at the door. It isn't her, he told himself. He got up and walked to the door.

"This is becoming a habit," Martha Ettinger said. "I drop by for a visit, and your eyes tell me you were hoping to see someone else."

Stranahan wasn't proud of himself for feeling a greater measure of relief than regret. He gathered himself.

"Martha, you look great," he said heartily. "Your hair is different. Are you blushing, Sheriff?"

"Nonsense," she said, "It's windburn. I've been out riding, getting my butt into shape for elk season."

"Right," Stranahan said. "Well, to what do I owe the honor of this visit?"

"Have something for you."

She unsnapped her breast pocket and reached inside.

"By the way, when are you going to have that removed?" She gestured with her free hand toward the subscript lettering etched on the frosted glass door. *Private Investigations.*

"A guy's coming in next week," Stranahan said. He hesitated. "I've been thinking about going back East for a while," he said. "I seem to get into trouble out here."

"Really," she said. "What the hell would you fish for?"

She handed him a small film canister.

Stranahan lifted his eyebrows in a question and opened the plastic lid. He shook out a small wet fly, a size 14 Gold-ribbed hare's ear. It was the fly Stranahan had caught the trout at the pond with, the one McNair had stuck into his lip.

"Been meaning to get around to it," Ettinger said. "But with the election coming up and all. . . . Anyway. I thought you'd want it."

"I do. I'll paint a self-portrait and hook it in my mouth, hang it on the wall to remind me to stick to my brushes in the future."

"You're really leaving us, huh?"

Stranahan shrugged. "I'm still trying to sort a few things out."

"Like Vareda Beaudreux? There's a lot of good women in the West. You need to get over her."

"The only other woman I'm interested in has a star on her chest. Where's the future in that?"

He saw Ettinger blush. She said, "Wait till they count the vote next Tuesday and maybe she won't."

"Martha, you're a rock star in this valley. Gary Cooper himself couldn't beat you in an election."

The tension between them was more in the open than it had been before. They bumped into each other every week or so and always were reluctant to part. But they had developed a teasing banter to deal with it, which kept them at a fixed distance neither wanted to be first to breach. The attraction wasn't as visceral as he'd felt with Vareda, not that he understood it and maybe there was nothing to understand beyond the fact that he liked the nearness of her.

Ettinger had brought some news. The manager of the hatchery had finally crawled out from the cover of his lawyer and decided to cooperate. He'd cleared up a point that had bothered Stranahan, who had never been able to understand what the diseased fingerlings were doing in a pond so close to the Madison, a river that already harbored the disease. The manager said that Ventura was using the pond as a staging area because of its proximity to Yellowstone Park. Ventura had intended to poison rivers there as well as in Montana. If the state wouldn't cooperate by stocking fish into affected rivers, maybe the feds would.

Ettinger said, "The good news is that the scheme was still more in Ventura's head than in the water. According to the manager, Apple McNair had dumped trout into no more than a handful of rivers— the Blackfoot, the lower Clark's Fork, a couple others I can't recall. But Ventura was gearing up for a much more widespread campaign, if you want to call it that, so it's a good thing he was stopped. You deserve a lot of the credit for that.

"The man wanted to be some kind of trout god," Ettinger went on. "He had this grandiose idea, but his ex-wives were milking the last of the movie money out of him. About all he had left were his name and some property."

Stranahan nodded, thinking of Sam, who'd be happy to hear that the scope of infection was limited. He asked Ettinger if they'd ever found the rifle McNair carried into the mountains during the manhunt, most likely the .243 he'd used to shoot Sam. She said no, in real life some of the threads are left hanging. But they did find Jerry Beaudreux's fly box, filled with flies his father had tied. McNair had slipped the box inside his own fishing vest.

"Just couldn't bring himself to do the smart thing and throw it away," Ettinger said. Stranahan understood McNair's reluctance. They were fine flies.

They talked a little longer, skimming surfaces. Hanging in the room was the unspoken thought that they might never see each other again. Finally Martha Ettinger extended her hand. He took it in both of his, pressed it.

"By the way," he said. "Where are you going elk hunting?"

"Bob Marshall Wilderness. It's God's country up there. You won't find anything like it where you came from. You get serious about leaving, you keep that in mind."

She turned and made good her exit.

Stranahan caught himself frowning at the reverse lettering on his office door. Maybe he'd call the guy and cancel. Think it over some. After all, he'd had a hand in solving the Royal Wulff murders. Nothing like that had ever happened to him in the East. Then too, he'd yet to fish Montana in the spring.

He picked up his brush, dabbed it onto the palette, and touched it to the canvas.

CHAPTER FORTY-FOUR

Two Medicine River

Martha Ettinger unfolded the hand-drawn map and stared at the directions scribbled in red ink, her truck idling at the trailhead. It was November 10, snow following snow for two weeks. She shut off the ignition, braced herself for the shock of the cold, and then walked back through a foot of powder to the tailgate of her truck camper. An envelope of steam issued through the slats of the horse trailer she'd hauled from Bridger.

"I'll be there in a jiff, Petal. Long drive, huh?" She straddled the trailer tongue and opened the camper latch. Saddle, saddle bags, bedroll, Winchester rifle. All there, no turning back now.

The one thing she'd insisted on was her own horse. She told herself she could always ride out if it started to feel awkward. Half of her, the half that sought the comfortable routine, had hoped that Harold Little Feather had forgotten the invitation he'd extended to her to join him, along with his brother Howard and Howard's wife, Bobby, for a week in elk camp up on the shoulders of the Continental Divide. The half that still remembered the silky feel of a once-worn blue dress had thought of little else as the autumn burned down, the larch trees rusting red and the needles feathering the snow. She told herself this would be elk hunting, nothing more. He'd said they would pack in a fifteen-pole Sioux teepee. One teepee, four hunters, no running water but the Two Medicine River tinkling under a pane of ice. It wasn't like he'd asked her to join him in Paris. How much trouble could a woman get into?

Snow was spitting when she touched Petal's ribs. The mare dipped her head, her tack creaking as she walked past the truck with Browning plates that Harold had driven in a couple days before. Up the trail were the sacred hunting grounds of the Blackfeet. Before the clouds closed in, Martha had cricked her neck gazing through the windshield at the swept escarpments and soaring peaks. From experience, she knew how wilderness swallows a person, that the toll it exacts on human confidence is in direct relation to the hours of light left in the sky. It was only a little past noon, but already the day seemed in decline. A pall fell upon her spirits. The deep imprints of the horseshoes that marked the trail left by Harold's hunting party filled steadily with snow.

An hour up the trail, Martha stopped to layer a down vest under her hunting jacket. She wrapped a silk scarf under her chin. Clucking to Petal, she squinted through eyelashes frosted with ice. According to Harold's map, she was supposed to take a fork in the trail eight miles from the trailhead, near the saddle of a ridge. A dotted line, bleeding ink where snowflakes had melted on the paper, indicated a path that left the trail to work through stunted aspens to a bench above the river. Harold had written that he'd leave his blaze on a tree at the fork, three slashes on the diagonal. But what if snow was driven against the trunk, obscuring the blaze?

She clucked to Petal. The snow was coming harder. When she stopped to let the mare blow an hour and a half later, she felt the hollowness that foreshadows human panic. She'd reached a saddle on the crest of a ridge—the right saddle, the wrong one, she couldn't be certain. Harold had written that from the saddle she'd have her first glimpse of Silvertip Peak to the west. But all she could see was wilderness rolling away in a sucking undertow, black timber waves cresting to a foreshortened horizon of falling snow. I can turn around now, she told herself, be out before the truck gets stuck. I can call Harold later and tell him the road to the trailhead drifted in with snow. Go back to radio static, Walt's crowing, cats twining at the foot of her bed.

She turned her head to look back at the forest she'd been climbing through, the pines grizzled with snow like the hump of a bear. It was all of a piece, a monotonous slope of dusted black timber. It was behind her and a part of her life now. But ahead the land was new, the air was thinner, the story unwritten. You heard yourself breathe this high.

"Oh for chrissakes, I'm the sheriff," she whispered to the void. "They gave me seventy percent of the vote." Gathering courage against several unknowns, she touched Petal's ribs and moved up the trail.

It was his horse she saw first, the big paint ghosting through a copse of stunted aspens. The arthritic snarl of branches obscured the silhouette of the rider until the horse stepped out onto the trail and turned broadside, steam rising in columns from its nostrils. She'd never seen Harold without his hair braided up. It was longer than she remembered, made his face look less civilized. Three black slashes crossed his sculpted cheek.

"Afternoon, Sheriff," he said.

"Harold, you look . . ." She was lost for words.

"Like an Indian? Don't worry. Just me. Have any trouble?"

"No."

"Come on, then. Camp's down the hill. Howard got an elk yesterday, fat spike bull. We're cooking liver."

Martha glanced at the scabbard against the paint's broad withers. Extending from the leather was a weather-beaten rifle stock and the exposed hammer of a lever-action rifle. The receiver had a pewter patina where the bluing had worn off from handling.

"Is that an .86 Winchester?" she said. She felt nervous and giddy, just making talk.

"You know your rifles," Harold said. "My father's gun. I had it rebarrelled to .450 Alaskan. Big bullet, but slow."

"Guess you have to get close."

"Well, I'm a tracker, Martha," he said, and turned to ride down the path. The words came over his shoulder. "The way I feel about elk hunting, it's like making love. You ought to do it face-to-face." A pause, the blood flushing through Martha's cheeks. "'Bout four times out of five, anyways," he said.

She felt the heat of her horse rise through her. She watched the black hair shifting in the hollow formed between Harold's shoulders, was aware of her breathing and the muffled clop of hooves. He had what looked like an eagle's feather tied into his hair, fluttering in the breeze.

When they came into the clearing, she saw the second teepee, the one Harold hadn't told her about. She saw it right off.

CHAPTER FORTY-FIVE

The Trout

In Montana, the first blush of spring arrives with the greening of riverbank willows. Stranahan felt the current swelling against his legs, the river running full and clouded with the blood of snowmelt. For the second time that afternoon, he peered down at his fly box. With the water cold, he knew he'd have to fish deep to coax a trout from its torpor. A bead-head Prince nymph had been his first choice. It had brought the whitefish out of their introspection, one after the other. Maybe, he thought, the answer was a bigger fly.

Wading to the bank, he sat down on an old drift log. Not a soul in sight. One thing you could say about a weekday in April, you owned the river, even the Madison. He pulled an apple out of his vest pocket and ate it, staring contemplatively at the water.

Winter had been a season of decompression for him, and a long time passing. Sometime after Christmas he'd finally gotten through to Vareda on the phone. She had seemed distant, her voice so soft he could hardly hear her. "Did you get my painting?' he'd asked. Yes, she'd said, but she wondered about the expression. "Do I look that sad to you?" she had said. He'd tried to make a joke, telling her that she was his Mona Lisa, and she had replied that he didn't know her at all. "I'm not sure that I want to talk to you," she said, and then a lilt had come into her voice, and she had said maybe, if he asked her nicely, she could change her mind. He heard her throaty laughter. It was a side of her that came and went like light reflected in a revolving chandelier.

After that his phone would ring late at night every other week or so. They would talk through the small hours, so that the next day became a hollow time when the town looked foreign and a long distance seemed to separate him from familiar faces. This would be followed by a lull. He'd immerse himself back into work and after a few days it would be Vareda who seemed far away. Maybe he could come down in May, she said once. She could show him where the redfish swam. Take him on a walk where the fireflies flickered under the willows. But was it just the hour speaking? He didn't know—most days he doubted he'd ever see her again.

In the meantime, he'd completed nine of the dozen paintings Summersby had commissioned. And, miracle of miracles, two watercolors he'd been shopping for limited edition prints were accepted by a respected agency with an office in the Flatiron district in New York City. He'd flown there in early March, ingratiated himself with the avant-garde colorist who condescended to manage the agency, and bar-hopped with the man's friends in Chelsea. Afterward, he had rented a car and driven to Vermont. He'd dreaded seeing Beth, but it was something that had to be faced. The expected pang of longing when she answered the door of the old farmhouse was akin to standing at the edge of a cliff.

Beth looked as lovely as ever, with stray hairs escaping from her curls and her arms crossed over a Norwegian-pattern sweater. She'd released her grip on herself long enough to peck him on the cheek. She invited him inside. It was no longer his house, he realized. They'd managed a civilized conversation over a cup of coffee. Afterward, she had followed him about the house, talking of this and that as he gathered up rolls of canvas and odds and ends of art supplies he hadn't been able to fit into the Land Cruiser when they'd separated. When he'd asked her, with rather transparent nonchalance, if she was seeing anyone, she shook her head no, and for an instant she fought back tears.

At the door, her face clouded over and she hugged him for a long minute, burying her face against his shoulder. Her expression, when she pulled back to hold him at arm's length, her cheeks glinting, was *Aren't we a pair?* But there was more sadness than love in her eyes, and in the end he'd felt relief to fly back to Montana, where he could feed his office mouse crumbs of a croissant, flirt with Sheriff Ettinger when their paths crossed, and shoot pool with Sam at the Cottonwood Inn.

Stranahan returned his attention to the river. He patted the outside of his vest. The box of nymphs and streamer flies that Vareda's father had tied was still zipped in a pocket. Nothing else seemed to be working. Why not try one? He opened the box and picked out a sculpin imitation with enough lead wire wrapped under the body to tap bottom. The first fish to grab the fly was a brown, hollow-bellied from the winter but athletic enough for a trout this early in the season. A few more casts and he had another, a chunky rainbow with dull silver sides. It surprised him a little. He'd expected that most of the rainbows would be up the feeders to spawn, that the river would be claimed by their Old World cousins. A second rainbow and then a third disavowed him of the presumption, and as he admired the fourth, which had brute shoulders and was perhaps a shade under three pounds, his eyebrows furrowed. A shallow V-shaped notch scarred its adipose fin. The fin had healed over with a thin white line edging the scar, but the V remained sharp-sided, as if it had been cut with the scissors of a fisherman's tool. Stranahan didn't have a camera and thought briefly of killing it, but what would that prove? He couldn't imagine sending Vareda a dead fish. She'd believed her father's story about marking the trout he caught—it was Stranahan who had needed convincing. Still, it seemed a bit of a miracle. She'd want to know.

Slipping the hook from the jaw hinge, he held the fish in the current so that the water worked over its gills. The rainbow marked the end of a story that had begun nearly nine months ago and he was reluctant to open his hand. Trout are the ghosts of moving waters, gone like the dreams one longs to remember. When this one glimmered away, he felt as if he'd caught smoke or that it had never been there in the first place.

Walking to the bank, he piled up a cairn of stones to commemorate the trout. He hooked the fly into the cork of his rod grip. Then he began his hike up the hill to retrieve the coffee can of ashes from the truck.

MYS   2/12

McCAFFERTY

ROYAL WULFF MURDERS $27.